SOMETHING
SPECIAL

*Also by Joan Hohl
in Large Print:*

Compromises
Another Spring
Ever After
Maybe Tomorrow

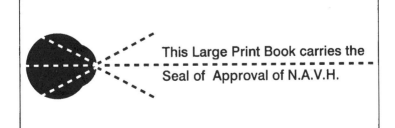

SOMETHING SPECIAL

Joan Hohl

Thorndike Press • Waterville, Maine

Published in 2002 by arrangement with Zebra Books, an imprint of Kensington Publishing Corp.

Thorndike Press Large Print Romance Series.

The tree indicium is a trademark of Thorndike Press.

The text of this Large Print edition is unabridged. Other aspects of the book may vary from the original edition.

Cover design by Deirdre Wait.

Set in 16 pt. Plantin by Minnie B. Raven.

Printed in the United States on permanent paper.

Library of Congress Cataloging-in-Publication Data

Hohl, Joan.
     Something special / Joan Hohl.
         p. cm.
     Contents: Snowbound weekend — Gambler's love —
The game is played.
     ISBN 0-7862-4055-5 (lg. print : hc : alk. paper)
     1. Love stories, American.   2. Large type books.   I. Title.
PS3558.O34759 S66 2002
     813'.54—dc21   2002019912

Dear Reader:

I have always believed that love stories — tales of the trials and tribulations of men and women finding each other and the true loves of their lives — were favorites, told perhaps by roving troubadours and, who knows, possibly even around fire pits in prehistoric caves, long before the advent of the printed word of romantic fiction.

I love reading those stories; I love writing them.

I wrote the three stories presented in this volume, *Snowbound Weekend*, *Gambler's Love*, and *The Game Is Played*, early in my writing career in the 1980s, under the pseudonym Amii Lorin — a name I created by combining the names of my two beautiful daughters, Amy and Lori, who were, and are, and will always be the enduring lights of my life and my proudest productions.

These stories focus on three independent women and the strong men they fall in love with. You will note, I'm sure, that the stories were written in a certain style, as dictated by the marketplace at the time. I could have made changes — but why, when, in essence, these stories are vintage, timeless stories of love and romance?

I sincerely hope you will enjoy reading them as much as I enjoyed writing them.

Happy Reading,
Joan Hohl

CONTENTS

SNOWBOUND
WEEKEND

One

The alarm rang at four-thirty. A soft groan preceded the slim, pale hand that emerged from under the brightly colored paisley comforter to depress the shutoff button. Yawning sleepily, Jen followed her arm out of the warm cocoon of bedding into the chill air of the bedroom. Still partially asleep, she pushed her way out of the tangle of covers and sat up. The sudden shrill ringing of the phone on the bookcase headboard of the bed brought her fully awake with a start. *Who in the world would be calling at this hour?* Eyeing the instrument warily, she lifted the receiver, hesitated, then said crisply, "Hello?"

"Jen?"

The dry, croaking voice was hardly recognizable as belonging to her friend Chris.

"Yes, of course it's me," she answered. Then, frowning, she asked, "Why are you whispering?"

"I'm not," Chris rasped. "Oh, Jen, I can't go."

Can't go? Chris's words didn't register for a second. *Can't go!* Then they sank in with a bang.

"What do you mean you can't go?" Jen exclaimed loudly. "The trip's been paid for for weeks. The bus leaves in an hour and a half. Four-thirty is a bad time of the morning for making jokes, Chris."

"I wish it was a joke," Chris wailed raggedly. "I'm sick, Jen. I've been up all night doctoring a sore throat, but it hasn't helped. My mother just took my temp and it's 101.6. She says there is no way she is going to let me go off into the mountains for a weekend." Chris paused to cough roughly, then went on, "And to tell you the truth, I don't have the strength to argue with her about it. Right now all I want to do is lie down and die." Again the dry, rough-sounding cough came over the wire. "I'm sorry, Jen."

"Don't be silly," Jen scolded gently. "You didn't try to get sick." Submerging her own disappointment, she sympathized, "What rotten luck. I don't suppose there's any way you can get a refund?"

"Mother's going to call Liz in a half hour to tell her I'm sick," Chris croaked. "I did take the insurance against just such a contingency." Her voice was beginning to sound reedy, tired. "Didn't you?"

"No," Jen laughed ruefully. "Or I'd call

12

and cancel too. The cost of the trip alone was enough, and as I hardly ever get sick, I never even considered it. But I'm glad you did."

"Oh, Jen," Chris half sighed, half coughed, "I feel terrible about this. I hope you have a good time."

Jen bit her lip at the sound of tears in her friend's voice. What was she thinking of, keeping Chris on the phone like this when her friend obviously belonged in bed?

"Of course I will," she replied bracingly. "There's bound to be a lot of young people on the bus and at the lodge, even though I *will* miss you. Now, I think you ought to hop into bed and take care of yourself. I'll call you when I get home, okay?"

Chris promised she'd take care, told her she'd be looking forward to her call, and then, before hanging up, wailed, "Oh, Jen, I was looking forward to this trip so much."

As she replaced the receiver Jen felt like wailing herself. The pleasurable glow that had filled her as she'd counted down the last few days had been extinguished with Chris's first words. What, she asked herself, did a young woman do on her own at a ski lodge? Never having been to a ski lodge, Jen didn't have the beginnings of an idea. But she was sadly certain that the long four-day weekend was going to be a total disaster. Glancing at the clock, she gave a soft yelp and jumped up. If she didn't get moving she'd miss the bus, and she simply could not afford that.

Jen had a quick breakfast of toast and coffee and, moving quietly through the small ranch house so as not to waken her parents, carried her second cup of coffee into her bedroom. Moving swiftly, she donned lacy minuscule panties and bra, stepped into designer boot jeans, pulled on buff-colored suede boots, and slipped into a bulky knit, roll-collared sweater in a shade of rust that should have clashed with her flaming red hair but didn't.

After checking her soft tan leather suitcase for the third time to make sure she hadn't forgotten anything, she locked it, tossed her key case into her shoulder bag lying on the bed, and headed for the bathroom on tiptoe to prevent her heels from clacking on the tiled hallway. All her tiptoeing and quiet moving around hadn't worked, for a light tapping sounded on the bathroom door as she put the finishing touches to her makeup.

"Are you just about ready, Jen?" Her mother's quiet voice filtered through the door. "It's twenty-five minutes after five."

"In a second," she called back softly. Her hand, poised to apply a strawberry-scented lip gloss to her mouth, hovered as Jen grinned at her reflection. Would the day ever come when she could slip out of the house unheard by her mother? She hoped she'd never find herself in the position of wanting to elope for, short of crawling out of her bedroom window in her nightclothes, she'd never make it.

The gold-flecked hazel eyes in the mirror sparkled with laughter at the thought, while the full, beautifully shaped mouth grinned back at her, revealing good-sized white teeth with just a hint of an overbite. Composing her well-formed features, Jen smoothed on the gloss, stuck her small pink tongue out at herself, and left the room. Her mother stood at the front door waiting for her, her suitcase beside her, her totebag in one hand and her ski jacket, purchased for this trip, in the other.

"You may break a leg," she said blandly as Jen reached for the jacket, "but at least I won't have to worry about you getting lost in the snow while you're wearing this beacon. I really think they saw you coming, Jennifer," she ended with a sad shake of her dark red head.

"Now, Mom, I was not sold a pig in a poke," Jen laughed softly, plucking the garment in question out of her mother's hand. "I loved it on sight and knew I had to have it." Shrugging into the shiny, bright silver jacket, Jen's laughter deepened as her mother squinted her eyes as if against a sudden glare. "And," she added with an impish grin, "as it was the only one like it they had in stock, I considered it a stroke of fortune that it was in my size."

"It will more likely give someone a stroke just looking at it," her mother quipped dryly. "Unless, of course, you keep dawdling. If you don't get a move on, you'll miss the bus."

"I'm going, I'm going," Jen laughed. Reaching for her tote and suitcase at the same time, she planted a kiss on her mother's still smooth cheek, teased, "Be good," and, slipping out into the cold morning, sent a soft "You bet" over her shoulder in answer to her mother's cautioned "Take care, Jennifer."

Driving along the dark streets, Jen threw a reproachful look at the car's heater. *Why is it things always seem to go wrong the minute you pay something off?* She had made the final payment on the Mustang the month before and now, suddenly, in late January when she needed it most, the dratted heater had decided to be temperamental. Moments later she sent up a silent prayer that the windshield wipers had not contracted the no-work malady from the heater as a light, misty rain clouded the window. Holding her

16

breath, she flicked the switch, then released her breath in a long sigh as the blades swished back and forth on the glass with reassuring regularity.

Stopping at a red light, Jen watched the wipers with a sinking sensation. *First Chris's call and now rain,* she thought dejectedly. *What next?*

Easing the car into motion again, she slanted a quick glance at her watch. Five thirty-five, and she should be at Barton's inside of ten minutes — plenty of time to make the bus.

Turning onto the road that led to the large office complex, Jen sighed with relief at the sparsity of traffic at that hour of the morning. The macadam gleamed wetly in the beam from her headlights and at patches slick with a fine film of forming ice.

The tension of hard concentration eased somewhat when her lights touched the sign reading BARTON'S — CONSTRUCTURAL ENGINEERS, INC. at the turnoff to the private road. The firm's parking lot comprised a large area, empty now but for the small group of cars parked at the far end.

Jen maneuvered the Mustang into a lined space beside a rather beat-up van and glanced around, wondering, *Where's the bus?*

At that moment, as if her thought was its

cue, the large vehicle turned onto the parking lot and headed for the parked cars, its high, strong headlights bringing the small group into harsh relief.

Before the bus had come to a full stop, car doors were flung open, and the early-morning stillness was shattered by the sound of excited, laughing voices as people left their cars and collected luggage. Following suit, Jen stepped out of the car, pulled her case from the back, and, depressing the lock button, swung the door to add to the cacophony of sound being made by the other doors being slammed shut.

Standing at the back of the line that had formed in front of the bus's open door, Jen caught snatches of the laughing banter being tossed back and forth as the group waited for their names to be checked on the guide's roster and their luggage to be stashed in the large compartment on the side of the bus.

"Yeah, if she ever gets off the beginner slopes," one young man gibed.

"Right now the idea of a hot cup of coffee in front of a crackling fire sounds like heaven," a slim woman of around forty laughingly told her tall, very thin male companion.

"This being engaged isn't all it's cracked up to be," the good-looking man directly in front of Jen said quietly to the equally good-looking man beside him. "Do you believe I had to swear I wouldn't look at another girl for the next four days?"

Hating to be an eavesdropper yet not knowing how to avoid it, Jen heard the other man ask softly, "Why didn't she come with you?"

"For one thing, she doesn't ski," the first young man replied disgustedly. "For another, she had to stay around this weekend as there's a shower planned for her. It's supposed to be a surprise, but she's known about it for weeks. Honestly, the games these women play are enough to drive a man to drink."

"Or to the ski slopes," the other man said, laughing softly.

The tiny smile that had begun to tug at Jen's lips disappeared when the man went on even more softly, "Of course, there are some games these gals play that drive a man to other things . . . I refer to bedroom games, naturally."

"Yeah, well, you can forget that once you've put the diamond on her finger," the first man murmured bitterly, taking a step as the line moved forward. "All of a sudden they become pure and want to wait. And that will drive a normal man over the edge completely."

Jen felt her cheeks grow warm in embarrassment, then her spine stiffened in anger at the advice the man's friend proffered.

"Well, as I'm sure there'll be plenty of more-than-willing females at the lodge, you'll have four days to work off your frustrations."

Thankfully their conversation was terminated before the other man could reply, as they were given the okay to enter the bus. *Creeps,* Jen thought scathingly as she moved up to a young woman holding a clipboard in her hands.

"Are you Jennifer Lengle?" the harried young woman asked. At Jen's nod she went on, "I'm sorry Chris couldn't make it. There must be a bug going around. I had six cancellations besides Chris's this morning, including the travel agency's guide." Then, as the bus driver indicated he had her case, the woman said, "Oh, well, I'm sure you'll have a good time anyway, Jennifer. You can get on the bus now."

With a murmured "Thank you" followed by a shiver, Jen gladly took the high step up that took her out of the cold, misty rain. Making her way slowly along the narrow aisle, Jen ignored an empty seat behind the ones occupied by the young men who'd stood in front of her in the line and stopped at double empties farther back in the bus. After sliding into the window seat, she placed her bag on the seat Chris would have occupied, then sat gratefully, soaking in the warmth from the bus's powerful heaters.

Settling her long frame as comfortably as possible in the confined seating space, Jen let her eyes roam over her fellow passengers. How many, she wondered, were employees of the engineering firm and how many were guests? Like many similar firms, Barton's had an employees association that, with the help of a travel agency, planned several trips a year for employees and their guests. The destinations of these trips were well chosen, and they were amazingly reasonable in cost.

This particular tour to a ski lodge in the Adirondacks in upper New York State was the first for Jen. Chris had taken advantage of several previous tour plans during the last few years. She had been to Williamsburg in Virginia; Mystic Seaport in Connecticut; New York City; and, the winter before, had enjoyed a skiing trip in Vermont. And on each occasion she had tried to coax Jen into going along. Jen would have loved to go, but somehow the trips had always seemed to be at times when she had other commitments. Chris had been delighted when Jen told her she could go on this trip. And they had talked of little else the last few weeks.

Sighing regretfully, Jen continued her perusal of the other passengers, hearing yet not registering their chatter. Although there were a few older people, it was, in the main, a young group, the females outnumbering the males almost two to one. Remembering the words about plenty of more-than-willing females the young man in the line had whispered to his friend, Jen grimaced. Promising herself she'd stay clear of that young man during the next four days, Jen dismissed him from her mind.

On the whole the group appeared open and friendly, calling to each other back and forth from one side of the bus to the other. There was no reason why she shouldn't enjoy herself, Jen mused.

At twenty-three Jen was happy with her life and it showed. Her more than just pretty face, given a wholesome look by the fine sprinkling of freckles across her pert nose, glowed with good health. Her taller than average, somewhat lanky frame had the firm, supple appearance that comes from plenty of exercise. And her crowning glory was exactly that: a long, glorious mane of flaming red, wavy hair that framed her creamy-skinned face beautifully.

Content with herself and her life, Jen viewed the world serenely. Not subject to extreme emotional moods, she was usually pleasant and outgoing. In her position of private secretary to two struggling young lawyers, she had to deal with people, old and young, from all walks of life. She had been in the office less than a week when she'd decided that, by and large, most people were basically nice. The idea that she might be observing the world through rose-colored glasses never occurred to her.

Glancing at her watch, Jen frowned. It was already ten minutes after six. *What could the delay be for?* Shrugging mentally, she rested her head back against the seat. At that moment the murmured conversation in back of her erupted into laughter and movement, and in the action the hair at the back of Jen's head was ruffled.

"Oh, gosh, I'm sorry!" The contrite exclamation came from directly behind Jen.

An understanding smile curving her generous mouth, Jen twisted around in the high-backed seat.

"That's okay, no harm done," she assured the worried-faced girl leaning forward in her seat. About Jen's age, the girl was small and cute. The smile that replaced her concerned expression was singularly sweet. Bright blue eyes studied Jen a moment, lingering on her hair.

"Are you Chris Angstadt's friend Jen?" she asked in a surprised tone.

"Yes, I am." Jen's smile widened. "How did you know?"

"Oh, Chris has mentioned you a couple of times," she said, grinning. "And she has described your hair." The grin broadened. "It's pretty hard to miss. But where's Chris?" Her grin was replaced by a frown. "If she doesn't get here soon, the bus will go without her."

"She can't go," Jen sighed, then explained why.

"That's too bad. I know how excited she was about this trip." The girl shook her head, then added, "Oh, that means you're on your own." At Jen's nod she offered, "If you like, you can kinda hang around with us. I'm Lisa Banks, and this is Terry Gardner." With a wave of her hand she indicated the young woman in the seat beside her. "We work in the same department Chris does."

"Hi," Jen said, returning Terry's smile. "And thanks. You're sure I won't be intruding?"

"Of course not," Lisa laughed. "But Terry and I do have an agreement not to cramp each other's style if something interesting turns up."

"Something male, you mean?" Jen teased. She laughed softly as both girls nodded emphatically. "I'll go along with that agreement."

24

"That is, if we ever get there," Terry grumbled. "What the heck are we sitting here for?"

Wondering the same thing, Jen turned to the front of the bus. At that moment Liz jumped up onto the high step. Shrugging disgustedly to the driver, she said tersely, "Go."

The door was closed, the air brakes were released, and the big vehicle began moving slowly across the parking lot. Before Liz could seat herself, her name was called from a half-dozen voices back through the bus. As one of the voices belonged to Terry, Jen turned questioning eyes to her.

"Liz is the head of the committee that arranges these tours," Terry answered Jen's unasked query. "And I'll bet everyone wants to ask her the same thing: exactly what was the holdup?"

Liz made her way slowly down the aisle, stopping every so often to speak briefly before moving on again. When she reached the empty seat beside Jen she smiled ruefully and launched into an explanation.

"Sorry about the delay." Her sweeping glance included everyone on both sides of the aisle. "I was waiting for two people." She shrugged. "I don't know if they overslept or what, but we just couldn't wait any longer." She started to move on, then paused. "Oh, by the way, the rain has changed to snow. And the bus driver told me the last weather report before he left the terminal called for snow all along the East Coast today."

All eyes, including Jen's, swung to the windows, but the darkness outside, combined with the tinted glass, made it impossible to see the fine snow.

"Well, if it's snowing out there," Lisa muttered, "it must be very fine. I'm darned if I can see it."

Fleetingly, Jen thought of her father's conviction that the bad snowstorms always start fine. *Oh well*, she thought, and smiled at her reflection in the window, *where we're going snow is devoutly to be wished for.*

After turning onto the highway, the bus picked up speed. Depressing the button on the underside of her right armrest, Jen tilted her seat back, shifting into a reasonably comfortable position. The excited buzz of conversation swirled around her for several miles, then petered out. Lulled by the steady hum of the engine and the now low murmurings of the other passengers, Jen's eyes slowly closed.

A sudden jolting of the bus awoke her. Sitting up stiffly, Jen gazed out the window at the gray morning. The snow could be seen now, still fine but falling steadily.

"Well, good morning, glory," Lisa

chirped directly behind her. "I was going to give you a few more minutes and then wake you. We'll be stopping for breakfast soon."

"Mmmm — sounds good." Jen covered a yawn and glanced at her watch. "Good grief, I slept over an hour!"

"I think most everyone on the bus did," Terry informed her cheerfully. "They're just starting to come alive now."

"Probably hungry," Jen commented, sitting up straight to ease her cramped back.

Smoothing her tousled hair, she peered out the window. The highway, though wet and slick-looking, as yet had very little accumulation of snow. As she studied the road, a gold Corvette drew alongside the bus. The rack mounted on the roof of the sporty-looking car held one pair of skis.

Someone else going skiing, Jen thought idly, staring into the interior of the car. The passenger seat was empty, and all she could see of the driver was part of one pants-covered leg and one hand on the steering wheel. Oddly, the sight of that hand sent a funny tingle through Jen's middle. In the few seconds the car paced the bus, the look of that right hand was imprinted on her mind. It was a big hand, the back of it broad, and somehow Jen knew the fingers that curved firmly, confidently around the wheel were strong. Yet the exposed wrist was very narrow, deceptively delicate-looking. For one uncanny instant Jen thought she could actually feel the touch of that hand. She shivered as the car moved ahead, passing the bus.

Chiding herself for being fanciful, Jen pushed the image of that male hand from her mind. Liz's voice, heard clearly over the loudspeaker, helped to dispell the picture.

"Listen up, people," she quipped. "We'll be stopping for breakfast in a few minutes. I'd like to keep our stopping time to an hour or less, so please don't dawdle over your food."

While she was speaking, the bus driver drove off the highway into the parking area of a fairly large restaurant.

"Don't let the number of cars here upset you. We are expected, and everything should be set up for us. Please sign the check the waitress gives you and hand it to me before coming back to the bus. Thank you and enjoy your meal." With those final words Liz clicked the mike off and sat down.

Glancing out the window as the driver maneuvered the bus around the fringes of the lot, Jen caught sight of the ski-topped gold Corvette parked near the front of the building. A picture of a hand flashed into her mind. Dismissing the tingle that came with the image, Jen smiled to herself. *Maybe now I'll be able to attach a body and face to the hand,* she reasoned in amusement.

On entering the restaurant, she was quickly disabused of that idea. The place was full, and the majority of the customers were men. Unless she could go from man to man examining right hands, Jen thought whimsically, she didn't have the slimmest chance of adding a body to that narrow-wristed appendage.

True to Liz's words, the restaurant's staff was expecting them, and they were swiftly herded into an empty dining room in the rear of the building. By the time Jen emerged from the building fifty minutes later, the Corvette was gone, as she had been sure it would be.

On the move once more, Jen settled into her seat for the long ride ahead. Mesmerized by the now large white crystals swirling in a downward slant, Jen stared out the window. The farther north they went, the heavier the snow fell, in spots so thickly she could barely see the countryside.

A chorus of "Jingle Bells" rang out from the very back of the bus, and within seconds everyone had joined in. Everyone except the driver, whose eyes studied the highway carefully, a small frown beginning to draw his brows together.

They had sung their way robustly through "Winter Wonderland," "Let It Snow, Let It Snow," and even back to "Jingle Bells" when the first blast from the suddenly risen wind hit the bus broadside. Silence fell as a shudder rippled through the large vehicle.

"I hope she stays afloat."

The quip, from a deliberately dry male voice, produced the results intended. Female giggles and male laughter eased the tension that had blanketed the atmosphere. The second windy broadside was not as strong and so was met with complacency.

Jen's eyes had flown to the window at the first shock from the wind, widening in disbelief at the absolutely white world they encountered. Not only could she not see the countryside beyond the highway, she could not see the highway. Driven before the wind, the madly swirling snow, now falling heavily, had closed in on the bus, cutting visibility to zilch.

Growing uneasy, Jen kept her eyes fastened on the window even though she couldn't see much of anything. *Where exactly are we?* Biting her lip, Jen strained her eyes in an effort to see the surrounding terrain. She knew they were in New York State as she had seen the sign some distance back when they had crossed the line dividing New York and Pennsylvania. A third shudder shook the bus, and Jen's hands closed tightly on the armrests of her seat.

"This is beginning to give me the creeps," Lisa quavered behind Jen. "I know we're in some mountain range, and the last time I could see the road it appeared very narrow."

"If you're trying to scare me," Terry squeaked, "you're succeeding very well."

Jen was mentally agreeing when the bus swayed, the back end fishtailing as it was buffeted by a fresh assault from the wind. All conversation ceased abruptly, and Jen felt a shiver feather her spine at the frightened stillness. That the bus was obviously moving very slowly up an incline added to the apprehension growing among the passengers.

A collective sigh of relief was expelled as the bus reached the summit and leveled off. But the sigh was followed by another collective gasp as it started its descent down the other side.

"Oh, God!"

The softly exclaimed moan came from a woman toward the front of the bus. A moment later Liz's voice, her tone even and steady, came from the loudspeaker.

"Please remain calm. Our driver — whose name is Ted, by the way — has enough to contend with just keeping this bus on the road. As you can see, we're in the middle of a full-scale blizzard. Driving conditions are getting worse all the time. What we don't want here is panic. From my vantage point up here I can honestly tell you that Ted is doing one fantastic job of driving. You can all help him by staying calm. Now, are there any questions?"

There were a dozen questions, all babbled at once. The mike came back on with an angry click.

"One at a time, please," Liz snapped. "We'll have to use the schoolroom method of raised hands."

Over a dozen arms shot into the air, the question-and-answer period commenced.

"Are we going to have to turn back?" This from one of the men who'd stood in front of Jen in line.

Liz had a hurried, murmured conversation with the driver before answering.

"There is no decision on that yet." Liz held up her hand to stem the tide of comments that followed her statement.

"Here's the picture," she said sharply, effectively cutting through the rumble. "We've been in the thick of this storm for over two hours. The big question is: Which way is this hummer moving? If we keep going, can we drive out of it? If we turn back, can we drive out of it? We simply don't know the answer. Ted's going to pull into the first service station we come to and try and find out. Until then, we keep going."

While Liz had been speaking, the bus had inched down the descent and was now on a level road. There was quiet for several minutes. Then, from behind Jen, Terry asked, "Does it look as bad through the windshield as it does from these side windows?"

Every person on the bus heard Liz sigh.

"I won't try and con you," she said quietly. "It is grim. I don't know if anyone could see them, but we've already passed several cars that have pulled off the highway. Ted has a slight advantage in both the size of the bus and his elevated position."

The mike clicked off, and she leaned close to the driver. After long, tense moments the bus lurched off the highway to the tune of one sharp outcry and several gasps.

"Hold the phone, gang," Liz soothed. "We're pulling into a gas station."

The minute the bus came to a halt the driver was out of his seat and through the door. At his exit the bus filled with sound. Everyone seemed to be talking at once.

Jen, sitting rigidly straight, peered wide-eyed out the window. She could see very little, but what she did see sent a shiver down her back. There were two cars parked haphazardly very near the bus, and she wondered in amazement how Ted had managed to avoid plowing into them as they were both nearly covered with drifted snow. The snow still fell heavily, spiraling in a wild and crazy dance before the wind.

"Scary, isn't it?" The frightened whisper came from Lisa.

Twisting around, Jen looked into the girl's pale face, knowing her own cheeks were as devoid of color.

"Yes," she murmured on an expelled breath.

Their driver was gone about ten minutes. On his return a waiting hush filled the bus. After a short conference with Liz, he took the mike from her and clicked it on.

"Okay, folks, here's the story." His brisk, confident tone went a long way in easing the almost tangible tension. "We are in a beauty. If you remember, Liz told you before we left Norristown that the report was for snow, but nothing like this. This storm ripped out of Canada and caught everyone with their pants down, so to speak."

A nervous twitter rippled through the bus.

"I think we should turn back," the woman across the aisle from Jen said loudly, nervously.

"We are not going to run out of it," Ted stated flatly. "At last report, this storm is dumping snow on the East Coast as far south as Virginia. Right now, apparently, the center of the storm is stalled over New York and Pennsylvania. The station owner has a CB, and he just told me he's been picking up reports of stranded motorists both ahead and behind us. There are, in fact, three cars stranded here now."

"We're surely not going to stay here?" the same woman shrilled.

"No, we're not," Ted answered quietly.

Watching him closely, Jen decided she liked the driver's style. A man in his early forties, he had a tested, competent look that was reassuring. Still speaking quietly, he ignored the outburst that followed his last words and went on.

"The station owner said there is a motel fifteen to eighteen miles further along this road." Ted paused for breath, his face settling into a determined mask. "I'm going for it."

Two

Over an hour later, the large bus hardly seeming to move as it crawled along at a snail's pace, Jen observed the very stillness of her fellow passengers and smiled around the apprehension gripping her own throat. The nail-biting quiet had settled on the group when the bus had begun its slow crawl forward.

What amused Jen was the contrast between this very stillness and the furor that had erupted on Ted's stated "I'm going for it."

Those four small words had sparked off pandemonium, albeit a very short-lived pandemonium.

"I think we should stay here," the woman across the aisle from Jen shouted, conveniently forgetting she had moments before protested that very idea. A chorus of agreement followed the woman's agitated shout.

"I want to go home." This teary wail, which came from a young woman near the front, received a look of scorn from Ted. Yet, illogically, a chorus of agreement, mostly female, also followed that statement.

"Dammit, man," an angry male voice rose above the other voices, "you just finished saying there were motorists stranded all over these roads. Why take a chance on becoming one of them? I think the lady's right. We'd be safer staying right here."

Just about everyone on the bus joined in vocal agreement with that advice. Everyone, that is, except Jen, who sat in mute fascination watching Ted's face harden.

"I am responsible for this bus and everyone on it." Ted's cold tone, amplified by the loudspeaker, silenced the uproar. "The decision is mine and I've made it." An angry murmur rumbled through the bus, cut short by Ted's next words. "Now, if you'll be quiet, I'll explain why I made it."

Her respect for the man growing, Jen's eyes shifted to study the sullen but now quiet passengers. When her eyes swung back to the driver she had to gulp back a surprised "Oh." Unless she was seeing things, Ted had winked at her!

"Thank you," he drawled when the last mutter had died out. "The reason I'm going to try to reach that motel is for your safety and comfort. I've been in storms like this before. No one can ever predict their duration or severity. We could be held up for as little as one day. Or we could be stranded for as long as one week. Think about it."

As he paused to let his words register, Jen watched the faces of the people nearest to her change from indignation to fearful astonishment. She could almost hear the same words ringing in their minds that were echoing in hers. *One week!*

"Now" — Ted's calm voice drew their complete attention — "the reason I think I can make it is the obvious one, and that is simply the very size of this vehicle. This sucker can plow through much deeper snow than a car can. Also, as it carries a hell of a lot more fuel, I can take it slow without the fear of running out of gas. It may get a little hairy," he warned softly, then underlined firmly, "but I'll make it. No more questions. No more protests. I want it quiet as a church in here. We're moving."

With that he had clicked off the mike, slid into his seat, and after flexing his shoulders, move they did, very slowly, very carefully — forward.

Now, over a tension-filled, tautly quiet hour and a half later, the bus was still moving. They had had a few hairy moments. The worst was when a strong gust of wind had caught the back end of the bus, sweeping it off the highway. Moans of fright and several screams had accompanied the bus's rocking swing. Thankfully Ted's cool actions and quick reflexes had brought the lumbering vehicle back under control and back onto the highway. At least what was assumed to be the highway by the occasional sign sticking up out of the deep snow that they passed.

Nervous perspiration beading her forehead, Jen, as frightened as everyone else, bit her lip against the demoralizing sounds of soft weeping that began suddenly with one woman and spread rapidly to others, including Lisa and Terry behind her. Nails digging into her palm, she hung on to her composure by hanging on to her faith in Ted.

Although there wasn't the slightest resemblance, he reminded Jen of her father. Like her father, Ted's quiet self-confidence instilled trust. Ralph Lengle was a taciturn, unassuming man who went about the business of getting a job done with tenacity. As she had inherited a strong streak of tenacity herself, Jen could recognize it in others. Ted had it.

The soft sobbing tearing at her emotions, Jen stared out the window with a new respect for the delicately formed crystals. They were pristine and pure, their white laciness beautiful, yet in accumulation, potentially treacherous. As, Jen mused, are many forms of nature unleashed in fury.

Eyes squinted against the continuing glare of white, Jen felt she'd lived through days as the seconds slowly slid into long, long minutes. God, if *she* felt exhausted, how must Ted be feeling by now? The thought drew her eyes to the not very broad but competent-looking back. The back moved as, hand over hand, the large steering wheel was turned and the bus lurchingly crossed the highway.

"What now?" the woman across the aisle from Jen sobbed.

The mike clicked on as the bus came to a complete stop. Liz's voice had the breathy sound of released tension.

"We're home free, gang," she laughed tremulously. "We're at the motel."

As if pulled by an unseen cord, they all, Jen included, rose in their seats, necks craning to see out of the wide windshield. Sure enough, its large bulk looming darkly through the swirl of white, the motel stood a short distance before them.

Blinking against the hot surge of moisture that filled her eyes, trembling with reaction, Jen sank back in her seat, mentally issuing a prayer of thanks. The next moment her tear-bright eyes flashed in astonished disbelief at the stupidity of a wailed

40

question that broke through the jerkily relieved, excited chatter.

"What do we do if they have no room and won't take us in?"

The shocked silence that followed that inanity told Jen she was not alone in her judgment of the woman's intellect.

"They will take us in." Ted's voice came cold and clear without benefit of the loudspeaker. "Even if they are already packed." With a disgusted shake of his graying head he dismissed the subject, saying crisply, "Okay, gather whatever hand luggage or paraphernalia you may have with you and get ready to leave the bus. No one," he said sharply, "is getting off this bus until *everyone* is ready. That wind is mean, so I suggest you walk in twos and stay close together. The men will lead off in order to blaze a trail."

Ted waited until the general hubbub of preparation had died down, then said briskly, "All right, let's go."

The door opened, and the line that formed in the narrow aisle inched forward slowly. When she reached the front of the bus Jen was not surprised to see Ted, in snow nearly up to his knees, standing stoically beside the door, giving a helping hand to his alighting passengers. Grasping hands or arms, he assisted and steadied each successive person. When he turned to take

41

Jen's outstretched hand a gentle smile touched his compressed lips. As she made the half step, half leap, into the snow, a strong gust of wind knocked her off balance. A strong hand at her back kept her from falling.

"Thank you," Jen laughed shakily.

"Thank *you*," Ted returned meaningfully.

Jen shot him a puzzled look, but he had turned to assist Lisa off the step. Hunching her shoulders against the biting force of the wind, she stood beside Lisa until Terry had joined them. Huddled together they made their way carefully along the uneven path in the snow, heads bent to protect their faces from the sting of the wind and the swirling wet flakes.

Blinking to dislodge some snow clinging to her lashes, Jen glanced up to see how much farther they had to go and felt her breath catch as her gaze encountered a partially snow-covered gold Corvette, minus skis. Again a clear picture of that male right hand flashed into her mind. A shiver rippled through her body, and hunching her shoulders even more, Jen tore her eyes away from the car.

When they reached the covered entranceway to the building, they paused to brush the clinging snow from each other before entering the roomy lobby. Joining the rest of their group, standing together off to one side, they were informed that Liz was at the reception desk inquiring about rooms. Ignoring the laughing, excited chatter around her, Jen's eyes took stock of the motel.

It was obviously newly built; Jen labeled the decor plushy rustic. Curving open staircases, one at either side of the lobby, indicated that the motel had two floors and that the rooms were reached from inside passageways. Jen registered that fact with a sigh of relief; at least they wouldn't have to plow to rooms with outside entrances. To her right, under the curve of the staircase, an archway with louvered swinging doors led into what Jen could see was the bar. Facing it across the width of the lobby, a matching archway led into a dining room, empty now and only dimly lit. To the rear two similar but smaller archways, without swinging doors, led into what Jen thought were hallways. Liz's voice drew Jen's attention from the large wagon-wheel style chandelier hanging by a thick chain from the high, open-beamed ceiling.

"Can I have your attention, please?" The sound of metal clinking against metal followed her words as Liz lifted a handful of room keys. "As you can see, they were able to accommodate us. As a matter of fact we've taken the last rooms available." She paused to allow the spattering of relieved comments, then said crisply, "Now, as I call your names, please step forward for your key."

The ensuing procedure was by necessity a slow one as Liz had to check and mark her clipboard after each key was handed out. When she got to Lisa and Terry, who had planned to share a room — as Jen and Chris had — she paused before glancing up at Jen.

"Jennifer, you are going to have to bunk with Lisa and Terry. I'm sorry, but" — she shrugged — "that's the only way we can get everyone in."

"It beats sleeping on the bus," Jen quipped dryly, stepping forward to join Lisa and Terry.

"No big deal." Lisa grinned. "Unless you snore, that is."

Key in hand, Lisa led the way to the stairway to their right. At the top of the stairs she swung down the hallway, checking room numbers on both sides against the one on the key tag. When she reached the one that matched, she unlocked the door, pushed it open, and, with a sweeping wave of her hand, ushered Jen and Terry in with a chirped, "It may get crowded, but it shouldn't get dull."

The large room contained two double beds covered with patchwork spreads, a matching pair of basic, sage-green arm-chairs placed one on either side of a tole metal floor lamp and a long combination dresser-desk against the long wall. A color TV/VCR unit sat on the end of the low dresser closest to the chairs. The bathroom was tiled in beige, the fixtures and molded Fiberglas tub-shower combination in white.

After they finished examining their temporary domain, Terry dropped onto one of the beds, declaring she was going to have a delayed nervous breakdown and then a nap. Grinning while she tugged her sweater over her head, Lisa opted for a hot shower.

Standing at the mirror, trying to brush her damp, curly mane into some sort of order, Jen said seriously, "Being scared always dries me up. I feel parched, so I think I'll investigate that bar downstairs." Dropping the brush onto the dresser, she scooped up her bag and left the room.

Jen pushed through the swinging doors, then paused to take a quick inventory of the bar, which was full. The end of the room closest to the entrance contained a large horseshoe-shaped bar manned by three bartenders. The center section contained a dozen or so tables covered with patchwork cloths and topped by candles set inside dark red glass globes. The far end of the room was set up as a lounge area with a long, low-backed sofa and several overstuffed chairs grouped around a wide fire-place in which a real fire flickered and sent out long fingers of orange-red light.

Laughter and conversation vied with the music from the jukebox. Unable to see one unoccupied seat, Jen sighed and was about to leave when she saw a raised arm beckon her to the bar.

Following the curving bar to the still-raised arm, a smile lit Jen's face when she saw the arm belonged to Ted.

Ignoring a softly called, "Hi, honey, looking for me?" from a man four stools away from Ted, Jen made for the one and only empty seat in the place, next to Ted.

"I believe just about everyone from the bus is in this place." Jen grinned as she slid onto the stool. "That was some fancy piece of driving you did, sir. But very, very scary."

"I know, I'm still shaking." Ted grinned back, holding up an exaggeratedly trembling hand for proof. "What would you like to calm your nerves?"

"A glass of white wine, please," Jen told the hovering bartender. Then, her face and tone serious, she looked into Ted's craggy face and murmured, "I knew you could make it."

The lines radiating from Ted's eyes crinkled as he smiled gently at her. "And I knew you felt I could," he said surpris ingly. "Your confidence and trust in me was written on your face. I could read it all the way up front. It's a look I've been blessed with on occasion from my teenage daughter."

"And I was thinking how much your determination reminded me of my father." Jen smiled back.

During their exchange Jen barely noticed that the man on the other side of Ted vacated his seat or that another had claimed it. But she did hear the deep, attractive voice that asked Ted if he was the driver of the bus in the parking lot.

Ted turned to answer in the affirmative, adding that after the ride he'd had that day, he might just look for a desk job. Ted's dry remark drew soft laughter from the unseen man; then Jen's heart thumped as a right hand was extended and the deep voice offered, "Adam Banner, and I know how you feel. I also drove through that mess."

"Ted Grayson," Ted replied, grasping the offered hand. "And this is Miss — ?" Leaning back, Ted raised his brows at Jen.

"Jennifer Lengle," Jen supplied somewhat breathlessly, finding herself staring into a pair of eyes the color of dark brown velvet.

The sight of his hand on the steering wheel had sent a tingle through Jen; the look of him set off a clamor. He was perhaps the most attractive man she had ever seen. His hair, though straight, was thick and full. The color reminded Jen of her morning toast, not dark enough to be brown, not light enough for blond. His features were even and regular, the jawline firm, determined. Dark brows slashed in an almost straight line above eyes heavily fringed with thick, dark lashes. And those eyes. If one were to imagine liquid velvet, Jen thought, bemused, it would look exactly like those eyes.

"How do you do, Miss Lengle?" His soft voice tugged at her wandering thoughts. "May I call you Jennifer?"

I'd rather you call me darling. The sudden thought shocked Jen, and yet it was true! She had never seen this man before. For all she knew he could be a criminal — or worse. But on his lips her name had sounded like a caress, and she felt a longing deep inside to hear that soft voice murmur an endearment. This feeling, never before experienced, confused and unnerved her. His soft, questioning eyes brought her to her senses.

"M-my friends — everyone calls me Jen," she blurted, feeling her face grow warm.

"I think I prefer Jennifer." Sharp now with consideration, his eyes probed her pink cheeks.

Tearing her gaze from his, Jen clutched the glass of wine the bartender had moments before placed in front of her and, bringing it to her lips, drank thirstily.

"I like Jen, myself," Ted opined teasingly. "It goes with the freckles."

It was obvious from Ted's easy, unaffected manner that he had missed Jen's slight stammer, the quickened sharpness of Adam's eyes. Had she imagined it? Jen asked herself. Had that electrical tautness that had seemed to sizzle between them been in her mind? She had to find out. The glass still at her lips, she turned her head very slowly, looking at him through the lashes of her demurely lowered lids.

He was waiting for her. The moment her glance touched him, he lifted his glass in silent acknowledgment and drank with deliberation and meaning, his eyes a warm caress on her face. *Zing.* The current ran, swift and hot, from his eyes to hers and down through her entire body, setting off sparks all along the way.

"It's stopped snowing, Ted."

The voice belonged to Liz. Dragging her gaze from Adam's, Jen turned to find the young woman at her shoulder, facing Ted.

"Some of the people from the bus have asked about their luggage." Liz grimaced ruefully. "I was delegated to come ask you if you could possibly unload it."

"What a bunch of sweethearts," Ted groaned. "I'll go take a look-see after I've finished my drink." Lifting his hand, he motioned to the bartender. When she came to a stop across the bar, he asked, "What'll you have, Liz?"

"A Bloody Mary," Liz replied grimly. "I need something strong to wash the bad taste away. Every tour I've been on has been the same. The majority of the people are pleasant and easy to get along with, but there are always a few who simply can't be pleased."

The bartender came back carrying the scarlet concoction, and Ted made a move to get up. Adam moved faster. Sliding off his stool, he reached around Ted and touched Liz on the arm.

"Have a seat and forget all of them for a while — Liz?" His brows went up questioningly.

"Yes — Liz Dorn, and thank you, Mr. — ?"

"Banner, Adam — and you're welcome."

The smile he gave Liz caused an odd, sharp little pain in Jen's throat. Glancing away quickly, Jen studied the stemmed wineglasses hanging upside down on a round rack above the space behind the bar. *What in heaven's name is the matter with me?* Jen actually felt envious of Liz because of a smile. *This is insane,* she berated herself, gulping the last of her wine. *You don't even know the man.*

"Would you like another?"

Adam's warm, whiskey-scented breath feathered her cheek. Jen had to clamp her teeth together to keep from trembling.

"I — I don't think I'd better." Jen swallowed back a groan of self-disgust. *God, did that stammered, garbled reply make any sense at all?* Drawing a quick breath, she went on more slowly, "I haven't eaten since we stopped for breakfast, and I'm afraid another would go to my head."

As a matter of fact, she added silently, *I'm afraid the one drink has gone to my head.* Could that be it? Could it be the wine causing this funny, squiggly feeling in her stomach, and not the man? He was standing behind her, very close, and Jen suddenly felt hot. Yet the fingers that played with the stem of her glass were like ice.

"You're right," Adam agreed. "It's not a good idea to drink on an empty stomach."

"Speaking of empty stomachs," Ted sighed resignedly, standing up, "I guess everybody's is, and as they'll probably want to shower and change before dinner, I suppose I'd better see about unloading the luggage."

"I'll go with you," Adam volunteered. He finished his drink in a few deep swallows. "Coming, Liz?" Leaning forward, he placed his glass on the bar. Turning to look at her, he murmured, "Jennifer?"

Jen's pulses leaped, pushing her spirits up out of the disappointed low they'd slumped into at his offer to help. Like a magnet, his eyes drew her off the stool. And like a puppet whose strings he controlled, she followed him out of the room, Liz at her side.

At the wide glass double entrance doors they stood side by side, Ted, Adam, Jen, and Liz. The motel's bright outside lights bathed the parking area in a glow that shot glittering blue-gold reflections off the snow.

"It looks like a Christmas card," Jen said softly.

"Oh, yes," Liz breathed. "Isn't it beautiful?"

"And cold," Ted grumbled. "And wet."

The deep chuckle from beside Jen ricocheted along her nerve endings.

"We're not going to get it done standing here looking at it," Adam drawled. "It would be a lot easier if you could bring that monster closer to the entrance. What do you think, Ted, want to give it a try?"

"If you can get it up here, just let it sit after it's empty."

All four turned to stare at the small man who had spoken with authority. Thin and balding, the man was about fifty, with a pleasant smile and shrewd, intelligent eyes.

"Bill Wakefield." He smiled, showing white, even dentures. "I'm the manager here."

"Ted Grayson," Ted said.

"Adam Banner." Adam smiled. "And this is Liz Dorn and Jennifer Lengle."

Handshakes were exchanged and Bill Wakefield, his smile wry, repeated, "If you can get it up, leave it sit. I don't suppose we'll be getting any more customers tonight. I'll put a man to work with the snow blower in the front. If you can get the luggage unloaded, we'll have to carry it in ourselves. I'm working with a skeleton crew, as some of my day people went home early, and most of the evening shift didn't make it in."

"Well, I may as well get my jacket and get at it."

Ted turned and strode across the lobby, Adam right behind him.

Feeling completely useless, Jen stood watching as the motel employee began blowing the drifted snow under the covered entranceway. A light touch on her arm drew her attention from the gleam of white.

"Here's Ted and Mr. Banner," Liz said quietly. "It was very nice of him to offer to help Ted."

"Yes, he seems like a nice guy." Jen forced a note of lightness around the sudden tightness in her throat caused by the sight of Adam walking toward them.

What was it about this man that affected her so strongly? True, he was exceptionally good-looking, but Jen was past the age of being impressed by mere good looks. No, it was more — much more — than looks. But what?

Her expression carefully controlled, Jen watched him approach, her breath catching at a sudden leap of excitement inside. He was not even looking at her as he fastened the zipper closing of the dark brown and white ski parka he'd donned, a simple procedure made difficult because he carried a knitted cap in one hand and gloves in the other. The closing made, he glanced up, and Jen felt warmth radiate through her body as his eyes captured hers. He didn't say anything as he passed her and pushed through the heavy doors. But then, he didn't have to say anything, for Jen received the message his eyes flashed to her as clearly as if he'd shouted it. The message was: Don't go away, wait for me here.

Shaken and confused by the strange telepathic experience, Jen's eyes followed his retreating back as, side by side, he and Ted plowed slowly through the knee-high snow. Without consciously trying to do it, Jen's mind sent out a plea to him of its own. *Please be careful, and hurry back to me.* That shook her even more.

She knew they had reached the bus when two bright lights, looking like the eyes of a huge monster, cut through the blackness that was the parking lot. Barely breathing, she watched those eyes move very, very slowly toward her. Suddenly those headlights blinded her, and with a small gasp she stepped back as the bus, looming out of the darkness, came directly at her. Then the lights arched away as the bus made a lurching swing and came to a stop parallel to the motel's entrance.

The moment the bus came to a halt Adam leaped agilely from the high step onto the now cleared area alongside which the vehicle had stopped. Ted was right behind him, keys dangling from his hand. The door of the storage compartment was opened, and the two men began hauling out the luggage.

"I think I'll go roust some of the men out of the bar to help," Liz declared in sudden decision. "Why should those two do all the work? Hell, Adam isn't even one of the passengers."

"Liz, wait." Jen's hand caught Liz's arm as she spun away. "If you go in there and call for assistance and they all troop out here, you're going to have nothing but mass confusion."

A rattling sound drew Jen's attention, and glancing across the lobby, she saw Bill Wakefield pushing a large luggage rack before him. Releasing Liz's arm, Jen walked to the doors, pushed through, then held it for Bill.

"Come on, Liz," she called. "If you and I help, we can have the bags loaded and inside in no time. Then you can call the others to the lobby to pick up their cases."

Jen didn't wait for a yes or no from Liz. Grabbing the front end of the rack, she guided it through the doors and over the cleared cement to the steadily growing pile of luggage. The night air was cold and damp, and Jen began shivering before she reached the pile of cases. Her teeth clenched together to keep them from chattering, she began stacking the cases onto the rack following Bill's directions, grinning at Liz, who had followed her out.

Jen knew the bus was empty when the compartment door slammed shut. Five pairs of hands made short shrift of the job. Jen was reaching for one of the few remaining cases when strong, gloved hands grasped her shoulders, turning her to the doors.

"We'll finish up and bring it in," Adam said firmly. "You're cold — go inside. You too, Liz."

Although his tone was mild, it was an order. Without protest Jen and Liz obeyed. Standing inside the doors, Jen watched as the three men maneuvered the ungainly rack across the cement. She was shivering again, only now it was from the touch of those leather-covered hands, not the cold.

Clipboard in hand, Liz checked the tags on the bags against the names on her list as Jen and the men unloaded the rack in front of the reception desk. When the conveyance was once again empty and the cases lined up into neat rows, Ted straightened.

"Thanks," he stated simply, then, his tone lightening, he asked, "How about having dinner together?"

"You're on," Liz said at once.

Jen, hesitating, glanced quickly at Adam, who nodded briefly at her before facing Ted.

"Sounds good." His gaze shifted back to Jen. "Jennifer?"

"Y-yes, of course," Jen agreed in a wavery voice. Why? Oh, why did the sound of her name on his lips unnerve her so?

"And I'll go and put a reserved sign on a good table for you," Bill said, heading for the dining room.

"Well," Liz sighed resignedly, "I guess I'll go call the thundering herd out of the bar." She started off, then glanced back.

57

"Jen, would you go tell Lisa and Terry their bags are in the lobby?"

"Will do," Jen answered, reaching for her own bag.

Scooping her case from under her fingers, Adam said, "I'll take them. Which ones belong to the other two girls?"

Ignoring her protests, he clamped a case under one arm and picked up the other.

"What time should we meet for dinner?" Jen's eyes shifted from one to the other.

Ted shot a glance at his watch.

"Seven okay?" At Jen and Adam's nod, he added, "We can meet in the bar. I'll tell Liz."

As they walked up the stairs, Adam slanted Jen a teasing grin.

"I think there's something developing between Liz and Ted; I can feel the vibes."

"But he's married!" Jen exclaimed, shocked. "He told me he has a daughter."

"He's a widower," Adam corrected gently.

"But how do you kn—"

"I asked him, while we were in the bus, if he'd gotten a call through to his wife," Adam answered before she'd even finished asking. "He told me his wife was dead, but that he had reached his daughter."

"And do you really think there is something brewing between him and Liz?"

They had reached the room Jen was

sharing with Lisa and Terry. Adam deposited the cases at the door before answering her question with one of his own.

"Haven't you seen the way they look at each other?"

"No." Jen shook her head.

"Well, I have." Adam's eyes stared straight into hers and the expression in them dried all the moisture in her mouth. When he spoke again she knew he was no longer talking about Liz and Ted.

"Every glance is a touch, a caress," he murmured. Turning away, he tacked on, "I'll see you at seven and — Jennifer — don't look so frightened."

Three

The hot, stinging spray from the shower overcame the chills that had attacked Jen's spine at Adam's parting words.

"Oh, glory," she groaned softly. "What is happening to me?"

The sound of her own voice, intensified by bouncing off the shower tiles, startled her and brought her up short. *Good grief! Now I'm talking to myself,* she thought wearily. *But, what is happening to me?* Nothing like this had ever happened to her before.

Oh, sure, she had been attracted to other young men — as well as repelled — on first meeting. But this confusing clamor of emotions and senses, this all-over warm sensation while chills skipped down her spine, this scary, exciting desire to hear him say her name, to feel his eyes on her, was beyond understanding, beyond reason.

Jen dressed slowly and carefully in a room that was, finally, blessedly quiet. Lisa and Terry had left moments before, going down to the dining room to eat and, as Terry put it, "To check out the male prospects of the motel's inhabitants."

Thankfully, her breathless, flustered state on entering the room had been overlooked by the other two girls simply because she had kept her head down while dragging the cases inside. On seeing their luggage, both girls jumped up with squeals of delight and began unpacking at once.

"I wonder if this is worth the effort," Lisa had mused shaking out a silky blouse before draping it carefully on a hanger. "Do you think there's any chance of going on to the resort tomorrow, Jen?"

"Well, it has stopped snowing, but" — Jen shook her head — "I doubt it. From what I could see of the parking lot, the snow looks pretty deep. I can't imagine what the roads are like."

"But suppose we unpack and they decide to go on tomorrow," Terry groaned. "We'll have to repack everything."

"I'm going to play it safe." Jen grinned. "I'm going to hang up the things that will crush and leave everything else in the case."

Lisa and Terry opted to do the same, and confusion reigned for several minutes as the three girls bumped into each other while moving back and forth between their cases and the room's one clothes closet.

"Would you like us to wait for you, Jen?" Lisa had called through the bathroom door as Jen prepared to take a shower.

"No, thanks, Lisa," Jen called back. "I'm having dinner with Liz and Ted." She hesitated, then added, "And a man we met in the bar."

"A man!" Lisa shrieked. "What man? Is he good-looking? Was he alone or was he with friends? Oh, why didn't I go down to the bar with you instead of —"

Jen had turned the shower on, effectively drowning out Lisa's voice. By the time Jen walked out of the bathroom Lisa and Terry had gone.

Now, putting the finishing touches to her makeup, a smile twitched at Jen's lips on remembering Lisa's questions. By the number of males evident in the bar, she thought wryly, Lisa should have no trouble finding company.

Stepping back to get a long view of herself in the mirror, Jen studied her reflection critically. Her long skirt, in a soft, cocoa wool, clung just enough to give her a leggy look. And her oatmeal cashmere turtleneck molded her high, full breasts while still managing to give her a somewhat fragile appearance.

With a nod of satisfaction she flipped back a fiery red tendril that insisted on falling across her cheek, picked up her bag, and walked out of the room, breathing slowly to combat the excitement tickling her throat.

As she had a few hours earlier, Jen paused inside the swinging doors of the bar's entrance, stepping to one side to allow an approaching man to exit. The man drew alongside her, hand raised to push open the doors. The hand dropped as turning to her he asked, "Aren't you on the Barton's bus?"

"What? — oh, yes." Jen had barely noticed him as her eyes had been busy searching for Adam. A smile curving her lips, she turned to face him. The smile wavered, but she managed to keep it in place. It was the man who had stood in front of her in line that morning — could it have only been that morning? — the one who had advised his friend to work off his frustrations.

"Well, hi." His right hand was extended. "I'm Larry Gordon."

It was the first really good look she had at him. Larry Gordon was an exceptionally attractive young man, almost pretty. About twenty-five or -six, he had a head full of soft blond curls that perfectly topped his boyishly innocent, baby blue-eyed face. His smile was warm, somewhat shy, and his eyes were guileless. If Jen had not overheard his words that morning, heard the

63

underlying disdain for women in his tone, she'd have trusted him on sight. But she had heard him; she didn't trust or like him.

After a brief hesitation while these thoughts flashed through her mind, she placed her palm against his.

"Jen Lengle."

Maybe it was foolish, but Jen had a sudden aversion to giving him her full name. After hearing Adam say it, she simply did not want it on this man's lips.

"Hello, Jen Lengle." His tone had a hint of intimacy that stiffened Jen's spine. "Since we both seem to be alone, how about having dinner with me?"

Good heavens! Jen thought in amazement. *Don't tell me his companion has found a playmate already?* Revulsion, combined with a hot shaft of anger, shot through her. Masking her face to keep it from showing, Jen felt her smile beginning to dissolve.

"I'm sorry, I'm meeting —" Jen began firmly, but a feathering shiver withered the refusal in her mouth. Her back to the bar as she faced Larry, she had not seen Adam cross the room, yet she knew he was there; the shiver told her.

"I've been waiting for you." Adam's quiet tone doubled her shivers. "Ted and Liz have gone into the dining room. As soon as you've introduced me to your friend, we'll join them."

Startled by the edge his tone had taken on, Jen's eyes flew to his face. His visage revealed nothing of what he was thinking, and his eyes looked flat, lifeless.

"Oh, yes — of course." Jen paused to draw a quick breath. What was the matter with her? She felt like a tongue-tied teenager caught in some guilty act. Guilty? For talking a few minutes with Larry? But why? The questions zapped through Jen's mind in the instant required to draw that calming breath. "Adam, this is Larry Gordon. He's one of the tour passengers. Larry, Adam Banner."

While the two men shook hands, exchanging the usual trite introductory conversation, Jen brought herself under control. Guilty indeed! But Adam's sudden appearance while she'd been talking to Larry had caused the strangest feeling, almost as if she were being disloyal. And she'd met Adam only a few hours ago! The word *strange* didn't seem strong enough.

Preoccupied with her confusing thoughts, Jen smiled vaguely at Larry when he excused himself and headed back to the bar, missing entirely the suggestive wink he sent her once he was beyond Adam's sight.

"Are you hungry?" Adam's quiet voice nudged her out of her musings.

"Starving." Jen walked by the door he was holding for her. "Are you?" she asked when he fell into step beside her.

"Yes," he answered shortly.

They were a few feet from the swinging doors into the dining room when Adam stopped moving and turned to her, a frown creasing his brow.

"Did you want to have dinner with him?"

Caught unaware by the abruptness of his query, Jen stared at him in perplexity. "With whom? Larry?" At his nod, she frowned. "Of course not."

"Good." The emphatic word seemed to be issued with a sigh of relief Taking her arm, he started moving again. "Do you know him well?" His tone was even, bland. Almost too bland.

"I don't know him at all." Jen preceded him into the dining room with a smile of thanks as he again held the door. "And I don't want to know him," she added emphatically.

Adam lifted a hand to acknowledge Ted's beckoning wave from the corner of the room, while at the same time he lifted questioning brows at her.

"He comes on a little too strong," Jen answered his curious look.

"Has he been annoying you?" he asked sharply.

"Not at all!" Jen exclaimed, startled by the fierceness of his tone. Returning Ted and Liz's smiles as they approached the table, Jen added in an undertone, "But I know the type and I don't appreciate them."

The table Bill had kept for them was at the very end corner of the crowded room at a large plate glass window. Every table was occupied, and the conversation and occasional laughter that floated on the air had a festive holiday ring.

Ted and Liz seemed to be in a festive mood as well. Liz looked decidedly sexy in a pale blue wool chemise. Ted, out of uniform, looked younger and casually terrific in a tan knit sweater and dark brown pants. With the weight of responsibility lifted from his shoulders, Ted was in a relaxed, teasing mood.

"What do you think, Adam?" he asked with feigned seriousness, his eyes moving from Liz to Jen. "Was it fate or pure blind luck that put us in the bar at the perfect time to latch onto the two loveliest women in this place?"

A slow, heart-stopping smile curved Adam's lips, and the warm velvet look was back in the eyes that followed Ted's from one pink-checked face to the other.

"I think it was a combination of both," Adam said softly. "A combination I have no desire to question but a strong desire to savor."

Jen felt her flush deepen under his melting gaze, felt her breath quicken as that gaze moved over her slowly, lingering first on her gently heaving breasts, then on her slightly parted lips.

God! He was making love to her with his eyes! Boldly, brazenly, in front of anyone who cared to watch, he was staking a silent claim on her. The response that quivered through Jen shocked her. Shaken by the intensity of her reaction to him, she tore her eyes away in embarrassment.

Incredibly, Liz and Ted seemed not to have noticed anything unusual. On closer inspection, Jen decided it wasn't all that incredible, as Ted and Liz had eyes only for each other.

Aware now, attuned to the vibrations, Jen, unable to tear her eyes away, watched the silent byplay between Ted and Liz. Ted's eyes, older but no less dimmed than Adam's, caressed her. Liz's reaction was much the same as Jen's had been.

What in the world was happening to all of them? The thought shot through Jen's mind like an outcry. Did being snowbound affect the mind, the senses? Feeling suddenly like an intruder, Jen lowered her eyes to the table. The tug of warm velvet drew her eyes from the

Wedgwood blue tablecloth to Adam's face. His expression was both understanding and compassionate. He *knew* the turmoil and confusion she was experiencing!

The appearance of their waiter shattered the intimacy that seemed to encompass the table.

"Good evening, folks." The young man smiled pleasantly. "Would you like something from the bar before ordering?"

"I'll have a double martini on the rocks," Liz replied in a strained, breathless blurt.

Although Ted's eyebrows went up, an indulgent smile tugged at his lips.

"I'll have the same," he told the waiter.

"Jennifer?" Adam nudged at her hesitation. "White wine?" She nodded and he turned to the waiter. "And I'll have a Manhattan — with a twist."

"Yes, sir." With another quick smile the young man handed menus around, then sauntered away.

Quiet prevailed for several minutes while they studied the bill of fare, then, closing the menu, Liz said stiltedly, "I think I'll have the shrimp cocktail and the flounder stuffed with crab meat."

"The shrimp cocktail sounds good," Ted agreed, "but I'll go with the broiled scallops." Glancing first at Jen then at Adam, he asked, "What about you two?"

"French onion soup."

Their replies came simultaneously and, strangely, breaking the tension simmering among all of them.

"And?" Ted laughed.

"Prime rib with baked potato." Jen grinned at Ted before prompting teasingly, "Adam?"

Broad shoulders inside a very expensive-looking off-white cable knit sweater lifted in a believe-it-or-not shrug.

"The same," he drawled softly.

The food was expertly prepared and delicious. Adam had cause to execute that elegant shrug once again when, taking the small boat of sour cream with chives Jen handed to him, he proceeded to pile every bit as much of it onto his potato as she had.

On leaving the dining room they encountered Bill Wakefield in the lobby and in a chorus congratulated him on his chef. Bill's slender face beamed at their lavish praise.

"Glad you enjoyed it and I'll be happy to pass your kind words on to the cook. It'll make his day." His smile turned impish. "Even though he knows he's good. Doesn't hesitate to tell me — regularly."

A phone rang, and from behind the registration desk the clerk called, "Phone for you, Bill."

"Coming," Bill called. "Enjoy yourselves." Then he added over his shoulder, "Oh, yeah, there's dancing in the bar tonight — to the jukebox."

"Well, at least the phones weren't knocked out of service," Liz observed as they strolled across the lobby.

"I never thought of that!" Jen exclaimed, stopping dead. "Look, you three go on ahead. I'm going to call home and let my parents know I'm all right and where I am."

It wasn't until the phone at her home was ringing that Jen realized she didn't know exactly where she was, and she couldn't ask the desk clerk as he'd disappeared on some errand. Her mother answered on the third ring.

"It's Jen, Mom. I just called to let you know I'm okay."

"Oh, Jen," Ella Lengle's voice sighed with relief. "We've been so worried. Are you at the lodge?"

"No, we're at a motel," Jen said ruefully. "But don't ask me where. All I can tell you is we're in New York State. Is it bad at home?"

"Yes." Her mother sighed again. "We've been listening to the radio, and reports of power and phone lines going down are beginning to come in. Everything has come to a standstill, and the call has gone out for volunteers with four-wheel drive vehicles for emergencies."

"Well, it has stopped snowing here," Jen reported. "Maybe we'll be able to go on to the lodge tomorrow. We can't be too far from there. I'll call you in the morning and let you know."

After hanging up the phone, Jen walked to the entrance of the bar, stepped inside, and for the third time that evening, paused while her eyes went skimming over the room. Beyond the bar a partitioning wall had been folded back to reveal a small dance floor, which was already full of couples gyrating to an upbeat tune throbbing from a large jukebox in the corner.

The bar was solidly packed two deep, although there were still several empty tables in the center of the room. Peering through the pall of gray smoke in the dimly lit room, a smile touched Jen's lips as her attention was caught by an upraised arm in the lounge area. The arm went higher into the air as Ted rose from the long, low-backed sofa. Waving back to him, Jen started toward the lounge area. Halfway across the room her name was called, and Jen glanced to her right to smile and wave at Lisa and Terry. When she turned back she found her way blocked by Larry Gordon.

"You're going in the wrong direction."

"What?"

"The dance floor is behind you," Larry

smiled, revealing even white teeth. "You *are* going to dance with me, aren't you?"

"I've just finished eating and I'm too full to dance," Jen hedged, deciding she disliked this cocky young man more with each meeting.

"Then come to the bar and have a drink with me," he ordered smoothly. "Then after your dinner settles, we'll dance."

For several seconds Jen stared at him in amazement. *Is this guy for real?* And was she actually supposed to be impressed by his takeover attitude? Biting back the scornful laugh that rose to her lips, she began softly, "I don't want —"

"Of course you do." He smiled insinuatingly, taking a step closer to her.

Fighting the urge to step back, Jen held her ground, lifted her chin, and insisted firmly, "No, thank you, I —" The words dried on her lips and her body stiffened as a hand curved around her waist from behind. The stiffness drained out of her with a warm rush of relief at the quiet yet commanding sound of Adam's voice.

"Back off, pal."

Larry's eyes flickered, and he did take one backward step before he caught himself in retreat and straightened with a fatalistic shrug.

"Sorry, man," he grinned knowingly. "Didn't mean to cut into your time." He started forward, and Jen turned aside to allow him to pass. As he did his arm deliberately brushed her breast, and he whispered, "Later, honey."

Not wanting to create a scene, Jen, swallowing the furious gasp that rose in her throat, glanced at Adam to see if he'd heard Larry's whispered gibe. It was more than obvious that he had, for his face was set in lines of cold rage and his eyes glittered dangerously from behind narrowed lids.

"That son-of-a—"

"Ignore him." Jen cut swiftly across his softly growled words. "Adam, please," she added urgently as his hand dropped from her waist and he made a move to follow Larry. It was only when she shifted to stand in front of him that she saw he was holding a bar tray in his other hand. On the tray were a carafe of white wine and four stemmed glasses. The glasses shivered on the tray, alerting Jen to the intensity of the anger rippling through Adam's body.

"Adam —"

It was a whispered plea, and with a sigh of relief Jen saw the glasses become still an instant before he tore his fierce gaze from Larry's back and focused on her upturned face.

"Ted and Liz are waiting for their wine," she said softly.

"If he touches you again, I'll —"

"He's not worth getting worked up over." Again she deliberately cut into his harsh tone. "And we're beginning to look conspicuous standing here." She laughed. "Don't you think we should join Ted and Liz?"

"Okay," he sighed, an answering smile twitching his lips.

Ted and Liz were ensconced at one end of the sofa, so deep in conversation, they had apparently not even noticed Jen's delay in reaching them.

"Your wine, sir," Adam murmured deferentially as he came to a stop in front of Ted. All evidence of his anger had disappeared, and a teasing light danced in his eyes. "Will there be anything else, sir?" he added with exaggeratedly raised brows.

"Not at the moment," Ted replied seriously, joining in Adam's nonsense.

"Then do I have your permission to escort this maid onto yon dance floor?"

"Yes — begone." Ted waved his hand impatiently. "And let me get back to the business of seducing this lovely lady."

Adam's soft laughter covered Jen's small gasp of surprise. Expecting some caustic comment, Jen glanced at Liz. But although her cheeks flushed becomingly pink, Liz lowered her eyes and remained silent.

Shrugging off the cloak of obsequiousness, Adam grasped Jen's hand and pulled her with him as he started to walk away.

"Each to his own method," he drawled sardonically. "Have at it, the couch is all yours."

Ted's laughter followed them as they made their way to the dance floor. Their progress was slow as the room was crowded. Every table was occupied, and the throng at the bar was now three deep. And over all a holiday atmosphere prevailed.

The area designated for dancing was even more dimly lit than the rest of the large room. The faces of the couples, moving slowly to a ballad, were barely discernible.

As they stepped onto the dance floor Adam released her hand and slid his arms around her waist. After a moment's hesitation, Jen placed her hands on his shoulders, ignoring the amused expression that crossed his face at her reluctance to encircle his neck with her arms.

They had taken no more than a few steps when the song ended, and yet it had been enough time for Jen to pick up his style. His hands holding her firmly at the waist, Adam waited until the next tune started. When the raspy voice of Bob Seger, singing something about his lady, came from the speakers, Adam's hands moved up her sides to her shoulders, then along her arms to grasp her wrists and draw them up and around his neck.

Following his steps automatically, Jen felt a shiver zigzag down her spine as his hands retraced their route to her waist. Then the zigzagging shiver splintered and sent stabbing points of excitement all through her body as his hands drew her closer to him. At least two inches still separated them, yet she felt suddenly breathless. Why, she wondered muzzily, did this man have this effect on her? She had danced in exactly this manner many times before, with many different men, yet never had she felt quite like this.

Tall as she was, Adam was several inches taller, and almost afraid to look at him, Jen fastened her eyes on the rolled neck of his sweater. As the music and Seger's sexy voice swirled around and through her, Jen felt Adam lower his head a moment before his warm breath teased the skin at her temple.

"Be brave, Jennifer," he whispered invitingly, his hands moving slowly, caressingly over her back. "Take that one tiny step necessary to bring your body against mine."

Gasping as much from the shaft of near painful longing that shot through her as from his words, Jen lifted startled eyes to his and was suddenly lost in a world of hot brown velvet. Thought suspended, she moved closer, feeling her breath catch again as his arms tightened to mold her softness to the hard contours of his larger frame.

Jen no longer heard the music or was aware of the other dancers around them. Melting warmth seeping through her, she stared in bemused fascination as Adam slowly lowered his head even more. By the time his mouth touched hers, her lips were slightly parted in acceptance.

Adam's kiss was brief in duration and gently experimental in nature. When he lifted his head Jen felt acute disappointment and dissatisfaction. Her feelings left her mind numb with shock. Sensing her mental confusion, Adam tilted his head back, his eyes narrowing as he studied her pale cheeks.

"Is something wrong?" His tone was soft but rough-edged, and somehow Jen knew he was wondering if she had been offended or turned off by his kiss.

"No, no." She shook her head to add emphasis to her words. "It's been a long day and I'm tired of dancing." It was a blatant lie. She wasn't in the least tired, merely surprised by her out-of-character response to him, and in truth, she could have moved to the musical beat, within the circle of his arms, for hours.

"Okay, let's go see what kind of progress Ted is making with his seduction of Liz." While he was speaking he came to a stop at the edge of the dance floor nearest the bar. His eyes, steady on her face, lit with laughter at the pink tinge his words brought to her cheeks. "I've shocked you?" he asked softly.

Feeling her face grow warmer still, Jen slid her arms from around his neck and lowered them to her sides. Lowering her eyes at the same time, she wet her lips and murmured, "Yes, a little."

"Why?" His one hand left her waist and came up to catch her chin, gently lifting it until she was looking at him again. "Why does the idea of Ted seducing Liz shock you? He has been seducing her with his eyes all evening. Why should saying it out loud shock you?"

"But they hardly know each other," Jen blurted, suddenly nervous because she felt sure that although he used Ted and Liz's names, he was talking about two other people, and she was one of those people. "They only met today."

"And a required amount of time must elapse for a man and woman to conclude they want to make love?" His tone was lightly teasing, but all the laughter was gone from his eyes. "Would you be less

79

shocked if they waited until tomorrow?" he prodded gently. "Or should it take a week or a month or a year?"

Beginning to feel badgered, cornered, Jen stared at him in confusion. Why was he doing this? What had she said to cause the fine, underlying trace of sarcasm that had entered his tone? She had the uncomfortable sensation that she had disappointed him, and she didn't know why. Had she no right to feel a little shocked at the idea of Ted and Liz spending the night together when they'd only met that very morning? Had she no right to her own principles of moral behavior? Anger stirred and she stepped back and away from him.

"I'm sure my views on the subject will have very little bearing on its outcome." Though she managed to keep her tone soft, there was a chill to it that betrayed her anger. She spun away from him but was brought up short by his arm snaking around her waist.

"Where are you going?" The mild demand in Adam's voice irritated her, and she made no attempt to hide it.

"Why, back to Ted and Liz!" she exclaimed curtly. "I wouldn't want to keep you from satisfying your avid curiosity about the progress Ted's making."

Before she could move away from him, his fingers dug into her waist, and with a jerk of his arm he pulled her to him.

"Jennifer" — Adam's soft voice now held a hint of his own anger — "let's have one thing clear. I don't give a damn what Ted and Liz do. And I'm sure as hell not going to pass moral judgment."

"But I haven't — !" Jen began in astonishment.

"Haven't you?" he cut in roughly. As if suddenly realizing where they were, he released her and said tersely, "I think we'd better go sit down."

With an angry toss of her fiery curls Jen swung away from him. Head high, she made her way through the crowded room, bewildered by the deflated feeling his rebuke had caused. Why in the world should she be hurt by his opinion? Why should she care what he thought? If they could leave tomorrow, she would probably never see him again. Jen had to smother the moan of protest that thought generated.

Eager to escape her confusing thoughts and emotions, Jen smiled brightly at Ted and Liz as she came to a stop in front of them.

"What happened to your dancing partner?"

Ted's mild inquiry startled her. She had assumed Adam was right behind her.

"I — I don't know," she answered faintly, biting her lip in disgust at the tremulous sound of her voice. Her eyes searched the crowded room without success; there was no sign of him. Sinking into a low chair facing the sofa, Jen stared blankly at the braided rug on the floor, unaware of the look that passed between Ted and Liz, or the understanding smile that tugged at the corner of Ted's mouth. For a brief instant Jen's expression had been as transparent as glass and had revealed more to Ted of her feelings than she was as yet ready to admit to herself.

Had Adam been so angry at her that he'd gone to his room without even bothering to say good night? But why take his anger out on Ted and Liz? She felt miserable, and suddenly very tired. *I may as well go to bed,* she thought dejectedly, *and leave Ted and Liz to get on with whatever they're going to get on with.*

"Lord, this is a thirsty crew."

Jen's head snapped up at the sound of Adam's quietly dry voice. One quick glance was enough to tell her that he was either no longer angry or masking it perfectly. He was carrying another carafe of wine in one hand and a large pewter mug filled with ice cubes in the other.

"We were wondering what had happened to you." Ted, in the process of pouring a glass of wine for Jen, lifted the carafe Adam had brought earlier. "I'm glad you decided to brave the bar, though. As you can see, Liz and I have just about killed this. How did you know?"

"Elementary." Adam grinned, setting the wine and mug of ice on the table that separated the sofa from the chair Jen was sitting on. "Every red-blooded male knows the first move in seduction is to create a seductive atmosphere."

"Good thinking." Ted grinned back at him, then laughed out loud at the color that rose in both Liz's and Jen's cheeks.

"Ted, stop it," Liz scolded gently. "You too, Adam," she tacked on as his soft laughter blended with Ted's. "You're embarrassing Jen."

Still laughing softly, Adam dropped agilely to the floor and sat, cross-legged, eyeing Jen wickedly. "Are we embarrassing you, Jennifer?"

Feeling her color deepen under his teasing gaze, Jen gratefully accepted the glass of wine Ted handed to her and took a sip before answering.

"Yes, a little." Although her cheeks were hot, Jen had somehow managed to keep her tone cool. "I've never heard anyone discuss seduction so casually before."

"Casual?" Adam's eyes pierced hers. "Believe me, I'm never casual about seduction."

Jen smothered her gasp inside her glass.

She gulped the cool liquid, then nearly choked as Ted concurred.

"No man worth his salt is ever casual about seduction."

Something in Ted's tone made Jen look up questioningly.

"Don't tell me you haven't noticed what's happening here?"

"Happening here?" Jen repeated blankly. "I don't understand."

The motion of Adam's head drew her eyes. His expression was rueful as he shook his head. "Look around, Jennifer," he said exasperatedly. "I mean, really look."

Following the direction of his waving hand, Jen glanced around the room. During the last hour the festive din of conversation had dropped to a muted hum as couples sat at tables and at the bar, talking softly. At first the significance didn't register. She was on the point of asking someone to explain when the word *couples* flashed through her mind. There had been very few couples when she'd entered the room. Slowly, carefully, her eyes made another circuit of the room before returning to Adam.

"Talk about casual seduction," he murmured. "This place has an epidemic."

"You really have been missing it, Jen," Liz chimed in softly. "It's like a chess game, every move well thought out and planned." Her pretty mouth curved wryly. "Most of them had never spoken to each other before they came in here tonight."

While Liz was speaking, Jen's shocked eyes watched Terry leave the bar arm in arm with a man. The man was Larry Gordon's complaining companion from the bus. Jen had to fight down the urge to run after Terry and tell her the man was engaged to be married. "What has come over everyone?"

"It's like a fever." Ted answered the question Jen hadn't even realized she'd asked aloud. "A fever that melts inhibitions. Caused by being snowbound."

four

"But we've only been snowbound for a few hours!" Jen cried incredulously.

"Makes no difference," Ted said quietly, handing Adam a glass of wine before emptying the first carafe by topping off Liz's and his own glasses. "I've been driving these tour buses for over ten years, and it's been an education." He took a long swallow of his wine before continuing. "When away, even for short weekends, some people act completely differently than when they're at home. And for some reason being snowbound makes them kick over any remaining traces of inhibition altogether. The first time I was snowbound my reaction was very similar to yours." He smiled gently at Jen. "I've learned a little about human nature since then."

"But —"

Jen's protest was interrupted by the arrival of a flushed, breathless Lisa. Jen was sure the young man with her had not been on the bus.

"Do you think we'll be going on to the lodge tomorrow, Liz?"

Jen frowned at the almost fearful note in Lisa's voice. Unless she had misinterpreted that note, Lisa was hoping Liz would say no. Yet Lisa had been eager to get to the lodge. Obviously the young man with her was the cause of her about-face. Liz's reply did little to relieve Lisa's anxious expression.

"I just don't know, Lisa."

"We'll have to wait until morning and see what condition the roads are in," Ted put in quietly.

"Okay." Lisa sighed. She started to turn away, then glanced at Jen. "Will —" Lisa hesitated before going on rapidly — "will you be going up to the room soon, Jen?"

Jen felt as if a spotlight had been turned on her, and she didn't like the feeling. That Lisa was hoping Jen would say no was as clear as if she had shouted it. *Dammit,* Jen thought irritably, *she's asking me to stay out of the room while they make use of it — and each other.* Disgusted anger warred with disbelief inside her mind. Cute, bubbly little Lisa, ready to jump into bed with a man she'd just met? And what about Terry? Had she gone to *his* room?

Jen had the uncomfortable feeling that by agreeing to stay where she was for a few more hours she'd be condoning the act. And she didn't condone it. On the other hand, she'd already been accused of making moral judgments once that night. What could she say? Adam made the decision for her.

"Jennifer will be here, with me, for some time yet." Adam's face and tone were devoid of expression. "Did you want her for something?"

"No — no," Lisa said hurriedly. "I just wondered."

"Don't wander too far, little lady." Adam laughed. "You may get lost."

Lisa flashed him an interested, impish look before walking away.

Jen was furious, both with Adam for interfering and, strangely, with Lisa for the parting glance she'd thrown him.

"You see what we mean, Jen?" Liz smiled wryly.

"Yes, I see," Jen mumbled around the anger choking her. "I still don't understand, but I certainly do see."

"Don't worry about it," Ted advised softly.

"And take that guilty look off your face," Adam chided.

"What do you mean, guilty look?" Jen bristled. "Why should I look guilty? I haven't done anything wrong."

"That's right, you haven't," Adam retorted. "But for a second there you were actually considering going up to your room just to thwart Lisa's plans. That's why I took the initiative." The mild emphasis he'd placed on his last sentence made it clear to Jen that he was very much aware of her anger, and at least one of her reasons for it.

"But my not going up is almost like saying I approve," Jen argued. "And I don't. She doesn't even know him and —"

"It's none of your business," Adam cut in harshly. "That woman is over the age of consent. Who she gives that consent to is entirely up to her." He paused, then sighed. "For God's sake, Jennifer, this place is full of consenting adults, not little kids. And if I read the signs right, they're all very eager to consent to almost anything. If it offends you, don't look. Sit back, drink your wine, and ignore it. It can't possibly hurt you unless you become a part of it."

"She's young, Adam," Ted interrupted imperturbably. "And she's entitled to her own opinion." Smothering a yawn behind his hand, he got to his feet. "I'm tired and I'm going to bed and" — he stretched his hand out to Liz — "regardless of anyone's opinion, I'm taking Liz with me."

Her eyes on Ted's, Liz rose, placed her hand in his, and after murmuring a soft

"Good night," left the lounge area with him.

"That wasn't exactly tactful," Adam admonished quietly.

The fact that Adam voiced her own uneasy thoughts put Jen on the defensive.

"I'm sorry if my 'young' opinions annoy you," she flashed scathingly. "Please don't feel you have to wait with me until Lisa and her friend vacate the room." With a wave of her hand she sneered, "Go join the mature, consenting crowd."

Feeling like a complete fool yet stubbornly refusing to back down, Jen watched as the muscles in his legs tensed before, straight-backed, he rose smoothly to his feet. As he turned away from her she had to bite her lip to keep from crying out a plea for him to stay. Closing her eyes, she let her head drop back wearily against the chair. What had come over her? With a few ill-chosen words she had shattered the camaraderie the four of them had shared. At the sound of ice tinkling against glass she lifted her eyelids a fraction.

Adam hadn't gone at all! Peering at him through her lashes, she watched as he poured wine over the ice cubes he'd dropped into his glass. After lowering himself onto the sofa he stretched his legs out, crossed his ankles, then looked directly at her. His gaze was pensive and held a hint of sadness.

"Are you still mad at me?"

His quiet tone seemed shaded by the same sadness Jen was sure she'd seen in his eyes. With a pang Jen wondered if he too regretted the loss of warmth that had surrounded them.

"No." Jen's voice was husky with remorse.

"Then why don't you come sit over here" — he patted the cushion beside him — "and talk to me?"

Jen needed no further urging. Pausing to drop an ice cube in her now warm wine, she sat down beside him and drew her legs up under her body.

"I" — she hesitated, moistened her lips — "I'm sorry for flaring up like that, Adam. I wouldn't blame you if you did walk away from me."

Adam was almost reclining, his head resting on the low back of the sofa. As he turned his head to look at her, he brought his hand up to her face and, with a feather-light touch, drew his long forefinger across her cheek and down her jawline.

"I'm never going to walk away from you, Jennifer."

Jen was unable to control the shiver his touch sent scurrying through her body, or the heat that followed at the low intensity

91

of his voice. *What did he mean by never?* She asked the question of herself because she didn't have the courage to ask him. Gathering her scattered wits, she drew a long breath to calm her suddenly racing heartbeat. Then her breathing and heart seemed to stop altogether as Adam's hand curved around her nape and drew her head to his.

Sharp disappointment washed over her when, her lips a bare half inch from his, he turned his head slightly and bestowed a chaste kiss on her cheek.

"I want to kiss you, Jennifer." Adam's throaty murmur replaced the disappointment with an exciting chill. "But later, when our audience has thinned out a little." The movement of his lips as he spoke teased her skin. "For now, talk to me, tell me about yourself."

Releasing her, he slid slowly into a sitting position and fixed her with that warm velvet gaze. Straightening, Jen gripped her glass with trembling fingers and brought it to her lips for a quick sip. The dryness in her throat somewhat relieved, Jen drew her eyes away from his compelling stare.

"What do you want to know?" The question was directed at the crackling fire.

"Everything. Anything. Whatever you want to tell me," his quiet voice prompted her. "Most importantly — is there a man in your life?"

"There are several." Jen's eyes swung back to his. "None of them serious."

"Good." There was a wealth of satisfaction in that one word. His eyes caressed her face a moment before he added dryly, "I'd have hated the idea of cutting another man out." Ignoring her soft gasp, he allowed a rough edge to tinge his tone. "I'd have hated it, but I'd have done it nonetheless."

"Do you think you could have?" Jen exclaimed, fighting the will-destroying pull of his eyes.

"I don't think so, I know so," he stated flatly. "You know it too."

Unable to deny his assertion, yet unable — or unwilling — to admit it, Jen again tore her eyes away from him. His soft, mocking laughter sent warm color flying into her cheeks.

"Am I going to have to drag every detail out of you?" Adam chided laughingly after she'd remained quiet for several moments. "Or did you want to play twenty questions?" Without waiting for her answer, he sighed exaggeratedly. "Okay, question one: Where were you born?"

"Right outside Norristown," Jen said to the fire.

"Now, that wasn't hard, was it?" he teased. "When?"

"What?" Jen turned her puzzled face to him. "Do you want the month, day, and year?"

"Jennifer" — he heaved another long sigh — "I'm trying to find out how old you are. Give me a number."

"Twenty-three."

"Ah, now we're getting somewhere." Adam smiled. "Parents?"

"Two." Jen smiled back.

"Cute." His smile stretched into a grin. "Siblings?"

"One." She returned his grin, her eyes beginning to dance with devilry.

"Male, female? Single, married? Younger, older?"

"A sister," Jen laughed. "Older by three years. Married — with a twenty-year mortgage and a two-year-old son."

"Careful, there," he intoned. "You answered two questions I didn't ask."

"Sorry."

"You're forgiven." He waved his hand airily, and Jen's eyes fastened on his slender yet strong-looking wrist. As it had early that morning, the sight of that wrist, and the hand connected to it, sent a thrill through her midriff. Shifting her eyes, she found him watching her closely.

"See something you like?" His voice had dropped to a low murmur.

His tone caused her breathing to grow

shallow. "Is — is that one of your twenty questions?"

"One of the most important ones." Adam's eyes followed the tip of her tongue as she wet suddenly parched lips. "Would you consider wetting my lips like that?"

Oh, Lord! Jen's lashes fluttered from the force of the anticipatory quiver that ran pell-mell over her skin. Suddenly too weak to break the hold his hot velvet eyes were imposing on her, she had the uncanny sensation that the electrical charge that had flashed between them from their first meeting had tautened and was drawing her slowly but inexorably toward him.

"Adam —"

Every tiny particle of moisture in her mouth and throat had been used up in her effort to articulate that softly moaned plea. Bemused, completely unaware of her action, her tongue again snaked out in an attempt to quench the fiery heat consuming her lips. Adam unwittingly broke the invisible cord pulling at her when his eyes dropped to her mouth.

The moment that had seemed to last an eternity was gone. Jen heard, and understood, Adam's harshly released sigh.

"God, I want to kiss you," he muttered raggedly. "I wish these would-be lovers would get on with it and coax their victims off to bed."

Jen felt a finger of ice pierce through her. Is that what *he* was? A would-be lover who just happened to need a little more privacy? And what about her? Was she an intended victim? No more, no less? A potentially willing female to be used as a bed warmer on a snow-filled night? The thoughts chilled her, stiffening her spine until her head snapped up rigidly.

"Are you anxious for them to finish their plays so you can make one of your own?" Jen's voice sounded cold and distant even to her own ears.

"Dammit, Jennifer." Adam actually seemed to growl with exasperation. "Don't go all uptight on me again."

Although Jen tried to avoid his eyes, they caught and held hers. Hard anger had replaced the dark brown liquid warmth.

"If I had wanted to make that kind of play, I'd have made it long ago." His tone smacked at her as effectively as a palm against her cheek. "If all I wanted was a quick roll in the hay I could have had you in the sack hours ago."

His overwhelming confidence angered her while at the same time it had her wondering if she would have been able to withstand him had he made such a play. Her own self-doubt inspired the impetus to challenge him.

"You're that good, are you?" she sneered

at him — and at her own uncertainty.

"I'm that good." His flat agreement, delivered without a hint of bravado, drew a shocked gasp from Jen. Before she could form the jumbled words of defensive ridicule that crowded into her mind, he added forcefully, "But my expertise — for want of a better word — has nothing to do with it. You have been mine for the taking from the moment we met. I know it, and although your mind's been dodging around in a frantic attempt to deny it, you know it too."

Damn him! Double damn him for making her face the fact that she had — as he so aptly phrased it — been dodging frantically. She didn't understand what was happening to her, and like everyone else, what she didn't understand frightened her. And, like some, being frightened called forth the urge to fight. Tossing back the fiery mane that exactly matched the color of the flames leaping in the fireplace, Jen forced a note of disdain into her voice.

"I won't even honor that claim with an argument. Now, if you'll excuse me?" Moving slowly, as if afraid she'd break if she moved too quickly, Jen carefully set her still half-full glass of wine on the table at the end of the sofa. "I'm going to bed — alone." Her final word was issued with hard bitterness.

"Stay where you are." Adam's hand, clamped firmly onto her shoulder, prevented her from rising. "That's better," he murmured with approval when she settled back without protest. "By the way," he began innocently, "what bed were you going to go to? Or" — Adam's tone remained innocent, but his eyes began to glitter devilishly — "were you thinking of joining little Lisa and her playmate? A sort of — ah — ménage à trois?"

"Adam!" Jen choked, outraged at the suggestion even though she knew he was teasing.

"Jennifer, really," he mocked sadly. "The laces binding you are very straight and exceedingly narrow."

"You consider me narrow-minded because I can't approve of indiscriminate sex?" she breathed in astonishment.

"It's not a question of approval or disapproval," Adam informed with a shake of his head. "It's a question of tolerance and understanding." He frowned at the look of distaste that crossed her face. "Will you tell me something, innocent one?" At her hesitant nod, he gibed, "Why the hell should you care who goes to bed with whom?"

"Why?" Jen cried in disbelief. "Why, because it's positively indecent, that's why!"

"No kidding!" Adam marveled sardoni-

98

cally. "You consider Ted and Liz indecent, then?"

"Well —" Jen felt trapped by her own hasty words. A vision of the quietly competent Ted and the patient, likable Liz rose in her mind. In no possible way could she truthfully label them indecent. "No — but —" Her moment's hesitation was all he needed.

"That's right, there are no buts. Ted and Liz are both very nice people." Adam paused, his hand sliding over her shoulder and down her arm to grasp hers tightly. "Why should the fact that they decided to advance their relationship from the social to the physical upset you? Don't you know the sex drive is the strongest of all?"

"Yes, of course," Jen snapped defensively. "But there is such a thing as pride and self-restraint."

"Bull," he snorted crudely. "At least in Ted and Liz's case. I recognized what was happening between them at once. Maybe because the exact same thing was happening to me." Lifting her hand he stole her breath completely by bringing her fingers to his lips, caressing them gently. "I want you." His warm breath feathered over her skin, setting off a delicious shiver that skipped up her arm. "I have wanted you since our eyes met, around Ted, at the bar. But I want more than one night. I want every night."

"Adam — I —" Jen swallowed painfully against the tightness in her throat, then blurted, "I can't go to b-bed with you tonight."

While she'd been stuttering her way through her refusal, Adam's tongue tasted the soft skin between her thumb and forefinger. As she finished speaking, his teeth nipped at the mound at the base of her thumb.

"Who asked you?"

"But —" Shocked at the sharp sense of rejection she felt, Jen had difficulty pushing words past her trembling lips. "I thought — you said —"

"I know what I said," Adam chided gently. "I also said I would not be satisfied with one night." He paused to lift his head and pin her with his eyes. "Jennifer, there is one thing I want you to remember always. And that is, unless I'm obviously teasing, I always mean what I say. And what I said was — I want every night."

Jen felt as if the flames in the fireplace had leaped from their food of logs to dance over her skin. *He couldn't mean — !* But what was he thinking of? Could he possibly have a long-standing affair in mind? And if not, that *could* only mean — marriage?

Her mind reeling with her confused conjecturing, Jen glanced around the room, unaware of the dark brown eyes filled with compassionate understanding watching her; her eyes darted back and forth like an animal that had caught the scent of danger. It required several circuits of the room before the realization hit her: except for a few hangers-on at the bar, the place was now empty.

Finally, not knowing where else to look, her eyes reluctantly came back to Adam.

"I don't understand," she whispered tremulously. "What, exactly, *are* you saying?"

Releasing her hand, he drew his legs up as he shifted his body to the edge of the sofa. Muscled forearms resting on his knees, he stared for long minutes into the slowly dying fire.

Tension coiling more tightly inside her with every dragging second, Jen found herself unable to tear her eyes from his sweater-clad broad back. When he did finally turn, it was so sudden that Jen jerked back against the sofa.

"I think you know *exactly* what I'm saying, Jennifer." His softly caressing voice reached out to encircle her with warmth. "But I also think it's too soon to put into *exact* words." His eyes left her to skim quickly over the room. When they came back they settled on her mouth. "Besides, my speech is never very exact when my lips are otherwise occupied."

The anticipation rising in Jen suffered a minor setback when, instead of moving closer to her, he turned away.

"Adam?"

Leaning forward, he set his empty glass on the floor.

"I'm only getting rid of the glass, darling."

On first meeting she had wanted to hear that endearment on his lips, and the effect of it on her senses was more devastating than she could ever have imagined.

"I — I like the sound of that," Jen offered timidly.

"That's good." Shifting his body on the edge of the sofa, Adam turned back to her from the opposite direction. "I intend calling you darling a lot." His hands came up to caress her shoulders before encircling her neck. "I liked the way you just said 'Adam.' " As he moved closer to her, his thumbs followed the line of her jaw. "It had a breathy, pleading sound. Very exciting." His head drew close to hers, and Jen's lids closed as her mouth opened. "Say it again, darling."

"Adam." Her voice was a mere sigh against his lips.

"That's even more exciting." The words were spoken on her lips, into her mouth.

His kiss began as gently as the one he'd

given her on the dance floor, but within seconds his lips hardened with command and his chest crushed her breasts. As the kiss deepened, long fingers slid into her hair, the tips pressing against her scalp as if to urge her closer, closer.

Jen's mind was beginning to feel disconnected from her body when her mouth was suddenly released. Lifting his head, Adam's eyes fastened onto the backs of the last two customers at the bar. Untangling his fingers from her hair, he slid his hands back to her shoulders.

"I don't want to be interrupted," he murmured as his clasp on her shoulders tightened. "Or watched."

Moving her gently, he slid her down until she was lying flat on her back. Fingers sliding back into her now disordered mane, he slowly bent over her.

Cold with a mixture of excitement and nervousness, Jen, her breathing growing more and more shallow, watched as his face came closer. *What am I doing here?* she thought distractedly. *I shouldn't be here.* A strange, desperate fear gripped her and her eyes flew to his. It was a mistake. Like a small, frantic animal caught in quicksand, Jen's eyes became caught in the hot molasses depths of his. She didn't speak — she couldn't — but she didn't have to; Adam read the panic in her hazel eyes. Inches from her, his head dipped lower and his lips pressed to the wildly fluttering pulse in her neck.

"Don't be afraid, Jennifer." Adam's voice, muffled against her skin, had a soothing, hypnotic effect on her. Feeling as though everything inside was beginning to melt, Jen moaned softly as his lips left a trail of heat up her neck to the ticklish, tender skin behind her ear.

"But I am afraid, Adam." Jen's whisper had the sound of a very young girl. "I've never felt like this before and — and I don't understand what's happening to me."

"Don't you?" His murmured tone challenged her ignorance. "You've never wanted a man, physically, before?"

Jen's breathing was so constricted, she could barely whisper, yet she had to answer, make him understand.

"No. Not like this, anyway. This — this frightens me, Adam."

"You are —" Adam paused while he lifted his head, his eyes searching her face — "you are still innocent?"

"Yes."

Jen's cheeks grew warm under his steady regard. Why did having to make that admission embarrass her? She knew the answer to that one, of course. How many times had she received pitying glances from young men she'd refused? And it wasn't just the men either. Although she was closed-mouthed about her personal life, her friends knew, somehow, that she'd never — in the words of one friend — "put out."

Hadn't she heard of the liberated woman? Jen had been asked repeatedly. Didn't she know she had as much right to sexual freedom as any male? Wasn't she — for heaven's sake — frustrated? Jen had answered yes, yes, and no to those questions — always basically the same, if couched differently — so often that her responses had reached the point of automatic flatness.

Now, with Adam's eyes searching her face, Jen questioned herself. Why had her admission made her uncomfortable? Was she frustrated? And had that unrealized frustration been the cause of her strange and immediate reaction to Adam? Did she, subconsciously, long to, as Ted said, kick over the traces, cast off the shackles of her state of innocence?

Her thoughts made her even more uncomfortable and she moved her head restlessly. On making her murmured reply Jen had lowered her eyes, unable to face the derision she was sure Adam would not be able to hide. Now, after his long silence, she lifted her lids.

"Why are you blushing?" There was not a hint of pity or derision in his tone or expression. "And why did you look away from me?"

Something about his stillness told Jen that he already knew the answers but wanted vocal confirmation from her. And what would he do if she gave him that confirmation? Laugh? Deride? Jen knew she could not take that. Not from him.

"Let me sit up, Adam." What had been meant as an order slipped out as an agonized plea.

"No." No lack of firmness in his tone. "Answer me, Jennifer. Why should admitting to your virginity make you this flustered?"

"Don't you know?" Feeling trapped, Jen flung the words at him defensively. "Don't you know that in this bravest of brave new worlds, in this sexually enlightened generation, I'm an oddity? A museum piece? A holdover from the Victorian age?" Her spark of defiance died, leaving her voice strained, shattered. "Don't you want to laugh or shake your head sadly and tell me I don't know what I'm missing?"

"No, I don't want to laugh or shake my head sadly." Adam's hands, grasping her head, forced her to look at him. "Actually I feel like shouting in sheer relief." A gentle smile curved his lips at her confused, wide-eyed stare. "What you've just said so bitterly is true. You don't know what you're missing, but I'm delighted you've missed it."

"Why?" Jen blurted nervously. "I thought — well, I've been told that men prefer a woman with some experience."

"I'm sure some do, and to be blunt, I've enjoyed my share, but —" Adam stopped speaking abruptly. Dipping his head swiftly, he caught her slightly parted lips with his. The feel of his tongue gliding along her lower lip drew a shuddering response from her. He pulled away at once.

"Did you like that?" he asked with almost clinical detachment.

If she was honest with herself as well as with him, there was only one answer she could give.

"Yes."

"That wasn't even the tip of the iceberg," Adam murmured softly. His fingertips gently massaged her scalp. "Jennifer, the world of the purely physical, the sensual, is a world apart. The only confines of that world lie within the individual imagination. It can range from a hurried, frantic, almost animalistic coupling to an exquisitely beautiful experience. I want to be the one to introduce you to that world." His mouth brushed hers gently. "You are my darling, and I want you." The uneven tremor of his tone sent an expectant shiver through Jen. "But I want more than mere willingness. I want even more than eagerness."

He paused to draw a ragged breath, affording Jen the opportunity to insert, more than a little fearfully, "Adam, I don't understand. What is it you want?"

"Exactly what I'm willing to give," he answered without hesitation. "Unconditional surrender."

Jen went stiff with apprehension. Did he mean now? This minute? But she couldn't, she thought frantically, she wasn't ready. His calming voice cut into her scuttling thoughts.

"Don't panic, Jennifer. I will not use force. I will not use coercion." A fleeting smile touched his firm lips. "I am not turned on by the idea of dragging you into that physical world. We will journey — together — or we will not journey at all." One dark eyebrow arched. "Will you go with me?"

"I — I —" How could she answer when she wasn't quite sure she even understood him?

"You may pause, or come to a complete stop, anywhere along the way, but" — his eyes bored into hers — "if you decide to embark on this venture with me, I expect your complete honesty."

"In what way?" Jen's voice was a shakily expelled whisper.

"If anything I do to you displeases or frightens you in any way, you must tell me." His voice grew husky, intimate. "By the same token, if I please you, you must let me know, either verbally or — or in any way that feels natural to you. Now do you understand?"

Closing her eyes against the hot velvet lure of his, Jen lay perfectly still. If this was a line — a new, refined way of making a proposition — it was a very effective one. For without knowing quite why, Jen trusted him implicitly. Still she hesitated.

"I may cry 'halt' at any time?" she asked softly.

"Yes." Adam didn't elaborate any further. He didn't have to. She believed him.

Taking him at his word she whispered, "When does this journey begin?"

"Now."

Jen felt the word like a wisp of silk ruffle her lips. Adam's mouth opened over hers invitingly. After a very brief hesitation Jen's lips parted to join with his.

There were no wildly ringing bells. No explosion of skyrockets. Unlike his kiss of a short time earlier, Adam's firm lips made no demand. Sweetly, gently, with a slowness that was, in its very languidness, exciting, Adam explored the outer edges of her mouth.

"Adam?" The pleasant, though uncertain, sound of Bill Wakefield's voice separated them. "Miss Lengle?"

"Right here, Bill." Releasing the cradling hold he had on her head, Adam straightened, placing a restraining hand on her shoulder when she made a move to sit up.

"I'm sorry to intrude," Bill said quickly, "but I wanted you to know that the bar's closing."

"And you'd like us to vacate the room?" Adam asked quietly.

"Not at all." Bill snorted. "Hell, I don't care if you stay in here all night. I just wanted to warn you that the lights in here will be turned off shortly, and to ask if you'll make sure the fire screen is in place before you leave."

"Will do, Bill."

"Okay, thanks. Good night."

Jen's soft voice blended with Adam's in wishing Bill a good night. A moment later his voice filtered through the empty room.

"Oh, by the way, it has started snowing again."

"Well," Jen murmured, "I guess that answers the question as to our going on to the lodge tomorrow."

Turning his head slowly, Adam stared down at her, his face free of expression.

"Does that disappoint you?"

Remembering his cautioning words about honesty, Jen shook her head.

"No." Then, with a teasing note, she added, "I don't ski very well anyway."

"I'll teach you to ski," Adam offered as he lowered his head to hers. "Among other things," he added as his mouth touched hers.

This time he let the kiss deepen, his lips hardening on hers when he felt her response. Caught suddenly in a maelstrom of new, exciting sensations, Jen curled her arms around his neck, her fingers digging into his hair. And now it was her fingers that pressed against his head, urging him closer. She was breathless and trembling by the time his mouth left hers.

Moving leisurely, his lips explored her face before, trailing moist fire across her cheek, they found her ear. She gasped when his teeth nipped gently at her lobe, and she moaned softly when the tip of his tongue followed the outer ridge of her ear. And all the while his hands slid caressingly over the soft material of her sweater, warming the skin of her shoulders, her arms, her waist.

Her breasts seemed to fill achingly as his hands moved slowly over her midriff. When his hands cupped the expanded mounds, she shuddered with the intensity of pleasure that skittered madly through her entire body.

His hands were removed instantly and

his breath tickled her ear as he softly questioned, "No?"

"Oh, yes." Jen's gasped reply was barely audible, as was her soft sigh as his hands returned to stroke her breasts. Turning her head, she kissed the corner of his mouth to draw his lips coaxingly to hers.

His mouth touched hers, retreated, touched again, over and over. First her lower lip was caught, caressed, inside his mouth, then her upper lip received the same loving attention. They were both breathing in short, ragged gasps when he pulled himself away. Turning from her, he slid off the edge of the sofa onto the floor.

"Cooling off period," Adam rasped tersely. "I think we'd better talk for a while."

fiue

Talk? Talk!! God, she could hardly breathe. And even if she *could* breathe, the way her mind was whirling, she doubted her ability to put together a lucid sentence.

Drawing his legs up, Adam sat, forearms crossed over his knees, chin resting on his arms, staring broodingly into the fire. Sometime during those mind-shattering moments while she'd been lost inside the euphoria of Adam's mouth, the lights had been extinguished and she had not even noticed.

Now, as her breathing leveled off and her rioting emotions cooled to languor, Jen studied the flickering play of dying firelight across Adam's face. What she viewed increased her pulse rate again. His strong face, alternately cast in shadow and light, had suddenly become the most important countenance in the world for her. Was it really possible, she mused dreamily, to fall in love within the time span of twelve or so short hours?

Yesterday she'd have laughed at the idea of love at first sight. Love grew as two people got to know each other, and deepened with the passage of time — didn't it? Yet she could no longer deny, even to herself, that *something* had happened to her the moment their eyes met. No, something had stirred inside her at the sight of his hand hours before their eyes met. But could it have conceivably been the first pangs of love?

Jen didn't know and at the moment was simply too lethargic to delve into it too deeply. What she did know was that merely looking at his shadowed profile sent the blood charging through her veins, making her fingers ache with the need to touch him. Wiggling her body, she shifted to the edge of the sofa. Her movement broke through his concentration on the crackling logs.

"Talk, Jennifer." Adam sounded as shaken as she felt.

"What should I talk about?" Jen asked huskily, her eyes arrested by a small, shallow indentation near the hairline at his temple. Before he could answer she murmured accusingly, "You should not have scratched."

"What?" He jerked around to stare at her, his back rigid with tension. "I scratched you?" His eyes moved swiftly over the exposed skin of her face and neck. "Where?"

"Not me," Jen corrected with a soft smile. Lifting her hand, she placed her fingertip on the tiny hollow. "You have a scar from scratching when you had chicken pox. How old were you?"

"Seven or so — I was in the second grade." His hand came up to cover hers, pressing it against the side of his face. Her palm felt the play of small muscles that tugged a smile from his lips. "Is it your turn to play twenty questions?"

"May I?" The tremor that ran down Jen's arm was revealed in her shaky voice. Hesitantly she moved her fingers to outline his eyebrow.

"Sure." Adam's hand moved with hers. "I want you to feel free to ask me anything." His long fingers slid along hers. "Touch me — anywhere."

"How old are you?" The words came out in a breathless rush.

"Thirty-two." Adam laughed softly.

Giving in to the urge to imprint his likeness on her fingers as well as her mind, Jen's fingers explored his forehead before moving on to trace his hairline.

"Where were you born?" she asked in bemusement as she drew a line from his hair to the bridge of his nose.

"Tokyo."

That caught her attention.

"You were born in Japan?"

"Yes." Adam's voice held a smile. "And spent the first ten years of my life there."

While she digested this bit of information, her fingers gently probed the soft hollow under his left eye. When his eyes closed she tested the texture of his eyelashes.

"You have very long lashes, you know that?"

The laughter that erupted from him momentarily dislodged her hand. The pressure of his fingers guiding hers away from his lids allowed him to open his eyes again. "Is that a note of envy I hear in your voice?" he asked around his laughter.

"Of course." Her soft laughter joined with his. "It isn't fair, you know. Do you have any idea what we females have to do to make our lashes look that long and full?"

"Life's cruel," he teased, drawing her hand down to cover his mouth.

"And you males don't apprecia— oh!" The tip of his tongue against her palm stole her breath. "I — I thought you wanted to talk," she gasped the moment she got it back.

"No, that isn't what I *want* to do." His hand moved away from hers. "But I think that is what we'd better do." When she

116

lifted her hand from his face he muttered, "Put it back. I didn't say we couldn't touch while we talk."

As he was speaking he shifted position. Turning to her, he imprisoned her loosely by placing his left forearm on the sofa on her right side and his right hand near her head. During the shifting, her hand slipped from his face. Bending over her he repeated, "Put it back."

His hand moved in time with hers, and she felt his fingers touch her face at the same time hers touched his.

"Talk, Jennifer."

"I — you —" Jen had never realized the skin on her face was so sensitive. Yet it must be, for the feather-light touch of his fingers could be felt clear through to the bone.

Marshaling her dissolving senses she whispered, "You came to the States when you left Japan?"

"Yes, to Philadelphia," Adam whispered back, a smile twitching his lips.

Covering the betraying twitch with her fingertips, Jen sighed. "Do I amuse you?"

"You delight me." The smile grew under her fingers. "You excite me," he murmured. "Talk, Jennifer."

"Your father was in the service?" Fingertips moving slowly, she delicately outlined his mouth.

"No." His breath tickled her palm. "Not then anyway. He was stationed there at the end of World War Two, before I was born. He fell in love with the country and its culture. When he came home, back to Philly, he formed a partnership with my mother's brother, opened a small showroom, and went into the importing business. As soon as the business was established he packed up most of his belongings, my brother, who was then two years old, and my mother, who was pregnant with me, and went back to Japan. I was born three months after their arrival there."

Adam's hand had not been idle while he was speaking. Moving slowly, his fingers had examined her facial features, as hers had explored his earlier. At the same time his left hand had awakened every nerve ending in her right arm with slow, caressing strokes from her wrist to her shoulder.

"And he stayed ten years?" Jen's voice had grown husky with the tightness invading her chest and throat. The incongruity of their conversation and the aura of sensuality surrounding them was creating havoc with her senses — physical and common.

"No, he never came home." Being very careful not to tug painfully, Adam put both hands to work arranging her hair into a fiery aureole around her head. "My mother brought me home when I was ten." Dipping his head swiftly, he rested his face against hers and murmured, "You have very beautiful hair, Jennifer." Lifting his head with obvious reluctance, he went on softly, "My father and brother remained in Japan. I've been back and forth like a swinging door since then."

"Your parents are divorced?" Jen stirred restlessly at the gaspy sound of her own voice. He was too close — much, much too close. Her movement brought his eyes to hers. A flame as bright as any in the fireplace blazed in their dark depths.

"No, they are not divorced."

"But —" Jen began, then paused, a frown betraying her confusion.

"Within the last twenty-five years they've seen each other approximately twenty-five times," Adam said quietly, steadily.

"But how can a marriage like that survive?" Jen asked in astonishment, visualizing the close, comfortable relationship her parents shared.

"Why shouldn't it?" Leaning back away from her, Adam shrugged. "They genuinely like and respect each other. How many couples do you know, married over thirty-five years, that can truthfully say they still have those feelings? Some quietly hate each other. Others are merely bored to numbness with each other. And that includes a lot of people married one hell of a lot less years. The only reason most of them stay together is their innate fear of change or being alone."

Jen felt chilled, both by his sudden withdrawal and the cool superiority of his tone. Perhaps that happened to some couples, but surely not the majority. Her own parents were proof of that. On the defensive, Jen plunged into the role of advocate for tradition.

"But without the day-to-day sharing, both of good and bad, there is no *real* marriage. There is no *real* communion, not only mentally but —" Jen broke off, the argument dying on her lips at the stonelike quality that had replaced the velvet warmth in Adam's eyes.

"Do you actually believe two people have to live together, endless day in, endless day out, to share that communion?" Adam asked austerely. "Believe me, they do not. My parents have shared the *important* things, including my brother and me."

"But that was so unfair to you!" Jen cried indignantly.

"In what way?" Adam replied coldly, moving even farther away from her. Before she could speak, he answered for her. "By not being subjected to the petty jealousies most parents indulge in? I can assure you, neither my brother nor I feel deprived about that. We had the best of both and of each other."

In one smoothly executed movement he turned away from her, leaned forward to scoop up his glass, rose with feline grace to his feet and, walking to the table, asked softly, "Would you like more wine?"

His sudden action, his soft tone, following so swiftly after his taut stillness and his cold voice, left Jen feeling disoriented and confused. Moving with much less grace than he had exhibited, she sat up, murmuring a hesitant "Yes, please."

He filled the glasses and handed one to her, then stood watching her as he drank half the contents of his glass in a few deep swallows.

Jen withstood his penetrating gaze as long as she could before protesting softly, "Why are you angry with me?"

"I'm not angry, Jennifer," he denied with a brief shake of his head. Sighing softly, he refilled his glass again before dropping onto the sofa beside her. "What I feel is impatience. Over the years I've become accustomed to the questions concerning my parents' lifestyle but" — he shrugged — "from you those same questions generate impatience in me."

"But why?" Jen's widened eyes mirrored her deepening confusion. "I'm very much like other people."

"You've just answered your own question." Adam's smile held self-mockery. "If you're honest, you will admit that from the moment we met, something — I don't know what, but *something* — happened between us." His eyebrows rose, and she answered his silent query with a nod. "Yes," he said softly, "and I guess I expected too much." Adam shrugged again. "I don't even know what I did expect exactly." A wry smile curved his lips. "Automatic understanding plus a deep sense of simpatico, I suppose." The wry smile turned sad. "Very unrealistic, I know — but the hope was there."

"Adam — I —" Jen paused, groping for the words that would banish the sadness from his eyes. She didn't even understand why his obvious disappointment in her should hurt her so much, but it did. And so, making no attempt to hide the hurt, she said wistfully, "I'm sorry, but I am very much like other people. I had a very ordinary upbringing. I have never even heard of the kind of relationship you have described to me." She bit her lip, pleading, "Help me to understand."

Adam's eyes studied her broodingly for long seconds before, sighing deeply, he leaned to her and kissed her mouth very gently.

"I'm sorry, too," he murmured against

her lips. "Okay," Adam said briskly as he sat up, "I'll make it as brief as possible. My parents *do* love each other. But they are both very independent people. My mother's a feature writer for a Philadelphia newspaper — has been since she graduated from college. She took a leave of absence when my brother, Luke, was born, and resigned when Dad decided to make the move to Japan. She worked for a while on a small English-language paper over there, but it didn't satisfy her." He paused to drink deeply from his glass before explaining, "She writes articles on vacation spots and places of interest on the East Coast. Places accessible, financially and timewise, to people limited to one or two weeks' vacation."

"What is your mother's byline?" Jen asked when he paused again to sip at his wine.

"Janet Elliot," Adam answered, one brow arching. "Have you read her articles?"

"I never miss them!" Jen exclaimed. "In fact it was because of an article she did on the ski lodge we were headed for that I decided to go on this tour."

Adam was nodding his head before she'd finished speaking. "I was headed for the same lodge." He laughed softly. "She is very good at what she does, and you can be sure if she claims a place is interesting, and worth the money, it will be. Anyway" — he shrugged — "as I said, she lasted ten years in Japan and then told my father she was going home, and back to work. Both Luke and I were present at that discussion. There were no accusations, no bitterness. If anything, my father seemed grateful for the ten years my mother had remained with him."

"Grateful?" It was impossible for Jen to hide her surprise and shock at that word.

"Yes, grateful." Adam's rough tone underlined the words darkly. "People can't own each other, Jennifer."

"I know that!" Jen exclaimed in protest. "But if there is real love between two people, then surely —"

"Surely, what?" he interrupted harshly. "One should be willing to sacrifice all ambition, all personal dreams, to the other? Subjugate themselves at whatever cost?"

Wincing, Jen shrank back, away from his lashing tongue. The look on her face drove him to his feet. Breathing deeply, his back to her, he placed his now empty glass on the table, then stood as if collecting his thoughts, one hand absently rubbing the back of his neck. When he turned back to her it was so sudden that Jen's body jerked.

"Dammit, Jennifer —" Adam stopped abruptly as his eyes caught the movement of her trembling hands. With an impatient grunt, he plucked the glass from her hand with a terse "Give me that before you spill it all over yourself."

Biting her lip, Jen watched him warily as he set her glass beside his own. When he again turned to face her, all signs of his impatience were gone.

"How can I make you understand?" He sighed softly, shaking his head. "If they had remained together they would very probably hate each other today. As it is, they still genuinely love and respect each other."

"But you said they've only seen each other about twenty-five times in the last twenty-five years."

"That's right," Adam replied quietly. "So?"

"Well — ?" Jen paused, searching for words, then she blurted baldly, "Adam, you reminded me earlier that the sex drive is the strongest of all. I don't see how —" Jen faltered, again searching for words.

"They have both had 'friends' over the years," Adam informed steadily.

"Friends?" Jen stared at him blankly a moment before, eyes widening, she asked faintly, "You don't mean — ?"

"I mean exactly that," he inserted flatly.

"But — but that's —" Words failed her,

and feeling her face begin to burn, she lowered her eyes.

"That's what?" Cradling her head with his hands, Adam forced her to look at him. "Immoral? Disgusting?" Bending over her, he stared directly into her eyes. "How do I make you understand?" he murmured. "I knew, and liked, every one of their 'friends.' There were only a few, on both sides. Their current friendships, or lovers, have been constant for several years now. My mother's 'friend' is a very prominent industrialist." His eyes grew soft, pensive. "My father's 'friend' is a gentle, exquisitely lovely young woman."

Jen was not so innocent or naive that she didn't know of the extramarital activities some people indulged in. But never had she heard of a situation quite like Adam had just explained to her. To Jen, it sounded cold-blooded and thoroughly selfish. In no way could she ever imagine herself loving one man while accepting another simply to appease the demands of the body. And she knew, without a shred of doubt, that the knowledge of the man she loved, and who supposedly loved her, performing that act of appeasement with another would be an unbearable reality she could not live with. Jen shook her head sharply in negation of the idea.

"I can't understand it, Adam," she whispered raggedly. "I don't even want to understand it. The thought that two people who claim to love each other could —" Jen's voice diminished to nothingness, and again she shook her head sharply inside the loose confines of Adam's hands.

Those hands, gentle till now, tightened, long fingers digging through her hair into her scalp. Holding her still, he grated, "I know it could not work for everyone. Ideally, each individual should be able to choose his own way, his own lifestyle. Females as well as males. But it usually comes down to one giving way to the other."

"But that's what marriage is all about, isn't it?" Jen cried. "The give and take of two individuals learning to live together?"

Why did she suddenly have the very uneasy feeling they were no longer talking about his parents? Jen wondered despairingly. And why did his opinion have the power to inflict the pain now clutching at her chest? She had no time to search for answers, for Adam, propping one knee on the cushion beside her, leaned very close to whisper harshly, "I should not have started this. I should have waited until we knew each other better." His digging fingers stilled a moment before beginning a sensuous massage down the back of her head. By the time his trance-inducing fingertips reached her sensitive nape, Jen was experiencing that all-over melting sensation again. Shivers skipping down her spine from quivering nerve endings, she was barely aware of Adam's words or the rueful tone of his voice.

"What I should have done is taken you to my room, bound you to me — at least physically — before attempting an explanation."

Jen's body grew rigid as the full context of his words registered on her bemused mind.

"No, you couldn't have." She moved her head restlessly from side to side in a useless effort to shake off his hands. "I would not have gone with you."

"Oh, Jennifer." Adam's voice had lowered to a caressing murmur. "Lie to yourself if you must, but don't try to lie to me. For while the words of denial whisper through your lips, the response of your body to my touch cancels them."

While he was speaking his hands moved as if to underscore his assertions. Trailing twin lines of fire, his fingertips followed the columns of her throat, paused a moment to explore her suddenly leaping pulse, then slid down to her waist and up underneath her sweater.

"Adam — stop —"

Adam's parted lips silenced her protest,

his probing tongue crushed the meager remnants of her resistance. The pressure of his mouth on hers drove her head back against the soft cushion. The searching tip of his tongue drove all reasonable thought from her mind.

Although Jen was sitting down she had the oddest sensation of dropping through space. Reaching out blindly, she grasped Adam's hips and hung on. Her mouth was released, then caught again, teasingly this time.

While Adam's lips played games with hers, his hands continued their caresses. The warmth of his palms sliding over the bare skin on her back drew a soft moan through her parted lips. The moan changed to a weak murmur of protest when his fingers deftly released the catch on her bra. Tearing her mouth from the drugging enticement of his, Jen gasped, "Adam, no!"

"I want to touch you." Adam's mouth moved along the curve of her neck to her shoulder with maddening slowness as his fingers examined her spine. His lips covered her shoulder, her collarbone, with moist, hungry kisses. "Touch you and taste you," he added huskily. "And I want you to do the same to me."

"No! Adam, I can't —" Jen's denial died as she realized the contradiction between her words and actions. As if she had no control over their movement, her hands had slipped under and inside his sweater to his waist and were urging him closer.

His tongue probing gently at the hollow at the base of her throat, Adam lowered his body next to hers. Sliding his right hand around her rib cage, he drew a shudder from her by outlining the curve of her breast with his long finger. When, finally, his hand cupped the aching mound, Jen released a sigh that swiftly changed into a moan of surrender.

Beyond caring about the consequences, Jen tentatively stroked Adam's smooth, warm-skinned broad back. Feeling his muscles tauten and grow hard in response to her lightest touch shattered the last of her reserve, and she let her hands roam freely.

Head flung back, eyes closed, trembling in response to the breath-stopping sensation radiating through her entire body from the hardening bud Adam's fingers gently caressed, Jen whispered a soft protest when he lifted his mouth from her throat. The next instant the protest became a murmur of delight as his lips brushed hers.

"Lie with me, Jennifer." Adam's wine-scented breath feathered over her lips deliciously. "Now," he urged, "here on the sofa."

"Here!" Jen's eyes flew open, became enmeshed in the hot velvet depths of his. "Adam, there's a clerk at the desk in the lobby. What if he should walk in here?"

The flame that leaped in Adam's eyes brought full awareness of her own words, left no doubt of his own understanding. Although she had not actually said yes, her question had betrayed her compliance. What had become of all her strong moral standards? she wondered sickly, her eyes shifting guiltily from the bright flame in his.

"Adam — I — I —" Pausing to search for words of repudiation she really didn't want to speak, Jen ran her tongue over her dry lips.

"I asked you earlier if you'd consider wetting my lips like that," Adam whispered, bringing his mouth to within a breath of hers. "Will you do it now?"

"Adam, please —" Jen groaned.

"Do it," he ordered softly, touching his mouth to hers. His fingers, for the last few moments stilled into a firm cup over her breast, began a sense-heightening stroking motion.

Hesitantly, using the very tip, Jen slid her tongue along his lower lip. Adam's low groan of pleasure instilled a boldness Jen had never felt before. Extending the tip almost imperceptibly when she reached the corner of his mouth, she started the return trip. When she paused to outline the center dip in his upper lip, his mouth opened.

"Enter, darling," he urged hoarsely. "Explore, go crazy. Make me crazy too."

His mouth crushed hers, forcing her lips wide. Slowly, with much trepidation, Jen slipped her tongue into the moist warmth of his mouth, then, growing brave, joined into a game of tag with his.

Without knowing quite how he had done it, Jen found herself flat on her back again, Adam's hard chest pushing her into the sofa's soft seat cushions. Giving in to demands and urgings from deep inside, she dug her nails convulsively into his back.

The following minutes were the wildest Jen had ever experienced. Adam's mouth, opening wider, consumed hers, filling her with desire, while his thrusting tongue drove her to acts she'd never contemplated.

Arching her back, she pressed her throbbing breasts against his possessive hands while her hands tugged at his sweater to bare his chest.

"Oh, God."

The harsh groan sounded as if it were torn from deep within his throat as Adam tore his mouth from hers. His sudden withdrawal chilled and frightened her.

"What's wrong?" Jen cried in confusion.

"Adam, don't you want me?"

Adam was on his feet, moving away from her. The tremulous note of fear in her voice stopped him in midstride. Swinging around, he came back to her, the expression of astonishment on his face answering her question before he opened his mouth.

"Not want you?" He laughed harshly. "Jennifer, I've got a hunger for you growing in me that will very likely take fifty years to appease." Bending over her, he grasped her shoulders and sat her up. Then, sitting beside her, he turned her so he was facing her back. His touch now coolly impersonal, he reached around her and expertly adjusted the lacy bra over her breasts before fastening the hook in back.

"Adam?"

"Shush, Jennifer." Lifting her hair to one side, Adam bestowed a tender kiss on the nape of her neck, then ordered softly, "Turn around, darling."

Obeying silently, Jen shifted around. Eyes lowered, she sat meekly while he pulled down her sweater.

"Look at me, Jennifer." His softly coaxing voice drew her eyes, shimmering with the threat of tears, to his. Now that her inflamed senses had cooled, sharp pangs of shame jabbed at her conscience, and as if that wasn't discomfiting enough, a deep feeling of rejection was poking holes in her confidence. The threat became the reality when two tears escaped to roll slowly down her cheeks.

Taking her face gently into his hands, Adam drew her to him with a murmured "Oh, my beautiful darling, don't cry. I want you so very badly, but not here, not on this sofa. When I finally make love to you I want everything perfect for both of us." His mouth touched her lips as tenderly as it had touched her nape moments before. Then, rising, he drew her to her feet.

"It's very late. Time for you to be in bed." Lifting his hand to her face, he wiped the tears from her cheeks, whispering, "Come, darling."

Six

The voices of Lisa and Terry, deliberately hushed so as not to disturb her, brought Jen half awake. The gentle click of the closing door as the two girls left the room imposed full consciousness.

Still sleepy, Jen pulled the covers up under her chin and, snuggling down, prepared to go back to sleep. The memory of Adam's parting words to her the night before sent her eyelids up.

"I think it's fairly obvious that no one is going anywhere tomorrow." Adam had murmured the words in between short, tender good-night kisses. "So sleep late, but when you do finally surface, search me out before you go to eat. I'll wait for you, and we'll have breakfast together." Nearly asleep on her feet, Jen nodded her agreement and gave herself fully to his last, lingering kiss.

Now, all thoughts of sleep forgotten, Jen tossed the covers back and slipped off the bed, her hand groping for her watch on the shelf that separated the room's two beds. A quick glance at the watch told her it was 9:05. It had been after four when she'd fallen into bed, yet surprisingly she felt completely rested.

After a hasty jump-in, jump-out-again shower, Jen stepped into brief panties, black corduroy jeans, and her boots. Opting for freedom of movement, she decided to go braless and tugged a heavy, cream-colored, cable knit sweater over her head. Swiftly but carefully, she applied light daytime makeup, ending with a pale peach lip gloss, then with impatient strokes brushed her unruly red mop into some semblance of order. A final few seconds were used to adjust a fine gold chain around her neck, and she was ready to leave the room.

At the bottom of the curving staircase Jen paused to glance out through the glass entrance doors. The view that greeted her eyes was starkly white, but it had stopped snowing and a weak, watery light was fighting its way through the remaining pall of dirty gray clouds.

Except for the clerk at the desk — a young woman this morning — the lobby was deserted. The combined hum of voices and activity from the direction of the dining room indicated that quite a few of the motel guests were up and about.

Standing before the swinging doors into the room, Jen moved her eyes slowly from table to table. Although she saw several of her fellow bus passengers, including Terry and Lisa, there was no sign of Ted and Liz, or of the only one she really wanted to see — Adam.

Sighing softly, she backed away from the archway and almost into Bill Wakefield. Bill's staying hand on her arm stopped her retreat and prevented a collision.

"Good morning, Miss Lengle," Bill said, smiling brightly.

"Good morning." Jen returned his smile, hesitated a second, then glancing around, asked, "You haven't seen Mr. Banner this morning, have you?"

"Adam?" Bill's smile deepened. "Sure. He's out in the parking lot digging out his car."

"Oh!" Spinning around, Jen headed for the stairs. "Thanks, Mr. Wakefield." Flashing a wide grin, she ran up the stairs. Within minutes she came running back down again, wearing the bright silver jacket, a white knit cap, and matching mittens. At the bottom of the stairs she came to a full stop, soft laughter shaking her shoulders. Bill Wakefield, grinning broadly, stood waiting for her at the entrance doors, leaning on a large snow shovel.

"I thought you might want to give him

a hand," he chuckled.

"If I can find him out there." Jen laughed as she walked to him.

"Oh, he'll be easy enough to spot once you get around that bus." He nodded his head at the large vehicle that blocked their view of the parking lot. "I've had men out there over an hour."

"Has there been any news on the road conditions?" Jen asked, taking the handle he held out to her.

"The road crews have been out since it stopped snowing around dawn. They were out last night but had to pack it in when it started snowing again." Bill shrugged. "The wind was blowing the roads closed as fast as they could clear them."

"Frustrating," Jen murmured. "Well, I'm no help to Adam standing here. See you later, Mr. Wakefield" — she indicated the shovel — "and thanks."

As Bill had promised, Jen had no difficulty locating Adam after she walked around the bus. The gold Corvette, now cleared of its white cover, gleamed dully in the watery sunlight. Beside it, wielding his shovel with smooth precision, Adam was making noticeable inroads into the snow around his car. And Adam's labors were not the only ones showing results.

With surprised eyes Jen surveyed the cleared area around her. Off to her left a man in a Jeep with a snowplow attached to the front was making steady progress in clearing the parking lot.

Toting the shovel, Jen walked to Adam and, without saying a word, set to work. As she straightened to dump her first shovelful of snow, an arm snaked around her waist.

"Good morning." Adam's quietly caressing tone sent a tremor down Jen's back. "You didn't sleep very long. Did you sleep well?"

"Yes." Turning inside the circle of his arm, Jen glanced up at him, feeling her breath catch at the warmth in his eyes. "Did you?"

"Not very." A rueful smile curved his lips. "I kept waking up, wishing you were with me."

"Oh, Adam. I'm —"

Adam's mouth, covering hers, silenced her. His lips were cold but every bit as exciting as the night before, and Jen responded eagerly. Adam began to deepen the kiss, then pulled back sharply.

"We're not going to get the job done this way." His eyes gleamed teasingly. "Even though I wouldn't be surprised if the snow is melting around my feet." Dipping his head, he stole another quick kiss before asking, "Have you had breakfast?"

"No," Jen exclaimed softly. "You said we'd have breakfast together."

"And we will," Adam chided at her reproachful look. "If and when we get the car dug out." Removing his arm, he stepped back. "So get to work, woman. I'm hungry."

Working silently, Jen matched Adam's pace until the area around the car was completely cleared of the heavy snow.

"I'm going to move the car closer to the entrance." Handing Jen his shovel, Adam slid behind the wheel and started the engine. "Go on ahead. I don't want to take the risk of having the thing slide around and slam into you."

Carrying a shovel in each hand, Jen walked to the front of the building, wincing at the stiffness in her back muscles caused by her unusual activity.

Adam carefully maneuvered the car into the part of the lot scraped clean by the snowplow, then joined her at the entrance doors. Relieving her of the shovels, he propped them beside the doors.

"We'll leave these handy for anyone else who might want to dig out. Now, let's go have breakfast."

After shedding jackets, caps, and gloves, and hanging them on a coatrack just inside the dining room, they made their way to the same table they had sat at the night before. They were no sooner seated when Adam lifted his arm to wave beckoningly to someone. Curious, Jen turned, then smiled a welcome to a very sleepy-looking Liz and a very satisfied-looking Ted.

"You two just crawl out too?" Ted drawled as he seated himself after seating Liz.

Jen felt her cheeks flush pink at the clear implication in Ted's question. He was assuming that, in the natural order of events, she and Adam had spent the night together in the same manner he and Liz had. Not bothering to disabuse Ted, Adam chided him disdainfully.

"I'll have you know, Jennifer and I have been industriously employed for the last hour" a little exaggeration there, Jen thought — "digging my car out of fourteen inches or so of snow."

"I humbly beg your pardon," Ted apologized dryly. "Who do you have to know to get a cup of coffee around here?"

At that moment, as if on cue, the same young waiter who had served them the night before came up to the table carrying a glass pot of coffee and four menus.

"Good morning," he chirped brightly. "Four coffees?"

As the table was preset with napkins, flatware, and inverted cups on saucers, the waiter had only to turn the cups over and fill them at their chorus of assent. After doing so he passed out the menus and promised, "I'll be back in a few minutes for your order."

Liz slowly came awake as they ate their breakfast, and by the time the waiter refilled their coffee cups she had joined in with the light banter. The meal finished, Ted indicated a third refill of their cups as the waiter cleared the table, and said smilingly, "Now I feel almost human. What do you think our chances are of getting out of here today, Adam?"

"Nil," Adam replied flatly. "The road crews are hard at it, but I doubt if we'll be able to go anywhere before tomorrow morning."

Liz frowned, then glanced questioningly at Ted. "I guess we may as well head for home, then."

"I'm afraid so." Ted shrugged. "I'll see what I can find out as to road conditions upstate, but I doubt they'll be any better than around here."

"Probably worse," Adam inserted.

"If we have to go home, we're going to have a very unhappy group of passengers," Liz sighed.

We have no control over the weather, Liz," Ted soothed. Then, deliberately changing the subject, he asked, "What do you do for a living, Adam?"

"I work for the oil industry." He named a large company. "Out of the Philadelphia office. I'm a sort of troubleshooter."

Ted's eyebrows rose. "I'd have thought you a little young for that."

"Not really," Adam answered easily. "But the fact that I speak several languages, including Arabic, doesn't hurt."

That sent three pairs of eyebrows up, and Jen exclaimed, "Several languages? How many?"

"Japanese, Spanish, and Russian fairly fluently," Adam said. "And a smattering of Greek and Portuguese — plus the Arabic."

"You studied languages in school?" Ted inquired.

"The Russian and Spanish, yes, through high school and college. As I spent half of my formative years in Japan, I picked up the Japanese as a matter of course." At the baffled expressions that had been growing on Ted and Liz's faces, Adam explained briefly. "My parents are separated. My father lives in Japan, and I spent six months of the year with him while I was growing up. Also, as my father is in the export-import business, dealing mainly in Asian art objects, he made numerous buying trips to the Middle East. He always took me with him. At times those trips took up most of my six-months' stay with him, and on several occasions included side excursions to Greece and Portugal." On noting the look of amazement on all three of the faces turned to him, Adam grinned.

"Sounds like a very erratic way to grow up, I know, but at the time I thought it was perfectly normal." The grin widened. "I enjoyed every minute of it."

"I guess!" Liz exclaimed. "By comparison, my life seems very sheltered and awfully dull. I've never been any farther away from home than Florida."

Liz had put Jen's own thoughts into words, except she hadn't even been as far as Florida.

"I was all the way to Virginia Beach once," she commented dryly. "How about you, Ted?"

"I've seen pretty much all of this country in the ten years I've been driving tour buses," Ted replied blandly. Rising, he excused himself from the table.

"I'm going to go and see what I can find out about the road conditions." He smothered a yawn with his hand. "Then, as I had very little sleep last night, I'm going to take a nap." He leered exaggeratedly at Liz. "Want to go with me?"

Although she blushed beet red, Liz's "Yes" was prompt and clear. As she stood up, Liz glanced from Jen to Adam. "What are you two going to do?"

Adam's quiet, serious "We're going to go play in the snow" drew surprised looks from both girls and a low chuckle from Ted.

"Each to his own games." Ted laughed and, grasping Liz's hand, he strolled away.

Finishing the last of her coffee, Jen studied Adam over the rim of her cup, a crawly sensation tickling the back of her neck. She *had* been longing to go romp in the snow, but how had he known?

"You do want to go out" — Adam's eyes as well as his tone teased her — "don't you?"

"Will you help me make a snowman?" Jen teased back.

"I haven't had much experience in the *man*-making line," Adam said, smiling wickedly, "but I'll do my best."

"You always madc snowladics?" Jcn fluttered her lashes over innocently widened eyes.

"Well, ladies, at any rate." Adam's soft laughter did strange things to Jen's breathing, while at the same time his words, though teasing, sent a tiny shaft of pain through her chest.

Why should you care? she chided herself as she preceded him out of the dining room. *Why should his none-too-subtle way of telling you he had made ladies bother you one way or the other?* A sharp memory of the melting feeling his mouth and hands had induced was all the answer she needed. Suddenly Jen hated the thought of any other lady knowing the feel of his mouth, his hands. *I'm jealous!* she thought in wonder. *I've known the man less than one full day, and I'm jealous of every other woman he has ever looked at with interest.*

Surreptitiously watching as he donned his outdoor gear, Jen acknowledged her feelings for what they were. *I'm in love with him. I barely know him and I'm in love. It's crazy. This doesn't happen in real life, does it? It's the situation,* she argued silently with her emotions. The snow. The proximity. Her eyes ran hungrily over his athletic frame, lingered longingly on his strong facial features.

Fighting the urge to reach out and touch him, she zippered her jacket with trembling fingers. The feeling of possessiveness that gripped her made a mockery of her inner arguments. All her previous beliefs went by the board. Whether it was supposed to happen "in real life" or not hardly mattered. She did love him, and the very thought of being separated from him now was unendurable.

In a somewhat shaken and unsteady state, Jen followed as Adam blazed a trail through the virgin snow around one side of the motel building. The large, even expanse of pure white was a blatant invitation, and shrugging off the unfamiliar depression that had settled on her mind,

Jen scooped up a handful of snow and tossed it at Adam.

Adam retaliated in kind, and that started a snow battle that soon had Jen shrieking with laughter and mock fear. The snowman was forgotten as the battle raged, wet and furious, for over an hour.

Stumbling away from Adam's too accurately aimed missiles, Jen came to a gently sloping bank near the rear of the motel.

"Oh, Adam, look!" Jen cried delightedly, staring at the bank. "A perfect place for angels in the snow."

"A perfect place for what?" Coming to stand beside her, Adam glanced at the bank then into her face in puzzlement.

"Angels in the snow," Jen repeated. "Haven't you ever made angels in the snow?"

"No." Adam shook his head. "How do you do that?"

"Give me your hand and I'll show you." Jen laughed up at him.

Ignoring the skeptical expression that crossed his face, Jen grasped the hand he held out and carefully lowered herself backward onto the smooth white bank. After extending her arms against the snow on either side of her body, Jen flopped them up and down while at the same time moving her legs in a scissoring motion. Then, jumping lightly to her feet, she turned to study the impression she'd made in the snow.

"Now, doesn't that look like an angel?" Jen indicated the effect of head, wings, and full skirt her movements had impressed into the snow.

"Surprisingly it does," Adam admitted. Lifting his hands, he caught the pointed ends of her upturned collar and drew her face close to his. "But I like my angels with a little more substance" — his cold lips touched hers — "and red hair" — the now warm lips trailed across her cold cheek — "and skin that's delicious even when it's been in the deep freeze."

"I'm no angel!" Jen exclaimed breath lessly.

Adam pulled her against his taut body. His lips moved with shivering slowness from her temple to her jaw. "Lift your head — I want to bite your neck." The order was whispered in a reasonably good impression of every actor's idea of Dracula.

With a breathless, shaky laugh, Jen flung back her head and exposed her throat to his mouth. The touch of his lips was the trigger that sent her arms around his waist.

Locked together, indifferent to the cold, damp bite in the air, they clung: Adam to her collar, Jen to his jacket. The sudden movement of Adam jerking his head up and back startled a soft "Oh" from Jen.

"Your collar is soaking wet," he growled softly. "You have got to be chilled to the bone. Why didn't you tell me?"

Without waiting for, or even allowing, her to answer, he released her collar and, clamping his arm around her shoulders, started toward the motel. As they approached the side of the building, an unmarked door opened and a motel employee struggled out with two large plastic trash bags.

Increasing his stride, Adam called, "Hold the door, please," then grinned a "Thank you" as they edged by the overstuffed bags. Within seconds they were standing outside the door to Adam's room. He inserted the key, then paused to gaze broodingly into her face.

"Okay?" he asked quietly.

Jen's hesitation was of a very brief duration, yet inside those fleeting seconds she became positive of two things. First, if she said "Yes" she would be agreeing to a total commitment, at least of a physical nature. Second, if she said "No," he would not insist but merely withdraw the key and escort her to her own room.

Without delving into her reasons, Jen gazed directly into his eyes and answered clearly, "Yes."

The door swung open, and Jen stepped into the room with an outward calm she was far from feeling. She had never been inside a man's room before. Excitement, coiling inside like an insidious reptile, vied with fluttering nervousness.

The room was a smaller replica of the one she shared with Lisa and Terry on the floor above, except there was only one bed — a double. Jen stared at the bed as if she'd never seen one before. The sound of the lock being set on the door sent a quiver of uneasiness zigzagging through her body. The sound of Adam's voice, for all its cool practicality, dried up all the moisture in her mouth.

"You'd better get out of those wet clothes."

They were standing just inside the door, and following his example, Jen pulled off her sodden mittens and cap.

"Just drop them where you stand," he directed quietly. "We'll collect them when we're dry."

Like a well-trained soldier she obeyed without question, her mittens and cap falling to the floor from nerveless fingers. Her jacket followed a moment later, and bending over, her trembling fingers went into battle with the wet zippers on the sides of her boots. By the time that tug-of-war ended, Adam had scooped up the wet garments and was busy draping them over the back of the room's lone chair.

"If you'll bring me the boots," he requested softly, "I'll sit them in front of the register." With a wave of his hand, he indicated the long, narrow heating vent in the far wall, below the wide window.

Jen carried the boots to him, then stood staring out the window while he lined them up along the wall. The window looked out of the rear of the motel, but the magnificence of the snow-covered, mountainous terrain was lost on Jen's unseeing eyes. Gazing in at the riot of conflicting emotions pulling in different directions, Jen blinked, startled when Adam's fingers, examining her collar, brushed her neck. Although impersonal, the physical contact made her shiver.

"You can't stay in these wet clothes," Adam stated flatly. "I think you'd better have a hot shower."

"A — a shower?"

Up until this point Jen had not spoken, nor had she looked directly at him. Now, hearing the faint, tremulous sound of her own voice and hating the timidity of it, she looked into his face — and melted. His eyes had that warm velvet glow, and a tender, understanding smile curved his lips. The hand at her collar slid around her neck, his fingers gently massaging the tension-tight muscles.

"There is no reason for you to be afraid,

151

Jennifer," he said softly. "I will ask no more of you than you're willing to give." Bending his head, he touched her mouth very lightly with his. "Now, go have a shower while I dig out something for you to wear." Turning her to face the bathroom, he gave her a gentle push, adding, "Then I'm going for a drink. What would you like?"

Pausing in midstride, Jen asked the bathroom door, "Could I have a cup of tea?"

"Jennifer" — Adam's beguiling voice coaxed her head around — "you may have anything that is within my power to give you." His eyes caressed her face with a touch she could actually feel before, turning away abruptly, he chided, "Now, go jump under a hot shower. I'll hand something in to you before I go for our drinks."

The "something" he handed through the six-inch crack she'd made between door and frame at his knock was a long-sleeved tailored shirt in blue chambray.

After a prolonged shower that went a long way in soothing her frayed nerves as well as chasing her body chill, Jen procrastinated further by cleaning her teeth with a dab of Adam's toothpaste on the tip of her finger and giving her unruly hair a vigorous brushing with his tortoiseshell-backed hairbrush.

She stepped back into her lacy bikini panties before sliding her arms into the soft sleeves of his shirt. The garment covered more of her than her short nighties, the front and back tails almost touching her knees.

She had fastened every button on the shirt when, lifting her head, she caught her reflection in the mirror and was gripped by silent laughter. *Some siren you are,* she ridiculed her image. Scrubbed clean of makeup, the sprinkling of freckles across her nose stood out on her shiny face. Added to that, the demurely buttoned shirt gave her a very young, very virginal look.

What in the world could a man who had been all over the world and had probably known — and made love to? — some very beautiful women want with you? she derided her reflection. The thought — more of the other women than her own innocent appearance — sent a fierce surge of competitiveness through her. *Something* about her had attracted him — he had admitted that — and right now he was waiting for her on the other side of the bathroom door. Was she going to go to him looking like a mature woman or a sacrificial lamb? With steady fingers she opened the top buttons to a point between her breasts, then raised her hands to her head and deliberately tousled her hair. Jen threw a final defiant glance at her image, then turned and walked calmly out of the bathroom.

Adam had thrown back the bedspread and covers and was stretched out on the bed. His eyes were closed, his head resting on his arms. A cup of tea and an empty glass sat on the small nightstand beside the bed. Opening his eyes, he stared at her expressionlessly before nodding at the stand.

"You'd better drink your tea," he murmured tonelessly. "While *it* still has some warmth." On the last word his eyes closed again.

Sitting down on the very edge of the bed, her back to him, Jen reached for the cup blindly, wondering if his words held a double meaning, and he was trying to tell her that his warmth had dissipated. She gulped thirstily of the tepid brew, emptying the cup in a few deep swallows. After replacing the cup on the saucer, she clasped her hands together on her lap and raked her mind for something to say. His still-toneless voice ended her fruitless search.

"Do you want to go to your own room, Jennifer?"

"No!" Jen blurted without thinking. Swinging around to face him, she rushed on tremulously, "Do you want me to?"

With the same gracefully fluid movement he'd displayed the night before, Adam sat up and gazed squarely into her eyes.

"You know the answer to that question," he grated softly. Circling her neck with one hand, he drew her face close to his. "Are you afraid, Jennifer?"

"Yes, a — a little," Jen finally managed to answer honestly.

"But you still want to stay with me?" Adam asked with low urgency.

His caressing fingers at her nape set off a tiny explosion that sent a spear of flame down her spine. The very closeness of his mouth brought a sudden dryness to her own.

"Yes," Jen whispered hoarsely and heard the hiss of his indrawn breath as her tongue slid over her parched lips.

"Do that to me," he groaned an instant before his mouth covered hers. As if to coax her own, the tip of his tongue teased the barrier of her closed lips until slowly, hesitantly, she parted her lips and let the tip of hers meet his.

The shudder that Jen felt ripple through Adam's body instilled confidence and, lifting her hands to clasp his head, she parted her lips still more as she urged him closer. Her small advance was rewarded by a full-scale attack on her senses.

His lips hardening with mounting passion, Adam's mouth plundered hers hungrily. His hands, sliding sensuously over her shirt, found, then swiftly opened, the four buttons she'd left closed.

Barely breathing, Jen waited for the touch of his hands on her bare skin. When he pulled away from her, her eyes opened wide in confusion.

"Adam — what — ?" The anxious protest died on her lips as she watched him tug his sweater over his head. The sweater went flying through the air, but Jen didn't see where it landed, for, as though drawn by a powerful magnet, her eyes clung to the naked expanse of his shoulders and chest. Her eyes continued to cling when he slid off the end of the bed.

With a boldness she had never before known, Jen watched as Adam flipped open the snap on his jeans, lowered the zipper, and, watching her watch him, deftly shucked out of them. The very brief shorts that covered his loins left little to her imagination. Desire, hot and demanding, surged through her and, lifting her arms to him, she whispered, "Adam."

Dropping back onto the bed beside her, he hauled her into his arms.

"Don't be afraid," he whispered against her lips. "I'll be as gentle as possible with you."

His kiss began very gently, but at her

eager response his mouth crushed hers and his tongue plunged with the swiftness of a rapier, tearing at the fabric of her natural reserve.

Her inhibitions melting under the warmth of his caressing hands stroking her skin, Jen sent her own hands exploring. The feel of his hair-roughened chest, the way his back muscles tautened against her palms, blurred all rational thought.

His arms tightened, flattening her breasts against his hard body, and Jen felt herself falling with him as he dropped back on the mattress. His mouth moved on hers, searching, devouring, like a starving man offered a banquet. His hands moved restlessly under the shirt until they found her hips. Grasping her tightly, he shifted her over his flat stomach until she was lying between his thighs. The evidence of his growing desire for her fanned the flame his mouth had lit into a consuming blaze.

When his lips left hers to forage hungrily down the side of her neck, she gasped his name over and over again. Jen felt his muscles bunch an instant before he rolled her over and their positions were reversed.

Sliding his hard, sinewy body along hers, his lips ignited small fires from her throat to her quivering concave belly, while his fingers teased her nipples into pebble-hard arousal.

He brought his mouth back to hers to play, to tease, to torment, and to whisper words that shocked at the same time they excited and turned the flame in the lower part of her body into a hard knot of aching need.

As if he sensed the ripe fullness of that need, Adam quickly removed her panties and his shorts. Moving between her legs, he grasped her hips and probed carefully at her maidenhead with his manhood.

"Adam! Adam, it hurts!" Jen silenced her hoarse cry by digging her teeth into her lips.

Adam's body stilled. "I know," he whispered, bending close to her. His lips touching hers, he grated, "Take hold of me and hang on." At his last word his mouth covered hers, and the swift thrust of his body drew blood.

Under his caressing hands the pain and fear that gripped her dissolved, then reformed into a driving urge toward fulfillment. When it came Jen cried out with the shuddering relief and, for a fleeting moment, teetered on the brink of unconsciousness.

The ragged sound of Adam's breathing drew her from the brink to awareness. His face was buried in her neck, and she could hear the rapid hammer beat of his heart against her chest. Lifting her hand from his back, Jen smoothed the sweat-damp hair from his forehead.

"Am I heavy?" he murmured against her throat.

"Yes." Jen's whisper held a smile. "A little. But it's a nice heavy."

She could feel his laughter rumble through his chest an instant before it touched her ears. Rolling off her, he sat up and pulled the covers up over them. Sliding his arms around her, he drew her tightly against his body with a teasing threat. "You'd better have a nap and rest up; I'm not through with you yet."

Seven

A hand nudging her shoulder shook Jen out of her seemingly drugged sleep.

"Up and at it, sleepyhead," Lisa chirped when Jen forced her eyelids to half-mast. "Liz has just informed everyone that we're leaving in as close to an hour as possible."

"An hour!" Jen's eyes flew wide open as she jerked into a sitting position. Adam! The thought of him caused a tightness in her chest. She had to see him! Shaking her head to clear the sleep-induced fuzziness, Jen focused her eyes on Lisa's grinning face. "But why?" Jen cried, jumping out of the bed. "What's the hurry? Are we going on to the lodge? What time is it anyway?"

Lisa stood patiently throughout Jen's bombardment of questions. When she'd finally run down, Lisa answered slowly and concisely. "We are leaving in an hour because, apparently, Ted has decreed it. And no, we are not going on to the lodge. The hurry, according to Liz, is Ted's; he wants to get us all home safe and sound." Lisa held up her hand when Jen opened her mouth to protest. "It seems Ted heard a weather forecast this morning calling for more snow by late this afternoon. That set the match to his fuse, and he sent Liz to roust us out. Liz assured me that he was not fooling around. He wants to get going as soon as possible." Lisa turned away, then tossed over her shoulder, "Oh, yes, it's now" — a quick glance at her watch — "nine thirty-five."

Jen stood blankly irresolute for several seconds. Adam. This time the thought of him galvanized her into action. Her need for haste overriding her innate neatness, she tossed her clothes carelessly into her suitcase, leaving out the things she'd need to get ready to leave.

After a quick sluice-down shower she pulled on underwear, jeans, a sweater, and the now stiff suede boots. Making do with a light makeup of tinted moisturizer and clear lip gloss, she then tugged her hair-brush impatiently — thus painfully — through her tangled red mop. Blinking against the tears that sprang to her eyes from the self-inflicted punishment to her scalp, Jen's fingers went to her naked throat and a small, soft smile curved her shiny lips.

Turning from the mirror, she tossed her brush and makeup pouch into the suitcase and locked it. Glancing at her watch, she nodded with satisfaction. The entire procedure of preparing to leave had taken her exactly thirty-two minutes, for it was now seven minutes after ten.

Having had a head start in their own packing, Lisa and Terry had left the room fifteen minutes earlier, Terry grumbling, "Ted or no Ted, I am not getting on that bus without at least a glass of juice and a cup of coffee to fortify me."

Now, her bag slung over her shoulder, jacket over her arm, mittens and cap in one hand and her case in the other, Jen, moving as swiftly as her incumbrances would allow, left the room without a backward glance.

After dropping her suitcase to one side of the entrance doors beside the cluster of others belonging to the tour passengers, Jen headed for the dining room. Feeling as though it was becoming a habit, she peered over the swinging doors, her eyes honing in on the table in the far corner. Although Ted and Liz were there, there was no sign of Adam.

Sighing softly, Jen turned away. Was he still sleeping? It had been very late last night — or, more correctly, very early this morning — before he'd given in to the need for rest.

Deciding he *was* still sleeping, Jen

walked purposefully to the reception desk. The clerk behind the counter was one Jen had not seen before.

"May I help you, miss?" he asked politely when she came to a stop at the desk.

"Yes, I —" Jen hesitated, then, her voice stronger, she went on, "I wonder if you'd know if Mr. Banner is still in his room."

"Mr. Banner checked out of the motel early this morning." The clerk's quiet reply held firm conviction.

"Checked out?" Jen exclaimed. Hearing the shocked tone of her voice, Jen swallowed against the sudden tightness of her throat, telling herself there had to be a mistake. Much more calmly, she put her thought into words.

"I'm sure you're mistaken. I'm referring to Mr. Adam Banner, in room one-twenty-seven."

"No mistake, miss," the clerk returned politely. "I accepted his room key myself. He left just after six this morning."

Stunned, not even remembering to thank the man, Jen turned away, took three steps, then stopped to stare ahead blankly, seeing nothing. On the edge of her numbed consciousness she knew that soon, very soon, the pain would start, but for these few seconds, a shocked nothingness encased her in unfeeling stillness.

"Miss Lengle. Miss Lengle?"

The concerned edge to Bill Wakefield's tone finally penetrated. Reluctantly emerging from her anesthetized state, Jen blinked against the strained, gritty feeling in her eyes and turned with a vague "Yes?"

"Are you all right?" The concern was sharply evident now. "You're white as the snow outside."

"I'm" — Jen moistened her lips — "I'm fine." At his disbelieving frown, she added with a forced, ragged laugh, "I — I didn't have enough sleep and I'm not quite alive yet."

"I see." Bill's tone indicated that he accepted her explanation with reservations. "I have a note for you from Adam." His eyes still narrowed on her pale face, he held a plain white envelope out to her.

"When — when did he give this to you?" Jen croaked as she took the missive from him.

"This morning, just before he left," Bill answered quietly. Then, more sharply, he asked, "Are you sure you're all right?"

"Yes, of course, I'll —" she began, then, catching sight of Ted and Liz, along with at least a dozen people from the tour, emerge from the dining room, she improvised, "I'll go have a quick cup of coffee to wake myself up." The envelope clutched in her hand, Jen made a beeline for the swinging doors.

164

After sitting down at a small table for two in a corner of the room that was nearly deserted, Jen tore open the envelope with shaking hands and withdrew the single sheet of motel writing paper. The note was written in a broad, neat hand, and the name *Adam* was slashed across the bottom. Teeth digging painfully into her lower lip, Jen read the words he'd left for her.

Jennifer, (Jen could almost hear the caressing sound of her name whispering through his lips)

I've received an emergency call that leaves me no choice but to go home at once.

I want so badly to talk to you and explain, but there is so little time, and I don't have the heart to wake you, knowing you have been in bed such a short amount of time.

Why did you go?

I'll ask that question again when I see you.

I must go.

I will *call you.*

Adam

An emergency call. I'll see you. I'll call you. The words stabbed in Jen's mind and heart like a blade heated red-hot. *An emergency call. I'll see you. I'll call you.* But would he?

Her teeth punishing her lip, Jen faced the possibility that she might have just read the lines of a classic brush-off.

No! The voice of reason denied that possibility. A similarly worded note from a man like Larry Gordon would have left no doubt of a brush-off. *But not from Adam.* Adam was the exact opposite of the Larry Gordons of the world. Wasn't he?

Fighting tears and a demoralizing sense of rejection, Jen hung on to the phrase *but not from Adam* through a glass of juice, the subsequent trip through the lobby, and right past the two people stationed at the entrance doors.

"Jen?"

The sharp sound of Liz's voice shattered the protective shell of concentration Jen had drawn around herself. Unaware that her face had a shockingly fragile look, or that her eyes betrayed her fear, Jen twisted her lips into a grim smile.

"Good morning, Liz, Ted," Jen greeted the couple in what she hoped was a carefree tone. Their facial expressions left little doubt that she'd failed.

"What's wrong, honey?"

Sudden tears, fiercely hot, filled Jen's eyes at Ted's tone; he sounded so much

166

like her father. Her poor excuse for a smile faded as she blinked back the tears.

"It's something to do with Adam, isn't it?" Ted went on softly.

"He's gone," Jen whispered starkly. "He left around six this morning." Swallowing convulsively, Jen looked around distractedly. "He left a note but — Ted, I'm afraid I've been a fool —" Her words trailed off as her voice became caught in the thickness of her throat. Moving jerkily, she put her hand out to push open the large door. A firm hand on her arm stopped her erratic motion.

"Jen, wait!" Though still soft, Ted's tone held enough of a command to halt Jen's flight. "I feel positive there's a good reason for Adam's sudden departure. He's not the type to —"

"How can you know?" Jen interrupted wildly. "How could any of us really know what type he is?"

Liz's softly gasped "Jen!" brought realization of the shrillness of her voice. Breathing deeply in an effort to control the surge of emotion over reason, Jen went on more quietly, "Maybe our judgment was clouded by what you yourself called 'snow fever,' Ted."

"I don't believe that," Ted disagreed sternly. "I think you're too levelheaded to be caught up in something like that, and

I've been in too many similar situations to get carried away with it."

And yet you latched onto Liz as quickly — no, more quickly — than that stranger latched onto Lisa, Jen argued silently. Aloud she murmured tiredly, "I want very much to believe that, Ted, but I — I have this fear that maybe Adam strung a line and I, very accommodatingly, swallowed the bait." Glancing up at him, she managed a weak smile. "I trusted him completely, and right now I'm trying to hang on to that trust. Please don't look so worried, Ted. Misplaced trust or not, I assure you I'll live."

Within the few steps required to reach the bus Jen somehow managed to compose her features into an expressionless mask. Smiling and nodding at the several greetings called out to her, she made her way along the bus's narrow aisle to the seat she'd occupied previously.

"You look like you're either still half asleep or stoned, and even knowing you such a short time, I'm sure it's the first and not the second."

Jen smiled bleakly at Lisa's teasing quip and nodded briefly at a crumpled-looking, sleeping Terry.

"It must be contagious. Terry looks completely out of it."

"Dance lag." Lisa laughed softly. "I

168

practically had to drag her off the dance floor at four thirty this morning."

Four thirty! A wave of despair washed over Jen at the sudden memory of where she'd been at exactly four thirty. Dropping her handbag, cap, and mittens onto the aisle seat, Jen slid into the empty seat next to the window with a muffled, "I'm about ready to join her in dreamland. Wake me when the bus pulls into Barton's parking lot."

Lisa's soft chuckle and easy "Gotcha" relieved Jen's concern that her hint that she didn't want to be bothered during the return trip had not been received as an insult.

After making herself as comfortable as possible in the limited space, Jen shifted her mental gear into neutral and closed her eyes, determined to sleep and not think. She was only partially successful. Drifting in and out of a doze, she heard the bus door close; heard the murmur of conversation as Liz moved slowly down the aisle counting heads; felt Liz's presence and ensuing perusal when she paused briefly at the empty seat beside Jen. The last thing she was aware of was the lumbering motion of the large vehicle when Ted drove off the lot.

"What time is it?"

Terry's question, issued around a yawn,

wakened her. Eyes closed, Jen waited for Lisa's reply. It came softly.

"Twelve fifty-one exactly, and we've been on the road for about two hours." Lisa's tone held a rueful note. "I sure hope we stop to eat soon. The toast and coffee I had for breakfast lost its power about an hour ago."

Jen grimaced at the mention of food and hunched her shoulders inside her jacket. At that moment she was positive she'd never want to eat again. Nevertheless, when Ted maneuvered the bus into the parking lot of a large restaurant some half hour later, Jen duly filed out with everyone else. This time they were not expected and the word was do your own thing, but please, do it within an hour.

Sitting in a booth with Ted and Liz, Jen pointedly avoided the subject of one Adam Banner. Shooting her worried glances but following her lead, they made a desultory attempt at conversation.

"Are we going to see anything of each other after we get home, Jen?" Liz asked somewhat hesitantly.

"Yes, of course," Jen answered quickly. "Call me some Saturday and we'll have lunch."

The look that crossed Liz's face, the way her fingers clutched the saltshaker she'd been toying with, made Jen realize how hollow and insincere her reply had sounded. Talk about classic brush-offs.

"I mean it, Liz," Jen insisted warmly, "I seldom work on Saturday, and then only in the morning. I could meet you for lunch somewhere, and then we could spend the afternoon shopping."

"And if I'm free, and you let me know in advance," Ted inserted, "I'll meet you later and take you both out for dinner."

Jen had to work at not letting her surprise show, for she had been sure that Ted and Liz had been indulging in a weekend fling. Hadn't Ted mentioned that he lived out near Harrisburg? Rigidly controlling her disbelief, Jen teased, "I never turn down an invitation for a free meal."

Surprisingly, Jen found her appetite restored with her first bite of the char-broiled cheeseburger the waitress placed in front of her. After polishing off the sandwich and the side order of french fries that came with it, she pushed her plate aside and drew her second cup of tea forward with a sigh of repletion.

"*Now* you look like you might live," Ted commented wryly. "When you sat down you looked like you'd been boiled, starched, and hung out to dry."

Jen obligingly gave him the smile he'd so obviously been angling for. With a nod of satisfaction Ted ushered them out of the restaurant and back onto the bus.

Jen's smile disappeared after she'd once again settled her long frame into the narrow seat.

"Going back to sleep, Jen?" Lisa inquired as Jen depressed the button that tilted the seat back.

"If I can," Jen replied softly, hopefully.

This time it didn't work. The numbing blankness of sleep, or even drowsiness, eluded her. Instead of lulling, the low murmur of conversation from the seat behind her tugged at her attention. Unwittingly she was cast in the role of eavesdropper.

"Believe it or not, he didn't lay a hand on me," Terry informed Lisa. "All we did was talk. That guy is so in love with his fiancée, he doesn't know which way is up. And I got the impression, more from what he didn't say than from what he did, that that sweet thing is leading him around like a trained poodle." Even though Jen mentally gave Larry Gordon's frustrated friend a pat on the back for decent behavior, she felt the same disgust for his fiancée that laced Terry's tone. For several seconds, as she mused on the stupidity of that sweet thing, the talk from behind swirled over her head, vaguely heard but not registering until a statement from Lisa made itself felt.

"Yes, I went to bed with him." The

boldly, if softly spoken words jolted through Jen like an electric shock. But there was an even bigger shock to come, for Lisa continued in a dreamy tone, "And he's serious, I mean really serious. We're talking marriage city."

Lisa's lightly flippant tone did not hide the underlying excitement and happiness bubbling beneath the surface. Jen's lids closed against the sting that attacked her eyes. As Lisa went on blithely, Jen's hands gripped the seat's armrest in silent protest.

"Keith's a salesman, and he lives out near Pittsburgh. He has to finish the sales route swing he is on now, but he's coming to Norristown to see me before he goes home."

God, the same routine, Jen thought sickly. Songs and dances and fancy repartee, only in this instance, the words to the song were changed to fit the situation. Jen could almost hear the man's oh-so-very-sincere voice. I've got to finish my route, baby, but I'll come to you as soon as I can.

Jen moved her head restlessly against the seat back. She didn't want to hear Lisa's story. It was much too similar to her own and, spoken aloud, sounded much too improbable, too brief encounterish.

"And you believed him? Oh, Lisa, that has got to be the oldest line going!" Terry exclaimed softly.

"Sez you," Lisa returned smugly. "And, yes, I believe him. Not only because I want to, but because he has proven himself to me."

"In what way?" Terry's skeptical question echoed the one in Jen's mind.

"By speaking to my parents when I called them to let them know I was safe," Lisa replied loftily. "He introduced himself to my father and mother in turn, accepted an invitation to dinner next Sunday, and then, after hanging up, he called his own parents and introduced me to them. And as if that was not enough proof, he asked his mother to call mine and assure her of his sterling character." Her soft, delighted laughter rippled raggedly along Jen's rigid spine. "But there's still more. He gave me, as a token, his class ring that — as you can see — I'm wearing on a chain around my neck."

Jen was electrified. Without her awareness, her hand released the armrest and moved to the base of her throat to begin a fruitless search. On Thursday night she had labeled Lisa a fool. In her arrogance, and from her citadel of virginity, she had made moral judgments on just about everyone. And then, less than twenty-four hours later, she had — Jen shifted uncomfortably as the word "eagerly" slithered into her mind — broken her own moral code. So maybe, she mused, in one form or another, we are all fools.

The motion of her fingers crawling agitatedly around her neck brought realization of their action — and the object of their search. With the realization came memories — sweet, painful, and a little bitter.

She had been awakened the previous afternoon by erotic tremors rippling through her body. The source of those tremors was the teasing play of Adam's lips. Moving with infinite slowness, his mouth explored the upper part of her back, inch by minute inch.

Still half asleep, Jen's body had moved sensuously in time with the rippling tremors. Her squirming had alerted Adam to her wakefulness. He had murmured something she didn't understand before brushing her hair aside to expose her neck. Now, a shiver feathered her nape at the memory of the sensations the touch of Adam's mouth against her skin had generated. So vivid was the memory, so intense the feelings inside her body, Jen lost all sense of time and place. She was no longer cramped into a narrow seat on a bus full of people. In the grip of memory she was warm and comfortable, curled lazily against Adam's smooth, hard body, his desire-husky voice barely reaching her ear.

"Do you like that?" Adam's warm breath, fluttering over the supersensitive skin at her nape, drew an involuntary moan from her throat. "Does it do funny little things to you?"

"Yes," Jen gasped softly on a quickly expelled breath.

"And this?" The warm, breathy flutter, the excitingly moist touch of his lips, moved down her spine.

"Oh, yes." Jen's gasp had a choking sound now.

"And this?" Adam's tongue, feeling to Jen like a hot, licking flame, drew circles in the hollow at the base of her spine.

"Ooooh — God, Adam!!"

Jen began to feel slightly delirious as Adam's mouth and tongue climbed back up her spine. By the time he turned her to face him, she had the uncanny sensation of floating inches off the bed.

"This time there will be no pain." Adam's teeth nipped playfully at her lower lip in between teasing kisses. "From now on it's sweet pleasure for both of us."

The truth in his promise was soon borne out. Jen had had no inkling of the varied and exquisite pleasure the act of making love could give. And the most delightful thing was that not only was the pleasure derived from Adam making love to *her*, the pleasure she derived from making love to *him* was every bit as wild, if not more so.

The tremors that awakened her the second time were of an altogether different kind. Jen knew it was late because most of the light had gone from the day. Except for the tepid tea, she had had nothing to eat or drink since breakfast. And the tremors rippling through her midsection were caused by her stomach's growling demand for food.

Slowly, carefully, she pushed back the covers. As she moved to sit up, Adam's arm curled around her waist, holding her still.

"Where are you going?" His voice was low, sleep-fuzzy.

"To my room," Jen answered softly, simply.

"Why?" Fully awake now, Adam's tone had grown an edge.

"Because I'm hungry," Jen laughed. Turning inside the circle of his arm, she leaned to him to kiss the side of his jaw. "And because I want to have a shower and get dressed." Having decided she liked the taste of him, she trailed her lips to his chin. The low growl her action drew from his throat gave her a feeling of power that enabled her to add, boldly, "And since it's your fault I missed lunch, I'm going to let you pay for my dinner."

"Really?" Adam's soft drawl was a delight to Jen's ears. "And here I had convinced myself that since I had brought some mild diversion to an otherwise dull afternoon" — he paused to nip gently at her lobe — "you would insist on repaying me by picking up the dinner check."

"Adam Banner!"

Rich male laughter followed her shocked exclamation. Pulling her tightly to him, Adam kissed her breathless before bothering to reply.

"You rang?"

"Your ears will ring from my blows if you ever again even hint that I would pay for —"

"You mean it wasn't worth the price of a dinner?" Adam interrupted in mock astonishment.

"Let me up this instant, you devil." Jen's command had very little force, issued as it was against his lips.

"A perfect match," Adam declared contentedly. "A devil and an angel." His mouth crushed hers for long moments, and Jen was beginning to have that floating sensation when he lifted his head to whisper, "I'd better let you go, my snow angel, or you'll be lucky to get out of here tomorrow morning for breakfast."

Jen sighed blissfully as she stood under the hot, revitalizing shower spray twenty minutes later. She was in love, and it was every bit as wonderful as she had hoped it would be. She felt fantastically good. Adam was perfect. The motel was perfect. The snow was perfect. Even she herself was perfect, if a little silly at the moment. Laughing aloud she shut off the spray and stepped out of the tub. As she patted at the rivulets glistening on her skin, Jen suddenly realized she was tinglingly aware of herself as a women.

Standing on tiptoe, she examined as much of herself as possible in the small bathroom mirror. *Not bad, I suppose,* Jen thought, her eyes noting in detail the upper part of her torso. A little lanky, maybe. Lips pursed, she cocked her head, her glance resting on her breasts. At least they are reasonably full, she mused, and high. Wide-eyed, she watched a rosy-hued stain creep up her neck and mount her cheeks as the echo of Adam's whispered, "Your breasts are beautiful, Jennifer. They fit my cupped hands exactly, and make my lips hungry for more" came back to her tauntingly.

The very depth of her response to his hands, his lips, and above all, to his body, had been a shocking revelation to Jen. She had gloried in his all-encompassing touch and, in turn, had reveled in the feel of him against her own hands and lips and body.

The heat stinging her cheeks, the tingling in the hardening tips of her breasts, and the leg-weakening tightness in her thighs startled Jen out of her erotic reverie.

"You are a bona fide diz," Jen chided her reflection softly. "And if you are not very, very careful, that very, very sexy guy is going to wrap you up and stick you in his pocket." Somehow the soft admonition had the opposite effect than the one desired, for the girl in the mirror grinned expectantly and begged, "When? When?"

The door to a room a short distance down the hall closed as Jen, finally composed and dressed to vanquish, left her room. Her emergence was greeted by a low, appreciative male whistle. Glancing up, Jen's smile changed to a frown of consternation. Larry Gordon ambled toward her, his hot-looking eyes insolently stripping her of the soft, clingy, spaghetti-strapped dress she'd moments before slipped into.

"You look good enough to eat," Larry praised unoriginally.

Not by you! Jen thought waspishly. Aloud she managed a tight "Thank you, Larry."

Coming to a stop beside her, he turned to face her, one hand reaching out to grasp her arm.

"Have dinner with me."

Jen's back stiffened at the command — for it had been a command.

"No, thank you, I —"

"C'mon, honey, loosen up a little," Larry cajoled in a tone Jen felt sure was calculated to melt the heart of the most frigid of maidens. "We'll have a good dinner, a few drinks, a couple of slow and easy dances and then" — he paused to grin boyishly — "we'll really have some fun."

Yech! Jen was hard put to keep the rude noise to herself. This creep, she thought scathingly, obviously believed he was Tom Cruise, Adonis, and Lord Byron all rolled into one irresistible entity.

"Larry," Jen began patiently, "I don't want to have dinner, or drinks, or dances or" — his grasp tightening on her arm snapped her patience — "or anything else. Now, take your hand off my arm," she finished icily.

"What's wrong with you anyway?" Rather then loosening, his grip tightened still more. "You hide out all day like some kind of recluse, you don't join in on the fun. I know, because I've asked, that you've barely spoken to any of the men on the tour. Are you made of ice, for chrissake?" His mouth twisted nastily. "Or do you like girls?"

Jen's outraged gasp was drowned by the deceptively pleasant voice that floated down the hall to them.

"I told you once to back off, Gordon."

Two heads, Jen's and Larry's, swung to face the source of that voice. Although Larry's fingers relaxed their punishing grip, he did not at once remove his hold.

"I'm not going to say it again." Adam's voice lowered as he drew near them — lowered and roughened. Jen had to suppress a shudder of fear when she got a clear look at his face. Larry's reaction must have been very like her own, for at that moment his hand slipped limply from her arm. Adam's face was set into frighteningly harsh lines that warned of icy rage and his eyes glittered chillingly from behind narrowed lids. His voice, so in contrast with his usually mellow, pleasant tone was commanding.

Larry needed no further urging. Without a word he took off down the hall like a scalded cat. The moment he was gone, Adam slid his hand around her neck and pulled her against his chest.

"Are you all right, Jennifer?" The transition from menacing to tender was so sudden, it threw Jen off balance and she sobbed, "Oh, Adam, I was so frightened."

"Did he hurt you in some way?" Stepping back, away from her, he swept his eyes over her. It was too much.

"Oh, Adam" — Jen couldn't stop the

laughter that gurgled from her throat —
"*he* didn't frighten me. *You* did."

"I did!" Adam nearly shouted. "How?"

"You looked so — so deadly." Jen covered her mouth with her fingers to contain
her laughter, but she couldn't cover the
brightness in her laughing eyes. "You —
you scared the hell out of me."

Adam looked at her disdainfully, but the
corner of his mouth twitched suspiciously.
"I think you're getting light-headed from
lack of nourishment. Come on, maybe if I
feed you, you'll regain your senses."
Turning her around, he marched her down
the hall.

As it was fairly late the dining room was
almost deserted. Sitting across the table
from him, Jen ate everything that was
placed in front of her and tasted nothing,
for Adam's eyes devoured her more thoroughly than his mouth devoured his food.

When they finished dinner they went
into the bar to find Ted and Liz waiting
for them at a table for four. On the table
were four glasses, a full carafe of wine, and
an almost empty one. Ted filled their
glasses as they sat down.

"As you can see" — he indicated the
empty carafe — "we've got a head start."
Cocking one eyebrow he asked, "Where
the hell did you two disappear to all day?"
Adam's muttered "Mind your own busi-

ness," combined with the bright flare of color that tinged Jen's cheeks, was all the answer he needed. With a murmured "Welcome to the club," to Jen, Ted lifted his glass in salute.

Their conversation was varied and far-ranging and flowed easily back and forth. In a surprisingly short amount of time she learned a lot about the others.

She learned that Ted was forty-three, a widower (which she already knew), had one child (a daughter), and was considering changing jobs as he was tired of being on the road all the time. He did woodworking as a hobby and admitted he was very good at it. He liked good food, quiet at-home nights, and George Strait's music.

Jen discovered that Liz, much to her surprise, was thirty-four, divorced, with no children. She worked in the reprographics department at Barton's and attended yoga exercise classes two nights a week. Liz admitted to being an opera buff who was happy as a clam to spend most of her evenings at home (a small apartment) listening to her large collection of opera recordings.

Although Jen already knew quite a bit about Adam, she found he liked cars (he owned two), skiing, all oceans, hiking, professional football, and history, from ancient to recent.

And the other three absorbed some things about Jen. Bits and pieces of information such as she was twenty-three, single, and lived at home with her parents. Also that she worked as a legal secretary, enjoyed most sports, loved live theater and old movies on TV, spent far too much money on clothes, and sang in the church choir.

A lull in the conversation came at the same time Ted poured the last of the wine. On his query of whether he should fight his way to the bar for a refill, Adam shook his head.

"Not for Jen and me, thanks." Standing up, he held his hand out to Jen. "We're going to fight our way onto the dance floor."

This time, when they reached the area set aside for dancing, Jen slid her arms around Adam's neck without hesitation.

"Good girl," he murmured against her hair as his arms circled her waist and drew her close to his body.

Enclosed in his embrace, Jen lost all sense of time and surroundings. The music throbbing from the jukebox swirled through her mind and carried her to a distant, flat plateau on which she and Adam were the sole occupants. Her face pressed to the side of his neck, eyes closed, she followed his lead around the minuscule floor, unaware of the couples around them.

"You look beautiful in that dress." Adam's warm, wine-scented breath ruffled the hair at her temple. His caressing tone ruffled every nerve in her body. "But I know you look even more beautiful out of it."

The ruffle swelled to a quivering wave that seemed to drain all the strength from her legs. Murmuring softly, Jen parted her lips and kissed his smooth, taut skin. His sharply indrawn breath was followed by the feel of his lips at the edge of her ear.

"Have you ever been in love, Jennifer?"

Adam's whispered question inserted a touch of reality into her dreamlike trance. Stirring restlessly, she sighed, "No." Then, with a deeper sigh, she lifted her head to look at him.

"I've had my share of crushes and infatuations," she confessed wryly. "But no, I've never been in love." Jen hesitated a moment, but she had to ask. "Have you?"

"I thought I was once," Adam replied, not hesitating at all. "It was a long time ago. While I was still in college. It was over before it ever really got started. That too turned out to be infatuation."

"I —" Suddenly nervous, Jen paused to swallow quickly. Was he trying to tell her that infatuation was all they had going between them now? Speaking carefully, she

186

continued, "I suppose it is easy to confuse the two."

"I suppose so," Adam agreed quietly. "At least I've heard enough people say they weren't sure if they were in love."

Suddenly scared, Jen felt she couldn't breathe for a tightness compressing her chest. They had stopped even a pretense of dancing and were simply swaying to the music. Unable to take her eyes from his, Jen stared at Adam fearfully. When he finally spoke, it took several seconds for the meaning of his words to register in her mind.

"I'm sure." The hard finality in his tone caused Jen to go limp with relief. Her gaze steady on his, she said clearly, "So am I."

A bright flame flared in Adam's eyes, and his entire body went still for a moment before he released her with a whispered, "Come."

With meek acquiescence Jen preceded Adam off the dance floor, out of the bar, and across the lobby, not knowing or caring how many pairs of eyes followed them knowingly.

With an outward composure that belied her mounting desire, she stood beside him calmly as he unlocked the door to his room. Adam himself appeared coolly unaffected as he pushed the door open and stood aside for her to enter.

The click of the lock automatically set-ting with the closing of the door was like an explosion that ripped away their facade of unconcern. Moving simultaneously, they reached for each other — tugging, yanking, pulling at each other's clothes.

Circling each other like hungry beasts, their movements jerky, their breathing ragged, they left a trail of crumpled, torn garments from the door to the bed where, divested of their cloaks of civilization, they grasped at each other savagely.

This time, their coming together held an element of violence. Imbued with a touch of madness in her need for him, Jen arched against his hard body wildly, teeth nipping, nails raking. As her body grew from warm to moist then slippery-wet from her frantic exertion, the soft moaning sounds in her throat grew into an outcry of sheer ecstasy that was echoed by Adam in the form of a harsh groan.

In sweet exhaustion, they lay side by side crosswise on the bed as their labored breathing slowly returned to normal.

"Good God," Adam whispered shakily. "That was absolutely the wildest experi-ence I've ever had."

Rising slightly, he leaned over her, his body supported by his forearm. Bending his head, he kissed her with a gentleness that bordered on reverence.

"You're perfect," he whispered as he leaned back to look at her. "An angel." A tender smile curved his lips. "My very own snow angel."

"Adam, I —" Jen could barely speak around the emotion clogging her throat. "I love you so much."

"You'd better," Adam growled, burying his face in her neck.

Jen felt his tongue glide over the fine gold chain that encircled her throat night and day. Lifting his head, Adam brought his hand up to finger the tiny loops.

"A gift from an admirer?" he asked tightly.

"No." Jen shook her head. "I bought it for myself over a year ago."

His fingers fumbled against her skin for several moments, and then he held the chain aloft.

"Loop it around my wrist," he ordered softly.

Without hesitation Jen took the chain from his fingers and did as he'd asked.

"Now you've chained me to you," Adam said with a smile when she'd fastened the clasp. "I'm yours to command. What's your pleasure, snow angel?"

The early morning chill creeping over her naked flesh wakened Jen. The luminous hands on Adam's small travel alarm told her it was four thirty, and the air in

189

the room was very cool.

A soft smile touched her lips at the half grunt, half snore that came from beside and slightly above her head. Turning her head, Jen studied the sleeping form that rested a few inches away from her. Adam lay sprawled on his back in an attitude of utter relaxation, one arm curved above his head, the other flung out to his side. His lips were slightly parted, and the taut skin that covered his face showed no sign of care or strain. On first sight, Jen had thought him handsome. Now, in his abandonment to oblivion, she thought him beautiful. Like countless numbers of lovers before her, Jen could find no fault in the object of her affection, for that beloved form had revealed to her a corner of heaven.

Eight

"Somehow I've always known it would happen like this." Lisa's soft but liltingly happy voice dispelled Jen's bittersweet reverie. "Everyone has always laughed at my belief in love at first sight, but I knew that when I fell, it would be at once — and hard."

Shifting uncomfortably in the narrow seat, Jen tucked in her chin and hunched her shoulders in an unconsciously self-protective position. Biting on her lower lip, she squeezed her lids together in a vain attempt to contain the hot tears that slipped beneath her guard to roll down her cheeks.

The action of her searching fingers added force to the stinging flood. In times of tension or stress she had played with her chain not unlike people do with a rosary or worry beads. And now that source of comfort was denied her, for the chain was still around Adam's wrist. At least it had been when she'd slipped out of his bed, and his room, before daybreak, unable to face the thought of boldly walking through the lobby and encountering early-risers later in the morning.

Had Adam been aware of her going? Had he been feigning that posture of deep slumber? Although it hurt like hell, Jen now conceded the possibility that he had been. It had been around four forty-five when she'd returned to her own room. The desk clerk had said Adam had checked out just after six. One hour and twenty or twenty-five minutes at the outside, Jen sighed.

His phrasing in the note he'd left for her seemed to bear out her conjecturing. He'd written, *Why did you go?* Not, *When did you go?* Jen shivered. If he had been awake he had let her go believing he loved her. Love! Jen compressed her lips to keep from moaning aloud. She wanted — no, longed — to believe he *had* been asleep, *had* received an emergency call from home, really *had* no choice. She longed to believe that he *would* call her, *would* come to her as soon as he could, *would* prove to her that the blind trust she'd placed in him had not been be-trayed.

She wanted to believe *all* these things, but the sense of betrayal, the feeling that she'd been used that had gripped her on first hearing he'd checked out of the motel, still nagged sickly at the back of her mind.

It was all too pat, had all come together too neatly, to be coincidence. Adam had to have realized, logically, that they would move on today, in one direction or another. God, she had made such a ridiculous ass of herself. Jen actually winced. After all her fast judgment making and moralizing, she had capitulated with an eagerness that was shaming, telling him, repeatedly, that she loved him.

Jen squirmed in her seat as the echo of her own strained voice, crying out the love words at a moment of sweetest agony, taunted her weary mind.

Was it possible Adam had chosen the path of least resistance? He was a man of the world. A man, Jen felt sure, who had known, and made love to, a number of women, all more beautiful and much more sophisticated than she could ever hope to be. And he had grown up with the belief that several lovers were acceptable — as long as one was selective. *And* — most searing thought of all — he had not actually said he was in love with her. With all the usual clarity of hindsight, Jen realized she had read what she'd wanted to believe into his avowed "I'm sure." Lord, for all she knew, he may have been thinking he was sure it was Friday.

Moving restlessly, Jen slid her hand into the slash pocket on the front of her jacket, her fingers curling around and crumpling the note Adam had left for her. At no time had he made any promises to her. *I will see you, I will call you,* hardly constituted a vow.

Wallowing in a quagmire of bitterness and despair, Jen stared sightlessly through the tinted glass window, totally oblivious to the murmur of conversation around her. Fingers mangling the envelope in her pocket, she thought distractedly, *Why didn't he, at least, toss my chain into the envelope?* She had had to save for months to buy it. She had seldom taken it off and felt naked without it. The absence of the gold circlet somehow intensified her feeling of rejection.

A tingling in the toes of a rapidly numbing foot alerted Jen to the necessity of shifting position once again. Drawn by discomfort out of her self-absorbtion, the rising note of excited chatter slowly registered in her mind.

Blinking away the remaining blur of moisture, Jen gazed out the window in surprise. The familiar environs of Norristown flashed by as the bus drew closer to Barton's — and home.

Cramped and both mentally and physically exhausted, Jen sighed with relief when

Ted brought the large vehicle to a stop in almost the exact spot in the lot as he had early Thursday morning.

Had it only been two and a half days ago? Was it really possible that so much had happened in so short an amount of time? Jen heard her own silent questions voiced aloud from several sources.

"God, I can't believe I got on this bus, right here, just two days ago." This from a man near the front of the bus who was standing in the aisle and unconcernedly massaging his rump.

"I feel like I've been away for weeks." This was from the whining woman across from Jen. "And confined to this damned seat for most of that time."

"If I don't get something to eat soon, I'm going to expire right here in this bus." This from the ever-hungry Terry.

"May I have your attention, please?" Liz's voice, magnified by the PA system, silenced the chatter. "I am sorry to have to inform you that there is every possibility you will all be receiving a bill for your lodging at the motel."

This statement was met by a barrage of angry exclamations.

"What?"

"Why?"

"The trip was paid for, dammit!"

"What the hell are you trying to pull?"

The last remark was followed immediately by Liz's exasperatedly snapped "If you will be quiet, I'll explain."

The melee subsided to a few disgruntled grumbles.

"Believe me, I understand how you feel," Liz assured them. "And as the gentleman pointed out, the trip *was* paid for." Liz paused to add emphasis to her next words. "It was paid *in full* to the ski lodge. During a three-way phone conversation this morning between our travel agency, Bill Wakefield, and me, arrangements were made to pay the motel bill." Liz paused to draw a quick breath before continuing, "We will, of course, be contacting the management at the ski lodge. If they will agree to a partial refund, it may be enough to cover the motel bill. But please understand that they are not required by law to make any refund."

"But it wasn't our fault we couldn't make it to the lodge!" Not surprisingly, the shrill protest came from the woman across the aisle from Jen.

"Nor was it theirs," Liz shot back angrily. Then more calmly, she added, "I'm sorry. I understand how you all must feel, but there is nothing I can do about it. Now, Ted has asked me to tell you that driving is still very hazardous, so please be careful on your way home."

Jen sat with outward patience while the muttering group filed out of the bus. At that moment the thought of possibly receiving a bill — or the death sentence — left her emotionally untouched. All she wanted was to get off the bus, get into her car, and get home as quickly as she safely could.

Saying good-bye to Liz and Ted turned out to be less difficult than Jen had feared it would be. As she stepped out of the bus she was caught and pulled against Ted in a bear hug.

"Take care of yourself, honey," Ted growled into her ear softly. "Keep the faith, Jen. *I* believe Adam will get in touch with you. You must try and believe it too."

Jen blinked against the renewed sting in her eyes. "I want to believe it, Ted," she choked as she disentangled herself from his arms. "I really do, but —"

"Don't even think *but*," Liz urged. "Think positive." She gave Jen a quick hug, then said briskly, "Now, go home and get some rest — you look beat. And call me soon — okay?"

"Yes, I will. I promise." Jen somehow managed a natural smile. "Drive carefully, both of you."

With a last wave of her hand, Jen picked up her suitcase and walked to her still snow-laden car. Thankfully Barton's maintenance crew had cleared the lot around the car, so all Jen had to do was clean the windows, back and front. Thirty nerve-racking minutes after she drove off the Barton's lot, Jen pulled onto the narrow driveway to the one-car garage attached to her parents' rambling ranch house. It was at that moment she remembered she'd promised her mother she'd call the day before.

Her mother, obviously, had not forgotten. She met Jen at the front door, a frown of disapproval marring her usually serene face.

"Jennifer Louise Lengle." Ella's use of Jen's full name was a clear indication of how upset she was. "Do you have any idea how worried your father and I have been? Why didn't you call?"

Even as she scolded, Ella's eyes grew sharp with concern as they noted Jen's pale cheeks and the dark shadows under her eyes.

"I'm sorry, Mom." Standing just inside the door on the mat her ever-tidy mother had placed there for the purpose of removing sloppy wet clothes and boots, Jen bent listlessly to tug at the zipper of her boot. "I have no excuse. I simply forgot."

Although Jen didn't notice, the look of concern spread from her mother's eyes to her entire face. "Jennifer" — Ella's tone of annoyance was gone, replaced by anxiety — "are you feeling all right?"

Her boots dealt with, Jen straightened. "I'm just tired." She smiled reassuringly as she shrugged out of her jacket. "And I think I may be coming down with a cold." This last remark she tacked on in an effort to stave off questions about her puffy, red-rimmed eyes. "Where's Daddy?"

A soft smile curved her mother's lips as she plucked the jacket out of Jen's hands and turned to hang it in the closet. "In his 'den,' asleep in front of the TV." Turning back to Jen, she ordered gently, "Leave your suitcase where it is for now and come have a cup of tea. You look like you need it."

As she followed her mother to the kitchen, Jen glanced down the long hall that led to the home's four bedrooms, a reflection of her mother's soft smile on her own lips. Her father's "den," as her mother had laughingly dubbed it, was located in the smallest of the bedrooms. Before her sister Vicki's marriage, the room had been used as a guest room. But two weeks after the wedding Ella began rearranging the rooms. Declaring, teasingly, that she was tired of listening to her husband snore as he ostensibly watched television, she turned Vicki's room into a guest room and installed a desk, a portable television, and a lounge chair in the small room and christened it "Dad's den."

The aroma of Yankee pot roast assailed Jen's nostrils as she entered the large kitchen, and with a surprised glance at the wall clock, Jen saw it was only a half hour shy of the usual dinner hour of six o'clock. *Lord!* Jen grimaced as she dropped onto a plastic and chrome kitchen chair. No wonder she felt wrung out. They had been on that bus all day!

"Did you run into any difficulty on the way home?" Ella asked as she placed a steaming cup of tea in front of Jen.

"No." Jen shook her head. "But it was slow going. We left the motel around ten this morning."

"There's my girl." Ralph Lengle's warm voice preceded him into the kitchen. Coming to a stop beside her chair, he slid an arm around her shoulders and gave her a brief hug. "Your trip turned out to be pretty much of a fiasco, didn't it?" he commiserated softly.

In more ways than one, Jen thought tiredly. Glancing up at him, she smiled ruefully. "I'm afraid so."

Becoming still, his eyes searched hers knowingly. For as long as she could remember, her father had been able to gauge her state of health — emotional and physical — from her eyes. Now he seemed puzzled. "What's up, Jen?" he probed gently. "Aren't you feeling well? Or is something troubling you?"

"I'm okay, Dad." Jen shook her head, as much to deny the moisture gathering in her eyes as his words. Always susceptible to his caring gentleness, Jen was even more so now. "I think I may have caught a cold."

Even though her father nodded, his expression left little doubt in Jen's mind that he was unconvinced.

Somehow Jen managed to eat at least some of her dinner and get through the clearing-away period after the meal was finished. When she was finally free to go to her own room, she walked down the hall determined to take a hot bath, crawl into bed, and have a good cry in an attempt to dissolve the tight knot of misery that had settled in her chest. She achieved the first two of her objectives, but after slipping between the covers, she was dead to the world before the first tear could fully form.

Uncomfortably for Jen, her hasty assurances to her parents that she was coming down with a cold proved to be prophetic. By Monday morning she was sneezing at the rate of what seemed to be three times within every five minutes; bleary-eyed; and red-nosed from her tender skin's constant contact with a procession of tissues. All that long week, Jen dragged her aching body from home to office to home again, sneezing and sniffling all the way.

Dousing herself with hot baths, aspirin, and a supposedly bracing tea concoction her mother brewed for her every night, Jen steadfastly refused to see a doctor. By the end of the week the sneezing and sniffling had stopped, but Jen felt exhausted and looked, in her mother's words, like warmed-over death. Even though her mother had made the statement teasingly, her eyes had revealed her growing concern. Jen had to fight the urge to confide in her mother, then have a good cry on her shoulder.

But she didn't. As each successive day passed without word from Adam, the fear grew inside Jen that she would never hear from him again. How could she tell her mother about him? What could she say? There was no way she could explain what had happened in that snowed-in motel. How could she make her mother understand when she didn't quite understand it herself?

Jen spent the entire week silently fighting the doubts that assailed her mind. Had she fallen headlong into love, she wondered over and over again, or had she been caught up in the snow fever Ted had talked about? Away from Adam's hypnotic, warm velvet gaze, his bone-melting touch, and his reason-destroying mouth, Jen was left with the knowledge of her own inexperience.

Had she, in her innocence, allowed herself to be led down the garden path? Had she, to be blunt, allowed herself to be used as a convenience — a bed and body warmer? The self-questioning seared her soul, but though she struggled to banish them, the questions persisted.

Never before in her life had she encountered anyone like Adam Banner. He was a completely unknown quantity to her, different from any other man Jen had ever come in contact with. His upbringing and lifestyle were the complete antitheses of her own.

Jen was, she knew, very much a product of the everyday middle class. Her own upbringing had been free of any disruptive influences or emotional upheavals. As she had honestly told Adam, she was very like other people.

Her moral code had been instilled by loving, concerned, God-fearing parents who believed in the sanctity of the marriage vows. The idea of divorce was unpalatable to them, but compared to divorce, infidelity was blasphemy. Jen had absorbed and accepted their beliefs unquestioningly. It was therefore unsurprising that she had been shocked at Adam's revelations. And now her own response to him held equal shock value.

As one day dragged itself into another, her head cold drained her energy and her confusing thoughts ravaged her mind, Jen felt torn in two by conflicting conclusions.

On the one hand was the emotional realization that what had been ignited inside her at the first touch of Adam's eyes had not been infatuation or mere physical attraction but the first, exciting spark of love — a spark that had flared into a vociferous flame, consuming all other considerations, by the time Adam's note had been handed to her.

On the other hand was the daunting voice of reason that told her that even if he were with her, they would be poles apart. Even though she was young, her character mold was set. Her dreams had been of a very prosaic nature. Very simply, she wanted a life like her mother had: a companionable relationship with her husband, a comfortable home, and children to love and enjoy.

By Friday morning Jen had reached the heartbreaking conclusion that even if Adam should still call or come to her, they had no future together. She loved him — almost desperately so — and she ached to be in his arms, to have all rational thought burned out of her mind by his searching mouth. But she knew that when his arms loosened and his lips left hers, the cold light of reality would still be there, glaringly exposing the fact that although opposites often attract, they are as often incompatible.

Sadly, Jen came to the decision that should he contact her, she would have to deny her feelings for him, for she truly believed that if she didn't, she would pay for a long time to come.

When Chris called while Jen was on her lunch break, she was so weary of her own thoughts she answered "Yes" at once when Chris asked if she wanted to go out that evening.

"It'll be the usual crowd," Chris said lightly. "At the usual place."

The usual place was a local night spot, frequented mostly by young singles.

"I'll be there," Jen promised firmly, suddenly filled with a need to get back into the normal swing of her life.

Jen informed her parents of her plans over the dinner table, feeling a twinge of guilt at the relief that washed over her mother's face. She had been aware of her mother's concern, of course, but now the full extent of that concern was clearly visible.

She should have known, Jen chided herself. She and Vicki had never been able to hide anything from their mother, and although her mother had no way of knowing what was troubling her, it was obvious she was aware that Jen was suffering from more than a common cold.

"It'll do you a world of good," Ella declared with a forced note of cheer in her voice.

"Other than to go back and forth to work, you've been cooped up in the house all week."

After dinner, having cleared the table and stacked the dishwasher, Jen and her mother were straightening the dining area when the phone rang.

"I'll get it," her father offered, coming in the back door after taking out the trash, and crossing the kitchen to the wall phone. Jen was bent over the table, replacing the flower-ringed candle centerpiece, when he called, "It's for you, honey."

Knowing Chris's genius for changing plans at the last minute, Jen was wondering what the change might be as she took the receiver from her father and said, "Hello?"

"Jennifer?"

Nine

The low, caressing sound of her name froze Jen in place. She was unaware that her parents had left the dining room. She did not hear the sound of the TV being turned up in the living room. For long seconds she could not think or hear or breathe.

"Jennifer?" Not so low now, Adam's sharp tone shattered her trancelike state.

Placing her hand over the end of the receiver, Jen drew a deep, ragged breath and released it slowly before removing her hand and answering huskily, "Yes?"

"Darling, you sound strange. Are you all right?" Adam asked in the same sharp tone.

"Yes, I'm fine. I've had a cold all week, but it's better now," Jen explained away the husky sound of her voice.

"Dammit," Adam muttered. "I kept you out in the snow too long last week. Have you seen a doctor?"

"No, it wasn't necessary." Jen sighed. "It was only a head cold, Adam," she ended somewhat abruptly. Why were they talking about a head cold! Adam was quiet a moment, and when his voice again touched her ear it held that low, caressing note that so affected her nervous system.

"I'm hungry for you, darling," he murmured roughly. "Cold or no cold, contagious or not, I want to kiss you so badly I get the shakes just thinking about it."

His blatantly sensual tone scattered the fog blanketing her mind, and with a start Jen remembered her decision of that morning.

"Did Bill give you my note, angel?" Adam's soft tone broke into her thoughts.

"Yes," Jen answered flatly.

"Jennifer, are you angry about the suddenness of my departure?" All traces of the sensuality were gone now, replaced by tight urgency. "There was a good reason for the abruptness of my actions."

"I'm sure there was," Jen replied in the same flat tone. And she really was sure, but somehow it didn't seem important anymore. If she was going to stick to her decision, the less she knew, the better. Forcing all expression from her voice, she murmured, "It's not important, Adam."

"Not important?" he repeated blankly. Then he almost shouted, "What do you mean, not important? And why isn't it?"

"Why is it?" she asked quietly.

"Why?" he repeated incredulously. "Wait a minute," he went on with forced control, "I'm tired, and I've got jet lag, and I think I'm missing something." He drew a long breath, then went on slowly, "Why isn't it important, Jennifer?"

"Because" — Jen swallowed around the painful tightness in her throat — "because what happened between us at that motel shouldn't have."

"Oh, hell," Adam groaned. "She's been passing judgments again — this time on herself," he muttered before demanding, "Is that why you left my room that morning?"

"That's not important either anymore," Jen sighed.

"Jennifer, listen to me," Adam said impatiently. "You're being ridiculous and childish. We have to talk about this."

His calling her ridiculous and childish stirred defensive anger in Jen. What did he want of her? Why was he even bothering? First he'd accused her of being too quick to judge. Then he'd scolded her for being tactless. Soon after that he'd called her narrow-minded and straitlaced. Now she was ridiculous and childish. The list of her character faults seemed to grow longer and longer. Why was he even interested? In comparison to the other women he knew, especially his mother, she had to appear appallingly gauche. That thought seared her mind and loosened her tongue in retaliation.

"I don't understand you at all, Adam," Jen cried through stiff lips. "Why did you call me? What interest can you have in such a morally uptight juvenile?"

"Dammit, Jennifer" — Adam's rough tone betrayed his anger — "will you stop this stupidity —"

"No, damn you, Adam." Jen's knuckles were white from gripping the receiver. Now she was stupid! The list grew longer every time he opened his mouth. God, what a bore he must find her. But then — why? The answer came glaringly simple. She had been so unbelievably easy. Was it possible he was between women, she thought wildly, and needed a diversion? The thought was crushing, and without actually forming them, words of repudiation poured from her trembling lips.

"I may be stupid and childish, but I'm not a complete idiot, even if I have given you reason to believe I am. I am not interested in being a part-time playmate to be used whenever there's a lull in your more sophisticated action."

A long silence followed her nearly incoherent tirade, during which Jen could only boggle at her own outrageous statement. She was wrong; she *was* a complete idiot! The bark of Adam's harsh laughter seemed to indicate his concurrence.

"Part-time playmate!" His laughter turned derisive. "I'm coming up there so we can talk this out."

"I won't be here."

"Where are you going?" Adam demanded. "Who are you going with?"

Jen bristled at his sharply possessive tone. How dare he question her?

Enraged, Jen choked, "None of your damned business," and slammed the receiver onto its cradle.

Shaken, trembling, Jen stood staring at the phone, fully expecting it to ring again. As the seconds dragged into minutes her shoulders drooped, and she had to close her eyes against the hot sting of tears. Leaning tiredly against the wall, Jen berated herself for the moisture that trickled from under her tightly closed lids.

A shudder rippled through her body as an echo of his voice whispered through her mind: "Jennifer, are you angry?" Angry? Good Lord, if it was only that simple. How much easier it would be if the only emotion she felt was healthy anger. She ached to see him, ached to be in his arms, while at the same time she was afraid to see him. She wasn't sure she could trust him not to hurt her again.

Sighing for what might have been, she

pushed herself away from the wall. She had taken three steps across the inlaid tile floor when a sudden thought brought her up short. Once before she had thought her words had driven him away. His reply to her then had been "I'll never walk away from you," and Jen knew now, positively, that before long he would be there, at her home, insisting she listen to him.

The thought generated action, and Jen practically ran down the hall to her room. She had over an hour until she was to meet Chris and the rest of her friends, but as she had no idea where Adam had been calling from, she could not, now, waste any time hanging around the house. She had to get ready as quickly as possible and get out. For if she saw him, if he got his hands on her, her resistance would dissolve in her need for him.

Eleven minutes later, every nerve in her body quivering, Jen backed her car out of the driveway. Instead of the long, hot bath she had looked forward to, she had made do with a quick sponge bath and a fresh application of makeup. A shimmery, clingy dress had replaced her tailored office clothes, and her comfortable low-heeled pumps had been exchanged for a few straps attached to a thin sole and narrow spike heels. She had shrugged into her short fake fur jacket as she headed for the door and had forestalled the questions she could see forming on her mother's lips with a brightly chirped, "I gotta run. Don't worry. I will not drink too much, I will drive carefully, and I won't be very late. Bye." Her last word coincided with the closing of the door.

Jen's breathing didn't return to normal until she was several blocks away from her home. Still shaky, she jerked to a stop as a light changed to red, and she sat gripping the steering wheel, wondering what in the world she was going to do for an hour. A short blast of the horn from the car behind her made her aware that the light had switched to green. It also made her aware of her distracted state of mind. *Better go to Chris's,* she told herself scathingly. *In the condition I'm in, I'm a menace on the road.*

Chris met her at the door with a frown and a wailed "Did I screw things up again?"

"What do you mean?" Jen asked blankly, her thoughts still on her rush to escape.

"Roger is picking me up." Chris bit her lip. "I thought you said you'd meet us at the club."

At that moment Jen blessed Chris's absentmindedness and her penchant for "screwing things up."

"That's okay." She managed to produce

213

a careless laugh. "I'll follow you and Roger, no major problem."

By the time they arrived at the night spot hangout, Jen had herself under control — at least on the surface. The others were already there and had pushed several tables together to accommodate the group that totaled ten.

Friday night — and the atmosphere was pure party, not only at their table but throughout the large room. The throbbing beat of the loud music, combined with the equally loud conversation and laughter, made thinking an impossibility for which Jen was grateful.

Laughing, joking, drinking, Jen threw herself into the spirit of revelry with a frenzy of desperation — although her drinking was limited. She had gulped down a glass and a half of gin and tonic when Roger literally dragged her onto the dance floor.

The colored, diffused lighting that bounced over and around the dance floor blended perfectly with the blare of rock music. What Roger lacked in expertise he more than made up for in enthusiasm. When, at the end of the fourth energetic number, Jen laughingly cried "Uncle," her already clingy dress was plastered to her perspiration-wet body in spots, and her face glowed with a moist sheen.

Still laughing as they walked off the dance floor, Jen lifted her head to glance around the room and felt her body go stiff with shock. Adam was standing with his back to the bar, his eyes fastened on her. The moment she saw him, he pushed himself lazily away from the bar and started slowly toward her.

Her first thought was to run, followed immediately by, where to? Adam's expression, hard with grim determination, brought her faltering steps to a halt. Forcing a semblance of lightness to her tone, she said, "Go ahead, Roger, I see someone I know," just as the lights dimmed and the strains of a ballad filled the room. All her senses centered on the man approaching her, Jen didn't even hear Roger's reply or see him move away.

When he reached her, he slid his arms around her waist and without saying a word drew her into the midst of the slowly moving couples. Without a thought, Jen's arms moved to circle his neck, and she felt a hot shaft of excitement as his arms tightened.

"Jennifer."

The familiar, longed for, whispered caress robbed her of all rational thought. Without even a pretense of dancing, Adam held her tightly against his hard body, swaying gently in time with the music. He didn't speak, but then he didn't have to; his body spoke volumes. And her body answered: yes, yes, yes.

One slow song followed another, all unheard by Jen. The darting colored lights that signaled the return to upbeat music pierced the mist of sensuousness clouding Jen's reason. Pulling away from him in disgust, she made a zigzag dash off the dance floor, half afraid he'd follow her, half afraid he wouldn't. He didn't, and Jen was back at the table several minutes before she found the courage to look around for him.

He was gone! Her eyes wide with disbelief, Jen made a second, slower search of the room even though she knew she would not have missed him on the first circuit. He simply was not there. Like a phantom conjured up by her imagination, he had disappeared. Fighting an eerie feeling of unreality, she gripped her glass with trembling fingers, unaware and unconcerned with the bantering chatter of her friends.

Other than to whisper her name, he had not spoken, had made no attempt to get her alone. Her face grew warm with anger and humiliation at the memory of how effortlessly he'd drawn a physical response from her. But why the disappearing act?

"Jen, are you feeling all right?"

Chris's sharp tone penetrated Jen's self-absorbtion before she could formulate an answer to her own silent question.

"Yes, of course." Jen smiled shakily. "But I'm suddenly very, very tired." It was true; she suddenly did feel very, very tired. "I think I'll go home to bed — it's been a long day."

The instant response of every male in the group to go with her was almost Jen's undoing. Swallowing painfully against the constricting tightness in her throat, she shook her head in rejection of their offers while choking out a none-too-articulate "Thank you."

Emerging from the building, Jen shuddered and hunched her shoulders against the sting of the cold night air on her overheated body. Clutching her upturned collar under her chin, she hurried to the protection of her car.

Her mind scurried from one inane, unrelated thought to another all the way home in a desperate but vain attempt to avoid thinking of Adam. Under all the surface thoughts, unanswerable questions hammered away relentlessly. How had he known where she'd be? Why had he disappeared as soon as they'd left the dance floor? Why had he remained silent when only a few hours earlier he'd insisted she listen to him? Where had he gone? And — damn him — what kind of game was he playing anyway?

By the time she turned onto the driveway and parked in front of the garage, she was too tired to notice the car parked along the curb in front of her home. As she stepped onto the macadam, the motion of the passenger door swinging open caught her attention. At the same instant she recognized the gold Corvette, she heard Adam's softly voiced order. "Come get in the car, Jennifer."

For one brief moment Jen considered ignoring him and making a dash for the front door. In the very next moment she dismissed the idea, certain he'd simply lie on the doorbell until she admitted him. The lone light left on in the living room gave evidence that her parents were in bed, and Jen did not want them disturbed. She didn't want to answer a lot of questions about Adam either.

Moving with obvious reluctance, she covered the ground to his car. "What do you want?" she whispered harshly.

"Get in the car," Adam repeated patiently.

"No."

"Why not?" he asked, still very patiently.

"I don't want to hear whatever it is you have to say." Jen heard his sharply indrawn breath and went on, "I don't trust you, Adam."

Adam was quiet for long seconds, then,

in a very even, very quiet tone promised, "If you don't get in the car — now — I will get out and put you in."

Deciding to be prudent, Jen slid onto the seat next to him, letting her anger show by slamming the door shut. Eyes blazing, voice frigid, she faced him squarely.

"All right, Adam, say your little piece — if you must."

"I don't think so."

"What?" Jen frowned at his flat, uncompromising tone.

"You may get out of the car, Jennifer." His tone was still flat but carried an inflection that tugged at Jen's memory. What was it? Unable to grasp the elusive memory, Jen shook her head.

"But — then why —"

"Why waste my time — and yours?"

The inflection was stronger now, and suddenly Jen was back in the motel, hearing him say, "Are you still mad at me?" in the same somewhat sad tone. At that time she had hurt Liz with her hasty condemnation. Was Adam hurt? Was it possible she had misjudged his actions? Had she, again, been too hasty? Hasty? After all *his* words of condemnation of her? Again Jen shook her head.

"Are you going to get out?" Adam's quiet voice ended her introspection. Glancing at him, Jen was struck by an odd, waiting stillness about him. *Waiting for what?* Jen wondered confusedly.

"Adam, I — What are you doing?"

What he was doing was sliding his hand around her neck as he leaned across the console dividing the seats. Bending his head, he muttered, "You should have got out while you had the chance." His lips brushed the skin in front of her ear. Although the touch was feather light, Jen could not repress the shiver that rippled through her, or the half gasp, half moan that whispered through her lips.

"Or didn't you *really* want to get out?" Adam's breath tickled her face as his lips moved from her ear to the corner of her mouth.

"Yes — no — I — ooh!"

Adam's mouth slid over her parted lips, silencing her vain attempt to answer him. It didn't matter. Nothing mattered except the wildfire that spread through her veins and sent her mind whirling. He was here. He was now. And everything else was, for the moment, forgotten in her body's clamoring response.

"Jennifer, Jennifer."

First against her lips, then against her cheek — over and over again — her name was whispered huskily as his lips explored her face. The overpowering need to touch him drove her hands to his head, sent her fingers spearing through the toast-brown strands. His hand at the back of her head urged her closer, closer.

"God, I've missed you." His tongue skipped along the edge of her ear. "Missed this," he groaned, trailing that tip of fire to her lips. "I want to touch you, kiss you, all over. Wet my lips for me, darling." The urgent whisper was followed by his hand cupping her breast.

An alarm went off in Jen's head, restoring reason and cooling her overheated senses. Turning her face away from the temptation of his mouth, his words, Jen cried, "Adam, don't!"

Long-fingers gripped convulsively, painfully, at her breast an instant before the hand was lifted to grasp her chin. Lifting his head, he tersely ordered, "Look at me, Jennifer." Without waiting for her to comply, he forced her to face him.

"What do you mean — 'Adam, don't'?" he asked harshly. "Adam, don't at all, or not here?"

"Not — not at all." Why did her voice lack conviction? Why now? Jen groaned silently. Now, when she had to make it clear to him that she would not allow him to use her again. Letting her hands drop into her lap, she clasped them together, drew a quick, strengthening breath, and added, "I told you earlier that I'm not interested in being a part-time playmate. And even if you think it's funny, I mean it."

"Oh, you're wrong, I don't think it's funny at all." Leaning back, he pinned her with a challenging stare. How about being a full-time playmate?"

"What — exactly — do you mean?" Jen asked warily.

"I can't keep my hands off you and you know it." That strangely sad smile touched his lips fleetingly. "And, although you'll probably deny it, you can't keep your hands off me, either. There's only one thing for us — isn't there?"

Jen was almost afraid to ask, yet of course she had to.

"And that is?"

"Marriage."

Openmouthed, wide-eyed, Jen sat staring at him, too stunned to speak. When, finally, she did find her voice, all she could manage was a croaked, "Marriage?"

"Do you have a better solution?" he asked imperturbably.

"But we don't even know each other. We —" She was going to add that they had nothing in common, but Adam's roar of laughter drowned her surprised protest.

"Don't know each other?" Still laughing, he shook his head in disbelief. "Jennifer, we know every inch of each other."

"I don't mean *that* way." Stung, Jen

flung the words at him.

"In case you don't know, *that* way is the most important way," he retorted. Grasping her shoulders, he gave her a gentle shake. "We have all the time in the world to explore each other's personalities, innocent one. And, personally, I'd prefer to do it in bed." Pulling her to him, he kissed her hungrily. "I think we'd better get married, angel. Very soon."

"H— How soon?" Jen whispered around the tightness in her throat.

"Next week?"

"Next week? Adam, are you out of your mind?" Jen gasped.

"Not yet," he murmured against her lips. "But I'm getting pretty close to it with wanting you." Drawing her as close to his body as the console would allow, his lips teased hers while his hands moved restlessly over her shoulders and down her back. "Why not next week?" he asked in a near growl.

Why? Where could she start? She didn't even know where he'd be after next week — or before, for that matter. Did he? she wondered fleetingly. To her, the way he lived seemed unstable and erratic. In no way could she see herself fitting into his life. What did they have, really, except this crazy physical attraction?

"Jennifer?" The whispered caress, combined with the mind-clouding, restless movements of his hands on her body destroyed her attempt at marshaling arguments. His lips almost touching hers crumbled her defenses entirely. "I said, why not next week?"

Jen blurted the first thing that came into her mind. "My parents! Adam, they haven't even met you." Pulling away from him, she wailed, "What on earth could I say to them?"

"How about the truth?" Adam murmured, moving back onto his own seat behind the wheel.

"What truth?" Jen asked uneasily.

"Why, while snowbound, you met a man, fell in love, and went to bed with him." Jen gasped, but Adam went on in a soft, rough tone, "Or have you forgotten you said you were in love?"

"No," she denied swiftly. "I haven't forgotten."

"Neither have I. Are you going to marry me, Jennifer?"

Every one of the reasons why she should say no rushed into her mind, only to become muddled and confused, and rendered useless against one irrefutable fact. She wanted him so very badly. Could it possibly work? If, given a little time to get to know each other — would it? Maybe, hope sprang wildly, just maybe. She tried to visualize the future, but the only image that came was of the two of them, locked together, on the bed in his room at the motel.

The picture made her heart thump, filled every inch of her being with need. *No!* she thought frantically. *That's not enough to build a future on. But — but if I can keep him at arm's length, at a distance, while we get to know each other? Could it work? I've got to give it a try, because I love him. Oh, God, how I love him.*

"Well?"

Jen started at the impatient edge in Adam's voice. She had been quiet too long, and he wanted an answer — at once.

"Yes," Jen surrendered.

"When?" Adam demanded.

"Adam, you must understand, planning a wedding takes time."

"How much time?" Adam asked grimly.

Jen wet her lips. "My mother would love a June wedding."

"Four months." His lips twisted wryly. "And you fully intend making me sweat out every day of it, don't you?" Before she could answer, he sighed, "Is this to be some kind of a test?" But again he didn't wait for a reply. "Okay, four months. I have some things to clear up anyway."

"What things?" she asked in confusion.

"Jennifer" — his voice held rough impatience — "do you want a husband that spends most of the year out of the country?"

"No, of course not!"

"That's what I thought. I'm changing jobs." Jen opened her mouth to question him, and he held up his hand to forestall her. "Not companies, Jennifer, just the job I do for that company. I've been offered a desk job several times over the last few years, and now I've decided to take it. But I will have to leave the country a few times before June."

Who is she? Jen hated herself for the first question that flashed into her mind. Nevertheless, there it was, and she had to face it; he was a very virile man. He had proved that — repeatedly — in a very short amount of time. The mental question that followed was equally as unsettling. Would he break with her entirely or — afraid even to think of an answer, she rushed into speech with the first thing that came into her head.

"Where are we going to live?"

"That's one of the other things I was thinking of." Adam glanced at her sharply, frowning, then he went on calmly, "I have a town house outside Philly." He named a rather exclusive suburb, causing Jen to raise her eyebrows in surprise. "If it doesn't suit you, we'll look around for something else." He shrugged. "But we can discuss all that later. Right now it's late and you'd better go in. I have to go into the office tomorrow morning to work on a report, but I'll call you after lunch, okay?"

Feeling suddenly very tired, Jen nodded and turned to the door, her hand groping for the release.

"No good-night kiss, Jennifer?" Adam chided softly.

Jen turned to meet his descending head with an eagerness that was shaming, her arms curling around his neck at the same moment his hands slid under her short jacket to clasp her waist. His mouth explored hers with an almost cool deliberation. She sensed it, and still she was powerless against the fierce surge of desire that drove her lips to beg him silently to deepen the kiss. When his hands moved up her sides to brush the outer curve of her breasts, Jen shivered in anticipation. Sharp disappointment drew a soft moaning protest from her lips when his hands moved back to her waist.

"My foolish angel." Adam's warm breath feathered her cheek deliciously as his lips sought her ear. "In punishing me, you'll be punishing yourself — don't you see that?"

"I don't know what you mean," Jen denied softly.

"I cautioned you once about lying to yourself." As if to underline his words, his hands slid over the silklike material of her dress, tantalizingly near but not touching her breasts until she, in an aching need to feel the possession of those hands, arched her back. "You need it" — one long finger drew a curving line up to a quivering tip — "every bit as badly as I do. If you persist with your present attitude, these next four months are going to be sheer hell — for both of us."

Anger at him as well as herself gave her the strength to tear herself out of his arms. What he'd said was true, of course, which made it that much harder to swallow. How, she wondered distractedly, had he known so positively that she had no intention of allowing that kind of intimacy again before the marriage took place? Feeling guilty — and made more angry for feeling so — she snapped, "You're wrong, Adam. I will be much too busy to think about it."

"Oh, you'll think about it." Adam's soft laughter fanned the flame of her anger. "In fact, I'll bet that by the time *the* day dawns, you will be thinking of little else."

"No!" Jen shook her head sharply. "I —"

"But console yourself with this thought," Adam interrupted harshly. "By then, I will have been on the rack for a very long time."

Refusing to listen to any more, Jen found the release and let the door swing open. "I can't think how I'll explain this to my parents." The sudden thought flashed into her head and emerged as a wail.

"I'm not going to disappear into a puff of smoke, Jennifer," Adam laughed softly. "I don't expect you to face them with this alone. Don't say anything until I can get here tomorrow."

"Adam!" Jen twisted around to him fearfully. "You won't tell them what happened between us? They have — certain ideas — rigid ones — and — and —" Jen floundered, her mouth going dry at the thought of her parents' reaction to that kind of news.

"I'm not a complete bastard, Jennifer," Adam ground out fiercely. "I don't make love — and tell."

Jen stared at him wide-eyed. Oh, Lord, how could they hope to make a life together when they became bogged down with misunderstanding at the first hurdle? She had been afraid that, in his honesty, he would be a little too frank with her parents. While he thought — what? That she believed him capable of viciousness? The very idea shocked her into stuttered speech.

"Adam, I — I didn't mean —"

The hard, unrelenting set of his features

told her that her plea wasn't reaching him.

"I know exactly what you meant." Then, his tone crushing, he turned and grasped the wheel. "Good night, Jennifer."

Feeling casually dismissed, her cheeks hot with embarrassment, Jen got out of the car, closing the door carefully.

Forcing herself to maintain a normal pace, she walked to the front door, unlocked it with trembling fingers, and, slipping inside, stood shaking like a leaf as she listened to the sound of Adam's car fade as he drove away.

Over an hour later, unable to sleep, Jen finally gave up her fitful tossing — and the effort not to think. After fighting her way out of the tangle of covers, she pushed her feet into furry mules and went slapping along the hallway to the kitchen.

She was pouring herself a glass of milk she didn't really want when her mother entered the kitchen. Wondering vaguely if a feather could fall to the floor without her mother hearing it, Jen sat down at the table and stared broodingly into the white liquid.

"What's the matter, honey?" Ella asked quietly. "Couldn't you sleep?"

"No." Jen shook her head briefly before glancing up. "I'm sorry if I disturbed you."

"Oh, Jen," Ella sighed, "you've disturbed me all week. Your lack of appetite, your listlessness, your sleeplessness. Oh, yes" —

she looked squarely into Jen's widened eyes — "I've known all week that you haven't been sleeping well." Her voice went low, coaxing. "Can't you tell me what's bothering you?"

Jen stared into her mother's concerned face for a long time, then, shifting her gaze back to her glass, she whispered, "There's this man."

"Ahhh —" Ella expelled her breath slowly. "I was somehow sure that there was. You met him while you were away?"

"Yes."

"He was a passenger on the bus?"

"No."

"Jen, will you look at me?" her mother ordered impatiently. "I do not like being cast in the role of interrogator. Now, if you want to talk about it, then talk. If not, say so, and I'll go back to bed."

Immediately contrite, Jen grasped her mother's hand. "I'm sorry, Mom," she apologized. Then, coming to a swift decision, she blurted, "He's asked me to marry him."

"And are you going to?"

Stunned by her mother's calmly voiced question, Jen gaped at her in astonishment.

"Well?" Ella prompted softly. "Are you?"

"Yes, but —" Jen's expression betrayed her bewilderment. "Is that all you have to say?"

"Hardly." Ella laughed. "But I wanted a definite answer before I bombarded you with questions."

They talked for nearly an hour over steaming cups of tea her mother insisted on making after pouring the untouched milk down the drain. Thankfully, her mother's questions did not probe too deeply, and with a sigh of relief, Jen willingly answered all of them.

By the time they bade each other a whispered "Good night," her mother knew what Adam looked like, what he did for a living, where he lived, and that Jen loved him very much. What she did not know was how impetuously Jen had responded to him, or any of the intimate, hurtful details that followed.

It was not until Jen was back in bed and beginning to drift into sleep that two thoughts — springing into her mind back to back — made her shift position restlessly. The first thought was what she would do if, after the way they'd parted, Adam did not call her. The second was much more irrelevant: Did he still have her chain? Not having the answer to either question, and by now dead tired, Jen closed her eyes tightly and fell asleep.

Jen's first thought on waking at ten thirty was an echo of the one held while falling asleep. Would he call? The very real fear that he would not lay on her mind heavily as she went to the kitchen for a bracing cup of coffee. She found her mother there watering the plants that lined the kitchen windowsill. There was no sign of her father anywhere. Emulating the breathless, happy tone that had colored her sister's voice for weeks before her wedding, Jen sang, "Good morning, Mom. Where's Dad?"

"He went to the hardware store," Ella answered placidly. "They're having a sale on electric hedge clippers."

"Did you tell him?" Jen asked tersely.

"No." Her watering finished, Ella turned to smile at her. "It's your bomb; I'll let you drop it." After replacing the long-spouted watering can in the cabinet beneath the sink, she frowned at the cup in Jen's hand. "Is that all you're having?"

"Are there any English muffins?" Jen asked, hoping there weren't.

There were, and Jen was determinedly chewing away when her father came whistling through the back door, a long package under one arm.

"Good morning, honey," he greeted her cheerfully. "Did you have a good time last night?"

Taking his question as her cue, Ella breezed out of the kitchen after bestowing an encouraging smile on her daughter.

Catching his wife's parting look, and not being in the least obtuse, Ralph leveled his eyes on Jen and prompted, "What's up?"

"I'm getting married." Jen bit her lip hard the minute the last word was out of her mouth. Calling herself a blithering nitwit, she watched her father anxiously for a reaction. When it came it left her as stunned as her mother's had.

"Anyone I know?" Ralph asked blandly.

Jen should have realized his tone was just a little too bland, even coming from her even-tempered father. But in her surprise she didn't realize it, and his second question hit her like a shock of cold water.

"I want some answers, young lady," he barked angrily. "Who the hell is he?"

His face set, his eyes hard, he listened as Jen repeated, almost word for word, what she'd said to her mother only hours before. In a desperate bid to wipe the rigidity from his face, she finished on a soft, appealing whisper.

"I love him, Dad."

Being a realistic man and loving his daughter very much, Ralph bowed to the inevitable.

"Okay, honey," he sighed. "When are we going to meet him?"

When, after exchanging hugs, kisses, and a few errant tears, Jen escaped to her room, it was with the conviction that if

Adam failed to call, she would leave home rather than try to explain.

The phone rang at exactly one minute after one.

Ten

Adam presented himself at the Lengle residence at exactly six thirty, having arranged — with Jen acting as go-between — to take her parents out to dinner. His appearance when Jen opened the door was a small assault on nerves that were already drawn too tautly.

Although up until now his clothes had been obviously expensive, they had been casual sport clothes. Now, the sight of him in a fashionably cut suit, silk shirt and tie, and a dark navy topcoat was just about enough to do her in entirely. Her reaction did not go unnoticed by Adam, although he did misinterpret it. Shrugging out of the topcoat as he stepped inside, he smiled wryly.

"It seems February is going to be every bit as bleak as January was. It is cold and it is windy."

In the process of handing his coat to her, the sleeves of both his suit and shirt inched up his arm, and Jen's glance was caught and held on the fine gold chain that encircled his left wrist just below his watch.

"May I have it back?" Jen inquired huskily, knowing full well she did not have to identify "it."

"No," Adam answered flatly and, in an obvious attempt to change the subject, asked, "Where are your parents?"

"They'll be out in a minute." Glad for an excuse to avoid his eyes, Jen turned to drape his coat over the back of a chair. "They are being tactful by giving us some time alone together."

"That's very thoughtful of them."

Jen shuddered. She had not heard him move, yet he was right behind her — not touching, but very close. The shudder increased when he turned her to face him.

"You look like you're ready to fall apart," he said softly. "Was it very bad?" He knew she had told her parents about their plans to marry. But that was all he knew, for all she'd said over the phone was, "I talked to my mother and father." When she didn't answer at once he insisted, "Jennifer, are they angry? — disappointed? — what?"

"No," Jen denied. "At least, not any more. There were a few uncomfortable moments, but . . . well, I think they're reserving judgment until they've had a chance to get to know you."

"A commendable trait, reserving judgment until you have a base from which you can render a *fair* judgment." Adam smiled sardonically. "One their daughter should have cultivated."

Was he going to start that again? Jen went stiff with swift anger that, while churning her emotions, clouded her common sense. Shrugging off the hands that still clasped her shoulders, Jen lashed out at him unthinkingly.

"Yes, I know — I am childish, stupid, narrow-minded, straitlaced, morally uptight, and" — she tossed her head back defiantly, setting her red curls to dancing like flames around a log — "worst defect of all — I make snap judgments." Suddenly aware that her voice was rising, she drew a deep breath.

"Jen—" Adam began.

"One might wonder," she went on as if he hadn't spoken, "exactly what it is you see in me." Jen glared at him silently, challenging him to answer. He met the challenge in a way that drained the color from her face.

"You're fantastic in bed."

Her parents' entrance into the living room prevented her imminent explosion. Gritting her teeth and forcing a smile, she managed to get through the introductions and the flurry of activity of donning coats and getting into the car.

By the time they were seated in the tastefully decorated restaurant Adam had chosen, Jen had her seething emotions enough under control to look at Adam without fighting the urge to hiss like a ruffled cat.

Adam's behavior was faultless. As they made their leisurely way through an excellently prepared dinner Jen barely tasted, he responded to her parents' sometimes probing questions with a charmingly open earnestness that had them smiling contentedly into their after-dinner coffee.

During the drive back to the house the final straw fell on Jen's delicate emotional state when her father invited Adam to play golf with him. Her father *never* invited anyone to play golf until he knew them inside out! Even her sister's husband, Ron, had not been invited to play until a few weeks before they'd gotten married, and Ron had practically been a fixture around the house for months by that time!

Back at the house, feeling as battered as an overworked tennis ball, Jen gave up all hope of retaliation against Adam that night. After being told to make himself comfortable by her mother and being given a drink by her father, Adam sat, his teasing eyes taunting her, happily joining in as her parents made wedding plans.

That evening set the pattern for the weeks that followed. When, on the following afternoon, Jen had finally gotten him alone long enough to attack him for what he'd said, he'd replied, unanswerably, "Why not say it, darling? You *are* fantastic in bed." Then, with a grimace, he'd launched his own attack. "And if I somehow manage to live through the next four months, I'm hoping the reward will be worth all the effort."

Jen would have dearly loved to argue with him. The only problem was, she wasn't quite sure she fully understood what he was talking about. And before she could marshal her thoughts, he had further confounded her by presenting her with a perfectly beautiful solitaire diamond set into an intricately wrought ring.

In the weeks that followed, Jen found they had more in common than a mutual physical attraction. She loved his town house on sight which, he admitted at once, was a relief to him as he loved it himself. Their preferences in furniture ran on parallel lines. Their taste in music was complementary, and they enjoyed the same sports. They had already discovered they liked the same foods while at the motel. Now Jen learned that liking extended to nearly everything edible down to the dark sweet chocolate that covered their favorite caramels.

The most delightful discovery came one night while they watched TV when her parents were out for an evening of cards at the home of friends. After roaring together at the offbeat sense of humor of a British comedy show, they had gone to the kitchen to raid the refrigerator for a snack. They reentered the living room just as the title of the late-night movie flashed onto the screen. The film was a classic from the forties and one of Jen's favorites. Studying her rapt expression as she read every one of the credits, Adam asked, "Do you want to watch it?"

"Would you mind?" Jen glanced at him quickly.

"Not at all," he grinned. "As a matter of fact, I love these old tearjerkers."

Up until that point Jen had kept Adam at arm's length as far as physical contact was concerned. And much to her surprise, he had shown remarkable patience. Not once had he even tried to deepen their usual passionless good-night kiss. But she was weakening. She had started out loving him, and as the weeks blended into months and their compatibility wove silken, enclosing threads over and around her senses, she discovered her love growing into frightening proportions. And undermining her determination to stick to her vow, she was gradually losing her fear of the future.

When the movie started they were seated over a foot apart on the sofa. By the time it came to a heart-wrenching end, Jen was wrapped in Adam's arms. The transition of being held close while sitting up, to being held closer while lying flat, was completed during the length of one mutually hungry kiss.

Partial sanity returned to Jen when Adam's trembling fingers began unbuttoning her shirt-style blouse. When the tips of his fingers brushed the exposed skin at the edge of her bra, she murmured an unconvincing protest.

"Oh, God, Jennifer," Adam groaned raggedly. "Being away from you again for two weeks is going to be hard enough as it is. Let me love you before I go, darling."

"Go!" Jen went stiff with shock. "Where are you going now?"

During the last months Adam had had to leave the country four times, and Jen had writhed with an uncertainty she couldn't control on each occasion. To add to her uneasiness, he had looked more harried and tired after each successive trip. And although her mind was filled with a riot of questions about his activities while he was away, she bit them back, sure he would resent them. The fact that he became cold and withdrawn for several days following his return each time was an added barrier to any open discussion. After his last trip, two weeks previously, he had told her that he most probably would not have to go away again before the wedding. In her overwhelming relief, Jen had conveniently forgotten his cautionary "most probably."

Now she added dully, "When?"

"I told you I might have to leave the country once more before June," Adam rasped. "I fly out tomorrow morning."

"You were going without telling me!"

"Of course not," he snapped. Swinging his legs to the floor, he stood up. "But being fairly sure of your reaction to my going, I decided to wait until the last minute to tell you."

Hating herself yet unable to keep the accusation from pouring from her mouth, Jen cried, "And was that last-minute telling to come by way of a note claiming you had an emergency call?"

The moment the words were out Jen wished them back. Not once during the preceding months had she questioned him as to why he'd had to leave the motel so precipitously that morning — simply because it hadn't mattered. He *had* called her. He *had* asked her to marry him. And as far as she was concerned, she had enough doubts in the present, worrying about the future, not to rake up the past. Why, she asked herself, had she brought it up now? Apparently he was asking the same question.

"Dammit, Jennifer, you —" Adam broke off to give her a hard stare, then, turning away abruptly, he ground out, "Oh, the hell with it." Striding across the room, he scooped up his jacket, growled, "Good night," and without looking back, slammed out of the house.

Time after time during the weeks that followed Adam's departure Jen berated herself for her foolish tongue. But always on the next thought she berated Adam for springing his news on her the way he had. And just when she was beginning to feel easy with him. His reaction to her charge, his abrupt departure, all seemed a little too suspicious to her. Mistrust of the necessity for his going reared its ugly head. The fact that she heard nothing from him did nothing to allay that mistrust.

Luckily her parents accepted Adam's absence with complacency, their attitude being, a man had a job to do and he did it.

As the wedding arrangements jelled and came together, Jen threw herself into the last-minute craziness with a frenzy that was mistaken for excitement. As the stated two weeks came and then passed, Jen felt she could show real excitement if she could be positive the bridegroom would show up.

In the short amount of time allotted, Ella

Lengle had outdone herself. Two weeks to the day of being told her daughter was getting married, she had hired the caterer and ordered the invitations.

The wedding and reception would be held in the large backyard, the food set out buffet style in the cool garage, along with a makeshift bar. Jen's only attendant would be her sister. Adam's best man was to be a close friend from his college days who Jen had met once. Ella's only fears were that the rose bushes would not bloom in time — and that it would rain.

Sixteen days from the day he left, Adam returned. Jen had had no word of any kind, and when the doorbell rang she ran to answer it, hoping against hope. When she opened the door there he stood, looking tired and a little drawn, a sardonic smile curving his lips.

"Were you afraid — or hoping — my plane had gone down over the Pacific?" he drawled.

The atmosphere between them was decidedly cool for several days.

Her mother had promptly invited him to dinner, and over their after-dinner coffee Adam said smoothly, "Oh, by the way, darling, I saw Mother while I was away, and she sends you her love, her regrets, and her promise of a fabulous wedding gift as soon as she gets back to the States."

Adam had informed them that first night that none of his family could make the wedding as they were all out of the country. At Jen's raised eyebrows and look of surprise, he'd explained that his mother was overseas on an extended leave of absence. He had then explained to her parents that his father and brother were permanent residents of Japan.

The ruffled waters between Adam and Jen smoothed out enough so that by rehearsal time — the night before the wedding — they were even smiling at each other again.

Jen's wedding day dawned pink and beautiful, the sky a sunshine-spattered, cloud-free blue.

Everything was perfect and went off like clockwork. The ceremony at eleven. The allotted thirty minutes for picture taking directly after the knot was tied. The announcement of luncheon being served at eleven forty-five, thereby allowing two hours and forty-five minutes for Jen and Adam to be duly toasted, have some lunch, cut the cake, and circulate among their guests before slipping inside to change and leave in time to make their plane, destination unknown to all but Adam and Jen.

Following the game plan like a well-trained soldier, Jen looked around for Adam at two twenty-five. When he was obviously not in the crush in the yard or at the bar, she headed for the house. On opening the screen door to go in, she encountered Vicki on her way out.

"If you're looking for Adam," Vicki said in an oddly strained tone, "he's in Daddy's den. He has a visitor, and when he asked me if there was somewhere they could talk privately, I told him to go in there."

"Thanks, Vic."

As she walked by Vicki, Jen gave a fleeting thought to her strange tone, but in too much of a hurry to linger and ask about it, she shrugged it off and headed for the den. The door was slightly ajar, and with a gentle push Jen opened it a few inches more, a smile and words of apology on her lips. The words were never uttered and the smile faded from her lips as Jen stood transfixed, staring at her husband of two and a half hours and the exquisitely lovely, sobbing woman he held so protectively in his arms.

The woman was obviously Asian, or at least partly so. Tiny in comparison to Adam, she had long, straight, shiny, raven-black hair and a face that belonged on a delicate silk wall hanging. And at the moment her dark, almond-shaped eyes looked heart-catchingly beautiful drenched in tears. Jen took one unsteady step back, then froze as the woman's soft, lilting voice came faintly to her.

"I-do-not-wish-to-sound-ungrateful-Adam-but-I-don't-know-how-I-can-bear-it."

Jen bit down hard on her lip as Adam's hand came up to stroke the silky black hair. Her teeth dug in harder when the afternoon sunlight struck glintingly off the fine gold chain looped around his wrist. The softly soothing sound of Adam's reply drove her back another step.

"The pain will ease, eventually, I promise you. And if you ever need me, I'll be there, always."

Numb, Jen was unaware of her bridal bouquet sliding out of her frozen fingers. Turning slowly, she walked blindly down the hall and into her bedroom. Standing at the foot of her bed, staring at nothing, her hands smoothed the material at the front of her gown over and over again. She was still standing there, smoothing, when Adam entered the room some ten minutes later.

"Jennifer."

The sound of his voice reached her; the tone of sharp concern did not. Blinking her eyes, she focused on him and saw the small bouquet he held in one hand.

"We have to change and get out of here or we'll miss our plane." Adam spoke slowly, carefully. "And you have to toss this" — he lifted her flowers — "to the single girls."

"Yes, of course." Her movements jerky, Jen turned away from him, her hands going to the zipper at the back of her neck. Then, except for the slight trembling in her fingers, she became still again. Her voice sounded gratingly harsh in the quiet room. "Has she gone?"

"Jennifer —"

"Has she gone?"

"Yes." Adam sighed wearily. "She had asked the cabbie to wait." He sighed again, this time from right behind her. "Jennifer, she didn't —"

"I think you said something about having to change," Jen interrupted sharply, her fingers tugging at the zipper. The bouquet flew by her, landing on the bed. Jen went stiff as his fingers brushed hers.

"Let me do that," he growled. Jen stood as lifeless as a mannequin until the zipper reached the end of its track, then she moved away from him with a terse, "Thank you."

Somehow she got through it. Changing clothes in the same room with him. Tossing her flowers to the laughing group of single girls and managing a teasing remark when Liz, blushing bright pink, caught it. Responding to the hugs, kisses, and good wishes of everyone. Smiling all the while. Somehow she got through it all.

Inside the car the atmosphere was electric with a tense silence. Unable to bare her highly imaginative thoughts, Jen launched into nonsensical chatter.

"Did you see the look that passed between Liz and Ted when she caught the bouquet?" Jen despaired at the false lightness of her trite tone, yet unable to face the strained silence, she went on. "I don't think it will be too long before they're facing a minister —"

"Shut up, Jennifer."

Her breath failed her as Adam's voice slashed across her jabbering. The very roughness of his tone produced the quiet he obviously wanted, for hurt by the harsh order, Jen withdrew, firmly hanging on to thoughts of Liz and Ted.

How perfectly suited to each other they seemed to be, she thought enviously. Liz had been the first person Jen had called about her and Adam's engagement.

"I knew he wasn't the one-night-stand type," Liz had exclaimed gleefully. "I can't wait to tell Ted. When can we get together, Jen?"

Although Jen had winced at the way Liz had phrased her opening statement, she had laughed and promised to get back to her about a dinner date for the four of them.

They had spent several evenings together during the last months, and the camaraderie they had shared at the motel had been solidly reestablished.

Jen had no idea how long they'd been driving before she realized they were not heading for the airport, or that Adam had not said a word since demanding that she shut up. Although she was sure she knew the answer, she asked, "Where are we going?"

"Home." Adam's tight lips hardly moved around the one word.

"But we'll miss our plane!" Shifting around, Jen looked directly at him, then wished she hadn't. His mouth twisted derisively, and the glance he shot her held cool contempt. He didn't bother to reply but returned his concentration to the road.

Jen didn't attempt to break the silence for the remainder of the ride to the house. Hands clenched in her lap, she nurtured her anger while trying to ignore the feeling of loss his glance had instilled.

When they reached the house she preceded him inside with a cool detachment she was nowhere near feeling. Inside she was a churning mass of emotions and urges, the uppermost being the urge to fling accusations at him. The only thing that kept her silent was her childish determination that he speak first.

Walking into the large rectangular living room, she stopped in the middle of the floor, back to him, and waited.

Still without a word to her, she heard him walk across the room and then the dull rattle of plastic against plastic as he lifted the mouthpiece to the phone and punched out a number. In disbelief she heard him cancel their flight reservations and then punch out another number. Unable to contain herself, she spun around to face him as he coolly canceled their hotel reservations in Hawaii. With a sigh of regret, she said good-bye to all the secret hopes she'd had for their time together at that hotel.

Adam's face was expressionless when, his phone call finished, he looked at her. "So much for that bright idea." He smiled wryly. "I don't think either of us are in the mood for the honeymoon suite now." One dark eyebrow lifted questioningly. "Are you ready to hear it?"

"No!" Spinning around, Jen walked jerkily across the room, lengthening the distance between them. In her blind haste to get away from him, and in her fear of hearing him tell her that the tiny beauty he'd been holding was a "friend," she scraped her leg on the corner of an occasional table as she hurried by.

"Jennifer!" Adam's warning, coming an instant too late, followed her sharp gasp of pain. With a few long strides he was by her side, his hands grasping her upper arms to steady her. "How long is it going to take you to realize what a foolish young woman you are?" His harsh tone was emphasized by a lightly administered shake.

"Adam, I don't —" What she'd wanted to tell him was that she didn't have the sophistication to live the way his parents did. That she was selfish, and possessive, and the idea of sharing him with someone else was unendurable. He didn't give her the chance to say it.

"Yeah, I know," he cut in bitterly. "You don't want to hear it." He gave her that oddly sad smile. "I thought I heard the gavel drop when I picked your flowers up off the hall floor."

"What?" Jen stared at him in confusion.

"You had made your judgment then already, hadn't you?" Adam rasped. "And the verdict was: Adam Banner, guilty as charged."

"Adam, stop —" Jen began, and again he cut in fiercely.

"Stop what?" Suddenly all the harshness was gone, in his hands as well as his voice. "Stop hoping, praying, that you'll begin to see sense?" His hands moved up her arms and over her shoulders caressingly. "Stop aching for the woman I know you can be?" Bending his head, he brushed his lips along the taut line of her jaw to her ear. "Jennifer

— Jennifer," he murmured. "This is our wedding day. You are my wife. I don't want to fight with you." His lips moved seductively to the corner of her trembling mouth. "I want to make love with you." Sliding his mouth over her slightly parted lips, he whispered, "And I know you want it too."

Jen's resistance was very short-lived simply because, with his mouth moving in drugging enticement on hers and his hands evoking a trembling response from her body, she didn't want to resist. Sighing softly, she let her forgotten handbag drop to the floor and, slipping her arms around his neck, parted her lips still further for him.

Adam gave a muffled groan and, sweeping her up into his arms, mounted the open spiral staircase to the second floor and their bedroom.

Slowly, taking time to stroke, caress, explore, they undressed each other until her only adornments were her wedding band and the engagement ring that complemented it, and his, a larger matching band that circled his finger and a fine gold chain that circled his wrist.

When, finally, he stretched his length beside her on the cool sheets, she lifted her mouth to his, eagerly, breathlessly.

"I was beginning to be afraid our interrupted journey was never going to be resumed," Adam groaned against Jen's hungry lips. The quivering response that sent the heat pounding through the pliant body she arched against him seemed to rob him of all control. His voice a hoarse incitement, he warned, "I don't know how much longer I can wait, darling. It's been so long and I want you so badly."

They spent their honeymoon week in seclusion in the house, the majority of the time in the bedroom. As if by mutual agreement the subject of the exquisite, dark-haired woman was studiously avoided. With an iron determination Jen had not realized she was capable of, she pushed all thoughts and fears of the future to the deepest reaches of her mind.

In the weeks that followed, their life fell into a pattern that Jen kept pleasant by simply refusing to acknowledge, let alone face, the uncertainty that hovered at the fringes of her consciousness.

Adam was kept busy and worked long hours settling into the executive position he'd been given by his company. Jen kept herself busy after working hours by playing housewife. That there seemed to be a hush-before-the-storm, waiting atmosphere surrounding them, she ignored with an unfamiliar adroitness.

As the days grew long and hot with

summer, Jen allowed herself the luxury of believing the growing closeness between them could cancel the necessity of an eventual confrontation. Her cocoon of complacency was shattered in mid-July, six weeks to the day from their wedding.

In an effort to more quickly familiarize himself with the routine of his newly acquired department, Adam had worked most Saturday mornings. On this fateful morning Jen was dawdling over her second cup of coffee while glancing over the morning paper when the phone rang.

After a coolly impersonal "Hello?" Jen's voice took on a sincere warmth on finding her caller was Liz. Although she and Adam had been out to dinner with Liz and Ted twice since their marriage, it had been over a week since Jen had heard from Liz. Jen soon learned the purpose of Liz's call was both urgent and exciting.

"Jen, please, *please* say you can go shopping with me this morning," Liz pleaded exaggeratedly.

"Okay," Jen laughed. "I can go shopping with you this morning. Now, do you think you could tell me why you sound like you're ready to explode?"

"We're getting married." Liz laughed. "Ted and I, I mean." Before Jen could get a word of surprise or congratulations in, Liz bubbled on, "He's been at me about it for weeks and last night, in a weak moment, I said yes. Jen, honey, you would not believe this man. When he decides to do something he doesn't horse around. He's picking me up late this afternoon, and we're taking an early-evening flight to Vegas. Vegas! Do you believe it?" Liz paused to gasp at a quick breath, then plunged on, "And I am determined to be completely outfitted. Can you be ready in a half hour? I'll pick you up, and we'll go into Philly to the Gallery."

It was not until after she was settled into the passenger seat of Liz's car that Jen remembered she had not called Adam. *Oh, well,* she smiled to herself, *it will be more fun to tell him in person anyway.*

It was after three when Liz stopped the car in front of the town house. Jen felt as if she'd been in a marathon race as they had dashed in and out of the many shops in the tiered shopping mall, pausing only long enough to gulp a quick lunch of sandwiches and iced tea.

"Oh, God, I've got to run or I'll never be ready when Ted arrives," Liz chattered, leaning over to give Jen a quick hug. "Thanks for going with me. Give Adam my love, and tell him we'll call when we get back."

Jen was smiling in anticipation of Adam's reaction to her news when she walked into the living room. The sight of Adam, still dressed in the lightweight business suit he'd put on that morning, a suitcase on the floor beside him, standing tense and tight-lipped by the phone, wiped the smile from her lips.

"Where the hell have you been?" His harshly impatient tone brought her to an abrupt halt. "I've been calling everyone I could think of, trying to find you. It's too late now, I've got to go." Shooting his left sleeve, he glanced at his watch and shook his head sharply before bending to grab the handle of his valise.

"Go? It's too late?" Jen repeated in shocked confusion. "Adam, what are you talking about?"

"Jennifer, I've got to go," Adam said gently. "The executive jet's waiting for me."

Anger spurred by renewed fear made Jen go hot, then cold. Where was this jet waiting to take him? Where or — the insidious thought crept into her mind — to whom? Watching him walk toward her, Jen was suddenly terrified by the thought that if he left now, their relationship would be irreparably damaged.

When he bent to kiss her, she stepped back, twisting her head aside. "I thought you were finished with the traveling part of the business," she accused.

"This is different." Adam sighed, raking his hand through his hair. "There is no time to explain now. I have no choice; I must go."

The four words *I have no choice* hit Jen almost like a physical blow. Her reaction to the pain and fear gripping her was totally human and completely contradictory. Her tone thick with sarcasm, she snapped, "Another *emergency* call, Adam?"

Adam's body stiffened, then, turning away from her, he walked to the door. "As a matter of fact, it was." He turned the knob and opened the door before adding, "Only *this* time my father's *dying*." Without a backward glance he walked out of the house.

Jen never knew how long she stood staring at the door, her eyes wide with shock and horror. Adam's father was dying, and she had sent him away in anger. The shudder that tore through her body broke the self-condemning trance that held her motionless. What had she done?

Adam was away for ten days. Ten long days during which Jen examined his parting shot, "Only *this* time my father's *dying*." Oh, the remark itself was fairly obvious. With those six terse words he'd told her clearly that his sudden departure from the motel had been due to his father's health. No, it wasn't his statement she

259

didn't understand, it was his tone that nagged at her. What, exactly, had that tone conveyed? Sadness surely, but there was something else. Exasperation? Anger? Defeat? She couldn't pinpoint it, and so it tormented her.

Feeling suddenly very young and not too bright, Jen lived through those ten days by telling herself that Adam *would* come back.

She was sitting on the sofa, staring sightlessly at the news on TV, when he came home after ten days of total silence. Without speaking, he dropped his suitcase to the floor inside the door, crossed the room, and, sighing wearily, sank onto the end of the sofa, stretching his legs out with another long sigh.

Jen's heart contracted painfully at the look of him. His face was pale, with lines of strain etched deeply around his mouth, and he looked exhausted. Her voice husky with compassion, Jen whispered, "Your father?"

"He's gone," Adam said quietly, his eyes studying the tips of his shoes.

"I'm sorry, Adam." Jen choked around the tears clogging her throat. "I'm — I'm sorry for everything."

"What does 'everything' mean?" Adam raised bleak eyes to hers. "Sorry you ever laid eyes on me? Sorry you married me?"

"Adam!" Jen exclaimed, shocked at the

utter defeat in his tone. "You can't believe that!"

"I don't know what I believe anymore, Jennifer." Getting to his feet, he stared broodingly at her a moment, then, swinging away, he walked out of the room with a muttered, "And I'm too beat to go into it now. Good night, Jennifer."

Good night! Good night? Stunned, Jen sat staring at the empty doorway. *No!* Anger ignited by fear catapulted her to her feet. *Dammit, no!* Tired or not, he could not let her hang like this. She would not let him. There had been too many things left unsaid. There were explanations to be given — by both of them. And the time was now. Scared but determined, she walked to the stairs.

Expecting to find Adam in bed, Jen was surprised to see him standing by the window, his hands thrust into his pants pockets. He had removed his jacket and tie and had opened the buttons on his shirt. He didn't turn around when she entered the room, yet she knew he was aware of her presence.

"Adam?"

"What?"

The flat, indifferent tone of his voice sent a shaft of unease through her.

"Why" — Jen wet her dry lips — "why didn't you tell me your father was ill?"

261

"Why?" Now he turned, and Jen almost wished he hadn't. His expression held both anger and disbelief. "Why?" He repeated mockingly. "Because you were so obviously uninterested, that's why."

"B-but I — I," Jen sputtered, unable to believe she'd heard him right. Had he really accused her of being uninterested?

"But hell," he spat savagely across her stuttering words, "you've made it very clear — from the beginning — what you wanted from this marriage, and interest in my father, or any other area of my life, wasn't part of it."

"What are you talking about?" Jen gasped.

"You know damned well what I'm talking about," he snarled. "Why did you leave my bed that morning?" he demanded.

"Be-because — I — I," Jen floundered at the suddenness of his question, her cheeks flushing pink.

"Because you were ashamed of what had happened there," Adam said flatly.

"No, Adam!" Jen protested. "I —"

"I needed you that morning." Adam's thickened voice cut through her protest. "My mother was damn near hysterical when she called me. She pleaded with me to come at once. You see, the doctors had told my brother they didn't know if he'd live until we could get there." His tone went rough. "I had to go, and I needed to see you, and you weren't there."

"But when you came back, Adam, you never said anything," Jen cried.

"I *did* try. You said it wasn't important." His lips twisted unpleasantly. "It didn't take long to figure what *was* important to you."

"What do you mean?" By the tone of his voice, Jen was sure she would not like his answer. She was right.

"That bed." Adam jerked his head at their bed. "I should have kept my hands off you. I should have left you unawakened and safe in your tight, moralistic world. You couldn't face it, could you? So in your shame you went sneaking away. And when I got back and called you, needing you even more, you were prepared to cut me dead, weren't you?"

"Adam, no! You don't understand. I was —" Jen got no further.

"You were hungry." He flung the accusation at her. "You have a hungry body and a greedy mouth, both of which very obviously drive me crazy. And when I asked you to marry me you said yes simply to make that hunger legal and moral. *That's* what's important to you."

"That is not true, Adam," Jen denied fiercely.

"No?" Adam's brows arched exaggeratedly. "Then why have you never asked any questions, not even about the woman who came to your parents' home the day of the wedding?"

"Because I was afraid," Jen shouted at him, goaded beyond endurance.

"Afraid of what, for God's sake?" he shouted back.

"Of losing you. Of boring you. Of not being able to hold your interest," Jen sobbed, brushing at the tears that were suddenly running down her face. "After the way you grew up, and the lifestyle you were used to" — she waved her hand in self-dismissal — "what could I possibly offer you?"

"Jennifer!"

"No, let me finish," Jen insisted. "Can you try and imagine how — how dull my life suddenly seemed while I was listening to you tell me about yours? Can you try and imagine how bland and uninteresting I felt? When I read your note the first thing I thought was that, having had your fun, you had decided to skip the good-byes — and possible recriminations."

"Dammit, Jennifer," Adam began angrily, but Jen went on doggedly.

"But — well — remembering how we'd been together, I — I just knew you were not like that."

"Thanks for that, anyway," Adam inserted wryly.

"Adam, please," Jen cried. "It was during the week you were away that I convinced myself that even if you did call or come to me, I couldn't possibly hold you. That's why I said it didn't matter. If you had let it go at that I would have gotten over you — eventually." She shook her head. "But once I saw you again, and you held me in your arms, and kissed me, I — I . . . What you said is true, Adam; I am hungry. But only for you." Her voice dropped to a whispered sob. "Only for you. And I've felt like I've been walking a tightrope all these weeks. I've been so afraid you'd come and tell me it was over, or that you wouldn't come at all. For you see, Adam, I thought that the physical thing was all we had going."

"Oh, God, angel!" Adam was across the room in a few long strides and pulling her into his arms. "I know I'm a little defensive about my parents, but I never dreamed I was giving you the impression I wanted to live like that. I don't." Lifting his hand, he wiped away the tears still trickling down her face. "I never did. And I'd grown tired of the traveling over a year ago. I even considered taking one of the desk jobs offered to me. The hang-up was, every time I came home this house seemed so damned empty, and I never met a woman who stirred enough interest in me to even consider the idea of installing her here." Suddenly his eyes darkened to that bone-melting look of warm velvet. "That is until I walked into that bar at the motel. You stirred all kinds of interest. The day I left the motel I told my mother I was going to marry you."

"She's been in Japan this whole time, hasn't she?" Jen asked softly.

"Yes," Adam sighed. "She's still there. She'll stay until all the legalities are straightened out. She can't wait to meet you. She told me no woman can be as perfect or beautiful as I've described you to be." Adam grinned.

"Oh, Adam," Jen stared up at him, her legs going weak at the expression of love on his face. "I love you so very much."

"And I love you." Sliding his fingers into her hair, he bent his head and brushed her mouth with his lips. "Why are we standing here talking?" he murmured huskily.

"Oh, Adam, I'm sorry," Jen cried contritely. "You must be exhausted."

"I'm tired, yes," he agreed softly. "But that isn't what I meant. I've been away ten days, and to a man in love who is as hungry for his wife as I am for you, ten days can seem as long as ten months."

It was later, as she lay replete and relaxed beside him, murmuring contentedly as Adam continued to stroke her skin as if he couldn't get enough of the feel of her, that Jen was struck by a sudden thought. Giving him a gentle push, she sat up and tried, unsuccessfully, to glare at him.

"Who was that woman, Adam?" she demanded softly.

Adam's soft laughter tickled her spine, and she couldn't even make a pretense of resistance when he drew her back down beside him.

"My father's 'friend.'" Adam's warm breath disturbed a few tendrils at her temple; it disturbed her pulse rate as well. "I had told you at the motel that she was an exquisite woman. She took his illness very badly. I pulled a few strings and got her a job in Dallas. She was on her way there, between planes, when she came to your parents' house." While he was speaking, his breath teased in a dancing, erratic line to the corner of her mouth. Jen's pulses seemed about to jump out of her body when the tip of his tongue began an exploration of that corner. "Any more questions?"

"One," Jen gasped.

"Mmmmm?"

"Aren't you ever going to kiss me?"

Jen woke to an empty bed and a silent house. Sitting up, she strained her ears to catch the slightest noise. "Adam?" *Strange,* she mused when there was no answer to her call. Adam had long since ceased going to his office on Saturday mornings. *Very strange. Is the honeymoon over?* she asked herself humorously.

All traces of humor had fled by the time she'd finished glancing over the morning paper, had consumed a glass of juice, two pieces of thin wheat toast, and two cups of coffee. Where the devil was he?

After making the bed she dressed in jeans, an old sweatshirt, and — remembering the full waste can in the kitchen and the snow on the ground — low boots, then went back to the kitchen to wash her breakfast dishes.

As she wiped the butcher-block table, Jen fought the images that flashed in and out of her mind. Images of icy roads and sliding tires and the carnage of wrecked cars and bodies.

She had been so ecstatically, unbelievably happy the last six months that sometimes it almost scared her. And although she wouldn't admit it even to herself, she was scared now. Pushing the growing feeling of unease to the very fringes of her mind, she hummed snatches of a popular song while shooting anxious glances at the clock. She was wringing her dishcloth over the sink when she heard the front door open and Adam call, "Jennifer?"

Fingers clutching spasmodically at the dishcloth, Jen slumped against the sink, weak from the rush of relief that washed over her. In the few seconds it took him to reach the kitchen she had control of herself.

"Where in the world have you —"

"Put your jacket on and come with me," Adam ordered, interrupting her. "I want to show you something."

"Adam, what —" Jen's voice trailed off, for after walking out of the kitchen, Adam went to the hall closet.

"Adam!"

"Come on," he urged, holding her jacket for her. "You'd better wear your cap and gloves too. It's cold outside."

Momentarily giving up the battle, Jen put on her jacket and, cap and gloves in hand, followed him to the car, glancing around to admire the sun-sparkling whiteness of the four inches of snow that covered the front lawn. As soon as the car was in motion, she tried again.

"Adam, where did you go this morning?"

"To look at a car." Adam flashed her a grin. "I woke up early and saw it advertised for sale as I skimmed the paper. I didn't have the heart to wake you, so I decided to run look at it myself and bring some Danish for breakfast on the way back."

"So, where's the Danish?"

"Oh — I forgot it," Adam answered vaguely.

"And now you're taking me to see the car?"

"No, I bought it." His grin flashed again. "For you. It's an early Valentine gift."

"A Valentine gift?" Jen exclaimed incredulously. "A car? Adam, are you crazy?"

"Sure," he answered complacently. "About you."

"Okay." Jen sighed. "I give up. Are you going to tell me where we're going?" He had made several turns, and now they were out of the more populated area on a back road where the homes were set much farther apart.

"I told you," Adam replied. "I want to show you something. I had to drive back this way to look at the car, and that's when I saw it." He paused, then smiled. "Ah, there it is."

They were approaching a bend in the road, and just before they reached it Adam drove the car off the macadam onto a flat, snow-covered verge about six feet wide. They parked at the base of a rather steep incline at the top of which was a high chain-link fence. Looking around in confusion, Jen said, "I don't see anything."

"Not here." Adam laughed. "We have to get out of the car. Come on."

After pulling her cap onto her head and tugging her gloves over her hands, Jen scrambled out of the car and through the snow to where Adam waited for her, hand outstretched. Grasping her hand, he strode off around the bend in the road at the foot of the incline, which became lower and lower as they walked. Where Adam came to a stop the incline had dropped to a low bank and Jen could see the chain-link fence surrounded a tot-lot, closed now for the winter.

"There." Adam nodded at the tot-lot. "That's what I wanted you to see."

"A tot-lot?" Jen exclaimed.

"No, the bank, Jennifer," Adam said softly. "A perfect place for angels in the snow."

"Angels in the —" Jen began in astonishment, and then she grew silent as the significance of his carefully spoken words hit her. They were the exact words she'd said to him exactly one year ago. "Oh, Adam." She choked around the emotion clogging her throat. Spinning around, she gazed up at him and felt her throat close altogether at the tender expression on his face.

"Come on," he challenged softly when he saw her blink against the moisture clouding her eyes. "I bet I can make a better angel than you can."

Turning around, he flung himself backward onto the bank, long arms and legs flapping vigorously. Laughing like a ten-year-old, Jen ran several paces below him and dropped into the snow on the bank. She had just begun to flap her arms and legs when Adam sprang to his feet and came to stand beside her.

"Now you ruined the skirt," Jen scolded, holding her hand out for him to hoist her to her feet.

Ignoring her hand, Adam dropped to his knees. His warm velvet eyes caressing her face, he pulled off his gloves — exposing a fine gold chain coiled around his wrist — and let them fall to the ground. Cradling her face in his hands, he lowered his head and kissed her gently.

"Who needs snow angels," Adam murmured as he lifted his head, "when they can have the real thing? You've made me very happy, Jennifer."

"I'm glad," Jen whispered huskily. "I love you very much, Adam."

"I know," Adam whispered back. "And the knowing fills everything inside of me to the point of bursting."

His mouth touched hers again, and with a groan Adam lowered his body and stretched his length on top of her. His lips grew hard with demand and, clasping his hands more tightly to her head, he kissed her with merciless passion until he heard her soft moan of surrender. Sliding his lips from hers, he teased, "Lift your head — I want to bite your neck."

The sound of a car driving by on the road brought Jen to her senses.

"Adam, stop," she gasped as his tongue went sliding down the side of her neck. "Anyone driving by can see us. What will people think?"

"That we are obviously in love and having a romp in the snow." Adam laughed, jumping to his feet. "And they'll envy us and wish they were so lucky."

Reaching down, he grasped Jen's hands and pulled her up in front of him.

"Come on, snow angel, let's go home." Adam grinned wickedly. "Those poor devils don't know the half of it."

GAMBLER'S LOVE

One

The drive seemed endless, and by the time she was finally east of the Mississippi, Vichy was beginning to feel like a prisoner of her own car.

A wry smile tugged at her lipstick-free mouth as she consciously loosened her death grip on the abused steering wheel. Being confined inside a Chevy Nova, she decided, was certainly not the ideal way to spend the better part of any week. But it would not be too much longer, and then she would be on the East Coast, and damned if she'd ever leave it again.

The highway unfurled before her like a cement ribbon, and Vichy kept her gaze on the sparse midweek traffic while her mind's eye looked back over the preceding weeks.

She had had it. On what day had she reached that decision? Had it been Tuesday? Wednesday? She couldn't remember, but, then, it really didn't matter. Having reached the decision, Vichy had hung on to it as firmly as she now hung on to the wheel of her car. She had had just about all the traveling she could take, all the smoke-filled rooms, all the night work. Had it really seemed exciting at one time? Yes, she conceded, it really had. A million years ago, when her eyes were still bright with ambition and her dreams were fresh off the assembly line — new. Back before the miles and the years had begun to pile up on her, weighing her down.

The highway blurred and Vichy blinked rapidly to expel the sudden hot moisture that filled her eyes. What good were tears, for heaven's sake? she chided herself scathingly. She was twenty-nine, going on one hundred and two, and if she had learned nothing else, she had learned that tears neither mean nor help anything. Uncurling the fingers of her left hand, she brought them up to her face to brush impatiently at her wet cheeks. *Coffee time,* Vichy told the swimming blue eyes that were momentarily reflected in the rearview mirror by a quick upward glance.

Her eyes scanning the terrain in the distance, Vichy sighed with relief when she spied the familiar red-tiled roof of a Howard Johnson restaurant. After parking in the nearly empty macadam lot, she automatically checked her appearance in the mirror, grimacing at her pale reflection before stepping out of the car and locking it.

Huddling inside the warmth of her Polartec jacket, she faced the sharp early-November wind and hurried across the lot to the welcoming light streaming through the restaurant's wide plate-glass windows.

The restaurant was quiet, as only one table and two counter stools were occupied by customers. Sliding onto a stool near the end of the counter, Vichy ordered coffee from a bored-looking waitress. Sighing softly, she smiled wanly at the waitress as the cup of coffee was placed in front of her, then stared moodily into the dark brew.

It was time she went home, she thought tiredly. Long past time. Time to wake up, face reality, no matter how unpalatable. There would be no fame or fortune for her in the entertainment world. Facing that truth had been one of the hardest things she'd ever had to do.

With another soft sigh Vichy lifted her cup. Sipping the hot coffee, she tried to visualize her parents' reaction to her unannounced arrival. Maybe she should have called and told them she was coming home, but, sure of her welcome, she'd plunged into the business of clearing up all the details of her life on the West Coast. She had been determined to leave no loose ends, as she was never going back.

Never going back. The thought stabbed at her mind, the poisoned tip inflicting a searing sense of failure. The known fact that she was only one of thousands who never made the big time brought no relief at all. Dreams die very, very hard.

Moving jerkily with self-impatience, Vichy paid for her coffee and hurried through the darkening afternoon to the now-too-familiar small car. Before sliding behind the wheel, she paused to study the lowering cloud cover. Before too long those enveloping clouds were going to split wide open and drench the landscape. Yet another sigh whispered through her pale lips. The prospect of driving through a downpour was disheartening. Why couldn't the weather have held for a few more days?

Why ask why? Vichy chided herself with a brief flash of humor. Why is a duck? The tiny smile that was just beginning to touch her lips at that nonsensical thought fled with the first cold drop of rain that struck her cheek. Glancing back at the motel complex, Vichy fought a short-lived, go-stay battle with herself. She hated to drive in the rain. The temptation to wait out the weather almost undermined her determination to drive until dusk each day. Squaring her shoulders, she slid behind the wheel and slammed the door closed beside her. Telling herself to get on with it, she turned the key to the ignition.

Two hours later, shoulder muscles tight from gripping the steering wheel, eyes achy from straining to see through the deluge of water pouring out of the sky, Vichy drove off the road with an overwhelming feeling of relief and into the parking lot of a new-looking motel. After checking in, she dropped into the molded plastic chair in the single room and allowed herself the luxury of groaning aloud. She was wet, and she was cold, and still she sat numbly until the sound of the rain slashing against the room's one window drew her attention. By the watch on her wrist it was not yet dusk, but the window she gazed at revealed nothing but darkness beyond its panes. With a shiver, Vichy stood up and walked to the side of the window to pull the cord that drew the flower-patterned drapes together.

Turning her back on the sound of the drops beating on the pane, she removed her sweater, then stepped out of her pants, shivering again as the sodden material brushed her ankles. Leaving her clothes in a pile next to her wet shoes, she went into the bathroom for a hot shower. After shampooing her rain-bedraggled hair, she stood under the hot spray until she'd stopped shivering completely. Thankfully there were two towels, and before giving herself a brisk rubdown with one, she twined the other around her head turban-style. When she was dry, she considered wrapping the damp towel saronglike around her body, but, then, remembering she'd drawn the drapes, she shrugged and walked nude into the small room. Opening the one valise she'd brought into the motel with her, she removed fresh underwear, a cable-knit sweater in a soft pink shade, and a pair of cream-colored corduroys. As she turned away from the suitcase, Vichy caught her reflection in the wide mirror above the desklike dresser.

Poised like a statue, she studied her reflection impersonally. The five-foot-seven-inch image was not bad, if a little too slender at one hundred and eleven pounds. Although the towel on her head concealed all but a lock of her hair, her matching brows proclaimed its rich dark brown color. Blue eyes gazed back at her out of an oval-shaped, pale face. Unselfconsciously, Vichy registered the fact that her face was more than just pretty. She was, she admitted, a knockout in the looks department. A twisted smile distorted her soft lips. But all her looks had ever brought her were heartache and advances from the opposite sex, both of which she could easily live without.

One man had even told her she was bewitching. The twist of her lips grew grim and with an impatient shake, she turned away from her mirrored image. Fool that she had been! She'd married that particular man. Even though it had now been almost six years since she'd seen or heard from her former husband, just thinking of him brought a bad taste to her mouth. The memory of that brief, turbulent marriage increased Vichy's feeling of defeat. It seemed she was a loser all the way around.

With a shudder, she forced the feeling away and concentrated on the more immediate need of getting dressed for dinner. She slipped her arms through the straps of the full-cupped, lacy bra and fastened the hooks, then adjusted the garment over her high, well-endowed breasts. She stepped into her cords and then pulled on soft cotton anklets and stylish but comfortable suede ankle boots. She removed the towel and then pulled the sweater over her head before digging through her suitcase for her blow dryer. Round brush in hand, she dried her hair while brushing the shoulder-length mass into soft waves. A light application of foundation, a quick wisk with the blusher brush, and a faint coating of pink lip gloss, and she was ready to leave the room.

Vichy didn't notice the man's bold stare until she glanced up at the waitress to give her her order. He was sitting with a lovely young woman several tables away from where Vichy sat, yet, even though the woman was speaking to him, his eyes roamed insolently over her body. When his eyes returned to her face, Vichy deliberately glanced away dismissively.

Vichy did not look in his direction again during her stay in the dining room, but his visage remained in her mind. He was so very much like Brad in appearance that without knowing anything about him, she felt sorry for the young woman with him. That man's face was too handsome, almost beautiful, the lower lip too sensuous, the eyes too slumberous. Even though she did not glance in his direction again, Vichy could feel his eyes on her. Irritated with his boorishness and humiliated for his companion, she hurried through her meal, leaving the room without a backward glance.

Back in her room, she draped her damp pants over the plastic chair, placed her wet shoes near the air vent, and prepared for bed. It was still early, but the tension of driving through the wind-driven rain had left her tired enough, she felt sure, to sleep.

She was wrong. Seeing the man who so resembled Brad had stirred a hornets' nest of memories that crowded in on her attempt to rest.

How excited she'd been about that engagement in Vegas. To be sure, it had been in one of the smaller rooms in one of the smaller hotels, but that hadn't mattered to her. The important thing had been that she was actually there in Las Vegas!

Brad had been in the audience the second night of her engagement. How very impressionable she'd been at twenty-two! And how very gullible. Brad, being ninety percent charm and one hundred percent opportunist, had taken full advantage of her gullibility.

Vichy could still hear the sugar-coated endearments that had rolled so naturally off his lying tongue. Lord! She shuddered in the darkness, thinking that she had actually believed every word he'd uttered. How she must have amused him! And how she paid for her belief and trust.

Within two weeks after that hurried ceremony she had been painfully aware that the only reason Brad had legalized their union was his awareness of the fact that there would be no union without the legality. Very simply, she had been a challenge to him.

Vichy, at twenty-nine, still felt pain for the dreamy-eyed innocent she had been at twenty-two.

"Damn it all!"

Vichy grumbled irritably as she thrust

her arm under the pillow and rolled onto her side. She hadn't thought about Brad or their short, disastrous marriage in years! And now, because of an insulting stare from a man who had a striking resemblance to him, she was once again examining one of her failures — the first of many, it seemed.

Sighing defeatedly, Vichy closed her eyes. How did that song go? she wondered, something about never falling in love with a gambling man? She was the living proof of that. She had lavished her first, eager love on that particular gambling man. For almost six months she had existed in a euphoric bubble of bliss. She had trusted him explicitly with her tender, young emotions. Finding him with another woman six months after their marriage had just about destroyed her. It *had* destroyed her trust in men, particularly gamblers.

Now, six years later, the pain she'd felt at that time had long ago subsided. All that remained was a residue of sadness for the trusting young fool she'd been.

A clear case of arrested mentality. A wry smile touched the lips that still possessed a young, vulnerable softness. At twenty-two, and an entertainer in the bargain, she really had been very immature. At the time, she'd been on the supper-club circuit for over a year and, apparently, had learned very little of the cold realities of life. She had been ripe for harvesting by an expert picker. *Comes from being raised in a protected environment,* she now excused the dumb bunny she'd been.

The thought of her early environment chased away the bad memories. She was going back to it, soon to stay for good. Not in triumph as she'd vowed she would when she left with such high, warm hopes, but with utter failure dragging at her fashionably high heels. The realization that she'd be welcomed with tears of joy and open arms by her elderly parents and younger sister allowed her to drift into a much-needed sleep. In triumph or defeat, Vichy knew she would be welcomed home joyously. It was her family's way.

Vichy awoke early, and after a quick juice-and-coffee breakfast was back on the road again, thankfully without a glimpse of the cold-eyed young man of the evening before.

Thoughts of the reception awaiting her at her destination kept Vichy's spirits bolstered during the long hours of driving over the following two days. As she crossed the state line into Pennsylvania, she drew a deep breath, telling herself whimsically that she could actually smell a difference in the air of her home state.

Fatigue weighed on her shoulders and her arms felt like lead when, finally, she turned off the macadam road onto the rutted lane that led to her parents' small frame farmhouse, located midway between Lancaster and Ephrata.

Misty-eyed, Vichy gazed at the home of her youth. Sparkling white paint was set off by the dark green trim on the window frames and shutters, a clear indication that her ever-busy father had very recently been at work with a paintbrush.

The yard surrounding the house, her mother's domain, had a pruned, ready-for-winter look, although the chrysanthemums banked against the house still blazed forth in all their rust and gold glory.

Off to the left, its paint every bit as fresh as that on the house, the barn, used now for storage and housing the family's two cars, stood square and solid-looking. Emotion closing her throat, Vichy blinked rapidly as she killed the Nova's engine and tugged on the hand brake.

Silly, she chided herself, *anyone would think you had been away a dozen years or so when, in fact, it has been less than a year since your last visit.* But, she mentally argued in defense of her tears, brushing at them with trembling fingertips, that was a visit; this is a homecoming.

At the fringes of the lawn to the right of

the house, Vichy's searching eyes softened as they came to a halt on the gnarled old apple tree. The sight of a tire, suspended from the tall tree's lowest limb by a sturdy rope, brought a rush of memories clamoring into her mind. A replica of that tire, the first of a long line, had been hung from that branch years before her coming into the world.

That first tire had been affixed for the amusement of the first of the Sweigart brood, Vichy's elder sister, Mattilda — so named for her paternal grandmother.

A tiny smile trembled its way onto Vichy's lips. How Mattie hated her given name! And how she and their brother Josh — named Joshua after their paternal grandfather — had tormented her about it. Yet, her smile deepened; to this day only she and Josh held that exclusive right, except their parents, of course, to the use of her given name.

"Vichy!"

Her younger sister's excited cry scattered the warm memories, and Vichy's eyes shifted to the small figure hurrying across the building's wide front porch.

The runt, as the baby of the four Sweigart offspring had been affectionately dubbed, was the only one of them to inherit their mother's small stature. One inch shy of five feet, she was also the only one of them not named in honor of a demised grandparent, Vichy being named Victoria after her maternal grandmother.

Stepping out of the car, Vichy chuckled softly in remembrance of her baby sister's christening. To her father's wondering shake of his iron gray head, Vichy's mother had named her youngest Bette, after a much-admired movie star!

All remembrance went flying as Bette launched herself into Vichy's arms, chattering thirty to the dozen.

"How did you get here? Well, that's obvious you came in your car, but how come? I mean, it's terrific that you're here, but how come you're here? You look super, but —"

"Whoa, slow down," Vichy cried around a mouthful of laughter. "I'll answer all your questions one at a time, but first, where are the folks?" Keeping a hold on Bette's arms, Vichy leaned back to look questioningly into her sister's heart-wrenchingly pretty face.

"Is it Friday?" Bette queried pertly.

"It was when I left the motel this morning," Vichy laughed.

"Well, then, where else would they be?" Bette chided on a return laugh. "They're at the Green Dragon."

"Where else, indeed." Vichy grinned, giving Bette a quick hug. How wonderfully normal and unchanged everything was, even down to Johanna and Luke Sweigart's weekly visit to the large market and auction held on Fridays on the other side of Ephrata.

"They're gonna flip when they get home," Bette broke excitedly into her musing. "Why didn't you let us know you were coming?"

"And miss out on seeing you bounce around like a Mexican jumping bean?' Vichy teased. "How about bouncing your way to the back and helping me unload my stuff?"

Having sold the few pieces of furniture and bric-a-brac she'd accumulated over the last ten years, everything Vichy now possessed was jammed into the car. Never slow on the uptake, Bette ran a sharp-eyed glance over the four suitcases and equal number of small cartons, then lifted her speculative gaze to Vichy.

"You're not going back to California?" she asked on a warmingly hopeful note.

"No." Vichy shook her head. "Except for two short running engagements in Atlantic City over the holidays, I'm home to stay."

The magnitude of Vichy's flat statement was not lost on her twenty-one-year-old sister. Bette knew how badly Vichy had wanted to make a success in the entertainment field, how very hard she'd worked toward her goal.

"You're really quitting?" she asked softly, obviously astonished.

"I'm really quitting," Vichy concurred firmly.

"But —" Bette began in protest.

"We'll talk it out later," Vichy cut in quietly. "But right now I think we'd better unload the car before it gets dark."

Bette talked nonstop while they carried the suitcases and cartons from the car to the bedroom that Vichy had occupied from her fifth year. Up until then she had shared the room with Mattie, who, on reaching her thirteenth year, declared dramatically that she needed privacy. As Josh, then eight, had squatter's rights on the only other bedroom on the second floor, that left the attic. Their father had spent that entire winter measuring, sawing, and hammering in the attic. When, in early March, he was finished, that one large attic had been converted into two small bedrooms and a good-sized storage closet.

On the completion of their father's remodeling, Josh had declared it "neat," and had promptly removed himself and his belongings to the floor above. Josh's bedroom on the second floor had remained empty until Bette made her debut eight years later.

It was fully dark by the time Vichy and Bette had unpacked the valises and lugged them and the cartons up to the storage closet.

"I don't know about you, Vich, but I'm starved," Bette declared as they clattered down the stairs.

"I could do with a cup of coffee," Vichy sighed. "But first I want a hot shower."

"Mom set a container of vegetable soup out to thaw for supper before she left," Bette said, heading for the backstairs that led directly into the large old-fashioned kitchen. "I'll warm the soup and make a pot of coffee while you have your shower."

"Thanks, hon." Vichy smiled tiredly. "I won't be long."

"Take your time," Bette called from halfway down the stairs. "I wasn't going anywhere."

Sliding her fingers into her long dark brown hair, Vichy walked into her bedroom and came to an abrupt stop on catching her own reflection in the mirror above the dresser. She was not particularly thrilled with the appearance of the young woman who stared back at her. That woman had a world-weary, defeated look about her.

Her hand stopped in midair, and Vichy's eyes made a minute inspection of her own image. At this moment she looked tired,

and every one of her twenty-nine years —
plus a few. There were dark smudges in
the pale skin under her dulled blue eyes,
and her cheeks and lips were totally devoid
of color.

Dropping her hand suddenly, she turned
away impatiently from that sorry-looking
female with a muttered, "That's entertainment?"

The shower went a long way in dispers-
ing the weariness, and a light application of
makeup restored at least a semblance of
color to her face.

Nose twitching, Vichy followed the mingled aromas of coffee, vegetable soup, and
baking powder biscuits to the warm,
homey kitchen, somewhat surprised at the
sudden sharp edge to her appetite.

Bette was bending over in front of the
stove, removing a cakepan of golden-brown
biscuits from the oven when Vichy entered
the room.

"Showing off your culinary skills?" she
teased as Bette straightened and turned to
face her. "Or do they come from a box?"

"Bite your tongue," Bette admonished
indignantly around a wide grin. "I made
these from scratch, as every home eco-
nomics major should."

"They smell heavenly," Vichy admitted.
"So does the soup. Did you create that as
well?"

"No." Bette shook her head. "Mom takes the honors for that." After gingerly plucking the hot biscuits out of the cakepan and dropping them into a napkin-lined bread basket, she glanced up, her grin widening. "Mom can still cook circles around me. Except" — she temporized — "where it comes to the *Cordon Bleu* stuff. There I shine." She grinned exaggeratedly. "Not that anyone's impressed with that. As you know, Dad still prefers things like Mother's vegetable soup and pot pies to any of the fancy concoctions I whip up."

Two places were laid on the long, Formica-topped table. A soft smile curved Vichy's lips as she seated herself at her place; for it was *her* place, and had been for as long as she could remember. With her first spoonful of the aromatic soup, she felt she was really, finally home. In Vichy's opinion, no one in the world made vegetable soup quite as well as her mother.

As she savored each successive spoonful, Vichy's gaze roamed lovingly over the large kitchen, which was a combination of up-to-the-minute appliances in old-fashioned country decor.

The line of cabinets above and below the sink were varnished, natural wood, carefully made and fitted by her father's clever

295

hands. Matching wood paneling covered three of the walls. The remaining wall was covered with a bright white- and tan-striped wallpaper. The ceiling was open-beamed, the plaster between sparkling white. Everything in the room, as, indeed, the whole house, was showroom clean. The very neatness of the property, both inside and out, was a clear indication that her sixty-year-old mother and sixty-one-year-old father were still fighting fit.

When they'd polished off their soup and most of the biscuits, Bette filled their cups with steaming, dark coffee and sat a pumpkin pie on the table.

"Fresh-baked this morning," Bette announced. "First of the season."

"Looks good enough to eat." Vichy smiled. "I haven't had good pumpkin pie since I was home for Thanksgiving two years ago."

"Well, then, stuff yourself," Bette invited with a proud, sweeping hand motion. "Plenty more where that came from. Mom made four of them this morning."

"Four!" Vichy laughed.

"You know Mom." Bette grinned. "She claims she still can't get used to cooking for only three. She slid one of the pies in the fridge and the other two in the freezer just in case Mattie or Josh drop in with their assorted broods."

"Drop in?" Vichy's eyebrows arched. "Mattie in Williamsport and Josh in Easton, and she expects them to drop in?"

"What can I tell ya?"

Bette's lifted shoulders displayed more elegance than her elocution. "Mom is — well, Mom. She'll never change. She'll probably stop the cortege on the way to her own funeral and declare she can't go just yet, as she has to get supper first."

Although Vichy shook her head in despair at Bette's corollary, she had to smile simply because it was so very near the mark. With cool disregard for the perfection of their mother's handiwork, Bette sliced into the pie.

"Mmmm, heavenly," Vichy murmured around the first bite. "Tastes like home."

"Maybe that's because it is." Bette laughed. "You sound like someone who's been very, very homesick."

"Maybe that's because I have been," Vichy admitted seriously. "Homesick, and just plain sick of it all."

Bette was quiet while she removed their empty plates from the table; then, after refilling both coffee cups, she asked softly, "What happened, Vichy?"

"Absolutely nothing." Vichy's smile held a hint of bitterness. "I just, finally, faced the fact that nothing was going to happen. In a word, hon, I've failed. At the moment,

I'm on my economic knees."

"You're broke?"

"Well . . ." Vichy grimaced. "Let's say I'm very badly bent. I have a little money — damn little — saved, and I do have the holiday engagement. But, come the first of the year, I am going to have to get down to some serious job hunting."

"Then you really did mean what you said!" Bette exclaimed. "You've given up your dreams of a Grammy?"

"I've given up my dreams, period," Vichy replied flatly. "The clouds have completely dissolved around my head. I know now there'll be no fame, no fortune, no Grammy."

"But, Vich —" Bette began in protest.

"No buts." Vichy cut her off with a sharp shake of her head. "I'm tired of it all — the piano bars, the dives, even the intimate little supper clubs, where no one is really ever listening." Her soft mouth twisted, as if with a sour taste. "I'm tired of men on the make who think I'm an easy target. God" — her laugh rang hollow — "I'm just tired of men and their predictable lines and come-ons."

A shocked silence followed her outburst.

"I'm sorry, hon," Vichy apologized softly. "I really had no intention of laying my grief in your lap." She hesitated, then laughed self-deprecatingly. "I guess what I was going to do was lay it in Mom's lap." She shrugged helplessly. "So much for the independent self-image I've been harboring."

"You really are tired of it all, aren't you?" Bette's face mirrored her concern.

"Yes." A genuine smile restored Vichy's lips to their natural, sweet line. "I'm somewhat like a runaway teenager in reverse. Instead of running away from home, I'm running back to it."

At that moment the back door opened and the one voice Vichy had been longing most to hear exclaimed: "Victoria Lynn Parks, why didn't you let us know you were coming home? Dad and I would not have left the house for a second if we'd known."

Two

Long after the voices of today had grown silent, Vichy lay in her bed listening to the voices of yesterday.

"Hurry up, slowpoke. You don't want to be late for your first day at school, do you?" The fourteen-year-old Mattie had chided her six-year-old self, right in this very room.

"Hey, bones," a ten-year-old Josh had called up the stairs to a thin, seven-year-old Vichy — then Vicky. "Your giggly girl friend Sue is on the phone."

"Is Mommy going to die?" Vichy's eight-year-old, tearful voice asked fearfully.

"Of course not, pumpkin." The maturing voice of the then-sixteen-year-old Mattie assured. "Mommy will be home before you know it with a brand-new brother or sister for us."

"Vic-key."

"Vich-ee."

"Vic-key."

"Vich-ee."

"No, no, Bette, it's like this," the four-teen-and-a-half-year-old Josh pleaded with his eighteen-month-old baby sister.

"Vic-key. Now you say that."

"Vich-ee." Everyone smiled at baby Bette's effort.

"Okay." Josh had figuratively thrown up his hands. "You win, bright eyes, Vichy it is."

And Vichy it had remained.

"Silly fool."

The words were whispered into the dark room through quivering lips. Blinking against the hot sting flooding her eyes, Vichy sat up and clasped her arms around her raised knees. All of a sudden she wanted, very badly, to hug Mattie and Josh close to her love-parched heart.

Yes, indeed, she thought wryly, rubbing her eyes against the comforter covering her knees, *you are one silly fool.* But, Lord, it was good to be home!

Tears sparkling in the shaft of moonlight that cast her bed in a pearl-like light, Vichy went over the hours following her parents' return from the market.

The waterworks had burst from her first look at her small, plump mother, standing just inside the kitchen door, a produce-stuffed shopping bag in each hand.

The moisture had slipped from between her eyelids a second time when, on entering the house moments after his wife, her father had caught Vichy close in a fierce, emotion-revealing bear hug.

At her mother's insistence, they made a call to Mattie in Williamsport. Vichy smiled shakily as the echo of her sister's voice sang in her mind.

"You're home to stay," Mattie had cried in delight. "Oh, Vich, that's wonderful. I'll bet Mom and Dad are overjoyed. And, oh, yes, has Mom told you?" she rushed on. "I'm going to be a grandmother in April, and now you'll be here — we'll all be together again."

Now the memory of her sister's happy voice drew a fresh deluge of tears. Reaching for a tissue from the box on the nightstand by her bed, Vichy assimilated Mattie's news.

Little Nan, the first of her parents' grandchildren, pregnant! It seemed impossible, yet Nan's wedding September a year ago had been the reason Vichy had made a quick visit home.

How beautiful they had looked, both the nineteen-year-old Nan and her seventeen-year-old sister, Brenda. Come to that, Vichy smiled in the darkness, Mattie had looked pretty darn beautiful herself at thirty-seven.

Vichy had no sooner said good-bye to Mattie than her mother was dialing Josh's number in Easton. Her brother's reaction to her news was no less enthusiastic than Mattie's had been.

"Hey, that's terrific," Josh had fairly shouted. "You've probably made Mom and Dad's day. Day, hell, you've probably made their year. I can't wait to tell Caroline."

Vichy chuckled in the still room, her amusement renewed at the memory of where Josh had told her that his wife, Caroline, and his young son were. It was too much! Tears surrendered to laughter. Rotten Robert, the scourge of the family, in a dance class! Oh, that poor dance instructor.

In the end, Vichy had not laid her problems in her mother's lap, nor had she cried, figuratively or otherwise, on her mother's shoulder. Her parents had accepted, without questioning, her explanation of being tired of working at night.

That she had not fooled them for one minute Vichy was sure. She was equally sure they would not pry or try to force the issue.

Sighing with contentment, Vichy slid back down under the covers. Her contentment was premature and short-lived. Eyes closed, composed for sleep, new voices intruded, shatteringly painful, even after six years.

"You have a beautiful body, made for love. There's nothing to be ashamed of. Let me love you, darling. I mean *really* love you."

How many times had Brad whispered those impassioned words within those short two weeks from the day they met until the day he'd slipped the ring on her finger? More times than Vichy cared to remember.

But, whether she cared to remember or not, the bittersweet memories flowed on. Eyes tightly closed, Vichy felt her cheeks flush as in her mind she lay in Brad's arms, innocently happy in the fulfillment of his physical lovemaking.

Defenseless in her love and trust, Vichy had made her handsome young husband the center of her existence, physically and emotionally. And for six months Brad had taken full advantage of that trust, gorging himself on her, coaching her on the ways and means of arousing and satisfying *him*.

At the end of those six months Brad had proved himself a rat. But, Lord, he had been a hot-blooded rat!

Vichy groaned aloud. She had found out, in a degrading and shocking way, precisely how hot-blooded and how very much of a rat Brad was, six months to the day of their wedding.

Moving restlessly under the suddenly oppressive handmade comforter, Vichy tried in vain to block the torrent of memories that should no longer have had the power to humiliate her, but did.

"You've become my life" — Brad had vowed fervently countless times during those months — "my only reason for existing." She had actually believed him.

His handsome face expressing tenderness, his hands gently caressing, Brad had bound her to him with his beguiling words.

"I need you every bit as much as I need air to breathe. No woman I've ever known has had the power to make me feel as complete as I feel with you."

There had been more, much, much more of the same. On and on, ad nauseam, Vichy remembered cynically. *And I swallowed the bait, hook, line, and sinker. But then,* Vichy exonerated herself, *I was so unbelievably innocent, and Brad was so very good at it that even a seasoned veteran could have been forgiven for eating up every one of his words.* But it was the last words he'd spoken to her that still stuck in her mind — festering, shaming her.

Giving up tiredly, Vichy allowed the memories free run, praying against hope that airing them would, at long last, expunge them.

Some four months after their marriage Brad's honey-tipped tongue had even soothed away the devastation Vichy felt on

305

being informed, during a routine visit to a doctor, that she would probably never be able to conceive a child.

"We have each other," he had crooned. "And you have your career." It was not until much later that Vichy was to wonder if his deep sigh had been one of disappointment or relief.

Vichy had considered it pure good luck when she had been booked into the same lounge, in the same hotel in which they'd met, at the time of their six months' anniversary. And even better luck that Brad had been able to secure the same room in which they had spent their wedding night.

Her engagement had called for two appearances a night, the first at dinnertime, the second later in the evening for the drinking crowd. Brad, a compulsive gambler who loved every minute of it, winning or losing, never appeared for the early show. But, every night for two short weeks, he would stroll into the room sometime during her last performance. Vichy always knew the exact moment he sauntered through the room, for wherever he went, female eyes followed his progress and lips murmured in appreciation of his passage.

Vichy had been only momentarily concerned the night he had not shown up at all. Only for a second had she considered looking through his favorite rooms for him, so sure had she been that he had planned some kind of six-month-anniversary surprise for her.

Wondering what form that surprise would take, excitement coursing through her, Vichy had hurried to their room.

Flinging herself onto her side, Vichy buried her face in her pillow to muffle the whimper of pity that escaped her lips for the shock her younger self had received on entering that hotel room.

Dupe that she had been, Vichy had not even wondered why the door to their room was locked. Fingers trembling in anticipation, she had still somehow managed to insert the key, turn the lock, and open the door silently.

The room was bathed in a soft light from the lamp on the dresser, illuminating clearly the couple locked together on the bed. As if turned to stone, Vichy had frozen in place two steps inside the room, her mind trying to deny the scene her eyes were riveted to. But there was no denying the position of the man and the woman, nor any question of their identities. The woman was a cocktail waitress in the lounge Vichy was engaged in. The man was most definitely Brad. Her Brad!

They had been so totally involved with pleasuring each other that even now Vichy had no idea what had alerted them to her presence. Had she cried out or gasped aloud? Vichy didn't know, but, then, what difference did it make now?

Choking with revulsion, Vichy had backed away from the sight of his sensuous face, the sound of the woman's excited laughter. To this very day, Vichy was unclear as to exactly where she'd gone that night. In a town that never seemed to sleep, she had walked, sightlessly, until, becoming aware of the time somewhere around nine a.m., she had walked into a lawyer's office. Within those lone nighttime hours Vichy had grown up — the hard way.

Lessons learned painfully are never forgotten. Vichy had not forgotten, nor had she been able to love any man since. To her way of thinking, except for her father and brother, the male of the species was simply not to be trusted.

Cold fingers brushed away the tears pooling under her eyes. Vichy was not crying for the woman she was today, but for the starry-eyed innocent she'd been six years ago. The death of that innocence had been painful in the extreme. Rebuilding her life at twenty-three after she'd received her divorce, six months after she had seen the lawyer, had been plain hard work. Being aware of the fact that she was the first member of her family to obtain a divorce had not made the rebuilding any easier.

Oh, there had been men in her life over the years, several in fact. But she never let any of them get too close. That in itself had not been easy, for while she held them off, she fought a silent battle with herself.

Brad had awakened her sensual being, had created in her a natural hunger. She had all the normal needs and urges of a healthy young woman. Fear lent her the strength to repress those needs. She'd vowed that never again would she leave herself open to the type of crushing hurt Brad had inflicted on her. Momentary appeasement, she'd reasoned, was simply not worth the price.

But abstinence by choice demanded its own price, and after six years the coin of frustration and loneliness had become bloated by inflation, its emotional weight growing heavier each year.

Another groan whispered through her lips and Vichy kicked impatiently at the suddenly confining covers. *Perhaps I should take a lover,* she thought despairingly. *A stranger for the night, chosen coolly and coldbloodedly with one purpose only: relief and assuagement — my own.*

Soft bitter laughter lived only seconds in the dark room. After all these years she wouldn't know how to go about it. And, even if she did, she knew without doubt that she'd lack the courage to go through with it.

Two weeks of her mother's gentle, bustling care, her father's gruff protectiveness, and her sister's sometimes zany humor went a long way in filling the emptiness Vichy had felt yawning inside herself.

The first weekend she was home, Mattie, her husband, Tom, and their youngest daughter, Brenda, came to visit. Most of the first day was spent on Vichy and Mattie catching up on the news of each other. Talk filled the house, sometimes everyone talking at once. Vichy was given a glowing report on her pregnant niece's health, Mattie's excitement over becoming a grandmother evident in every word she spoke.

The second day found them settled into comfortable conversation, broken at intervals by the high-spirited banter between Bette and Brenda, who were separated in age by only four years.

The second weekend Josh descended on them, Robert in tow. During that weekend pandemonium ran rampant, and by the time Josh and Caroline departed for Easton with the scourge, Vichy was beginning to feel like the self she had once been.

All of which made it that much harder

for Vichy to leave again to honor her commitment in Atlantic City. But, telling herself she had only two short runs to go, leave she did the weekend before Thanksgiving.

At the boardwalk the atmosphere bubbled and sparkled like champagne, and was just as heady.

Buses, cabs, and limos disgorged passengers everywhere. Female laughter rose above the babble of voices, punctuated regularly by the shrill whistles of hotel doormen.

Vichy located the hotel she was to perform in without difficulty and, following the instructions she'd received, made her way through the throng of people inside to the designated office.

Vichy found the small lounge she was to sing in just that — small and intimate. After a brief consultation with the manager of the lounge, Vichy went to her room. A hot shower dispensed with most of the tension tightening the muscles at the back of her neck and her shoulders, caused by a combination of nearly three hours of driving plus the apprehension of walking cold into a new job.

The first set on Sunday went smoothly. It was at the beginning of the second set, as Vichy's eyes scanned the sparsely populated room, that her glance collided with the piercing one of a dark-haired man sitting alone at a front table.

After ten years of performing in rooms very much like this one, Vichy was not unused to being stared at, but there was something about this man's riveting gaze that made her uneasy.

Time and again, while she went through her numbers, as if being compelled by a force too strong to deny, Vichy found her glance straying back to the man. And each time, for the length of a sigh, her glance was caught by his steady stare.

His face, rather harshly chiseled, even in composure, wore no expression. Did he hate the sound of her voice? Did he enjoy it? Vichy could not tell, for he didn't smile, he didn't frown. He just sat there, regarding her with that cool, unsettling, straight-on stare.

By the time Vichy had finished for the night and made her hasty retreat to her room, she had decided that if, for whatever reason, the man's goal had been to rattle her, he had achieved his purpose; she was thoroughly unnerved. If his desire had been to make her aware of him, in that he had also succeeded; she had hardly been aware of anyone else in the lounge.

Her dreams that night were peppered with an unsmiling countenance that stared numerous holes right through her.

When she began her last set on Monday night, she was almost afraid to scan the room. She had not seen even a hint of him during her earlier sets, but . . . Telling herself to grow up, Vichy launched herself into a popular, upbeat song, her eyes beginning a slow perusal of the scattered faces fanned before her. At the opposite side of the room from where she'd begun, her gaze came to a jolting stop. He was back!

Fighting a sudden, inexplicable urge to run for cover, Vichy, a hard-fought-for smile cracking her face, plodded through her repertoire, her glance dancing to encompass the room — except for one spot.

As the last note of her final number faded away, Vichy began a slow circuit of the room, pausing to greet the customers, bestow a smile, and murmur a soft "thank you" if complimented.

Studiously avoiding the section of the room where her tormenter sat, Vichy smilingly turned away from a young couple near the back of the lounge to find her way blocked by the very person she'd so carefully tried to steer clear of. His words were as direct as his staring eyes had been.

"You have a very sexy voice," he said softly. "But, of course, you know that."

Before Vichy could even begin to form a reply, he murmured an invitation that sounded more like a command.

313

"Come have a drink with me." His harshly cast features relaxed with a spine-tingling smile. "Let me flatter you into having a late supper with me."

Without waiting for an answer, in fact while he was still speaking, he curled long, slender fingers around her arm and began leading her in the direction of the table he'd occupied.

Bemused by the startling change his smile made to his visage, Vichy moved dazedly, allowing him to not only draw her with him, but seat her at the table as well! Her wits returned as he seated himself opposite her.

"Look, Mr. —" Vichy hesitated, eyebrows arched questioningly.

"Larkin," he supplied quietly. "Bennett Larkin."

"Look, Mr. Larkin," Vichy began again, "thank you for your offer, but —" She got no further, for he cut in smoothly.

"Surely you eat?" The corners of his beautifully sculptured if somewhat thin lips twitched with the beginnings of another smile.

"Yes, of course, but —" she began again, only to have him cut in once more.

"Well, then, why not eat with me?" he queried, his tone mild.

"I don't even know you!" Vichy exclaimed softly.

"Not yet," he parried. "That's the point in having supper together."

"Mr. Larkin, I —" Vichy paused, her mind searching for polite words of refusal; after all, one did not antagonize the paying customers.

"Ben," he said softly.

"What?" The very softness of his tone had been lost to the muted murmurs of the other patrons. His tone rose half a notch.

"I said, my name is Ben."

"Yes, well" — Vichy swallowed against her strangely parched throat — "I'm sorry, but —"

"Have you a date for supper?" he rapped in a suddenly rough tone.

"No!" Vichy denied it at once, then chided herself for not ending the matter by giving an unqualified yes.

"There you are, then." His tone lifted with the corners of his mouth. "Why should we both eat alone, when we can keep each other company?"

Three

Why indeed? Vichy wondered. If she was honest with herself, she had to admit that she was tired of constantly being alone.

It was strange, she mused, regarding Bennett Larkin from behind the barrier of self-imposed detachment, considering how many years she'd been, for the most part, alone. She had made friends, of course, but all of her relationships had been of the surface, casual type. Except for Brad, whom she refused to even count.

Why, now, had these past few days on her own seemed so barren? Very likely, she concluded, because of the fullness of her days during the two weeks she'd spent at home, with her family around her.

"Was the question too difficult?" Bennett Larkin's somewhat sardonic tone demanded she sit up and pay attention.

"What? Oh, I'm sorry, but where were you thinking of having supper?" Vichy hedged.

"Wherever." He shrugged. "Does it matter?"

"No, uh, I suppose not," Vichy finally answered.

"We could eat in one of the rooms right here." He waved his hand languidly to encompass the building. "Or," he paused, then asked, "are you hungry? I mean really hungry?"

"Well," Vichy hesitated, then answered honestly, "yes, as a matter of fact, I am." She had not rested well the night before, then had compounded the resultant edginess by pouring cup after cup of coffee into her tired body. At this moment she suffered from three afflictions — nervousness, hunger, and an unsettling sense of lonesomeness.

"There's a Japanese restaurant not far from here." He mentioned one of the casino hotels. "For a set price they serve a seven-course meal. There is no mulling, or indecision, over a menu. The majority of the food is prepared in front of you, on a grill set into the table, by a very dexterous chef. The meal is served in a courteous, leisurely manner. Does the idea appeal to you?" he finished quietly.

"Very much," Vichy admitted.

"Then why are we sitting here?" Rising abruptly, he came to help her out of her chair, not exactly rushing her, but giving her no time to change her mind either.

"I must get a coat," Vichy said as Ben

317

started toward the steps that led out of the lounge.

"All right." He gave her a measuring glance, then added, "While you do that, I'll call ahead to make sure they can accommodate us." Again that measuring glance swept over her. "If you want to meet me at the lobby entrance, I'll have a cab waiting."

"Couldn't we walk?" Vichy asked, feeling the need of some exercise outdoors.

"Certainly, if you prefer," he concurred at once. "A stroll in the sea air might sharpen the appetite. I'll meet you at the boardwalk exit."

When she went for her coat, Vichy caught a glance of herself in the mirror and decided she'd better remove her stage makeup if she didn't want to be stared at like some sideshow freak. Aware of the minutes slipping by, and of Bennett Larkin waiting, she worked swiftly, but carefully, creaming the heavier makeup off and applying a lighter coat more suitable for being seen in public. And all the time she worked, she tried to avoid thinking about the fact that she had just made a date to have dinner with a perfect stranger.

As she approached the appointed exit, Vichy spied Bennett Larkin before he saw her and used the short interval to study him.

In the dimly lighted lounge, his hair had simply appeared to be dark brown, much like her own. But in the well-lit area before the exit doors, Vichy could see his hair was actually a deep shade of auburn, the red highlights gleaming in the artificial illumination. He was taller than most of the men who passed him going in and out, and his shoulders were wide, his chest broad. His well-cut, perfectly fitted suit revealed a narrow waist, slim hips, and long legs. His arms hung limply at his sides, the fingers of one hand snapping impatiently, belying his relaxed stance.

In the darkened lounge his face had seemed somewhat harsh. Now, in the light, his features appeared chiseled, the cheekbones high, the nose almost hawkish, the jaw jutting out aggressively.

The well-shaped head turned, his eyes sweeping over the faces of the people in front of her before fastening onto her own. Suppressing a shiver, Vichy forced a small smile, asking herself: *What am I doing?* His expression was so fierce it actually frightened her.

"I was beginning to think you weren't going to show," he murmured as she walked up to him. "Did you have to fight second thoughts?" Vichy did not care for his tone or his fierce look. What was she getting into here? she asked herself nervously. His tone had had an underlying note of possession that sent a chill of warning down her spine. Should she try and beg off? she wondered. Would he give her an argument if she did? The answer came without hesitation. Yes, he would. Vichy didn't know quite how she knew, but she did.

"No," she answered simply. "I'm sorry I kept you waiting. I had to remove my stage makeup." Vichy had never before seen eyes the color of the ones studying her now. His eyes were brown, yes, but they actually had deep red flecks in them. Were these what she had heard referred to as sherry-colored? Giving an imperceptible shrug of her shoulders, she preceded him through the door he held open for her.

After the warmth of the smoky lounge, the sharp salt air had an invigorating effect. Sliding her hands into the slash pockets of her all-weather coat, Vichy walked beside Ben, only vaguely aware of the clacking sound her heels made on the almost-deserted boardwalk.

"Are you tired, or are you always this quiet?" Bennett Larkin angled his head, slanting her a questioning glance.

Vichy swallowed against the sudden odd something tightening her throat. "I am a little tired, but, yes, I'm usually this quiet." *Comes from being alone so much,* she could have added, but didn't.

"That's a relief," he drawled. "I was beginning to think my company had stifled your power of speech."

Glancing at him quickly, Vichy caught a flickering, sardonic curve that touched his lips.

"It's a rare quality in women, quietness," he went on softly. "Most of the females I know chatter incessantly, usually about nothing of any importance."

"Importance to whom?" Vichy couldn't resist the small dig. Why did men always think that the topics that concerned them were important?

"Ah, she's quiet, but she does have claws." A note of satisfaction underlined his smooth tone.

"Oh, yes," Vichy warned lightly. "She does have claws. Teeth too."

"Indeed?" His sherry eyes lit from within. "Very intriguing. I'll keep it in mind."

Something in his tone sent a tingle sliding down her spine and started a small fluttering in her midsection. *Careful, Vichy, this one knows his way around the distaff side.* At that moment they reached the hotel, relieving her of her fruitless search for an effective retort.

On their arrival at the restaurant they were seated at once by a pleasant, soft-spoken maître d'. The table was rectangular and set for eight, the place settings arranged on three sides around a large grill.

A young couple, so obviously in love that Vichy wondered if they were on their honeymoon, were already seated at the table. They glanced up curiously, and Ben extended his hand to the young man.

"Bennett Larkin," he informed quietly. "And this is Victoria Parks." He recited the name that was on the lounge's advertisement board.

"Kevin and Donna Wheatley." The young man smiled before turning his attention back to his pretty wife.

"Honeymooners," Ben murmured, echoing her own thoughts.

Although their drink order was taken and quickly brought, the meal was not begun until the table had a full complement of eight, which consisted of an elderly couple and two women Vichy judged to be somewhere between forty and forty-five.

As Ben had informed Vichy, most of the meal was prepared on the grill before them by a charming young man. The rest of the meal — the sake and a clear, green tea — was served by a lovely, whispery-voiced young woman who looked like a delicate Japanese doll in a colorful kimono.

During the course of the meal, and the

ensuing conversation around the table, Vichy learned that the young couple were on their wedding trip, that the two women were on a one-day bus tour, that the elderly couple had stopped off in Atlantic City on their way from New Hampshire to Florida on a driving trip, and, most important to Vichy, that Bennett Larkin was in the city for one reason — to gamble.

Vichy had, of course, suspected as much, but having him so casually confirm her suspicions tightened nerves that the comfortable atmosphere had just begun to relax. But that didn't mean that gambling was his life, Vichy reminded herself. Oh, why was she trying to make excuses for this man, she wondered then, when he could very well be Brad all over again?

After bidding their table companions good night, Vichy and Ben left the restaurant.

"Do you want to take a cab or walk back?" Ben asked as they rode the escalator to the ground floor.

"After all that food, I think I'd better walk." Vichy smiled. "I can't remember ever eating so much in one sitting."

Holding her coat for her at the exit doors, Ben's eyes ran over her figure consideringly.

"It would appear to me that you have been eating hardly anything at all at any one sitting," he observed dryly.

"Is that a roundabout way of telling me I'm too skinny?" she demanded. Vichy was more than a little touchy on the subject of her weight, or lack of it, having been chided about it by every member of her family at least once over the two weeks she'd been at home.

"Not at all," he denied smoothly. "More a roundabout way of giving a compliment. Your figure is just about perfect, at least for my taste it is."

Vichy's pulses leaped erratically, startling her. After all these years performing in front of the public, she was used to compliments, honestly given or not. Why should this stranger's offhand remark have the power to fluster her? And there was no denying to herself that she was flustered. It was weird. She didn't care what this man thought of her figure or anything else. Did she?

Her shoulder being jostled made Vichy realize that they were still standing in front of the exit doors, hindering traffic. Bennett Larkin's amused expression made her uncomfortably aware of the fact that he knew of her confused state and was enjoying every minute of it.

With a stiltedly murmured "thank you," Vichy swept past him out onto the boardwalk. Without pausing to see if he was beside her, she started walking as fast as her heels would allow.

"What's the rush?"

His fingers curled around her arm, halting her headlong pace, before sliding slowly down to capture, and entwine with, hers.

Vichy opened her mouth, then closed it again, shocked speechless by the riot of sensations radiating from her imprisoned hand all the way up her arm to her shoulder.

"It's very late," she began. His soft laughter stopped the rest of whatever she was going to say in her mouth. Good Lord! What was happening to her? Vichy could not remember feeling this way while in the company of a man since . . . No! She would *not* think about Brad. She tried to disentangle her hand, but Ben's fingers tightened around hers.

"Don't panic, beautiful," Ben advised softly, close to her ear. "I'm not going to make any sudden overt moves or shocking suggestions." He shook her hand slightly. "I'm not going to let go either. Enjoy our stroll," he urged, "and this perfect fall night." His tone went very low. "Relax and let nature take its course."

Vichy had a very good idea exactly which course he referred to. The very thing she'd been so carefully avoiding all these years. A shiver of — of apprehension or anticipation? — rippled through her body. Bennett Larkin felt it, of course.

"For God's sake, woman," he growled impatiently, "ease up." He came to a complete stop and turned to face her, his expression baffled. "You're as nervous and uptight as a teenager on her first date. But, as you are very obviously *not* a teenager, what's your problem, anyway?"

Vichy stiffened at his exasperated tone. Who did this guy think he was? And did he think that buying her supper gave him the right to question her? Or make remarks about her age and attitude? And she didn't like being called "woman" either! Once again she tried to pull her hand from his — and failed.

"Let go of my hand, please." Vichy was proud of the cool tone she'd managed.

"No." His tone held flat finality. "Answer me."

His implacability shattered most of her cool. "You're right," she snapped. "I'm far from being a teenager. I have been around, as the saying goes. If I have a problem, it is men, like you, who take entirely too much for granted. Now, let go of my hand — and don't call me 'woman.' "

"My, my, you're even more uptight than I thought," Ben marveled infuriatingly. "Some jerk rake you over the coals, did he?"

326

"That is none of your business," Vichy ground out through clenched teeth.

"True," he agreed easily, which incensed her even more. "But that doesn't stop me from wondering what he did to you."

"You can wonder until the cows come home," she spat out angrily. "I have no intention of pandering to your curiosity." Again she tried, and failed, to disengage her hand. "And if you don't mind" — she gave another unsuccessful tug against his grip — "I'm tired. I want to go to my room."

"Okay." He sighed deeply, exaggeratedly. Without warning he began to walk, tugging her along.

An uneasy silence hung between them like a tangible presence all the way back. A silence that went unbroken until, standing before the door to her room, his hand covered hers as she attempted to insert her key into the lock.

"Victoria, wait," Ben urged softly. His other hand came up to grasp her shoulder and turn her to face him. His somewhat austere features betrayed confusion. "I'm damned if I can figure out why what I said upset you. But as it obviously did, I'm sorry. If I promise to ask no more personal questions, will you have supper with me again tomorrow night?"

Vichy's pulse leaped. Good grief, she

chided herself in confusion, hadn't she just gone out of her way to discourage him? She knew that if she had any sense at all she'd say no.

"Yes." So much for sense.

"Good." His warm breath feathered her forehead as he lowered his head.

He was going to kiss her; she knew it, and yet she stood unable to move, her eyes fastened on his firmly outlined mouth as it drew closer to her own.

"Ben!"

Her whispered protest was too late. His mouth touched her parted lips for gentle seconds, and then he lifted his head and stepped back. His fingers plucked the cardkey from hers and a second later the door swung inward.

"Good night, Victoria."

Leaning to her, he lightly brushed his lips across her cheek, and then he was gone, striding down the hallway.

Jerking like someone coming out of a trance, Vichy hurried into the room, closed and locked the door, then, breathing deeply, leaned back against the wood panels weakly.

What is it about this man? she asked herself blankly. Her chest felt constricted and she had a strangely hollow feeling inside.

Shaking her head sharply, Vichy pushed herself away from the door. No, she was overreacting, she assured herself bracingly. She was attracted to him, yes, but it was purely a physical attraction, nothing more. Surely she could handle that.

As she moved around the small room preparing for bed, Vichy rationalized her totally out-of-character response to Bennett Larkin. Never before had she gone off with a complete stranger as she had tonight. Hadn't she even kept Brad at arm's length for several days after they'd been introduced before agreeing to go out with him? But, she was so childishly homesick and lonely, much more so than she'd been at twenty-two. Then she'd had the fullness of the promise of the future to combat the occasional pangs of emptiness. Bennett Larkin had lit the first spark of life in her in what seemed like ages.

On the verge of sliding into bed, Vichy went still with a cautioning thought: *Be very careful, Vichy Parks, that the spark Ben Larkin fired doesn't flare into a full-blown blaze. You've been burned before; play it cool.*

After settling herself for sleep, Vichy deliberately conjured up a mental picture of Ben Larkin, again asking herself, *What is it about him?*

She had met so many men over the years, some of them almost unbelievably handsome that, comparatively, Ben was merely very attractive, and that in a harshly masculine way. A tiny, live wire of excitement shot through her body. Was that it? Was it that raw masculinity about him that appealed to something within her? Vichy shivered. She knew nothing about him but one thing — he was all male.

Vichy's last thought before drifting off to sleep was, all male or not, he's a gambler, and not to be trusted — or was he?

four

Tuesday was much like Monday, except for one major difference — all day long thoughts of Ben stole into Vichy's mind, bringing with them a mixture of excitement and trepidation.

Periodically swinging from feeling breathless to foolish, even she heard the new nerve in her voice as she sang her way through her first performance.

Touching up her makeup before her final set, Vichy couldn't help but notice the flush of color in her cheeks. Stroking a brush through her mane of dark hair, she studied her appearance critically. Her dress had cost a great deal, and it was worth every penny. In a pale lilac, the soft silk material clung to her full breasts and small waist, then swirled out enticingly around her slender calves.

Finally satisfied with the smooth shine of her hair, Vichy stowed the brush in her bag, wet her lips with the tip of her tongue, and, swallowing to relieve a sudden tickle in her throat, went back to work.

A quick inspection of the lounge left her feeling as flat as a bottle of uncorked, week-old champagne. Ben wasn't there!

Never missing a beat, or forgetting a word, Vichy sang, talked to the audience, and laughingly bantered with the combo that backed her up musically, all the while upbraiding herself for the depth of disappointment she was experiencing. He was a gambler. Hadn't she learned the hard way that gamblers could not be trusted? But the same nagging thought she had tried to push out of her mind kept coming back. Maybe he was different, maybe she had misjudged him. . . .

The set seemed endless. Lord, had she really rehearsed all these numbers? At last, only one more song to go! Then she could go back to her room and cry, or throw something or curse all gamblers out loud.

Flashing her listeners a brilliant smile, Vichy opened her mouth and very nearly missed the first note. Moving casually and looking extremely attractive, Ben Larkin made his way to the table he'd sat at the previous two nights.

Felling her anger in its path, joy welled up inside and voiced itself through her music, drawing from the audience the most enthusiastic round of applause she'd received since beginning her engagement. Ben was equally appreciative.

"I'm doubly sorry now that I arrived so late." The smile that revealed his even white teeth sent an expectant chill along her spine. "I fear I've missed a very exciting performance."

Lackluster, Vichy silently corrected him while aloud she murmured, "Thank you," and returned his smile.

"Don't sit down." Ben took her arm as she made a move to do just that. "I've had the car brought around. Go take your makeup off as quickly as possible."

"But —"

"Go," he ordered gently. "We wouldn't want the doorman unhappy with us. The car's taking up space."

Vichy removed her makeup in record time. Carrying her coat, she went back to him and, without a word, he ushered her to the lobby and out of the building. Slipping a bill to the uniformed doorman, Ben led her toward a sleek-looking black Lexus. Allowing the doorman to seat her, he strode around to the driver's side and slid behind the wheel. Vichy remained quiet until they were through the worst of the congested traffic and headed away from the city. Now, after being tense and jumpy all day, a sense of contentment enfolded her like a warm pair of arms.

"At the risk of sounding nosy," she taunted lightly, "might I be permitted to ask where we're going?"

At her easy, teasing tone, Ben shifted his eyes from the road to her face in a swift, encompassing glance. His slow smile carried the impact of a sledgehammer.

"Feel good, do you?" he teased back, his sherry eyes lit from within. "We're going to have supper at a steak house along the road, several miles inland." He went on without waiting for a reply from her. "Does that meet with your approval?"

Vichy's soft laughter was a clear indication of her suddenly lighthearted mood. "Would it matter terribly if it didn't?"

"Terribly," he intoned with mock seriousness. "I'd be devastated."

"I think you're pulling my leg," she accused laughingly.

"Oh, no," Ben drawled, slicing her a glinting look. "If I ever pull on your leg, beautiful, you won't have to think about it — you'll know."

His tone as well as the innuendo sent a shaft of warmth radiating through her body, and Vichy was grateful for the darkness that concealed her flushed cheeks from him.

Whatever had come over her? she wondered, studying his relaxed profile from under lowered lashes. If any other man had made that remark to her in just that suggestive tone, she'd have withdrawn behind a wall of ice. *What is it about this man?* Vichy asked herself for at least the hundredth time. *Why does he have the power to reduce me to a blushing inarticulateness?* He was only a man, and probably a gambler at that. If she had any sense at all, she would not even be here now.

"Am I receiving that silent treatment for being brash?" Ben's quiet taunt jerked her out of her introspection.

"Was I expected to respond to that crack?" Vichy parried.

"Crack?" Ben laughed aloud. "Oh, sweetheart, that was no crack. That was a promise."

Now, how in the world was she supposed to respond to *that?* Thankfully, she was spared the effort, as at that moment Ben brought the car to a near stop; then, his long hands controlling the wheel easily, he drove off the road into the parking lot of a long, single-story building which boasted a neon sign that proclaimed it a steak house.

Very likely due to the fact that it was a Tuesday night and fairly late, there were only a few patrons in the large, dimly lit dining room. They were greeted at the door by a smiling hostess, smartly dressed in a straight long black skirt and a crisp, long-sleeved white blouse. She escorted them to a secluded corner table, asked if they'd like to order a drink, then, after presenting overlarge menus for their perusal, went gliding away to place their drink order.

"That is a very classy-looking woman," Ben opined, his eyes following the swaying, retreating form.

"Yes," Vichy agreed tightly, appalled at the flash of annoyance his attention to the woman's appearance generated in her.

"But she can't hold a candle to you," he added teasingly, obviously not missing the strained note in her tone. His eyes dancing with devilment, he examined her face and the upper part of her body, lingering long seconds on her silk-draped, suddenly quivering breasts.

"Ben, s-stop it," Vichy pleaded constrictedly, glancing around nervously.

"Why?" Leaning back lazily, he raised gleaming eyes to hers. "Are you wearing a bra?" he asked softly, outrageously, chuckling softly at her quick gasp.

"That's none of your —" she began in a strangled groan, only to gasp again at his soft laughter.

"I don't believe you are," he laughed, his eyes betraying the amusement he felt at bringing a rush of pink to her pale cheeks. "Of course," he drawled consideringly, "to be absolutely sure, I'll have to play the intrepid explorer — later on."

"You'll do nothing of the kind!" Vichy exclaimed in another shocked gasp.

Ben's delighted laughter bounced around the nearly empty room, drawing the eyes and smiles of patrons and staff alike.

"Oh, Victoria, you're an absolute gem," Ben teased around the laughter that still rumbled in his muscled chest. "You snap at the bait like a starved fish."

"Better be careful," Vichy teased, falling under his playful spell. "You could find you've hooked a barracuda, with very tiny, but pointed, teeth."

"Ah, ha," he shot back. "But the barracuda is no match for the shark, who has very *large,* pointed teeth." His voice dropped to a low growl. "And this shark is already tempted to gobble up the barracuda." His eyes raked her like a rough caress. "And this particular barracuda is a very tasty-looking morsel indeed."

Catching sight of a waiter approaching their table, Vichy purred, "Luckily, this particular fish is about to have her scaly skin saved by a fisherman in the disguise of a waiter." She fluttered her long eyelashes innocently. "Are you going to order a barracuda steak?"

"Barbs like that only make the shark hungrier," Ben managed to jibe softly before the waiter came to a halt beside Vichy.

Suddenly famished, Vichy ordered a full-course dinner, from soup through dessert, and ate every bit of it. In between her first spoonful of broccoli-cheese soup and her last forkful of pecan pie, the conversation flowed easily between them.

"Victoria is such a straightlaced sort of name," Ben mused around his own spoonful of the rich soup. "Haven't you ever been called Vicky, or even Vic?"

"Vichy," she supplied.

"What?"

"Vichee," she repeated distinctly, shrugging lightly. "I have a sister eight years my junior. When she began to talk, she could not articulate Vicky. It always came out Vichy. The name stuck, even after she could have pronounced it correctly."

"I'm glad," Ben decided, after munching and swallowing a piece of his filet mignon. "It's different, like you."

"How am I different?" Vichy asked, glancing up from her plate in surprise.

"In many ways," Ben smiled. "I'll tell you sometime."

"Sometime?" Vichy echoed. "Why not now?"

Ben glanced around the room, empty now except for the employees. "Too

338

public," he was teasing again. "You'll have to remind me to tell you when we have a little more privacy."

"Were you always a tormentor?" Vichy chided. "Even as a little boy?" Before he could answer, she tacked on, "*Were* you ever a little boy?" finding it hard to picture him any way but the way he was this minute.

"Of course I was a little boy once." His tone held effrontery. "I was even a baby at one time."

"Really?" Vichy breathed, wide-eyed.

His eyes glittered back at her.

"Had you thought that, perhaps, my parents had found me, fully grown, under a large boulder somewhere?"

"Natural offspring of a rock, you mean?" Vichy queried sweetly.

"I'm as hard as one." Ben's grin held wickedness. "Better be careful you don't bruise yourself against me."

The mere idea of being against him was enough to fluster Vichy all out of proportion, and sidestepping, she stammered, "Have you, ah, any brothers or sisters?"

"Coward," he mocked, then, with lifted brows and bland face, asked, "Sibling stones, so to speak?"

"If you will," she laughed helplessly.

"Oh, I will," he taunted, deliberately twisting her meaning. "I will, *anything*."

"Ben, be serious," Vichy admonished.

"I'm very serious," he answered her. "There are a number of things I will, with you — eventually. And that's another promise."

"Ben, please," Vichy begged, her dinner forgotten for the moment, lost, as she suddenly was, inside his sherry eyes. Those eyes, she decided vaguely, could be positively intoxicating.

"Is the barracuda ready to concede the battle?"

"Not on your fishhook," Vichy retorted.

"Just hiding out in the shallows, eh?" he wondered aloud. "Okay," he almost crooned. "I'll cut bait for a while." He speared a french fry, his eyes laughing at her. "I have one brother, no sisters." Popping the slice of potato into his mouth, he showed his teeth in a grin. "He's younger, not quite as hard as I am."

"Does he gamble too?" Vichy was sorry the moment the harsh-sounding words were out of her mouth, for Ben frowned, and the light in his eyes dimmed. His expression quizzical, he stared at her a long time before answering with a question of his own.

"Doesn't everyone?"

"Of course not!" Vichy exclaimed. "I don't."

"I think they do," Ben stated adamantly.

"Yourself included."

"No," Vichy shook her head in denial. "I never —"

"Forget it," he interrupted brusquely. "I never argue over a meal." The light went on in his eyes again, and he smiled meltingly. "It's bad for the digestion, you know."

"But, Ben —" That's as far as she got, for Ben again cut determinedly across her attempt at protest.

"You mentioned a younger sister. Are there any others?"

"One other sister and a brother." Vichy sighed in defeat. "Both older than I."

"And is there a husband waiting at home?" he asked overly casually.

"No." Vichy kept her tone every bit as casual. "Is there a wife?"

"Not anymore," Ben declared grimly. His tone sent her eyebrows up in question. With a shrug, Ben clarified, "I've been divorced for three years."

"I've got three years on you." Her flat statement sent his brows arching. Emulating his careless shrug, Vichy explained, "It's been six years since I received my divorce decree."

"You must have been very young." It was a deliberate probe to ascertain her age, and Vichy knew it. She smiled wryly.

"I was twenty-three."

"I was thirty-one," Ben offered her the knowledge of his own age. "It's a bad experience at any age."

"Yes," Vichy nodded soberly.

"Were there any children?" he probed further.

"No." *Thank God,* she added silently. "You?" she sank her own probe.

"One, a boy." Ben's expression was suddenly so fierce Vichy felt chilled with apprehension. The feeling deepened when he went on harshly, "I have custody."

Good Lord! A shiver slithered down Vichy's spine. He was frightening. His chiseled features had set into granite hardness. This would be the wrong man to cross, Vichy thought nervously. At that moment, without knowing any of the facts concerning the affair, Vichy felt compassion for his former wife.

"Chad's seven."

Ben's quietly voiced statement scattered Vichy's thoughts. Glancing at him quickly, she tried to discern his mood. A sigh of relief whispered through her lips. His expression had softened a little — and the gleam was back in his eyes.

"And is he as hard as you are?" she blurted out before she could stop herself.

"Not yet," he laughed without humor. "But he will be." His laughter subsided into a bitter smile. "No woman is ever going to rake him over the coals. I intend to see that he goes into the world fully prepared."

"To do the raking, instead of being raked?" Vichy asked bitingly.

"Bad, was it?" Ben queried softly.

"Very," Vichy clipped, revealing her impatience with him.

"Okay." He held up his hands in surrender. "Point taken. But, in my own defense, I must say that I have been instructing him on the proper way to treat a — a lady."

His deliberate pause was not lost on Vichy. *Holy cow,* Vichy thought wildly, *was he also instructing him on the proper way to treat a non-lady?* A second shiver followed the first one down her spine. Ben saw her involuntary movement.

"Something bothers you?"

Vichy smiled uncertainly. "I suddenly find myself hoping you consider me a lady."

Amusement twitching his lips, Ben lifted his stemmed wineglass that still contained an inch of the Merlot he'd ordered, and tilted it toward her.

"A very special lady," he murmured assuringly.

By mutual if silent agreement, their conversation was kept to generalities for the remainder of the meal.

Over coffee and liqueur Ben broke the tacit agreement to remain impersonal. Raising his tiny glass, he studied its contents for a moment before, glancing up at her, he touched his glass to hers. He took a sip, then waited, brows arched, until she had followed suit. Vichy nearly choked with his murmured words.

"Amaretto, the drink of lovers." His smile invited — all kinds of things. "And we will be. That's another promise."

"Don't bet on it, gambler," Vichy advised angrily. She was furious, yet, underneath that fury, excitement sizzled scaring her.

"I am betting on it," Ben said imperturbably. "Heavily."

"Ben —"

"Drink your coffee." His eyes roamed over the deserted room. "I think the hostess is trying to tell us something. She's positively glaring at us."

It was raining when they left the restaurant, not a downpour, but a steady rain Vichy's father would have called a land rain.

"I like to ride in the rain," Vichy announced after they had settled into the car. "But I hate driving in it." She shuddered, remembering the deluge she'd struggled through on her way east.

"Well, sit back and enjoy it," Ben invited

expansively. "I don't mind driving through it."

Made drowsy by all the food she'd consumed, Vichy dismissed the uneasiness Ben's last promise had aroused and snuggled into the soft leather upholstery. Assuring herself he could do nothing about fulfilling his outrageous promisc without her compliance, she closed her eyes and allowed herself to be lulled by the swish of the windshield wipers.

"Vichy."

Ben's soft, gentle tone roused her out of a half-sleep. Sitting up quickly, Vichy blinked against the glare of light illuminating thc hotel forecourt.

"I'm sorry, Ben." Vichy had to pause to smother a yawn behind her hand. "I'm not used to so much food at such a late hour. It sends me right to sleep," she avowed, conveniently forgetting her wakefulness of the night before.

"Apology accepted" — Ben smiled warmly — "but entirely unnecessary. You work hard, you get tired. You owe no one an apology for that." He hesitated, then underlined darkly, confusingly, "Most especially me."

The ensuing activity of leaving the car prevented Vichy from inquiring into his meaning. But why him especially? she asked herself, wondering. She put the question to him as he escorted her to her room.

"Why, because I've witnessed the amount of energy you put into each performance," Ben explained glibly. But, as the seconds of quiet lengthened, Vichy had no option but to accept his answer at face value. Shrugging off the certainty that he was being less than truthful, Vichy let the matter rest.

As they approached her room, Vichy slipped her cardkey from her purse to have ready in case she had to make a quick escape. Her forethought was wasted, for Ben, aware of her every move, simply took it from her fingers and unlocked the door, allowing it to swing open before turning to face her with mocking eyes.

"Are you going to offer your mouth?" he taunted. "Or must I play the kiss thief again?"

"Ben, I —"

"Okay," he sighed deeply. "Have it your way." All the harsh angles and planes of his face settled into iron determination as he lowered his head toward hers.

"But, if I have to steal it, I may as well make it worth the effort."

His lips touched hers and the effort he put forth was shattering. Never in her life had Vichy been kissed quite like Ben was kissing her now. There was no slow build-up to possession. His mouth attacked, devoured, vanquished. His tongue raked hungrily for every drop of sweetness. His arms crushed her softness into submission to the hardness of his body.

Knowing herself beaten before she could launch an offensive, Vichy surrendered to his superior forces. At her first sign of the white flag, Ben's tactics switched to a new field of battle.

Bringing into play every sensual weapon he possessed, he proceeded to annihilate her faintest hope of resistance.

His mouth moving, his tongue teasing, his hands restlessly caressing, he lit a spark that ignited a sexual explosion, the effects of which singed to life every inch of her quivering body.

Without thought, without caution, Vichy's arms circled his waist convulsively as she arched herself to him, moaning a protest when his mouth slid from hers.

"Vichy," he groaned, the tip of his tongue exploring the corner of her mouth before trailing across her cheek to her ear. "Do you know what you're doing to me?"

"Yes," she admitted. Held so very closely against him, she could hardly deny the evidence of his arousal.

"Then invite me into your room," he urged unsteadily. "I can't make love to you here."

Every one of Vichy's inflamed senses froze. What was she doing? Was she out of her mind? She was not that kind of woman, was she? Cold, shivering with re-action, she struggled to free herself.

"You can't make love to me anywhere," she cried in a strangled croak. "Ben, please," she begged. "I can't."

His arms dropped away from her and he stepped back, his face a study in disgust.

"Why did you respond like that?" he de-manded coldly.

"I — I —" What could she say? How could she defend an action she didn't un-derstand?

"Don't strain yourself," Ben almost snarled. In an abrupt movement he turned to walk away from her, but he didn't walk away, or even move, for long seconds.

Barely breathing, Vichy watched him, a soft sigh easing out of her when she saw the tautness in his back slowly relax. When he turned back to face her, all sign of his blazing anger was gone.

"I don't think I've ever wanted a woman quite as badly as I want you," he said softly. "Fair warning, Vichy. You might as well know I intend having you — and soon." His eyes narrowed on her suddenly trembling, kiss-bruised lips, and he smiled. "You, beautiful, are every bit as aroused as I am. I'm not the only one who will have trouble getting to sleep." His smile taunted pitilessly. "I won't say good night, because we both know it won't be." With that he turned and walked away, his long stride widening the distance between them.

fiue

Over three hours later Vichy ruefully acknowledged the truth of Ben's parting barb. It was not a good night; in fact, it was a very bad night.

Vichy ached in places that had not felt the stirring of life for a very long time. Her body throbbed with a demand for release, making rest impossible. Her mind darted around like an animal in a cage seeking sleep-inducing, tranquil thoughts in vain.

Her mouth still savored the taste of Ben, her skin still tingled from his touch, and her body still felt his imprint. And most discomforting of all was the realization that she wanted him with near desperation.

This is beyond sense, she thought wildly, in an effort to calm her churning emotions. Frantically, she sought excuses for her own out-of-character behavior. *I've been alone too long. I'm tired. I'm losing my mind.*

Nothing worked. Near dawn, exhausted both physically and mentally, Vichy faced the unpalatable truth her mind had been dodging since Ben had walked away from her.

He had said he'd never wanted a woman as badly as he wanted her. Vichy knew what he meant, for the truth she'd been so studiously avoiding was that her own desire equaled his.

She had loved Brad with all her heart and mind and yet, not even at the zenith of their lovemaking, had he had the power to bring her to this degree of awareness of herself as well as of him. That Ben so very obviously possessed that power shook her to her foundations.

Vichy moaned and buried her face in the mangled bed pillow. There had been several altogether different types of men interested in her over the years — a constructional engineer, a successful businessman, a live-wire from the advertising field, even her agent had made a play for her attention. She had liked all of them, and in the case of the engineer and her agent, very much. Yet none of them ever dented the barrier of reserve she'd erected around herself after Brad's betrayal.

Now, this stranger, another gambler, had, within a few minutes' embrace, not only dented that barrier but shattered it completely.

What was it, Vichy wondered despairingly, that drew her to this reckless type of man? Unconscious rebellion against her own protected, moralistic upbringing? An unrecognized urge deep within her to throw caution to the winds and either soar or crash with the careless toss of a pair of dice or the turn of a card? Latent idiocy?

Vichy did not know nor could she be sure that Ben was as obsessed with gambling as Brad had been. Her thoughts revolved unceasingly as the room emerged from blackness to pearl-gray predawn and no rational answer presented itself.

One thing she did know: She would have to be mad to get within fifty feet of him again. He could hurt her badly. And if she saw more of him, she would be inviting the pain, for one concrete truth stood boldly unsinged in the ashes of her burned-out thoughts. It had been hours since he'd taken his leave, and she still wanted him.

Against all reason, against all sensible judgment, she still ached to be enfolded in his strong arms, still yearned to be drawn close to his hard body, still hungered for the taste of his marauding mouth. And with that urgency still burning along her nerve endings and through her veins, Vichy finally slipped into a deep, dreamfree sleep.

Vichy had never been overwild about

Wednesday, coming, as it did, in the middle of the week. It had always been *the* day to get through. Friday, she had always maintained, she could do standing on her head, but Wednesday was a drag. This particular Wednesday was worse than most.

Three hours of sleep definitely did not leave one bright of eye and dewy-skinned, Vichy concluded as she deftly camouflaged her face with cosmetics.

During the process of preparing herself to venture outside the relatively safe confines of her room, Vichy raked her mind as to how she was going to accomplish her objective of avoiding Bennett Larkin.

Lord, just thinking his name had the effect of a feather-light massage with icy fingers. Vichy shivered, and, repressing a sigh, examined the finished product of her labors in the mirror above the room's single dresser.

With blatant bravado, she had chosen a pair of narrow-legged, camel's-hair wool slacks and topped them with a champagne-colored cashmere V-neck sweater. The thin, soft wool outlined her perfect figure. Chocolate brown leather high-heeled boots enhanced her long legs.

Even in a place where lovely women were the norm, eyes followed Vichy as she made her way to the coffee shop where she'd breakfasted every morning since her arrival at the hotel. As she sat in the same section each day, she invariably was served by the same waiter, and this morning he was quick to comment on her appearance.

"Morning, Ms. Parks." His bright young eyes made a detailed inventory of her entire person before he quipped, "You look good enough to be listed on the menu under desserts."

"Thank you." Vichy smilingly returned his boyish grin. "I think."

Even though the waiter was about her sister Bette's age, his obvious admiration bolstered her spirits and she left the coffee shop with a much lighter tread then when she'd entered.

Rehearsal, and the usual give-and-take that ensued over it, ate up the hours till her first set. Being cloistered with the musicians prevented any contact with other people, which suited Vichy. In her mind other people represented one person: Ben Larkin.

After making a wobbly start, Vichy settled down, and the rest of the set went smoothly. During her breaks she hid out in her tiny dressing room, endeavoring to convince herself that she was not nervously anticipating the last set.

After a day that seemed at least seventy-five hours long, the time for her last set did arrive, and with it the man who had claimed the major part of her thoughts through every one of those hours.

Torn as she was by the conflicting urges to run to him and run for her life, Vichy somehow managed to render every one of her numbers without faltering.

Then the last song was finished, and, while aloud she said her thank yous and automatically rattled off her usual chatter to her audience, silently she shouted down the voice that suggested she take the coward's way and flee.

She had only three more days of her engagement to get through; then she could run to the safety of her home. Surely she could handle him, and her own traitorous emotions, for a few days, couldn't she? Of course she could!

Looking like a gift from the gods in gray trousers, navy blazer, and a crisp blue shirt, Ben stood waiting at the table she now thought of as his.

"You're very sexy tonight, both in voice and dress," he complimented softly when she came to a stop in front of him. "If the intention was to turn me on, it worked." Ben ignored her sharp indrawn breath and went on dryly, "But, first things first. I haven't eaten since early this morning and I'm famished. Run along and get rid of your makeup so we can get out of here."

Tell him now, the warning voice whispered from a deep recess of her mind. *Tell him you're too tired to go out. Tell him you're not feeling well. Tell him you're on the verge of a nervous breakdown. Tell him anything, but tell him now.*

Vichy knew very well that she should heed the advice of that tiny voice of alarm. *Then why,* she asked her reflected image in the makeup mirror, *did I so meekly obey him?* For obey him she had. At her slight hesitation, Ben had simply said, "Go," and she had. *I was right earlier,* she decided as she wiped makeup remover off her face. *It must be a case of latent idiocy.*

But, surely, if I play it cool, keep the emotional temperature low, it will be safe to share a meal with him? The blue eyes in the mirror stared back at her reproachfully. *But I want to see him.* She defied those eyes. *I can control the physical thing,* she assured herself before swinging away from the mirror.

Oh, sure, that tiny voice mocked persistently.

Ben was waiting for her, leaning indolently against the wall across from the dressing room. As she closed the small distance between them, Vichy felt her pulses leap at the slow, lazy-eyed glance he sent roaming over her body.

356

"I grow hungrier and hungrier," he murmured, reaching out to clasp her hand as he straightened to his full height. "But, for the moment, I'll have to satisfy myself with food."

Vichy could not even pretend she'd misunderstood his meaning, for just looking at him aroused her own sexual appetite. She was playing with fire, she knew it, yet, when he started to move, tugging on her hand, she followed him without protest.

As it had been the night before, his car was waiting for him. Unlike the night before, as if deliberately avoiding an intimate atmosphere, he took her to a brightly lit all-night dincr. The food was plain, but very good, and Ben ate like he was indeed very hungry. Surprisingly, after her first forkful, Vichy found her own appetite whetted and managed to eat almost as much as Ben.

After the table had been cleared and their coffee cups refilled. Ben slid a long flat box from his pocket.

"I have something for you," he said warmly, sliding it across the table to her. "A little Thanksgiving gift."

"But gifts are not given for Thanksgiving!" Vichy exclaimed softly, eyeing the box warily.

"That depends on what you're thankful for." He smiled enigmatically. "Open it. I assure you it won't bite you."

Handling the case gingerly, as if it might do just that, Vichy lifted the hinged lid, a small gasp parting her lips at the sight of the exquisitely wrought gold bracelet nestled inside. The word *expensive* was, figuratively, written all over it.

"But, Ben" — Vichy lifted shocked eyes to his — "I can't accept this. It must have cost an enormous amount of money." She started to push the case back toward him and his hand shot out to cover hers.

"Its cost is none of your business," he chided, his fingers snaking the shimmering adornment from its bed of satin. "Besides," he went on teasingly, clasping the bracelet around her slender wrist, "the dice were hot for me early this evening. This bauble is by way of a celebration of my run of luck."

Vichy's supper was suddenly a heavy weight in her stomach. How many times had she heard similar words from Brad? True, Ben's voice had not contained the note of feverish excitement Brad's had always held, but, then, Ben was older, more mature, than Brad had been.

Fighting the sickness of despair rising inside, Vichy's trembling fingers tried to undo the bracelet's clasp. Brad had always exacted payment for his winnings gifts. Payments that, at the time, she'd always

358

been eager to meet. Did Ben expect the same type of payment?

Ben's covering hand stilled her fingers' fumbling action, and as if he could monitor her anguished thoughts, he said, almost harshly, "The damned thing has no strings on it, Vichy."

"Ben, I —" The words died on her lips as, glancing up, she caught the grim expression on his face. Was it possible she'd hurt his feelings? Had she offended him?

"I won't be able to meet you tomorrow night." Ben's smoothly controlled voice scattered her questioning thoughts.

"Why?" Vichy could have bitten her tongue. Her tone held a wealth of possessiveness she had no right to feel. Yet, the query seemed to please Ben, for the harsh angles of his face relaxed into a heart-melting, sweet smile.

"Because I promised Chad I'd be home for Thanksgiving," he explained. Leaning back against the plastic-covered booth seat, he nodded at the waitress when she stopped at the booth to ask if they'd like more coffee. "He has been staying with my brother, Mike, and his family," he went on when the waitress had completed the service. "He's content there, but he expects to see me when he wakes up tomorrow morning." He flicked a glance at the slim gold watch on his lightly haired wrist and grinned. "Or, I should say, *this* morning.

"Of course he does," Vichy murmured in understanding. Then, smiling wistfully, she asked, "Will there be the traditional groaning board at your brother's home?"

"Without doubt." Ben laughed softly. "Shelly, my sister-in-law, is a fantastic cook. I wouldn't be surprised to learn she's been preparing goodies all week, just for the one day. And she'll really outdo herself for Christmas. Actually," he went on seriously, "Shelly is pretty fantastic, period. Besides being a great cook, she's a wonderful mother and a meticulous housekeeper." A tiny smile twitched his firm lips. "She must know how to keep a husband happy, too, for my brother smiles a lot."

Hearing Ben extol his sister-in-law's virtues caused a strange twinge in Vichy's chest. What did it signify? she wondered in surprise. A touch of envy? Surely not jealousy? Thankfully, Ben saved her from having to identify her own emotions.

"You're going to miss being with your family for the holiday, aren't you?" he asked, obviously having picked up on the wistful note in her voice.

"Yes," Vichy replied honestly, then laughed sadly at herself. "It's silly really. I have spent very few of my holidays with them since I started performing professionally ten years ago." She shrugged, as if ridding herself of her sadness. "At least I'll be able to spend Christmas at home."

"You're not booked in the lounge through the holidays?" Ben rapped sharply, causing Vichy to blink in surprise.

"No." She shook her head, confused by Ben's intent expression. "I was hired as a fill-in for this week, and then again for the weekend after Christmas through New Year's Day."

"So that means you'll be going home — when?" Ben's eyebrows arched.

"I was planning to leave early Sunday morning," Vichy answered. "I want to be home by the time my folks get home from church."

"And where's home?" he probed quietly.

"Pennsylvania," she finally supplied after a long pause.

"Pennsylvania is a large state." Ben nudged at her obvious reluctance to reveal the exact location of her parents' home.

"Near Lancaster," she hedged.

"How near?" he insisted.

"Ben —" Vichy drew his name out in exasperation.

"Vichy —" Ben mocked softly.

Vichy smiled in spite of herself. "The price of a few dinners does not entitle you to a life history," she told him with prim severity.

"I haven't asked for your life history," Ben retorted sardonically. "Just your address."

"Fresno, California," Vichy lied promptly, blandly.

"You just said Pennsylvania," he sighed wearily.

"My parents live in Pennsylvania," Vichy explained blithely. "I'm visiting with them while I fulfill this engagement. I haven't been a resident of Pennsylvania for over eight years." That much was true; she hadn't been.

"Okay, what is your address in Fresno?" Ben asked doggedly.

Vichy hesitated, then shrugged, giving him her former address. It didn't matter anyway, she assured herself; she had not left a forwarding address with the superintendent or any of the other tenants at the apartment house.

Vichy watched as Ben entered the information into a small black leather address book, full, she felt sure, of a good number of female names and addresses. Every gambler she'd met — and there had been plenty in the few months she'd been with Brad — had all seemed to know scads of women, Brad included. It would appear, she thought bleakly, that gamblers liked variety in all the games they played. Vichy was unable to repress the shiver that shook her slim shoulders.

"Are you cold?" Ben asked at once.

"A little. It must be getting colder out, there's a draft creeping in under the windows." It wasn't a complete untruth. She *had* felt a draft from the windows.

"Then let's get out of here." He cast another glance at his watch. "I have to hit the road for home soon anyway."

They were almost back to the hotel before Ben broke the silence that had enveloped them since they'd left the diner.

"Are you going to be all right on your own tomorrow?" he asked concernedly.

After all the years of being alone, his solicitude was touching. The problem was, Vichy didn't want to feel touched — not by a gambler. Never, never by a gambler.

"Oh, I'll be lonely," Vichy admitted. "But, I assure you, I'll survive." Her short laugh held bitterness. "If nothing else, I am a survivor."

Ben shot her a sharp glance but, as they had reached the turn that led to the front of the hotel, he made no remark.

In less than five minutes after leaving the car, Vichy was standing before the door to her room, watching Ben unlock it, and flick on the light switch as the door swung in. He turned to her, and she felt her breathing become constricted.

Would he try a repeat performance of last night? Could she resist him if he did?

Did she really want to? *Yes! No. I don't know.* He was standing very close and the nearness of him was clouding her reasoning faculties.

As he lowered his head she did make a weak protest: "Ben, no . . ."

"Just a little kiss to see me on my way," he murmured an instant before his mouth touched hers. His lips remained unhardened by passion, and within moments he lifted his head. "I'll miss seeing you tomorrow," he whispered, caressing her cheek with the fingertips of one hand. "And I'll be back Friday, okay?"

Vichy nodded, fighting against the sudden heat in her eyes.

"Will you miss me?" His lips had replaced his fingers and the question was murmured close to her ear.

"Yes," she gasped, telling herself she was *not* aching for him to kiss her again, properly this time.

"Vichy," he groaned, then suddenly stepped back, away from her. "I've got to go, I promised Chad, but —" He took a half step toward her before becoming still. His sherry eyes seemed to burn over her face. "You'll be here?"

"Yes, of course." Vichy's voice wobbled with the riot of emotions coursing through her.

His hand, strangely unsteady, came up to

lift her face to his lowering one and he brushed his mouth roughly against hers.

"I'll see you Friday," he whispered. "Now, go inside before I change my mind and pull you into my arms."

He stood there, rigid with tension, until she'd closed and locked the door. Leaning back against the panel weakly, barely breathing, Vichy heard him curse softly before turning away.

Trembling with reaction, Vichy walked slowly, carefully to the bed. Sitting on the edge of the bed stiffly, hands clasped tightly on her lap, she stared sightlessly at the door, fighting the urge to jump up and run after him.

What was happening to her? she cried silently. What was he doing to her? She was not an impressionable teenager to be thrown off balance by the lightness of caresses. Yet that was exactly how she felt, off balance, unsure, near tears.

Dragging her fixed stare from the door, she lowered her eyes to her painfully clasped hands and her vision blurred. Glinting wickedly in the glare from the overhead light, the gold bracelet on her wrist seemed to wink mockingly at her.

A "winnings" gift. A shudder shook her hunched frame, and a soft moan went whispering into the still room.

In her parents' third-floor storeroom, at

the very bottom of one of her cartons, was a locked leather jewelry box. Inside that box were some dozen pieces of very expensive jewelry: rings, necklaces, bracelets, earrings, all "winnings" gifts. Vichy had turned the tiny key in the equally tiny lock on that box six years ago. She had not opened it since then. She could have sold the pieces. She could have given them away, for they meant nothing to her any longer. She had done neither for a very deliberate reason. She had kept the jewelry as a reminder of how little real value such things possessed when given without true affection. Brad had never really loved her. His baubles had been offered as an inducement. And from the moment she'd backed out of that hotel room they'd held no meaning for her.

Now another man, another gambling man, had tossed his winnings at a salesclerk in exchange for a shiny bauble. The very night before he'd told her bluntly that he wanted her. Was his gift yet another inducement?

A sob tore at Vichy's throat and she flung herself facedown on the bed. What was it about her that attracted these men? What was it about them that attracted her? For she was attracted to Ben Larkin, strongly attracted. It would be pointless to deny it, even to herself. She was worried —

no, terrified — that what she felt went beyond mere physical attraction.

Rolling into a ball of misery, Vichy cried herself to sleep.

Thanksgiving was just another day to be gotten through.

After waking, stiff and uncomfortable from sleeping in her confining clothes, Vichy set her chin at a determined angle and told herself, scathingly, that she had to go on. That resolution firmly set in her mind, she showered and dressed for her performance.

Surprisingly, there were more patrons in the lounge than Vichy had imagined there would be on a family holiday. Grateful for their attention, she psyched herself up to giving them the best performance she was capable of. The enthusiastic response of the customers sustained her through the seemingly endless hours between the start of her first set and the final number of her last. And all through the day, with every slightest movement of her wrist, she was reminded of Ben.

In a bid to put off having to face her empty room, Vichy joined her back-up musicians at the bar for a nightcap, much to the surprise of all four of them. They had issued the drink invitation every night, and every night Vichy had politely declined.

Seconds after she'd slid onto a barstool next to the drummer, she was left in little doubt that they were aware, to a man, of her reason for accepting this night.

"It's a bummer, isn't it?" the lead guitarist grumbled. Obviously, he never expected anyone to reply, for he muttered on, "This working every holiday is the pits."

"Yeah," the drummer concurred. "My working on holidays is about the only thing my old lady and I argue about." He paused, then laughed. "Except money, of course."

"What happened to the high roller who was putting the rush on you, Vichy?" The lead guitarist inquired in a bored tone.

Vichy stiffened, but somehow managed to keep her tone light.

"He went home to spend the holiday with his family." As she answered she slid off the barstool. The one thing she didn't need now were questions about the "high roller." Shaking her head at the drummer's offer of another drink, Vichy proffered her thanks for the one she'd had, wished them all a good night, and made her way reluctantly to her room.

Tired but not sleepy, Vichy had a hot, tension-easing shower, then, after slipping into a silky nightdress and matching robe, she curled up on the bed with the romance novel she'd bought in the hotel gift shop the previous Monday.

Vichy was at a very touching scene in the story when a light tap at her door startled her so badly that she dropped the paperback onto the floor. The tap sounded again and Vichy's eyes flew to the face of her small travel alarm. Eyes widening at the lateness of the hour, she swung her glance back to the door fearfully. Who in the world. . . .

"Vichy?"

Although the voice was pitched very low, there was no mistaking it, and with a smothered gasp of joy, Vichy scrambled off the bed and went running to open the door.

"Ben!" She gasped his name as she swung open the door, and that was as far as she got, for Ben leaned forward and placed his cool lips against hers.

Without breaking the contact, he backed her into the room, kicking the door closed behind him. A bulky, crackly object he was holding in his arms prevented Vichy from getting close to him. When he lifted his head, she saw he was holding a supermarket-size brown paper bag.

"What in the world?" As she raised her eyes from the bag to his face, her voice deserted her. Ben's sherry-colored eyes caressed her face and a knee-weakening smile curved his hard mouth into tenderness.

"This?" he prompted, rattling the bag. At her nod, he murmured, "I had a feeling you'd skip supper tonight. Was I right?" Again she nodded in answer, and his smile deepened. "This" — he held the bag aloft — "my beautiful songbird, is your Thanksgiving supper, complete with wine."

"But the time . . ." Vichy began laughingly.

"Means nothing," Ben inserted softly, "now that I'm here."

Vichy wanted to dispute his assertion, but in all honesty she could not. Nothing outside her small room held any meaning for her, now that he was here.

"But I have no table in here." Vichy laughed, indicating the lack of furniture with a wave of her hand.

Ben's eyes surveyed the room, then looked down at the beige carpet.

"So we'll have a Thanksgiving picnic," he decided, setting the bag on the floor and shrugging out of his overcoat.

Vichy's breath caught in her throat, as much from the look of him as from his suggestion. Always before, he'd been dressed rather formally in suits or a jacket, complete with dress shirt. Now he was wearing faded jeans that fit snugly around his slim hips and flat stomach and clung to his muscular thighs. An equally faded sweat shirt with a barely discernible college emblem on the front enhanced the width of his shoulders and the breadth of his muscled chest.

Tearing her gaze from him, Vichy squeaked, "A picnic? In here? How?"

"Do you have a clean bath towel?"

"Yes, but —"

"No buts," Ben overrode her protest. "Get the towel and leave the rest to me."

Vichy retrieved a large white towel from the bathroom and following Ben's ordered, "Spread it out on the floor next to the bed," she smoothed it out carefully, frowning all the while.

Dropping to his knees at the edge of the towel, Ben placed the bag beside him and proceeded to pull foil-wrapped packs from it, somewhat like a magician pulling rabbits from a hat. As he placed each item on the towel, he disclosed its contents.

"Turkey breast sandwiches. Lettuce. Sliced tomatoes. Pickles. Olives. Potato chips. The plastic container contains cole slaw. Plastic forks. Plastic knives. Paper plates. Paper napkins. Two real wine-glasses. And" — he paused for effect — "the pièce de résistance, a chilled bottle of pinot grigio."

Six

Vichy rested her back against the side of the bed and sighed with repletion. She had not even realized she was hungry, yet she had insisted Ben toss a coin to see who got the last half of the last turkey sandwich. She won the toss.

Vichy brought her glass to her lips and sipped her wine, gazing at Ben over the rim of the glass. He was stretched out on the floor across the towel from her, his fingers laced behind his head. From where she was sitting he looked long and slim and shatteringly attractive. Her gaze ran the length of him and back, coming to a crashing halt when her eyes met his.

"You have already eaten," he murmured teasingly.

"Wh—" Vichy had to clear her throat. "What do you mean?"

"That was a hungry look you cast over my person, songbird," he taunted. "Made me tingle — all over."

Incapable of coming up with a suitable

retort, Vichy lowered her eyes and took several deep swallows of the cool wine.

The atmosphere around them had undergone a none-too-subtle change. Up until now they had behaved like two carefree youngsters on an unexpected vacation.

Ben had teased and beguiled her by relating amusing, and highly colored, she was sure, incidents and misadventures of his growing-up years.

"My mother always insisted she was afraid to take her eyes off me for even a moment whenever I actively participated in any sport," he'd laughed in remembrance. "If I was playing basketball, and she happened to glance away from me for a second, when her eyes returned to the court, they invariably found me on the floor, usually all entangled with another player, fighting for possession of the ball." He'd grinned ruefully. "She always claimed I suffered more bruises, sprains, and broken bones than any six other boys."

"Played hard, did you?" Vichy laughed.

"Well, let's say I put everything I had into it," he conceded. "I remember one baseball game in particular," he'd reminisced. "Mother was in the stands, of course. I was defending first base, and I mean, I was *defending* first base. The batter hit a grounder to the second baseman and came galloping down the base line toward me. The second baseman scooped up the ball and made a wild toss over my head. I jumped for the ball and came down directly in the path of that charging runner."

"What happened?" Vichy asked breathlessly, completely caught up in his narrative.

"He charged right into me. He flew to the right of the line. I flew to the left." He shook his head. "Hell knows whatever happened to the ball! *I* wound up in the hospital with a fractured wrist and a mild concussion. Poor Mom. I'm sure I'm responsible for every gray hair on her head."

At that point Vichy had softened, for Ben had thrown back his head, laughing delightedly.

"Mom always said I'd get mine someday, and she was absolutely right. I have had Chad in the hospital emergency room so many times, we're all on a first-name basis."

"Sounds like the apple didn't fall far from the tree," Vichy had observed dryly, and then had become totally confused because he'd answered grimly, "I guess not." Then he'd immediately changed the subject, becoming lighthearted and amusing again.

Vichy could not remember when she'd

laughed so much at such ridiculous utterances, but it had been fun, and she'd enjoyed every minute of it.

Now, with one teasing thrust, Ben had created a charged awareness between them.

Gulping down the last of her wine, Vichy straightened up and began clearing away the debris from their impromptu picnic, all too aware of Ben's hooded eyes following her every move.

When the carpet between them was returned to normal, Ben caught her around the wrist and drew her down to the floor beside him.

"Ben, it's very late. I really think you should leave now." Suddenly nervous, Vichy tried to sit up. Ben simply rolled over and pinned her to the floor with his body. Startled, a little frightened, Vichy lay perfectly still, staring up at him.

"I've thought about you all day." Lowering his head, he brushed his lips back and forth across hers roughly, then blazed a trail of quick kisses to her ear.

"While I watched the Thanksgiving Day parade on TV with Chad, I thought about you," he murmured, circling the outer edge of her ear with his tongue.

"While I ate Shelly's delicious dinner, I thought about you." He nipped at her lobe, sending a shiver down her back.

"While I watched the football game with

Chad and Mike, I thought about you."

His voice was muffled against the side of her neck.

"And when I lay in bed, trying to sleep, I thought about you." His lips had found the wildly beating pulse in her throat, and his tongue was busy increasing its fluttering rate.

"You" — Vichy, her breath ragged, could barely articulate — "you were in bed for the night?"

"Oh, yes." Ben laughed softly. "Wanting to get an early start in the morning, I went to bed soon after I'd settled Chad for the night." His mouth climbed back up her neck to her ear. "It was a waste of time. I hadn't a hope in hell of sleeping. All I could think about was you and how much I wanted you there, beside me."

Fear, and all caution, gave way to the warmth invading Vichy's body. The scent of him muddled her thoughts, confusing her. The feel of his long body excited her past all reasoning. His murmuring voice touched a responding chord in her.

"I thought about you too."

His fingers twined in her hair and he turned her face to his.

"Hold me," he whispered. "Kiss me. Show me you missed me as much as I missed you."

Without pausing to think, Vichy curled

her arms around his tautly held neck and touched her mouth to his.

"Vichy."

Her name was groaned into her mouth and her lips were crushed beneath his.

The feel of his fingers tugging at the loop in her belt sent a momentary flash of sanity through her mind, and she tore her mouth away from the seduction of his.

"Ben, no!"

"I'm a man, Vichy, not a boy," he whispered harshly. "I don't turn on and off on command." Pulling back to break his gripping hold, he gave a final tug on the belt, then, with trembling fingers, separated the edges of her robe.

His sherry eyes, glittering with dark red shards of fire, burned their way over her quivering body, entirely visible through her filmy lingerie.

"You want me every bit as badly as I want you," he said raggedly, his eyes fastened on the thrusting tips of her breasts. Lowering his head slowly, he touched his lips to one hardened tip.

The flash of sanity was doused by a surge of sensual pleasure. His tongue, moving the sheer material over her aroused nipple, was exquisitely erotic, and, whimpering his name, Vichy arched her back to him.

She had surrendered, and he knew it.

Sliding one muscle-tightened leg over hers, he moved his body slowly, while his hand made a caressing path from her waist to her thigh. As if savoring the feel of her, he very carefully slipped his hand under the hem of her nightie and ran his palm up over her hip and across her quivering abdomen.

The warmth of his hand on her naked skin set off an alarm in Vichy's head. Cringing away from him, she moved her head restlessly back and forth on the hard floor.

"Ben, stop, I — I'm frightened," she cried softly.

"Frightened?" Ben's head jerked upright. "Vichy, you're a mature woman. You've been married, and there had to be another man over —"

"No!" Her frantic denial cut across his confused tone. "There have been no others. I couldn't let anyone touch me." A shudder shook her body.

"Good God," Ben muttered. Then, dipping his head to nuzzle her neck, he whispered, "How long has it been?"

"Almost six years," she admitted reluctantly.

"There is nothing to be frightened of," he crooned into her ear. "I won't rush you. I won't hurt you." Lifting his head, he ordered gently, "Look at me, Vichy."

"Ben, I —"

"Look at me."

His hand was moving again under her gown, stroking, soothing, coaxing softness back into her stiffened body. With a soft sigh Vichy turned her head and looked into his shadowed eyes.

"You want me," he whispered. "I know you do. And God knows I want you. Don't think of the past. Let it go. Wrap your arms around me and cling. I'll take you to a place where there is no fear or pain, only pleasure, for both of us."

The warmth of his voice melted the chill permeating her mind. His gentling hand re-awakened the sleeping tiger of need inside.

"Kiss me, Ben," Vichy sobbed, giving in to that growing need. "Love me. Take me to that place."

Vichy's first thought on waking was that it had to be midmorning, as the sunlight pouring through the room's single window was strong and brilliant. Her second thought was, *Good grief; I'm naked as a jay bird!*

Fully awake now, she became aware of the weight of an arm laying at an angle across the upper part of her body, and, more important, a warm hand cupping her breast.

Ben.

Memories of the hours she'd spent in his arms rushed into her mind and, sighing contentedly, Vichy closed her eyes, reliving them.

He'd promised her a place without fear or pain, and gently, tenderly, murmuring softly words without clarity but with infinite meaning, with his hands and lips and his lean, hard body, he'd kept his promise.

Vichy had visited that place many times before, of course, during the six months of her marriage to Brad, yet with Ben it had all seemed so very different, exquisitely new, unexplored.

Perhaps, Vichy mused dreamily, that place, that realm of the purely sensuous, was like a kingdom with many provinces, each a part of the whole, yet different. A whimsical smile curved her lips, and perhaps — she drew her thread of thought out fancifully each province had its own designated label — from ecstasy, through pretty good, all the way down to why bother? A bubble of laughter was tickling her throat when a stirring of movement beside her put an end to the fantasizing.

"Good morning."

Softly, his warm breath caressed the sensitive skin below her ear. Reacting instantly, Vichy moved closer to the lips that had released that breath.

"Good morning."

Turning her head a fraction, she touched those lips with her own.

"Did you rest well?" he asked, punctuating every word with a kiss on her mouth.

"Beautifully," Vichy gasped as his hand moved, palming renewed life into her breast. "Did you?"

"Beautifully," Ben mimicked, gasp and all, as her hand began a timid exploration through thc hair on his chest.

His hand moved, seeking, creating new, exciting sensations. Turning to him, Vichy deliberately brushed the tips of her sensitized breasts over his chest, to be immediately crushed against the hard flat plain.

"Did I make you happy?" he growled into the hollow at the base of her throat.

"Very," Vichy confessed softly, sliding her fingers into his crisp, auburn hair.

"Shall I make you happy again?" he invited, sotto voce.

"Yes, please."

The warm jet spray of water from the showerhead cascaded over her body, clearing her sleep-fuzzy mind. She had wakened, again, only moments before, gasping in disbelief as her glance came to rest on her small travel alarm. The day was more than half gone, and if she didn't hurry, she wouldn't even have time for a cup of coffee before going to work.

Stepping out of the tub, she dried her body carefully before pulling the showercap

381

off her head. With a single sharp shake of her head, she tossed the thick, dark mass of hair back off her face and, sitting on the closed toilet-seat cover, smoothed her way into sheer panty hose. Slipping into her robe, she pulled the belt tight, opened the door, and walked into the bedroom just as Ben was coming to life.

"Hi." He grinned, his sleep-clouded eyes roaming over her slowly.

"Hi, yourself," she grinned back, returning his encompassing glance with one of her own. Ensconced in the disgracefully rumpled bed, his body naked from the waist up, he looked infinitely inviting. Reminding herself of the time, Vichy tore her eyes from the lure of him and went to the dressing table to begin applying her makeup. Out of the corner of her eye, she saw him stretch contentedly.

"All that physical activity builds an appetite," he teased around a huge yawn. "I'm famished. What about you?"

"Mmmm," Vichy murmured, carefully blending blusher into the foundation over her cheeks. "I'm dying for a cup of coffee."

Leaning back, Vichy picked up her hairbrush, a frown creasing the smooth skin between her brows as she contemplated her tangled mop of hair.

"Bring that brush over here and let me do that," Ben ordered, pushing himself into a sitting position.

"Ben, the time!" Vichy protested unconvincingly.

"It's not going to take any more time if I do it or if you do it," he decided firmly. "Now get over here."

Sighing her defeat, Vichy crossed to the bed, avoiding his devilishly bright eyes. Handing him the brush, she sat down on the edge of the bed, her back to him.

With slow, gentle strokes, Ben smoothed the strands he'd tangled with his thrusting fingers into a gleaming curtain that framed her face and lay docilely over her shoulders.

"I love your hair," Ben said softly. "It reminds me of sweet dark chocolate." Leaning forward, he buried his face in her hair, drawing the clean scent of it in deeply. Then, parting it, he planted a shiver-causing kiss on the nape of her neck.

"I love dark chocolate."

A sharp pain jabbed searingly through Vichy's chest and she had to bite her lip to keep from crying aloud. How many times had he murmured the word *love* over the preceding hours?

"I love the feel of your skin under my hands," he had murmured at one point.

"I love the shape of your mouth," he'd whispered, outlining her lips with the tip of his finger.

"I love making love to you," he'd groaned as his breathing slowly returned to normal.

But never once had he committed himself with the words, *"I love you."*

Of course, it was much too soon. They had known each other less than a week. Vichy shivered as Ben bestowed another lingering kiss on her neck. The attraction between them was strong, very strong, but Vichy was long past the age of believing physical attraction indicated the presence of love.

Unsettled by her thoughts, Vichy moved away from the reason-clouding touch of his lips.

"What's the matter?"

Vichy didn't have to see his face to know he was frowning.

"Nothing."

She avoided her own eyes in the mirror. *Nothing, except that I'm very much afraid that I am in love, and I don't know quite how to handle it.*

"Why did you move away from me like that?" he demanded.

Vichy was not about to reveal her thoughts to him. She might be in love, but she was definitely not addlepated.

"I want a cup of coffee, Ben," she answered with forced easiness, "and I'm running out of time." Pulling the slipknot on her robe, she added, "Didn't you say something about being famished?"

It was not until the belt ends fell apart and the robe gaped open that Vichy remembered she had nothing on except sheer panty hose. *Oh, Lord,* she moaned silently, *why doesn't he go into the bathroom?* Hesitating with embarrassment, she slid him a quick, nudging glance.

"I thought you wanted a cup of coffee." he nudged back, letting her know he was well aware of why she hesitated.

"Ben, please."

"Of course, if you've changed your mind . . ." He ignored her plea, settling himself more comfortably. "Why don't you come back to bed for another half hour?" He held a corner of the covers away from the bed invitingly.

Impatience, frustration, and a flash of anger stiffened her spine. Not bothering to answer, she walked to the clothesrack on the wall. Keeping her back squarely to him, she slid the robe off her shoulders and let it drop to the floor.

"Turn around, Vichy."

It was a soft command, but it was definitely a command.

"Ben!"

"Turn around."

If anything, his voice was even softer, but the tone of command was harder.

Lifting her head proudly, Vichy slowly turned to face him, unable to control the flush of color that heated her cheeks.

Ben was silent as his eyes did a survey of her body from head to toe and back again. It was not till his eyes came back to her face that he saw her own eyes were closed.

"Look at me, Vichy," he ordered impatiently.

Vichy felt her face grow even hotter as she lifted her lids.

"You are a beautiful woman," he said emphatically. "There is no reason for you to feel embarrassed. Especially with me." A teasing smile twitched his lips. "Okay, you may get dressed now, but I fully intend watching you. I find watching a woman dress is one of the biggest turn-ons there is."

"Ben, really!" Vichy exclaimed, made even more embarrassed by his taunting revelation. His delighted laughter sent her spinning around to grasp blindly at the clothes hanging on the rack.

Luckily she grabbed the right garment and, nervously conscious of Ben's eyes watching her every move, fumbled and tugged her way into the dark apricot, form-hugging sliplike sheath. To complete the outfit, she stepped into bronze-toned sling-back, slim-heeled sandals. Smoothing her hair nervously, she turned to again face Ben.

"Sensational." He approved her choice warmly. Then, to her horror, he threw back the covers and leaped from the bed, his amusement-filled eyes leaving her in little doubt he fully expected her to avert her gaze. Rebellion rose and, clenching her hands, she forced herself to run her eyes over him in an outwardly cool appraisal.

God, he was gorgeous! Not an ounce of excess weight marred his tall, muscular frame. Did he still participate in sports? she wondered fleetingly.

"Well?" he prompted, working hard at keeping a straight face.

"Sensational," she managed to drawl shyly.

Once again the delightful sound of his laughter filled the small room.

"You're precious, you know that?" he asked when he could again speak. Knowing she wouldn't reply, he warned, "Get out of here while you still can, songbird. I'll meet you in the coffee shop in fifteen minutes flat."

Amazingly, he was not only on time, he was two minutes ahead of his promised fifteen. Having finished her juice, Vichy was munching on a toasted English muffin and sipping at her second cup of coffee when he joined her at the table.

"Is that all you're having to eat?" He frowned at her meager breakfast.

"I never eat a big breakfast," Vichy replied imperturbably, drinking in his freshly showered and shaved appearance. He was dressed casually in dark brown cords and a caramel-colored pullover with a brown stripe running across the shoulders and down the sleeves. The stripe accented the width of his shoulders, and Vichy had to repress a shiver at the memory of how the muscles had rippled under his smooth skin. The palm of her hand tingled at the remembered feel of him.

Vichy felt her cheeks warming up again and was grateful that Ben was busy studying the menu and had missed her loving perusal of him.

Lifting her cup, Vichy, suddenly parched, took several deep swallows, for loving was the only way to describe the way she felt when she looked at him. *Oh, boy, you have really walked straight into it this time,* she told herself bleakly. At twenty-two one can be forgiven for acting the fool. But, to engage in the same foolish impetuosity at twenty-nine one was to be pitied.

No, Vichy mentally shook her head, *I can't be in love — can I? It's nothing more than a case of blatant physical attraction — isn't it?* In an effort to escape answering her own questions, she glanced casually around the interior of the coffee shop and had to bite her lip to keep from gasping aloud at the flash of unfamiliar emotion that ripped through her entire being.

Through a haze she heard Ben ordering his breakfast and she lifted her gaze to the waitress's face. The girl's expression mirrored what Vichy had seen on the faces of several young women seated in the room; the expressions revealed overt interest in an attractive male, and that interest was directed at Ben.

Although the burning emotion she was feeling was unfamiliar, it was by no means unrecognizable. With a sigh smothered inside her cup, Vichy admitted that what she was experiencing was common, garden-variety jealousy. She also admitted that, yes, she was undoubtedly in love.

Suddenly needing to be away from Ben for a while, Vichy, finishing her now-unwanted coffee, placed the cup in its saucer and pushed back her chair.

"Hey," Ben protested quietly, "where are you going?"

"To work," Vichy answered, avoiding his eyes.

"But there's time yet." He shot a glance at his watch, frowning. "Why the sudden rush?"

"No rush," Vichy lied. "I'm having some difficulty with one of my numbers and I want to go over it with the guys."

Although his frown darkened, Ben accepted her hastily conjured explanation and rose to his feet. As she moved away from the table he caught her wrist.

"I'll see you later, okay?" he asked quietly, his gaze holding hers.

"Yes, of course," she began, then gasped, "Oh, Ben!" as he deliberately bent his head to kiss her on the mouth in full view of everyone. With his soft laughter burning her ears, Vichy fled the coffee shop and the curiously amused glances of its patrons.

The remaining hours of that day and night and the following one seemed to run through Vichy's fingers like precious grains of gold. She had told Ben of her intention of leaving for her parents' home early Sunday morning and, although he didn't seem too happy with the idea, he did not try to dissuade her.

Ben, sitting at the same table, was at every one of her performances, complimenting her quietly each time she finished and joined him.

On both nights he insisted she go with him early in the evening for a light snack between sets. And on both nights he took her to one of the restaurants in the hotel for a late supper. And on both nights he ignored his larger, expensive room in favor of hers.

They didn't talk much, but they held hands and touched a lot. Late Saturday night, hours after they'd returned to her small room, Ben broached the subject they had been studiously avoiding.

"Stay with me for the entire day tomorrow," he urged in a deep, growling tone. "There's no reason you have to be home earlier, is there?" He didn't wait for a response, however, pressing on. "And I don't have to be back on the job until Monday morning."

"You have a job?" Vichy blinked in sudden attention and surprise, believing, since Brad, that *all* gamblers worked at nothing but the odds.

"Well, of course I have a job!" Now it was Ben who stared in surprise. "I . . . ah . . ." His eyes took on a gleam of amusement. "I deal within the realm of probability, so to speak. Did you think I existed on a private income or something?"

"No, well, er . . ." Vichy stammered. "I don't know what I thought." She knew exactly what she'd thought; she just was not about to reveal assumptions to him now. And, anyway, he certainly had been unencumbered by employment all the past week.

"Uh-huh." He gave a slight shake of his head as if clearing it. "I assure you I do work." His tone scolded. "At any rate, I'll be involved in a new project starting Monday morning and that, combined with all the holiday plans Chad's made, which he filled me in on on Thanksgiving, means my time's going to be pretty limited as far as getting away before Christmas." He paused to nip at her lobe. "Sunday will be our last day together until after Christmas. Stay with me."

"But, Ben, I told my family I'd be home by noon," Vichy explained. "Besides, I really would prefer not to drive home at night."

"All right, I can understand that," he conceded. "But you could stay until early afternoon. If you waited to leave until after we've had lunch together, you'd still be home before it got dark. It shouldn't take you more than three hours at the outside to drive to Lancaster."

As he had interspersed the request in between light kisses, dropped at random over her face and around her lips, Vichy, her senses going haywire, gave in. Early Sunday morning Ben made love to her so fiercely it bordered on violent. Murmuring husky words she could barely hear, but really didn't have to, caressing her in a manner that brought her to the edge of exquisite pain, he defined, in action, the word *ecstasy* for her.

For all they tried to hold on to the hours

of Sunday morning, lunchtime came and passed, and the moment arrived when she could not put off her departure any longer. Ben carried her valises to the hotel entrance and relinquished them to an employee before turning to her to grasp her hands.

"You'll be here the day after Christmas?" His voice had a harsh, strained sound.

"Yes," Vichy whispered, feeling strained to the limit herself.

"So will I," he promised. Bending his head, he kissed her very gently on the lips, then, releasing her hands, he stepped back. "Merry Christmas, Vichy. I'll see you in four weeks."

"Yes," Vichy said again. Then, throwing caution to the wind, she stepped to him, placed her parted lips against his muscle-knotted hard jaw, and whispered, "Merry Christmas to you and Chad, Ben," and, turning away quickly, hurried to her car.

It didn't strike her until she was an hour out of Atlantic City that she had completely forgotten to ask him what kind of job he had.

Seven

All the way home Vichy had to fight the desire to turn around and go back to Ben. But she knew she would not turn around. She also knew it would be pointless if she did, for Ben had told her that he would be leaving himself as soon as he packed his things and paid his bill. Nonetheless, the urge persisted.

The day had started out crisp and clear, but by lunchtime wisps of smoky gray clouds had moved in to dot the expanse of blue sky. The farther west Vichy drove, the more overcast it became.

She was less than five miles from home when it started to rain. At that point she ceased berating herself for not giving in to Ben's plea that she stay with him for the entire day. She didn't particularly enjoy driving at night when she had any real distance to cover, and she particularly disliked driving in the rain.

Vichy allowed herself a long sigh of relief when she turned into the private lane that led to her parents' home. As she had a few weeks previously, Bette came out to the car to greet her.

"Hi," she called, skipping down the porch's three steps. "You're just in time for supper. How did the engagement go?"

"Very well, actually." Vichy smiled. "Better than I expected."

Opening the trunk, she removed her cases before adding, "The back-up group was first rate" — her smile spread into a grin — "it made me sound good."

"Baloney," Bette snorted, grasping one of the cases. "You always did sound good to me."

"Yes, but you're just a wee bit biased." Vichy laughed as they stepped under the protection of the covered porch.

"That does not preclude my being objective," Bette retorted, holding the door open for Vichy to enter first.

"Perish the thought that a college junior would be anything but objective," Vichy teased.

They were laughing companionably when their father came out of the kitchen.

"What is this?" he asked the room at large, "the giggle hour?" When the only reaction he received were two wide smiles, he grinned in return. "Hearing you two laughing together again sounds good," he admitted, taking Vichy into his arms.

"Welcome home, honey." He greeted her warmly, when at last he released his tight hold. "How did it go?" He echoed Bette's question.

"A piece of cake." Vichy laughed with the realization that she'd receive the same query from her mother. "I'll tell you all about it during supper." *Except for a few details,* she qualified mentally, *which I intend to hug to myself.*

As Vichy had expected, the first words out of her mother's mouth were, "Did everything go all right?"

As they consumed the usual Sunday night fare of homemade soup and sandwiches, Vichy outlined her week for them, then, as none of them had been to Atlantic City, she culled forth as many details as she could remember about the glitzy atmosphere.

Over coffee and her mother's out-of-this-world, wet-bottom shoe-fly pie, her mother shot a frowning glance at the window, now streaming with water from the rain that had become a downpour.

"I hope this rainstorm isn't the front-runner of a cold spell," she observed worriedly. "I was keeping my fingers crossed for the mild weather to hold through next weekend."

"Why?" Vichy asked idly. "What's happening next weekend?"

"Josh and his family are coming down for the day next Sunday," her mother explained. "He's going to help Dad put up the outside Christmas lights."

"Won't that be fun?" Bette cried, her eyes fairly twinkling. "A whole day of rotten Robert."

"Now, Bette, stop it," her mother scolded, fighting a smile. "Your nephew is not rotten. He's just — well — more boy then most."

Her mother's description of her grandson sent a memory whispering through Vichy's mind.

She always claimed I suffered more bruises, sprains, and broken bones then any six other boys.

Had Ben, she wondered dreamily, been the same as rotten Robert at the age of five? Vichy had to repress a soft trill of laughter. It was darn near impossible to imagine the austere-faced Ben as a holy terror of a little boy. But, on the other hand, Vichy mused on, he had displayed a devilish facet of his character more then a few times since Thanksgiving night.

"Are you falling asleep at the switch, Vich?"

Bette's quip corraled her wandering attention and, blinking away the memories, Vichy smiled in apology.

"Sorry." Her glance encompassed the

three others at the table. "I'm a little tired. As soon as I've helped with the cleaning up, I think I'll go up to bed."

"You don't have to help. I, being the absolute sweetheart that I am, will do the cleaning up," Bette offered magnanimously. "You can go up to bed now, if you like," she went on. "I will even lug one of your valises up for you."

"Oh, Bette, you are just too good to be true," Vichy praised straight-faced. "The only possible reward must be canonization."

"I've thought the same myself," her mother concurred, getting into the act. "Many, many times."

"Good Lord," Luke groaned. "Spare me a house of flighty females." He fixed a blue-eyed stare on first his wife and then Vichy. "Two of which are old enough to know better." Shaking his shock of white hair sadly, he headed for the living room, mumbling, "I guess the only escape around here is the Sunday paper."

Vichy, Johanna, and Bette exchanged glances, then collapsed into a fit of laughter, like three teenagers.

After she finished unpacking her suitcase, Vichy slid between the covers on her single canopied bed, and lay staring up at the frilly "roof," as she'd called it when she was a little girl, missing Ben more than she would have believed possible.

What was he doing now, this minute? she wondered longingly. And, belatedly, where exactly was he doing it? She had never gotten around to asking him where his home was. His casually mentioned "central New Jersey" had been less then concise. But, come to that, she had never corrected the erroneous information she'd given him either. As far as Ben knew, she made her home in California. He didn't even have her parents' phone number!

Talk about ships passing in the night! Vichy sighed aloud. It certainly didn't bode too well for any kind of lasting relationship.

Nevertheless, whether wisely or unwisely, Vichy harbored the hope of a lasting relationship in her heart.

The day after Christmas. The words, like a silent prayer, skipped in and out of Vichy's mind. Her last thought before falling asleep was that not since she was a little girl had she wished for Christmas to hurry up and come.

Vichy had been sure the days would pass with grinding slowness but, thanks to her mother, they did not.

With no place to go and nothing to do, Vichy dressed in jeans and a rather shapeless baseball jersey Monday morning. When she walked into the kitchen, she was glad she had. Her mother, dressed in sweats and an old flannel shirt of her father's, sleeves rolled to the elbow, was standing on a ladder, cleaning the paneling.

The kitchen looked like it had been struck by a minitornado. The windows looked naked without their curtains. The chairs had been pushed into one corner, and the clock and other decorations that had hung on the wall now littered the table. Stunned by the upheaval, Vichy asked the obvious.

"Mother, what are you doing?"

"Dancing," Johanna returned placidly.

Vichy grinned appreciatively. At sixty her mother's sense of humor was every bit as keen as it had been at thirty. Johanna's eyes twinkled as she returned Vichy's grin.

"There's juice in the fridge, raisin bread in the bread drawer, and coffee in the pot. Help yourself." With that she turned back to the wall.

After clearing and wiping a corner of the table and retrieving a chair, Vichy dropped two slices of raisin bread into the toaster and poured herself a small glass of juice. Standing at the refrigerator, she sipped the juice and frowned worriedly at her mother's back. "You shouldn't be up there," she advised.

"It's the only way I can reach the top,"

Johanna retorted dryly, then, turning to face her daughter. chided gently, "I'm not decrepit, you know."

"I know," Vichy shook her head in wonder. "You can work rings around most people half your age, but it makes me nervous to see you up there." She smiled coaxingly. "Why don't you come down and have a cup of coffee with me? Then, after I've eaten, I'll do the paneling."

Vichy and Johanna spent that entire week housecleaning. From the kitchen they proceeded to the dining room, and from there the rest of the house, up to and including the third floor. By Saturday morning Vichy's respect for her mother had grown to near awe. Seldom-used muscles Vichy hadn't even known she possessed complained achingly from abuse, while her mother, who had not only kept pace with Vichy, but had blazed the way, bustled around getting breakfast as if she'd never heard the word *housecleaning*.

"You look like you've had a hectic week of debauchery," Bette, who had escaped the week's arduous labor by hiding out at school, teased when Vichy entered the kitchen. "Mom would make a great field marshal, wouldn't she?"

"A little hard work never hurt anyone," Johanna said blandly from the stove, where she was frying scrapple for break-fast. "*You* can set the table, young lady," she told Bette, then, "Vichy, go to the door and give your father a yell. He's out in the barn."

Feeling as though she should tiptoe over the tile floor so as not to mar its freshly waxed beauty, Vichy did as she was told, fully enjoying the sensation of time having slipped back to when she was a young girl.

Sunday dawned bright, clear, and mild. At mid-morning the quiet serenity of the house was shattered by the arrival of Josh, his wife Caroline, and rotten Robert.

As she clasped the five-year-old's body to her in a brief, welcoming hug, Vichy assured herself that Robert was not rotten, simply more curious than most.

By late afternoon her own assurances had been sorely tested. Robert had managed to get into just about everything, keeping not only his mother but Vichy and Johanna running after him. Bette, having gone out with a friend after dinner, had once again escaped.

As soon as it was dark enough for the lights to be turned on, they all trooped outside to admire Luke and Josh's decorative handiwork. And, as if on cue, they all sighed appreciatively at the magical quality the strings of staggered red and white lightbulbs gave to the house.

"I can't believe there are less than three weeks left till Christmas," Caroline groaned as they drifted back into the house. "I have *so* much to do yet to get ready for it, and I know the weeks are going to fly by too quickly."

For you maybe, Vichy replied silently. *But, for me, the weeks will seem to drag by.* Suddenly afraid her yearning to see Ben, be with him, would overwhelm her if she didn't do something, Vichy hung her sweater in the living room closet, then hurried into the kitchen to begin preparing supper.

"Seeing the house lit up gave me an idea," Josh said over his hot roast beef sandwich during supper. "After we've finished eating, why don't we all drive to the Christmas Village in Bernville? Robert would love it."

Robert would not be the only one, Vichy thought in amusement. Unlike many men, Josh did not suffer through the frantic preparations for the holidays. He loved every minute of it, and his enthusiasm was contagious.

"That sounds like fun." Luke agreed at once, thereby revealing from whence came Josh's love for the trappings of the season. "I'll even let Vichy drive," he added teasingly.

"You're much too good to me," Vichy

responded to his teasing dryly. "But, you're right, it does sound like fun. It must be at least fifteen years since I was up there."

"You're in for a pleasant surprise," Bette, having arrived home just in time to sit down for supper, joined in.

"I was up last year with a couple of the kids and it's really been enlarged. The night we were there, there were at least twenty tour buses parked in the lot."

Bette's assertion was proved when Vichy, Bette in the seat beside her, her parents in the back, followed Josh's station wagon up to the crest of a small hill on the country road from where they got their first glimpse of the brightly lit tourist attraction.

It was not a real village, but a miniature one, with small houses and pathways all gaily decorated and illuminated, all of it on the private property of a farmer who began it as a hobby and wound up with an attraction that drew crowds of people every year.

Strolling the arrow-marked lanes, smiling at Robert's delight in the life-size cutouts of cartoon and Disney characters, Vichy suddenly ached to be walking, arm-in-arm — in exactly the same way Josh and Caroline were — with Ben, both of them smiling as Chad eagerly ran to view each new sight.

Which was pretty silly, she admitted ruefully, considering she'd never even seen as much as a picture of Ben's son. Nevertheless, the ache persisted the entire length of time required to see everything.

Vichy was ready for a hot cup of coffee when, cold and rosy-checked, they entered the building with a lunch counter. The room was crowded with tourists, and as she waited her turn at the counter, Vichy glanced at the clock on the wall in disbelief. They had been strolling around for nearly two hours! No wonder Robert had coaxed to be picked up and carried. And now she could appreciate Caroline's forethought in putting Robert's pajamas on him under his snowsuit. With approximately an hour's drive home, Robert would be ready to be tucked into bed if he fell asleep on the way home, which, from the look of his droopy-lidded eyes, he would.

After giving and receiving good-bye hugs and kisses in the parking lot, they went their separate ways. By the time Vichy pulled into her parents' driveway, she was wishing she had on her own nightwear.

The hours of the second week were every bit as full as the first week had been. With the housecleaning out of the way, Johanna declared her intention of getting down to the serious business of baking Christmas cookies.

For the better part of that week Vichy

and Johanna kept busy sifting, mixing, rolling, or dropping by spoonfuls. Luke contributed by shelling nuts, chopping candied fruits, and telling endless anecdotes.

The centerpiece of fall foliage and the delicate lace tablecloth were removed from the dining room table to be replaced by a worn but clean, plain cotton cloth in preparation to receive the mounds of cookies as they came from the oven.

By Thursday, the square, solid table had been covered, then cleared many times of its light burden of crisp cutout cookies, buttery melt-in-the-mouth sand-tarts, chocolatey-rich Toll House, fruit-and nut-filled Michigan rocks, and many others in all shapes and sizes.

Vichy had not helped with the Christmas baking since the winter she was nineteen, and she loved every minute of it.

By the time Bette came home from the college she attended in Reading, every room in the house was redolent with baking odors. The minute she walked into the house, Bette put into words what Vichy was feeling.

"Mmmmmmm, it smells Christmasy in here. Makes me feel like a little girl again, all excited, and wishing for the days to fly by."

Of course, Vichy's Christmas wishing had nothing to do with visions of sugar plums, or elaborately wrapped packages. Her visions revolved around a tall, lean form, a pair of strong, enfolding arms, and a well-shaped mouth that could drive all other visions from her mind.

Friday evening she sat at the kitchen table with her mother, boxes of Christmas cards between them. While her mother signed the cards and Vichy addressed the envelopes, Johanna filled her in on what had been happening in their many friends' lives since Vichy had been home last.

That weekend the four of them, Johanna, Luke, Bette, and Vichy, decorated the inside of the house. Kitchen, dining room, and living room all received their share of a variety of ornaments from homemade to "store boughten," as her father described them. Every carton of decorations was emptied except the one containing the tree ornaments, as the tree would not be put up until the week before the big day.

The Monday of the third week, almost as if her mother somehow sensed Vichy's need to keep busy, Johanna announced over breakfast that she was ready to start her Christmas shopping.

Luke responded with a loud, exaggerated groan. Although he fully enjoyed decorating, baking, and even wrapping the gifts, Luke Sweigart hated the shopping necessary for all of them.

"Relax, dear," Johanna advised serenely. "You're off the hook this year. Vichy and I will do the shopping." She raised questioning brows at Vichy, who nodded her silent agreement. "All *you* have to do," she went on sweetly, "is provide the money."

"There's always a catch," her father grumbled, laughing.

The morning was bright and sunny, but there was a definite chill in the air that warned of approaching winter. As she walked to the car, Vichy drew a deep breath, and when she released it, a small vapor cloud formed in front of her.

"Where to, madame?" Vichy asked her mother after they were seated in the car.

"We'll start in Lancaster," Johanna answered blandly, giving no hint of the miles Vichy would cover before the end of that week.

Driving toward Lancaster and its large shopping mall, Vichy's eyes caressed the countryside she'd grown up in. The fields, some dull brown, some with a dark yellow stubble from last summer's crop, lay resting and waiting for spring, and the expertise of the world-renowned Pennsylvania Dutch farmers to bring them to pulsing, green life.

Near the turnoff road to Lititz, Vichy carefully passed a box-shaped, black, horse-drawn buggy, the occupants of which were attired in the traditional dark Amish garb.

"They're still risking life and limb in those things, I see," Vichy observed, shaking her head.

"Yes," Johanna replied quietly. "It's their way. But I'm sorry to say that with the crazy way some people drive today, they are struck with increasing regularity."

Shifting a quick glance to the buggy's reflection in the rearview mirror, Vichy smiled sadly. *It's really a shame,* she mused, *for, probably more than anything or anyone else, these people and their picturesque conveyances are the trademark of eastern Pennsylvania.*

Vichy and Johanna began what turned out to be a shopping marathon in downtown Lancaster. By the time the week, and Vichy, had waned, they had combed the area. Collapsed into the overstuffed living room chair Friday evening, Vichy recounted their stops for Bette.

"After we'd plumbed the possibilities of Lancaster's shopping district, we buzzed over to Park City and spent the remainder of the day, and a fair amount of money, there." Vichy sighed. "Tuesday we drove to Reading," she went on, to Bette's amusement. "Not only did we hit just about every one of the city's outlet stores, but we also shopped at both the Berkshire Mall and the Fairgrounds Square Mall, on the outskirts of Reading, as well."

As, at this point, Bette was nearly convulsed with laughter, Vichy cut through the rest of her long list of places she and Johanna had stopped at, to end on a groan. "And do you believe we even drove all the way up to Allentown and the Lehigh Shopping Mall?"

"Of course I believe it," Bette laughed. "I went through the same leg-killing routine last year. But, 'fess up, it's fun shopping with Mom, isn't it?"

"Yes, it is," Vichy admitted, laughing with her. "I enjoyed every footsore minute of it. And, everywhere we went, the Christmas decorations were absolutely beautiful."

What Vichy did not admit were the number of times she caught herself thinking a particular article was perfectly suited to Ben. Should she, she'd wondered repeatedly, buy some small gift to give him on the day after Christmas?

In the end she gave in to the desire to give him something, and bought him a gold money clip, fashioned in a dollar sign.

Saturday evening Luke fastened a six-foot blue spruce into a metal tree stand, and within hours its aromatic scent permeated the entire first floor of the house.

Directly after the Sunday dinner dishes were dispensed with, Luke, Bette, and Vichy, following Johanna's expert supervision, trimmed the tree.

Vichy remained downstairs for some time after her parents and Bette retired for the night.

With a glass of white wine and a CD of Fred Waring's Pennsylvanians singing carols on the stereo for company, she sat curled up in one corner of the wing-back Early American sofa, staring dreamily at the glittering tree. As had happened on her first night home from California, haunting voices from yesteryear came stealing into her mind, drawing her back in memory to previous Christmases.

"Mattie, if you don't hurry up, we're going down without you," an eight-year-old Josh yelled through the bathroom door as he fairly danced back and forth in the upstairs hallway early Christmas morning. Vichy, every bit as excited and eager to go downstairs as Josh, sat squirming on the top step of the living room stairway. It was out of the question that any one of them would venture downstairs alone on Christmas morning. They always waited for each other and went down together. At five, Vichy could have no idea that the thirteen-year-old Mattie was deliberately stalling in the bathroom to give their father time to plug in the tree lights and get the camera ready to catch their expressions at their first glimpse of the pile of gifts under the tree.

"That's the most beautifulest tree ever." The awe-filled voice belonged to a four-year-old Bette. She had come to a dead stop at the foot of the stairs. Vichy, Josh, and Mattie lined up behind her in that order. It had been her first sight of the tree, because up until the time she no longer believed in Santa Claus, the tree was not put up till after Bette was sound asleep Christmas Eve.

"Oh, Tom, it's absolutely beautiful," an eighteen-year-old Mattie whispered in a tear-choked tone as she gazed misty-eyed at the diamond engagement ring her future husband had presented to her in front of the whole Sweigart clan on Christmas day.

Vichy blinked, and the tiny, shimmering lights came back into focus. Brushing impatiently at the moisture on her cheeks, she drank deeply from her stemmed glass. She had felt on the edge of tears all day, without knowing why, and now she told herself the tearful feeling was caused by the season and the realization of time slipping away.

Vichy had never been a regular-as-clockwork, every-twenty-eight-days female. And so it was that she, foolishly, had given scant notice when her cycle date passed early in the previous week. Her mother had kept her so busy, she had hardly had the time to do any counting, but she should have.

The final days before Christmas were filled to overflowing with wrapping of gifts and visiting friends and neighbors Vichy hadn't seen in over a year. The house rang with laughter the day before Christmas with the unexpected arrival of not only Mattie, Tom, and Brenda, but a glowingly lovely Nan and her obviously proud husband Mitch.

When, soon after supper, with hugs and kisses and cries of "Merry Christmas," they departed for Williamsport, Vichy again had to blink against the onrush of tears.

Christmas morning was a quiet time. The gifts under the tree went unopened as, by mutual agreement, they awaited the lunchtime appearance of Josh and his family.

The afternoon and evening was something else again. Once more laughter prevailed as Robert, being the center of everyone's attention, frolicked his way through the remainder of the day.

As swiftly as the day flew by, the hours

could not pass fast enough for Vichy who, at least a hundred times during the day and evening, found herself thinking: *To-morrow, I'll see Ben tomorrow.*

Eight

Ben.

His name was the first thing that popped into Vichy's mind on awakening the morning after Christmas.

Forcing down the desire to toss her clothes into her suitcases and jump into her car, Vichy joined her family at the breakfast table.

"Won't you change your mind about leaving today?" her mother asked from the stove, where she was stirring her father's favored oatmeal. "Uncle John and Aunt Katie are going to be very disappointed if we arrive without you."

"Not to mention Mark," Bette added slyly.

"By all means, let's not mention Mark," Vichy drawled teasingly. Bette laughed and, although she tried hard not to, Vichy laughed with her.

"Now, girls," Johanna scolded gently. "Don't be unkind. Mark is a very nice young man."

"But dull." Bette grinned.

Ignoring Bette, Johanna went on, "He's a conscientious, hard worker —"

"With both feet planted firmly in cement," Bette inserted, her grin widening.

Turning from the stove, Johanna leveled a quelling glance on Bette before plowing ahead. "Mark is kind and considerate. He's a good son, and will make a good husband and father."

"If dull," Bette, braving her mother's look, passed judgment. "And old dull Mark has been wacko over Vichy forever."

With a sigh Johanna turned back to her pot of oatmeal. Vichy hid behind her small glass of juice. Neither one of them dared challenge Bette's statement, simply because they both knew it was true. Mark Hartman had been "wacko" over Vichy, if not forever, almost as long as Vichy could remember. And, although every word of praise Johanna had uttered was true, Bette's judgment was also true; Mark was dull.

There was no blood relationship between the Sweigart and Hartman families. Luke Sweigart and John Hartman had grown up on neighboring farms and were lifelong friends. The titles of Uncle and Aunt were honorary ones, and worked both ways. To Mark Hartman, Vichy's parents were Aunt Johanna and Uncle Luke.

Mark, at thirty-five, was as set in his ways as a man twenty years his senior. Being the only Hartman offspring, he had been babied and cosseted by an overprotective mother every one of those thirty-five years.

Vichy had a sisterly affection for Mark, and it saddened her to admit that he could be summed up in one condescending condemnation: Mark never went out in the rain without his raincoat, umbrella, and rubbers. In a word — dull.

"I'm sorry, Mother —" Vichy began belatedly, only to be interrupted by her father, as he entered the kitchen through the back door.

"Sorry about what?" he asked, his glance shifting from Vichy to Johanna as he shrugged out of his plaid jacket.

"I've asked Vichy to reconsider her decision to leave for Atlantic City today," Johanna answered for Vichy. "I know John, Katie, and Mark are going to be very disappointed if we arrive there without her."

"There" being the large farm John owned in Bucks County, for which Johanna, Luke, and Bette were planning to depart directly after breakfast.

"I know they'll be disappointed," Luke agreed, but then, in defense of Vichy's decision, added, "but I can understand Vichy wanting to leave today. By going today she won't feel rushed."

"Exactly," Vichy jumped in, relieved at having found an ally. "If I wait until tomorrow, I'll have only a few hours to settle in before I start working. If I go today, I can take my time, both driving down there and settling in," she explained patiently, for what seemed like the twentieth time. "I can have a good night's sleep and be fresh to start working tomorrow."

What Vichy did not say was that, short of a major family catastrophe, nothing was going to keep her from meeting Ben today as planned.

"May as well give up, Mom," Bette advised. "Poor old Mark will just have to grin and bear his disappointment." She tossed Vichy a look of pure devilry before quipping, "That is, if he knows how to grin."

"That is more than enough out of you, Bette Sweigart!" Johanna exclaimed. "I thought you liked Mark."

"I do!" Bette defended herself, choking against the laughter bubbling in her throat.

"She's baiting you, Johanna," Luke said quietly, pausing in the act of spooning oatmeal into his mouth. "If you're lucky, and you ignore her, maybe she'll go away."

"How can I possibly ignore someone who is mostly all mouth?" Johanna inquired sweetly.

"O-kay." Bette grinned unrepentantly.

"I'll shut up. I can take a hint."

The subject was changed and the rest of the meal was finished companionably. The name *Hartman* was not spoken again until Vichy mentioned it when her parents and Bette were ready to leave.

"Give Uncle John and Aunt Katie and Mark my love," she requested of her mother. "And tell them I promise I'll visit them early in the new year."

Finally, after assuring her mother for the third time that she would drive carefully, Vichy was alone. Turning from the door, she ran up the stairs and into her room to pack. Glancing at the small travel alarm by her bed, she calculated that if she could be ready to leave within the hour, she could be in Atlantic City by lunchtime.

Would Ben be there when she arrived? she wondered as she hurried back and forth between her closet and the open suitcases on her bed. What if he didn't show up at all? Vichy stopped dead halfway between her large double dresser and the bed. He would show up. He had to show up! Vichy bit her lip at the intensity of the anxiety that rushed over her.

She had not seen him in four weeks, yet just thinking about him made her tremble all over. Was it possible to fall so deeply in love in such a short time? Vichy was very much afraid that it was not only possible, but it was exactly what had happened to her. What scared her was knowing full well she had fallen head over heels in love very quickly once before. She had paid, painfully, for her impetuousness that time. Would she have to pay again?

Shaking herself out of her reverie, Vichy resumed her packing. Except for the fact that they both enjoyed gambling, there was no comparison between the two men. In complete opposition to Brad, Ben was mature, settled, and secure in the life he'd made for himself.

He'll be there, Vichy assured herself, beginning to hum snatches of a Christmas song she'd heard repeatedly over the previous week.

Vichy wasn't on the road too long before she decided that everyone and his brother were making Christmas visits. Although the traffic was heavy on the Pennsylvania Turnpike, it moved at a steady, even flow and she was making good time until she left the Turnpike and got onto the bypass around Philadelphia. The bypass was bumper-to-bumper with cars, and every one of those bumpers was attached to a machine with a horn. It seemed to Vichy that at least half of those horns were being leaned on by irate drivers.

By crawling, inching, and softly cursing, Vichy finally reached the Walt Whitman

Bridge over the Delaware. After she'd crossed the bridge and driven onto the Atlantic City Expressway, the traffic was moving in an even flow again and Vichy was able to maintain the speed limit straight into Atlantic City.

After making her presence known to the management, Vichy went to the same small room she'd occupied four weeks previously and began unpacking, jumping in expectation at every sound of movement in the hallway.

Now what? Her unpacking finished, Vichy stood indecisively in the middle of the room. Had Ben arrived? Was he, at that moment, in his own room unpacking?

Just the thought that Ben could be that close set her pulses hammering and, unable to stay still another minute, Vichy smoothed the sides of her hair, which she'd coiled back into a neat chignon that morning, applied a fresh coat of shimmering gloss to her lips, then, scooping up her handbag, left the room.

The lobby was an absolute madhouse. Vichy could barely see the carpeting for the mass of humanity that filled the large area, After making her way to the desk, with repeated pleas of "Excuse me, please" and "Pardon me," she waited her turn with forced patience until the harried clerk glanced at her, a warm smile curving his lips in response to her own.

"May I help you?"

"Yes, thank you." Vichy hesitated, then rushed on. "Do you have a Mr. Bennett Larkin registered?"

"Larkin," he repeated, his eyes making a quick, expert perusal of the computer screen. "No, ma'am, no Larkin. I'm sorry."

No Larkin. Vichy repeated the words dully to herself, shocked at the feeling of desolation that swept through her. Biting on the inside of her lower lip, she made a half turn away, then, on inspiration, turned back to the clerk. "Could you tell me if you're holding a reservation for Mr. Larkin?"

"Just a moment." He brought up another screen and scanned it quickly. His answer was written on his sympathetic expression.

"I'm sorry, but I have no reservation under that name."

"I see." Forcing her lips into a semblance of a smile, Vichy murmured, "Thank you," and walked away from the desk aimlessly.

Ben was not here, and he was not coming. The phrase, circling around in Vichy's head, affected the nerves in her stomach. She felt sick, and suddenly very, very tired.

Moving without purpose through the

crush of laughing people, she fought a silent battle against the overwhelming urge to weep like an abandoned child. It was not until she noticed the odd glances being sent her way that Vichy, straightening her spine, made a concentrated effort to pull herself together.

Coffee! Find someplace that you can get a cup of coffee. Vichy admonished herself sharply. *And don't you dare cry!*

Vichy made a beeline for the nearest restaurant. She ordered coffee then, as a tiny frown made an appearance above the haughty waiter's slightly hooked, long nose, added weakly that she'd have a chef's salad with the house dressing as well.

Ignoring the salad, she sipped at her coffee while trying to calm her rioting thoughts. Ben's last words to her had been, "I'll see you in four weeks." So, where was he? Had something happened to detain him? Or, and here she winced, hadn't he meant to keep his promise to join her today?

Vichy motioned the waiter to refill her cup and suffered the grimace he aimed at her untouched salad.

"The salad is not to your liking, ma'am?" he asked through lips that looked like they'd been sucking a lemon.

"The salad is fine, thank you." Vichy sighed, half tiredly, half exaggeratedly, picking up her fork. "Don't go away mad," she pleaded bitchily. "Just go away, please."

The affronted waiter withdrew stiffly, and, pushing the salad around with her fork, Vichy went back to thinking of the cause of her anguish — one Bennett Larkin. Dammit, where was he?

Possibly signing in at another hotel this very minute! Vichy brightened at this new thought. Of course! What an absolute nit she was being. She had seen for herself on her way in how crammed full the city was. The possibility was very real that Ben had been unable to secure a room in this hotel. But that did not preclude the possibility that he'd booked into another hotel.

Her reasoning had the effect of not only lightening her mood, but of sharpening her appetite as well. Suddenly hungry, Vichy dug into her salad. When she lifted her cup to drain the last of her coffee, the light became tangled in her gold bracelet, causing the metal to glitter as if it were winking at her. At least that was the whimsical thought that sprang into her mind with the reflecting gleam.

Hiding her smile behind the cup, Vichy told herself that she had no more sense than a teenager, yet her optimism was restored to the point that she bestowed a brilliant smile on the now-confused waiter as she paid her check and left the restaurant.

Vichy stayed in her room all day, doggedly hanging on to her optimism as the day waned. At seven, her confidence slipping rapidly, she left her room long enough to have a quick meal. She was gone less than an hour, and after she returned she paced restlessly, berating herself for her lack of pride. It would have been obvious to everyone but a besotted fool that he simply was not going to show up, she told herself scathingly. And still she paced — waiting, waiting, waiting.

A few minutes after ten, tired, yet unable to sit still, Vichy stamped into the bathroom to brush her teeth before making an attempt at going to bed. *You just don't learn, do you?* She chided her reflection in the mirror above the sink as she scrubbed her mouth with her toothbrush. *Men, in general, are not to be trusted,* she advised her bleak-eyed image, *and gamblers more so than most.*

She was wiping her lips with a hand towel when she heard the light tap on the door.

"Vichy?"

Ben! The hand towel dropped to the floor — and her own advice dropped from her consciousness — unnoticed as Vichy went running out of the bathroom as if the skirt of her robe were on fire.

She wasted several precious seconds fumbling with the lock, and then she pulled the door open, exclaiming softly, "Where have you —" That was as far as she got before she was cnveloped in a bone-cracking embrace.

"Oh, God, I thought I'd never get here," Ben groaned as his mouth honed in on hers. His lips were cold, but they warmed rapidly on contact with hers.

Vaguely, Vichy heard the door close before she gave herself to the sensations his hungry kiss was creating. Inside the protection of his crushing hold, she forgot the hours spent waiting.

"You taste like toothpaste." Ben grinned as he lifted his head to stare into her face. "You weren't going to bed without me, were you?"

Vichy felt her throat close with the emotion that welled up inside. Oh, God, he looked so, so — beautiful! She had known she was in love with him. But how very deeply in love became evident now. She had never been the clinging type, yet now, suddenly, she wanted to cling to this man for all she was worth. The strength of the emotion raging through her was frightening. Grasping at her swiftly dissolving sense of self-preservation, she loosened her hold and attempted to move away from him.

"What's wrong?" Ben demanded softly, his arms tightening to keep her close. His grin vanishing, he frowned down at her.

"Nothing's wrong." Vichy shook her head to emphasize her denial. "I — I thought you weren't coming," she rushed on in a whisper.

Ben's hand came up to capture her chin and give it a light shake before be dipped his head to kiss her mouth gently.

"I told you I'd be here, didn't I?" he growled softly.

"Yes, but —"

"But I got hung up in a family day at my parents'," he cut her off. "I had planned to take Chad there early this morning, stay a short time, and then leave to come here." He sighed. "Besides Mike and his family, the house was full of assorted aunts, uncles, cousins, nieces, and nephews. I hadn't seen some of them in years, and I just couldn't walk out on them." He smiled ruefully. "As it was, I spent the majority of the day glancing at the clock. I finally escaped after supper."

He paused long enough to steal a quick kiss. Then, releasing her, he ordered, "Get dressed and pack up. We're getting out of here."

"Dressed? Pack? Getting out!" Vichy repeated stupidly. "What do you mean? Getting out to where?"

Ben walked across the room to pull her suitcases from the top of the clothes rack. "I've booked a room in a motel on the outskirts of the city, practically on the beach." He tossed the cases on the bed and opened them before adding, "We'll be more comfortable there."

"But, I —" Her protest stuck in her throat when he whipped around to face her, his expression settling into harsh, austere lines.

"But what?" he clipped. "You *had* planned on us staying together, hadn't you?"

Had she? Vichy smoothed her hand over her tangled hair. She had really not consciously thought about what their sleeping arrangements would be, but, yes, she admitted to herself honestly, subconsciously, she had known they would stay together. Vichy felt her face grow warm as she whispered the admission. "Yes."

"All right then." Ben's locked tight expression relaxed. "Surely you didn't think we could stay here?" A wave of his long hand indicated the confining area of the small room. "We'd be bumping into each other every other time we turned around. I stopped to check out the place and drop off my own stuff before coming here. It's

428

large and roomy." A teasing smile pulled at his lips and his sherry eyes glittered at her. "And the bed's almost twice the size of this one." He jerked his thumb at the bed beside him. "Now, come on, Vichy. Pull a pair of jeans on over your nightgown, throw your things in these suitcases, and let's get out of here." He grinned rakishly. "I've got the car sitting where it shouldn't be, and I asked to have your car brought out."

"Pull a pair of jeans over my nightgown? Are you crazy?" she cried. "I can't go out like that."

"Sez who?" Ben retorted. "You're going to wear a coat, so who'll know?" Now his grin was downright wicked. "Besides, it'll save time once we get to our room. If we even get there," he added pointedly.

It was the "our room" that did the trick. Vichy so liked the sound of it, she did exactly as he'd directed. The entire move, from packing to unpacking again, was completed in less than an hour.

As Ben promised, the room was large, an efficiency with a tiny kitchen area at one end and the rest a combination bedroom-living room.

"There's another reason why I was so late getting here," Ben said after he'd stashed their valises out of the way. Strolling into the kitchen area, he opened the cabinet above the sink and the door to the small boxlike refrigerator. "I stopped to do the grocery shopping." He grinned, indicating the full shelves. "Are you hungry?"

Suddenly she was, ravenously. "Starving," Vichy admitted, grinning back at him.

"And me," he agreed in a husky murmur that sent little tingles up Vichy's back. Walking to her slowly, he slid his arms around her waist and drew her close to his hard body. "But that will have to wait." Bending his head, he tasted her mouth with his tongue. "Mmm, yes," he whispered. "I'll have you for dessert."

All thought of food went flying out of Vichy's mind. In fact all thoughts of any kind dissolved, replaced by a burning need to appease the four-week-long hunger of a more earthy nature.

Sighing his name, Vichy curved her soft body to the rigid length of his, a fresh flare of excitement surging through her at his immediate and obvious response.

"God, I want you," Ben groaned huskily against her parted lips.

"I have wanted you continually for the last four weeks."

Very slowly, as if to savor every minute, his trembling fingers betraying the intensity of his arousal, Ben removed her robe and then her nightgown. Without touching her, his sherry-colored eyes sparking with red shades of light, he stood still, his gaze drinking in the sight of her like a man dying of thirst.

Motionless, her breathing painfully shallow, Vichy withstood his devouring glance until she began to tremble visibly.

"Ben, please," she pleaded in a throaty whimper. "I need you so badly, I hurt. If you don't touch me, love me soon —"

The room tilted as, with a half growl, half groan, Ben swept her up into his arms and carried her to the bed.

There is something extremely erotic about the glitter of gold when it is the only adornment on a woman's unclothed body.

Vichy came to life with the touch of cool metal against her exposed skin. The air was chilly, and even before she opened her eyes she moved with unconscious sensuality toward the warmth of the body beside her. Her movement intensified the feeling of metal against her skin and, frowning in confusion, she opened her eyes and glanced down.

She had not been imagining the metallic coolness! Eyes widening, Vichy stared at the length of gold draped across the rounded fullness of her breasts. It was a necklace, the match to the bracelet that even now circled her wrist, unclasped and strung across her body.

Stiffening, Vichy stared at the expensive, glittering trinket that looked almost indecent lying there against her naked breasts.

What was this, some sort of payment for services rendered? The sickening thought jolted through her mind, freezing her already stiffened form.

"Merry Christmas."

The tenderness embodied in Ben's soft tone banished the degrading question. Twisting her head, Vichy stared up into eyes so warm that the chill was banished from her body as well.

"I couldn't resist." A devilish smile pulling at his lips, his eyes shifted to the adornment, then back to hers. "It was wrapped so beautifully too." His smile grew to reveal even, white teeth. "Like a little kid, I couldn't wait for you to wake up and open it. I wanted to see it against your soft skin." Now his smile held pure wickedness.

"In my shifting around while opening it, the covers kinda slipped to your waist. And I just couldn't resist placing it on such an enticing spot." His face sobered and his tone took on the sound of an anxious little boy. "Does it please you?"

"Yes," Vichy whispered around a sudden tightness in her throat. "Very much. Thank you."

He was lying beside her, propped on his elbow, and now he lowered his head to bury his face in the side of her neck.

"I'm glad," he murmured huskily. "Because you please me in so many different ways."

Trailing tiny, exciting kisses, his lips explored her neck, her face, and then her mouth before he lifted his head again.

"You appear so calm, so self-contained, almost detached." Ben's eyes smiled, as if with a secret. "No one looking at you would believe that behind that cool exterior hides a very passionate woman."

Vichy's cheeks flared with warmth and she lowered her lashes at his teasing chuckle. She couldn't deny his assertion. How could she after last night? Her flush deepened as she relived in her mind the hours she'd spent in his arms.

After laying her gently on the bed, he had undressed with slow deliberation, his eyes compelling her to watch him. Once again Vichy had been struck by the beauty of his tall, slender, yet muscular form.

She had been burning for him by the time he came to her, and the fire consuming her had met its equal in the blaze inside him. Together their hungry fires had caused a sensual explosion. Touching, with hands and mouths and their entire bodies, they had driven each other to the very edge of pleasurable madness before, in silent agreement, they had joined together in a near frenetic search for shattering completion.

Now, her whole body warm with memory, a shiver feathered her skin as Ben's forefinger lightly outlined the ribbon of gold adorning her breasts.

"You're so very beautiful," he whispered against her parted lips. "And I'd love to spend the entire day right here with you, but" — he paused for effect, his warm, sherry eyes beginning to dance — "I'm positively weak from hunger for *real* food."

Feigning indignation, Vichy gathered her strength and pushed him out of the bed, onto the floor.

"Just for that, you get to cook breakfast," Ben growled in an attempt to conceal the laughter that erupted from his throat.

Nine

Thus began what was to become for Vichy a week out of time.

It was a slice of life's rarely offered perfection, beginning with the breakfast she served Ben that consisted of eggs, bacon, juice, toast, coffee, and his Christmas present, which he accepted with genuine surprise and delight.

After breakfast, bundled up against the cold late December wind, they walked the deserted beach arm in arm. The walk was to become a morning ritual for them, one that was always followed by another, more basic and warming ritual.

"I wish you didn't have to go to work," Ben sighed that first morning when they were once again cocooned within the warmth of the bedcovers and each other's arms.

"But I do have to go to work." She softly forestalled the request not to go that, she could discern from his expression, was hovering on his lips. "I have signed a contract." Her eyes begged him to understand. "I have never broken a contract, Ben. Not for illness or any other reason. I can't now." She did not add that, as this particular contract was her last, it was a matter of pride for her to end her professional career with her record unblemished.

"Okay, I'm sorry." A rueful smile curved his lips. "And your assumption was correct. I was about to ask you to renege." He kissed her mouth lingeringly. "We'll just have to make the most of the time we do have together."

And make the most of it they did. They laughed a lot, and made love a lot, and, during the hours she was not working, behaved as if they were the only two people in the world.

In effect, what they were doing was playing house. Vichy knew it, but refused to examine it too closely.

Ben had made no commitment to her, nor had he asked for one from her. Yet, like a bud slowly unfurling to full bloom under the warmth of the sun, Vichy's love for him blossomed with each succeeding day.

They talked, at times casually, at others animatedly, about anything that came to mind, sometimes agreeing, other times arguing on a range of subjects, including politics and religion. And, although their conversation covered both the impersonal and the personal, not once did either of them venture into the future, beyond Vichy's present engagement.

If she allowed herself to think about it, it hurt, so she simply did not allow herself to think about it. Hanging on to each moment greedily, Vichy pushed all outside considerations to the very back of her mind. Included within those considerations was the beginning of a twinge of doubt concerning her irregular monthly cycle.

During her working hours at the hotel, Vichy's entire person, including her voice, reflected the happiness Ben so lovingly created inside her when they were closeted together in their so carefully guarded hideaway.

Ironically, now that she had made the decision to quit, her audiences responded to the new life in her voice with what amounted to wild enthusiasm. Being normal, Vichy lapped up their enthusiasm like so much cream. Also being normal, Ben displayed a delightful tendency to be jealous of every male member of her audience who evidenced the slightest interest in her.

Ben sat at the same table he had occupied weeks before, through every performance, glowering and scowling — to the growing amusement of her same back-up group of the weeks before.

By Tuesday, barely able to contain her own amusement any longer, Vichy, her lips twitching, advised him to go lose some of his money at the tables, adding, chidingly, "Then you'll really have reason to scowl."

Ben had the grace to grin sheepishly. "Have I really been scowling?"

"Enough to break up the group." Vichy nodded, her blue eyes bright with laughter. "Especially Ken, on the drums. I half expect him to fall off his perch momentarily."

If being the cause of her back-ups' hilarity bothered Ben at all, he hid it well. Lifting his hand, he caressed her smooth cheek with his fingertips. "Okay, sweetheart." He smiled tenderly. "I'll make myself scarce." He turned to walk away, then paused and glanced back, his sherry eyes glittering. "And, Vichy, you can tell Ken I said he should go take a flying leap."

After that Ben's attendance at her performances was sporadic, but when he did show up, he made a point of buying her back-ups a drink after the set, bantering back and forth with them easily.

When the last set was finished Wednesday, Vichy had to go on the hunt for Ben. Up until then she had skirted around the casino in her comings and goings, as if the floor had been implanted with land mines.

Her progress was slow, as the room was packed with people, all apparently eager to risk their hard-earned money in hopes of pulling off a fantastic coup.

Mentally shrugging in her bewilderment over the number of people who were avid gamblers, Vichy inched her way through the spacious room, her glance bouncing off the faces of strangers in her search for one dear and familiar.

As she passed one row of slot machines a telltale ringing and a woman's excited scream alerted Vichy to the fact that a machine had been "hit." Pausing, she glanced down the narrow aisle, amazed at the crowd that had gathered around the laughing winner. Silently advising the woman to grab the winnings and run, positive the advice would be ignored if tendered aloud, Vichy moved away from the excited chatter.

Vichy finally spied Ben at one of the craps tables, the sight of his tall form bringing a catch to her throat and increasing her pulse rate. He was standing rather indolently, leaning against the side of the table, and his expression bespoke boredom. Lord, he looked elegant. His stylish suit hugged his wide shoulders and slim body as though it were in love with him. His shirt was the color of thick, rich cream, and contrasted perfectly with his dark suit and hair. His tie was almost the exact same shade as his sherry brown eyes.

As if mesmerized, Vichy walked to him, her fingers itching to touch him, her arms aching to hold him, her body quivering in its need of his possession.

And to think I really believed myself in love with Brad, she marveled. Compared to what she was experiencing now, what she had felt for Brad took on the shadings of a teenage infatuation. What she felt for Ben was more than love, it was total devastation, and it frightened her. She could, with this man, lose all sense of self. And that was not good. There had been no mention of a future together and, with the way she felt, she was very much afraid she was going to be left completely shattered. And that was worse. Every ounce of common sense she possessed urged her to gather the pieces of her self that were left and run. But, as she had suspected of the woman at the slot machine, Vichy would not heed the advice either. She loved Ben as compulsively as any gambler loved pitting himself against the odds. She had to stay until the dice were tossed for the last time.

"Hi."

Ben's soft greeting drew her out of her introspection. Raising emotion-clouded eyes to his, she repeated him.

"Hi."

Suddenly his eyes took on the bright sheen of alertness, and she heard him inhale sharply. His attention to play was called from midway down the table, and with a quick motion of his hand he indicated he was out of it. Not once did his eyes leave her face.

"You want me, now, this minute, don't you?" he breathed in a tone that reached her ears alone. Past all subterfuge, Vichy nodded.

"Yes."

"And I you," he admitted unsteadily. He drew a deep, calming breath, then moved abruptly. Scooping his chips off the table, he jammed them into his jacket pockets, saying tersely, "I'll cash these in later." Turning away from the table, he slid his arm around her waist and, bending his head, whispered close to her ear, "Let's go home."

Later, wakeful as she lay quietly curled against Ben's relaxed, sleeping body, Vichy decided that home, with Ben, was the most wonderful place in the world, no matter where its location.

Ben's lovemaking had completely immersed her in a hot pool of sensuality, washing away all lingering traces of shyness and inhibition until, in mutual hunger, she had taken possession of him as forcefully as he had taken possession of her.

His experience in the art far exceeded hers, as he had proved by his expert tutelage. That he had known, intimately, many female bodies before her own, Vichy had no doubt. That knowledge truly did not bother her. Ben was a mature man. It was the fear of how many women would follow her in the future that kept her wakeful. For, even at the most intense moments, when Ben's hoarse voice had whispered all kinds of exciting love words, not once had he uttered a word of commitment.

Did Ben feel anything for her beyond the pull of a very strong physical attraction? That was the question that was beginning to torment Vichy to the exclusion of all else. There were times she felt positive he returned her love in equal measure. Yet he never said the words aloud and, until he did so, Vichy could not believe he loved her.

Don't be a greedy fool, she chided herself, blinking against the acidy sting in her eyes. *He has made no demands of you; you have no right to make any of him. Don't cry for the entire sky when you have your hands full of stars.*

By morning Vichy had her emotions under control. She would, she had vowed before falling into a fitful sleep, not ask for more than Ben was willing to give freely. That she had fallen in love with him was her problem, not his.

Her engagement at the hotel would be over with the last set Friday night, and though she had originally planned on leaving for home Saturday morning, she had subsequently agreed to stay at the motel with Ben through the weekend. All she could do, she decided now, was hold her love close to her heart and pray that by the time that weekend was over, Ben would have made clear his intentions regarding the future.

New Year's Eve was a gala time at the hotel, starting early and ending late — or rather early New Year's morning.

Although Vichy joined in the fun with the patrons who drifted in and out of the lounge, and she observed Ben doing likewise, they saved their real celebration until they returned to their room in the wee hours of the morning.

There, ensconced in the wide bed stark naked, they shared an expensive bottle of champagne and each other. If Vichy had cherished hope that Ben would make some personal declaration with the advent of the new year, she was sorely disappointed, for he did not. He drank to her health, to her beauty, and to her passion, but not a word about their future together passed his lips.

Friday Vichy woke disheveled and with a headache. Groaning in protest at the tiny hammers beating at her temples, she rolled over and forced her eyelids to half-mast. The sight that met her gaze was thoroughly disgusting.

Freshly showered and shaved, looking delicious in tight jeans and a bulky knit pullover sweater, obviously without any residual fallout from the champagne or the activity that had accompanied it, and grinning like a damned devil in the bargain, Ben stood by the bed, a glass containing a nauseating red concoction in his hand. When she fastened her bleary gaze on him, he held the glass out to her like an offering.

"What's that?" she groaned, fuzzy-tongued.

"My secret blend," he replied with twitching lips. "Drink it down; it'll clear the cobwebs out of your head."

Grimacing, she grunted "Ugh," but she took the glass from him and sipped at the red liquid. Actually, it was not too bad, Vichy decided after the third small sip. Tomato juice, obviously, but what else? Tabasco? And? This morning her attention span was short, and, giving up the guessing game, she drank it down, as Ben had suggested.

"You're not much of a drinker, are you?"

Ben observed in amusement. "You had only a few glasses of champagne. I can't imagine what you'd be like after an entire night on the town." One dark eyebrow shot up in question. "Or had you been drinking with the customers all evening?"

Vichy started to shake her head, and then stopped, gasping at the increased tempo of the hammering in her temples.

"No," she croaked. "I carried around a glass of iced tea all night." She paused to wet her parched lips with the tip of her tongue before adding, "I rarely drink anything other than a glass of wine with dinner."

"I'd say it's a good thing," he laughed. Sitting down on the side of the bed, he leaned to her and gently kissed her pale cheek.

"But I am relieved," he teased. "For a scary minute there, I was afraid it was the — ah — vigorous activity that had done you in."

"You're a wicked man, Bennett Larkin," Vichy accused reproachfully.

"Yeah, I know." Ben grinned complacently. "Isn't it fun?" Before she could retort, or even gasp at his outrageousness, Ben jumped to his feet. "I'll tell you what," he declared expansively. "Being the all-around terrific person that I am, I'll make the coffee while you have a reviving shower. What do you say to that?"

"Big whoop."

Ben's laughter followed her into the bathroom.

Surprisingly, the shower did revive her — at least partially. Then Ben insisted she eat something with her coffee, and the toast she opted for revived her even more.

By the time they left to go to the hotel, the hammers had stilled in her temples and, except for a gray dullness blanketing her mind, she was feeling almost human. Ben — the rat — was still highly amused by it all.

His amusement carried through her first and second acts. During the break after the second set he grinned at her once too often and Vichy, having walked the fine edge of impatience all day, slipped to the wrong side and ordered him to "get lost."

Not even looking offended, in fact looking more amused than ever, Ben drawled, "Whatever you say, sweetheart," and with a careless wave of his hand sauntered toward the casino.

Tormenting herself with wondering if Ben's attitude was an indication of his tolerance of her, or his unconcern for her, Vichy watched him until he was swallowed up in the crowd, a strange foreboding settling over her like a shroud.

Ben did not put in an appearance for her

final performances. And Vichy, torn between the desire to stretch out the seconds of her last professional engagement and the urge to have it over and done with, grew moody and depressed as the hours ticked inexorably away.

Finally it was the last set, and then the last song, and then she was thanking her audience with tears in her eyes.

It was over — the career she'd embarked on with youthful enthusiasm and high hopes had come to an end with a feeling of dullness and depression.

She had to find Ben. Now, more than at any time since she'd met him, she needed his confidence, his coolness, and, yes, even his teasing amusement. Perhaps, she mused, she needed the last more than anything else.

Declining Ken's offer of one last drink — for although the men in her back-up did not know this had been her final performance, they did know it was the end of this particular engagement — Vichy left the lounge and entered the casino.

As usual the room was crowded, and wondering irritably if half the population of the East Coast had suddenly had the urge to test their skill in this casino, Vichy picked her way at a snail's pace through the room.

The holiday spirit still prevailed, as was

evidenced by the good humor of the majority of the people Vichy observed. At one point she was jostled by a young man at least eight years her junior, and her ego was given an unexpected lift when, after running his eyes the length of her and back, he said smoothly, "Sorry, gorgeous. No, on second thought, I'm not sorry at all. You're the best-looking thing I've clapped eyes on in weeks." Although his words were bold, his grin was shy, and Vichy couldn't help smiling at him. "I guess you wouldn't care to have a drink with me, would you?" he finished hopefully.

"No, thank you," Vichy refused gently. "I'm meeting a friend."

"Well, I can't be shot for trying." Smiling broadly, he winked and then moved on, in search, Vichy was sure, of more available game.

However, the brief exchange had lightened her mood, and with a small smile curving her lips, she wound her way along the narrow expanse of floor space around the gaming tables.

She was beginning to despair of ever finding Ben when she was forced to come to a dead stop by a group of elderly ladies totally blocking the way at intersecting aisles.

"You girls should have gone with me to

the cashier's cage," one blue-haired lady said excitedly to the others.

Resigned to being held up until they completed their conversation, Vichy unabashedly listened in.

"What's so thrilling about cashing in ten dollars' worth of chips?" a second gray-haired lady grumbled.

"It wasn't *my* chips I was referring to," Blue Hair snapped back smartly.

Controlling her smile valiantly, Vichy glanced around in assumed disinterest and waited for the mystery to unfold.

"Well, what or whose chips *were* you referring to?" this from a bespectacled, brown-haired lady.

"You see that young man at the cage window? The one with the lovely young woman hanging around his waist?" Ms. Blue Hair asked excitedly.

Five necks were craned around the corner of the intersection in the direction of the payoff cage.

Vichy was humorously aching to view a man with a woman hanging around his waist, lovely or otherwise. She knew she would be unable to see the cage window even if she did crane her neck, and she was too polite to shove any of the elderly ladies aside, so she stood still, waiting patiently for the explanation she knew was coming.

"Well, I never!" a fourth member of the

party of five exclaimed. "Kissing in a public place!"

"Oh, that's nothing." Blue Hair waved her hand airily. "You should have seen them a few minutes ago, when I was at the next window. I swear, that young miss was all over him like a wall-to-wall rug. Laughing, and crying, and kissing him all over his handsome face."

Vichy choked back her laughter just in time to hear Madame Gray Hair query her friend.

"Why? Do you know?"

"Oh, yes, I know why." Blue Hair paused to make sure she had their full attention, which she did, Vichy's included. "I would imagine that young woman's display of affection has something to do with the thirty-four thousand dollars' worth of chips he's just cashed in."

"Thirty-four thousand dollars!" four awe-struck voices repeated aloud.

Thirty-four thousand dollars! Vichy repeated in awestruck silence. The small dramatic moment over, the five ladies went on their merry way, and Vichy quick-stepped to the end of the narrow aisle, curious for a look at the winner and his solitary cheering section. The sight her eyes encountered froze her in place.

There was only one couple at the row of windows. The ash-blond young woman was very lovely and, with her arms clasped around the man's waist, she did give the impression of hanging on for all she was worth.

In between stuffing bills into his pockets, the smiling man allowed the woman to kiss his mouth. The man was indeed handsome. Vichy had never seen the young woman before. The man was Bennett Larkin.

Her body rigid as stone, eyes widening with an expression akin to horror, Vichy stood, barely breathing, watching the "happy couple." As the first tears rushed to blur her vision, another picture swirled around and formed to superimpose itself upon the scene before her.

Trapped forever in that mental image Vichy had tried so very hard to banish from her consciousness were a naked man and a naked woman, intertwined on top of Vichy's marriage bed.

The picture grew clearer, only now the naked man on the bed was Ben.

Much the same as she had done six years before, Vichy slowly backed away, her head moving as if in slow motion from side to side, the protesting words, no, no, no, coming in whispered tones through her taut lips.

"Hey, lady!"

Vichy had lost all awareness of the people around her and she jerked to a stop

451

when she backed into a man. The face she swung around to the stranger was starkly white.

"Hey, lady," the man repeated in an altogether different tone. The former had held hard impatience, the latter, sharp concern. "Are you sick?"

"What?" Vichy blinked her eyes and, thankfully, the vision was gone. "Oh, no, I'm all right."

"You don't look all right to me," the middle-aged man insisted, grasping her upper arms as if to keep her upright.

"I — I'm fine, really," Vichy choked. "It — it's so very hot in here, don't you think?" she improvised. "I'll just go and get some fresh air and I'll be fine."

"Well, if you're sure there's nothing I can do."

"No, thank you." Desperate to get away, she added, "I'll hurry out and get some air, if you'll let me go."

"Oh." He actually blushed, and at any other time Vichy could have appreciated the fact that her would-be rescuer was a very nice man. "Sure, but you take care now, you hear?"

"Yes, I will." Free of his hold, Vichy dashed away.

Huddled in the back seat of the taxi, Vichy had only a jumbled memory of her flight through the casino. She was wearing her coat, and clutching her handbag, so she knew she must have stopped long enough to pick them up before making a beeline for the hotel's front entrance. She clearly remembered getting into the cab and giving the driver the name of the motel.

Once inside the efficiency unit, tears washing her face, Vichy tore around like a demented wild thing, flinging her belongings into her suitcases. She was not thinking. She was reacting to a host of emotions; every one of those emotions screamed: run.

The door to the unit was open. The handle of one suitcase gripped in one hand, Vichy reached for the other case and went still, her eyes fastened on the glittering gold bracelet on her wrist. Releasing the handle, she unclasped the bracelet, and then its counterpart around her neck. Walking to the bed, she dropped the shiny pieces onto the smooth bedspread.

"You can go to hell, Ben Larkin," Vichy whispered bitterly. "And you can take your winnings trinkets with you."

Spinning on her heel, she crossed the room, scooped up her valises and walked out, closing the door quietly behind her.

Somehow she managed to get to her car, unlock it, and drive away from the motel, even though she could see very little through the tears that kept filling her eyes. After she was clear of the city, she pulled to the side of the highway and had a good cry.

Damn him, damn him, damn him. The words circled around and around in her head unceasingly.

How long she would have remained sitting there if a state patrolman had not stopped to ask if she needed help, Vichy had no idea. But, after she had assured him that she was all right, she pulled herself together. She didn't have time to cry, she told herself bracingly. *Wait until you get home. Wait until tomorrow. But, for now, get your act together, and get out of here.*

Ten

Vichy spent what was left of the night and most of Saturday morning in a motel on the outskirts of Philadelphia. Up until she dropped, exhausted, onto the bed, she had, through sheer willpower, managed to keep a tight rein on her emotions. The reins went slack when her body hit the bed.

Fully clothed, her arms wrapped tightly around her midsection, she released the agony tearing at her insides through great, racking sobs that rent the silence in the room for hours.

Vichy woke around dawn, cold and cramped, wondering where she was. For a few blessed moments, blankness covered her mind. Then memory rushed back with all its attendant pain.

Groaning softly, she dragged her slender frame off the bed. Shivering, her movements stiff end not too coordinated, she stripped down to her panties and bra, then, ignoring the untidy heap of clothes on the floor, she crawled between the covers and escaped into a deep, dream-free sleep.

The slamming of the door to the room next to hers woke Vichy late in the morning. This time she was fully aware of exactly where she was, and exactly why. The image of her Ben laughing down at the young woman clinging to him like a leech was clear and concise in her mind.

Her Ben! Vichy blinked angrily against the resurgence of moisture in her eyes. *Stop it. At once.* Her Ben indeed! Her Ben, and that young woman's Ben, and probably a half-dozen other women's Ben as well. Damn all gamblers!

Suddenly she exploded into action. Flinging back the covers, she jumped out of the bed. She had to move. She had to get a shower and get dressed. She had to go home. She had to begin the process of eradicating him from her mind.

The fuel tank in her car was still half full when Vichy turned into the rutted driveway to her parents' farm. The power generator in her body hovered at empty. She had eaten nothing since lunchtime the day before. She was operating on nerves and guts, and it showed.

How badly it showed became evident to Vichy by her family's reaction to her appearance. Her mother fussed. Her father grumbled. Her sister, all mouth and no tact, was blunt.

"You look like you've been hit by a sixteen-wheeler. What the heck kind of week did you have in Atlantic City?"

"Hectic," Vichy understated dully. Had it really only been a week since she'd rushed out of this house, eager to fly back into her lover's arms? Her lover. Vichy shivered. The metaphorical needle in her body bounced on E. The elasticity of her nerves had been drawn to full tautness, courage conceded the battle, and Vichy knew that if she did not lie down very soon, she would fall down.

"I've had very little sleep the last few days," she offered by way of an explanation. "If you don't mind, I'll skip supper and go right to bed. I'll tell you all about it tomorrow."

Tomorrow. The word haunted Vichy in the days that followed. So many tomorrows, and every one of them empty, meaningless. And the hardest thing for her to bear was the realization that throughout every morning, noon, and night of every one of those tomorrows she would continue to love Bennett Larkin. She wanted to hate him. She tried desperately to hate him. With ruthless determination, she recreated the setting in which she had last seen him. She remembered everything in minute detail, down to the shimmering gleam in Ben's eyes, and the tiny mole on

457

the ash-blonde's temple. It hurt to review the scene, but it changed nothing. She loved him.

Thankfully, her parents accepted her hastily formed explanation of a week filled with work as she knocked herself out entertaining wildly celebrating crowds of people. But Vichy was not too sure of Bette. Bette was definitely casting her some very pained glances.

Two weeks after her flight from Atlantic City Bette's glances were the least of Vichy's problems.

It was on this Saturday morning in mid-January that the seed of doubt Vichy had buried in the farthest reaches of her consciousness reached full germination and poked its questioning sprout into the fore-front of her mind.

Telling herself her suspicions were ridiculous, she nonetheless took out her personal calendar and flipped through the pages until she came to the last one with a date circled in red. One careful count forward from that circled date was all the confirmation she required.

She was pregnant!

Feeling like she had received a stunning blow to her solar plexus, Vichy sank limply onto the edge of her bed. *Fool, fool, fool,* she berated herself mercilessly. But she *had* been told she would probably never be able to have a child and, even though that had been almost six years ago, she had had no reason to suspect that conditions had changed.

Had there been a minute tear in one of the condoms Ben had used? No method of contraception was foolproof, of course, but it was ironic that precautions she'd thought of as probably unnecessary had failed her.

What am I going to do? she cried silently. *You're going to have a baby,* the answer came from within. *Ben's baby.*

Ben's baby.

A small flicker of anticipation tickled her stomach. She had very little money, and though she had had several job interviews this last week, she had no definite prospects of employment. Yet, suddenly, she didn't care. She was going to have Ben's baby!

Sunday the Hartman family came to visit. John and Katie had changed very little since the last time Vichy had seen them. Mark had not changed at all; he was gentle, he was kind, he was considerate — he was dull as old dishwater.

Distracted by thoughts of her condition, and how to go about handling it, Vichy was totally unaware of the soulful glances Mark shyly cast at her.

Bette, however, had witnessed every one of Mark's longing looks. After the Hartmans' departure, she launched a teasing attack on Vichy.

"If worse comes to worst," she grinned impishly, "you can always marry old Mark."

"What do you mean if worse comes to worst?" Startled, Vichy stared at Bette. Had her sister, somehow, guessed her condition?

"I mean, if you have no luck finding a job." Bette laughed. "Poor old Mark is positively besotted with you."

"Don't be ridiculous," Vichy retorted, weak with relief.

"I'm not!" Bette protested. "He's always been crazy about you and, unbelievably, he has not changed a bit in all these years. When we visited them the day after Christmas, he bent my ear all day with questions about you."

"I like Mark, I really do," Vichy offered seriously. "But . . ."

"Yeah." Bette filled in where Vichy trailed off. "I know what you mean."

Early Monday morning Vichy drove to a clinic in Lancaster to have a pregnancy test to satisfy any lingering doubt. The results were positive. Strangely, it was not until after Vichy was faced with the reality of her condition that she experienced her first bout of morning sickness.

Saturday morning she was in the bathroom, hanging over the bowl, when Bette came tearing into the room without knocking.

"Vichy, do you —" She broke off what she was going to ask to exclaim, "Hey, are you sick?"

Waving with a backward swing of her hand, Vichy, appalled at being caught, gasped, "Bette, please, go away. It's just a stomach upset." She barely got the last word out when a racking heave shuddered through her body.

"That's more than a stomach upset," Bette declared worriedly. "You have probably got some kind of virus. I'm going to tell Mom to call the doctor."

"No!" Vichy ordered sharply. "Don't bother Mom, I don't need a doctor." But again her body betrayed her with its violent roiling.

"We'll let Mom decide," Bette said, turning to the door.

"Bette, wait, please!"

"But you're sick, I —"

"I'm pregnant." Defeat coated Vichy's whispery voice.

"You're —" Bette cried in disbelief. "Does Mom know?"

The spasms over, Vichy shook her head as she straightened. "No. I just got confirmation myself a few days ago." Vichy sighed wearily. "Look, wait for me in my

461

bedroom while I wash my face and brush my teeth. We'll talk then."

Bette was waiting, a frown creasing her smooth young brow. "This is incredible," she said softly when Vichy had closed the door. "How did this happen?" With a wave of her hand and a grimace she canceled the question. "Well, I know how it happened. What I mean is, when? Who? Were you seeing some man in California? Is that why you came home?"

"No, no," Vichy answered, sinking onto the bed. "It happened when I played Atlantic City in November. I — I met this man . . ."

"You hopped into bed with a stranger!"

Vichy winced at her sister's shocked expression.

"Please, Bette, keep your voice down," she urged. "And, no, I didn't just hop into bed with a stranger." Yet, wasn't that exactly what she had done? she accused herself. The thought hurt, and she rushed on, "He — I — oh, Bette, what difference does it make?"

"Well, what does he say about it?" Bette asked bluntly.

"He doesn't know," Vichy murmured. "And he's not going to know," she added much more firmly.

"Not going to know?" Bette repeated in confusion. "But, why? He's the father. He

462

has every right, not to mention responsibility, to know."

A tormenting vision, never far from the front of her consciousness, of a lovely young woman kissing Ben's smiling lips swam before Vichy's eyes.

"He has *no* rights," she said harshly. "And I'll take the responsibility."

"You're not thinking of doing this alone?" Bette demanded in a tone of shock.

"Why not?" Vichy countered. "A lot of women do." If her own voice lacked conviction, Bette's did not.

"Certainly *not* in this family," she underlined darkly.

There was the crux of Vichy's concern. In a sense, she had been the pioneer of the family. She had been the first ever to enter the field of entertainment. The first ever to divorce a mate. Now Bette had just confirmed her own fears. Her latest *first* was going to go over like a lead balloon. Biting her lip, she eyed her sister wearily.

"I'm going to do it, Bette," she sighed. "They'll just have to get used to it. I know they'll all be shocked, but . . ." Her voice whispered away.

"I don't think shocked quite covers it," Bette warned. "I can imagine Josh's reaction, and *Mattie!*" Bette shuddered. "I used to envy you," she confessed. "I don't anymore." She lifted her shoulders helplessly. "When are you going to tell the folks?"

"Soon."

Nodding, Bette walked to the door. "I — I wish there was something I could do," she said softly, not looking back.

"There isn't." Vichy swallowed against the lump in her throat. "But, thanks, anyway."

After that, Vichy knew she would have to talk to her parents very soon or take the risk of betraying herself to her mother in the same way she had to Bette. Yet, the day slipped by, and still she hesitated.

While her parents were in church on Sunday, Vichy, cooking the midday meal, decided she'd speak to them as soon as dinner was over.

Growing more tense by the minute, Vichy greeted the appearance of Mark Hartman at the door, like a stay of execution, while she and Bette were finishing up the dishes.

After exchanging small talk with her parents, Mark, ever the same, challenged Vichy to a game of checkers, exactly as he had when they had both been teenagers. Sighing in a combination of amusement and frustration, Vichy accepted his shyly worded challenge, exactly as she always had.

They were into their fourth game when the doorbell rang. As she was losing for the fourth time, Vichy, glad for any distraction, sprang to her feet.

"I'll get it," she cried, forestalling her father, who had begun folding the paper he was reading.

Vichy walked out of the room into the vestibule and opened the door. She froze, her hand gripping the knob.

"Hello, Vichy."

Ben looked leaner than ever, and meaner then a midwinter blizzard out of the northwest.

"If you slam that door, I'll kick it in," he warned softly, correctly reading her intentions.

Vichy moistened her lips. "What do you want?" she croaked.

A cynical smile twisted his lips and Vichy shivered. He looked tired and exasperated and mad enough to chew nails — very large ones.

"I want an explanation," Ben gritted out. "In fact, I want several."

"I can't t-talk now," Vichy, actually frightened, stuttered. "We — we have a g-guest, and —"

"Vichy, invite whoever it is in, and close the door," her father called impatiently. "I'm not paying to heat the front porch."

Rebellion flared. She couldn't bear to be

in the same room with him. It hurt her just to look at him. How could she possibly go through the motions of introducing him to her family as a casual acquaintance? She was pregnant with his child, for heaven's sake! She just could not. Her arm moved to close the door in his face.

"You heard the man." A small, unpleasant smile tugging at the straight line that slashed his face, Ben stepped forward, forcing her to back up to avoid physical contact.

"Do you know what you're doing?" she muttered as he passed her.

"Yes," Ben hissed. "Do you?" There was no time to try even to formulate an answer, for Bette came clattering down the stairs, a questioning grin on her face.

"Hi, I'm Bette . . ." She paused expectantly, her grin widening.

In an instant, Ben's entire mien changed. Returning her grin, he offered his hand. "Hi, Ben Larkin."

"Well, Ben Larkin, why don't you take your coat off and come inside?" Bette invited.

Up until that moment Vichy hadn't even noticed that he was wearing a coat. But, of course he was wearing a coat, she chided herself as she held out her icy cold hand for the garment. It's January.

Clamping down firmly on a rising feeling

of hysteria, Vichy led the way into the living room and managed to get through the ensuing introductions coherently.

With every one of her senses alive to the smallest nuance about him, Vichy felt rather then saw him tense when she introduced Mark. Yet, nothing about his demeanor betrayed that tension.

He was all charm as he accepted her mother's offer of a cup of hot coffee, and smiled with devastating effect when Bette eagerly requested the honor of performing the small task of bringing it to him.

Before he was in the room five minutes he had not only Bette but her parents as well hanging on his every word.

As to the contents of his words, Vichy hadn't a clue, until she heard, and registered, the word *California*. Gathering her emotion-rattled thoughts, she forced herself to attention.

"The plane landed in Philly a few hours ago," Ben was saying. "I thought since I was this close, I'd drop in and see Vich."

His use of her shortened nickname was a dead giveaway. He might appear easy and relaxed to every other person in the room, but Vichy knew better. The only times Ben had ever called her Vich was when he was annoyed or angry with her. Vichy had the sinking sensation that he was very, very angry with her. Once again she dragged her attention to what he was saying.

"No, we didn't meet in California," Ben answered a question posed by her mother. "Actually, I met Vich while she was performing in Atlantic City Thanksgiving week."

Attuned only to Ben, Vichy completely missed Bette's suddenly electrified appearance.

What was her father asking now? Something about whether Ben had much more driving to do today.

"The weather service is predicting snow for early this evening, you know," Luke cautioned.

"Yes, sir, I did know," Ben replied respectfully. "I'm not going to be driving anymore today." He smiled. "At least, no more than to get to the room I booked for the night." He mentioned a motel on the highway less than ten miles from Vichy's parents' farmhouse.

Vichy's spirits hit rock bottom. She had been harboring a hope that he'd be starting for home when he departed. Now that hope was shattered, and she knew there was no way she could avoid the coming confrontation between them.

Mark, sitting across from her on the other side of the table that still held their unfinished checkers game, stirred restlessly, catching her eye. Unbelievably, until he moved, Vichy had forgotten he was there.

"I guess I'd better be going," he said in his halting, shy way in answer to her questioning glance. "I hate driving in the snow."

Ignoring the sardonic expression that passed fleetingly over Ben's face, Vichy rose to see Mark to the door.

As he put on his jacket in the comparative privacy of the vestibule, Mark proved that though he was dull, he was in no way dense.

"He's important to you, isn't he?" Mark asked softly, giving evidence that while her family had centered all their attention on Ben, he had been observing her.

Loath to lie to him, Vichy nodded reluctantly.

"I thought so." Mark stared at her, his dying hope reflected in his eyes. "Is there anything I can do?"

Strangely, dull old Mark was apparently the only one who had sensed trouble between Vichy and Ben. Grateful for his offer, Vichy nonetheless shook her head.

"You're a good friend, Mark," she murmured. "But . . ." Again she shook her head.

"Well . . ." Mark fiddled with the doorknob. "If you need a friend anytime, call me."

Even though she knew she never would,

Vichy promised, "I will. Thank you, Mark."

When she stepped through the archway into the living room, she found Ben on his feet.

"No, thanks anyway. I had a late lunch," he was saying to her mother, who had, apparently, invited him to supper. "I have to be going too." Striding across the room, he put a staying hand on Vichy's arm as she turned to show him out. "I can find the door by myself," he clipped. "I'll call you," he added in a tone that warned: You'd better answer.

Vichy fielded her parents' questions about Ben through supper. At least she didn't have to parry Bette's blunt queries, as her sister had gone to visit a girl friend. She was beginning to grow desperate for innocuous answers when the phone rang.

Tossing down her dishtowel, she volunteered, "I'll get it," as she headed for the vestibule and the small table on which the phone rested.

"Get over here," Ben ordered an instant after she'd said hello. "And I mean *now*."

Why had she assumed he'd wait until tomorrow to call? she wondered wildly. Did he ever do anything she assumed he would? He didn't even give her time to refuse. Harshly repeating, "Now, Vich," he slammed down his receiver after growling a room number.

I won't go, Vichy thought defiantly. *He can't order me around like a recalcitrant child. I will not go. What can he do about it, anyway? Come back here and raise all kinds of hell,* the answer came loud and clear to her mind. Releasing thc death grip she still had on the receiver, Vichy walked to the vestibule closet for her coat.

Vichy's headlights cut through the darkness of the cloud-shrouded early evening, and in her preoccupation, Vichy was unaware of passing her father's car, Bette behind the wheel, moving in the opposite direction.

There were only four cars parked in the motel lot. Her palms damp, Vichy maneuvered into the lined slot beside Ben's familiar Lexus. He must have been watching for her, for the door of his room was pulled open as she hesitantly lifted her hand to knock on it.

Her feet responding to her shaky order to move, Vichy walked into the brightly lit room.

Eleven

"Are you pregnant?"

The harshly worded question hit her with all the force of a hurtled missile. The slam of the door was an indication of the fury riding the man who had flung the verbal stone.

Struck speechless by the swiftness of his attack, Vichy stood motionless, her spine rigid with apprehension and the beginnings of a fury of her own. Bette! It had to have been Bette. When she didn't respond, he moved to stand in front of her, hands on his slim, jeans-clad hips, his eyes blazing with red sparks, his expression grim.

"Answer me, damn you," he ordered between teeth clenched in rage.

"Yes." Vichy spat the admission at him. "Yes, I'm pregnant . . . so what?" Her question held a degree of bravado she was far from feeling.

"So what?" he repeated incredulously. "So what?" His lips twisted in an ugly way. "So when were you planning to tell me?"

472

"You're assuming it's yours?" she retorted, with hard-fought-for coolness. The look that came over Ben's face turned Vichy's blood to ice water.

He snorted. "You know damned well it's mine. Who else could have fathered it?"

"Mark Hartman." The moment his name passed her lips Vichy regretted uttering it. It wasn't fair of her to even verbally involve Mark in this mess. The impact of that name on the man standing in front of her made her doubly sorry she'd mentioned it.

"Don't push it, Vich. I'm not in the mood to be hassled." He drew a long, calming breath, then said flatly, "We'll get married as soon as possible."

"No!" Vichy exclaimed. "We will not."

"What the hell do you mean, we will not?" Ben rapped sharply.

"Exactly what I said," Vichy retorted, every bit as sharply. "I won't marry you, Ben."

"I'm good enough to go to bed with, but not good enough to marry? Is that it?" Ben nearly shouted, his tone sounding strangely hurt as well as angry.

His response, so traditionally feminine, should have been funny; Vichy wasn't laughing. In fact, she was very close to tears.

"That's it," she concurred over the constriction in her throat. "Now, if that's all

473

you wanted to see me about, I'll be going." She turned, only to have her arm grasped and her body spun back to him.

Although it hardly seemed possible, Ben looked more furious than before. "You're not going anywhere," he grated. "At least not until we settle this."

"There's nothing to settle," Vichy cried, attempting unsuccessfully to pull her arm from his grasp. "I'm not going to marry you."

His fingers tightened, yet not enough to cause pain through the heavy material of her coat. "And what about the child?" he demanded.

"It's mine. I'll take care of it." Again Vichy gave a sharp tug of her arm. Again she was unable to free herself. "I want nothing from you."

"You already *have* something from me," Ben corrected her roughly. "And it is as much mine as it is yours, and I want it."

Vichy went numb with a sudden premonition. "What do you mean, you want it?" she asked through lips that had gone bone dry.

"Exactly what I say." Ben's smile closed her throat with fear. His voice matched his smile for grimness. "If you won't share it with me through marriage, I'll take it from you."

"You can't do that!" Vichy cried.

His reply came hard and fast and scathingly. "Do you want to bet?"

"You would say that! No, I don't want to bet, simply because you'd lose."

"No, Vich, I would not." Ben's tone held total conviction.

"But . . . but you can't!" Vichy stared at him in confusion. "How could you? You don't mean you'd try and abduct . . ."

"Don't be ridiculous," he snapped. "I mean I'd sue you for custody. I'd win too," Ben added arrogantly.

He was threatening to take her baby! Her baby! Fighting the panic building in her chest, Vichy managed a scornful snort. "I am, or will be, the baby's mother. No judge is going to award you custody if I countersue. And I will."

"And you'll lose," Ben said confidently. It was his very confidence that shook her. Before she could refute his statement, he began firing questions at her. "Have you any money? Are you employed? Do you have any solid prospects of employment? Can you provide a decent home and environment for the child?"

"I — I . . ." She got no further.

"The answer to every one of those questions is no, and you know it," he cut into her futile attempt at defense. "And every one of those questions would be asked in

475

front of a judge. On the other hand, I can truthfully answer yes to all those questions and more." He smiled almost pityingly, then taunted, "Whom do you think the judge will favor?"

"There's my parents," Vichy cried desperately. "They'll help me."

"Oh, great," Ben scoffed. "You'd lay that kind of responsibility on them at their age." His voice dripped sarcasm. "How very thoughtful of you. You're all heart."

Without her conscious volition, Vichy's free hand moved to cover her still flat abdomen protectively.

"Ben, please, don't do this to me," she begged raggedly. Begging was all she had left. She knew that without any visible means of support, if he carried through with his threat to sue, she would very probably lose.

"How badly do you want this baby?" This time his tightening fingers caused pain in her arm. Refusing to let him see the pain she was feeling, both mentally and physically, Vichy swallowed the gasp that rose to her lips.

"Very badly," she admitted in a whispery voice. Her tautly held body swayed when he suddenly released her. "Very badly," she repeated hoarsely.

"Badly enough to marry me?" Stepping back, he fixed her with a narrow-eyed stare, closely watching for her reaction. "And sleep with me again?" he asked very softly. His close scrutiny was rewarded when her body jerked spasmodically.

"Ben, I told you —" Vichy began in renewed anger.

"There is no other way in hell you'll get to keep it," Ben cut her off brutally. "Hard as it may be for you to believe, I want this child every bit as badly as you do."

"But why?" she cried despairingly. "You have Chad."

Shrugging dismissively, Ben turned away from her. "You may as well take off your coat and sit down," he advised, lowering his long frame into one of the room's two molded plastic chairs. "It's beginning to look as if you're going to be here awhile."

Although Vichy did remove her coat awkwardly with trembling fingers, she did not sit down. She could not; she was far too tense, too nervous. Standing before him, her hands clasped tightly in front of her, Vichy tried again to change his mind by reminding him of his son.

"Ben, you do have Chad," she said with a minimum of control. "Let me have my child."

"All to yourself?" he asked with deceptive quiet. "I'd have no rights at all? No visitation privileges? No say in the way he, or she, is raised?" Ben's lips twisted. "No

477

financial obligations?"

For one wild moment Vichy actually thought the idea of having no financial obligations might sway the argument in her favor, but then his expression told her that for one wild moment she wasn't thinking at all. Still, she had to try one more time. "You *do* have Chad," she reminded him frantically.

At first Vichy thought he would make no response at all. Then, to her dismay, she saw a muscle ripple in his jaw an instant before his face settled more harshly into place.

"Yes, I have Chad," Ben replied in a tone every bit as harsh as his expression. "And I am his father in every sense of the word but one." He paused, as if not quite sure if he wanted to go on. Then, in words clear and distinct, he said, "I am not Chad's natural father."

Vichy stared at him in sheer disbelief and confusion. Then she gave a nervous little laugh. "But that's ludicrous! You told me you got custody at the time of the divorce. If he wasn't yours, why would you have . . ."

"I didn't know." His tight voice sliced across hers. "My wife told me in the hall just outside of the room in which the verdict was rendered." He laughed unpleasantly. "She didn't want to be tied down, she said, so she let me believe Chad was mine, knowing I'd fight for him, fight for everything I was worth. She was absolutely right."

Vichy opened her mouth, but he forestalled her questions as though he'd read her mind.

"I had the blood work done. He is definitely *not* mine." His eyes sharpened on her face. "I *will* have my own child, Vich. One way or another. It is entirely up to you."

Vichy felt trapped. Trapped in a motel with a man who was totally unbending. Restlessly, she paced the width of the room, once, twice, raking her mind for a way out. If she could get some money, she thought irrationally, she could disappear. If only . . . Josh! Josh would loan her some money, she knew it!

"May I have some time?" she asked warily, coming to a stop in front of him.

Ben was way ahead of her. "So you can run away again?" He laughed. "You have got to be kidding. I had enough trouble finding you this time. I don't care to repeat the exercise. I'm not your basic Sherlock Holmes type."

"Oh, I'm well aware of that," Vichy retorted. "You're more the basic gambler type."

"What the hell does that mean?" he

snapped, backing her up abruptly as he stood up.

"It — it doesn't matter," Vichy answered vaguely, her mind working on something else. "How *did* you find me?" She put her thoughts into words.

"Elementary, my dear," Ben drawled. "First I went to the address you had given me," he paused to smile nastily. "The super told me you'd moved without leaving a forwarding address. That was two weeks ago." He thrust his hands into the pockets of his jeans in a way that left her in little doubt he was fighting the need to shake her, or worse. His stance was intimidating, and Vichy backed up a step. Her movement brought a parody of a smile to his face. "Last weekend I drove back down to Atlantic City." He went on calmly. Too calmly. "I went to the hotel management. They refused to divulge any information at all about you." His smile turned sardonic. "By the time I thought of talking to Ken, I wasn't even sure anymore why I wanted to find you."

"But Ken didn't have my parents' address!" Vichy exclaimed.

"But Ken did know the name of your agent," Ben shot back.

"Bernie!"

"Yes, Bernie," Ben retorted. "I flew back out to California yesterday. He didn't want

480

to say anything at first but after I'd convinced him we'd had a lovers' quarrel, he opened up. He told me all about how you had decided to quit the entertainment business and go home to stay. He also told me where home was." He bowed mockingly. "And here I am, at your service."

"You had no right —" Vichy began angrily.

"I *thought* I had every right," Ben again cut her off harshly. "I *thought* the time we'd spent together gave me that right, at least to an explanation of why you took off without a word the way you did."

Vichy stood perfectly still. It was very close, but then, it was always very close: that memory of Ben's laughing, and the woman so eager to kiss him. Shaking her head to dispel the scene, Vichy looked him straight in the eye and lied, "I — I just decided it was time to go home; the affair was over."

"Affair?" Ben's icy tone chilled her. "Affair?" he repeated cuttingly. "Well, sweetheart," he sneered the endearment, "I'm afraid the 'affair' is going to have to continue. That is, if you want to keep this child."

Everything about him told Vichy that argument would be futile, yet she had to try one more time. "Ben, please, don't go through with this. Can't you see how unfair it would be to the child? I mean, to bring a child into a home where there's dissension just would not be fair."

"And you're so sure there will be dissension?" Ben rapped. "We weren't doing too badly in that motel room, you know."

Not as long as I was foolishly believing that I was your only woman, Vichy cried silently. *How could I bear to live with you, sleep with you, and wonder day and night how many others there are?* Aloud, all she said was, "I don't want to get married. I've *been* that route. I didn't like the scenery."

"Damn it, Vich!" Ben exploded. "I didn't give you a rough time, he did. If we both work at it, we can make a go of it. We have to." He sighed, and for a fleeting second Vichy thought she saw a hint of sadness, or disappointment, flicker over his face. Then it was gone and his expression was harsher. "Besides which," he sighed again, "there's no other way. You want the child. I want the child. We will just have to share it . . . legally."

Still Vichy argued. For over an hour she ranted, raved, and even cried, all to no avail. Ben remained adamant; he would not bend. Either she married him, or she fought him in court. In the end she gave in, as he very likely knew she would.

"All right, all right!" she shouted, when

she finally realized he was not going to budge. "I'll marry you, damn you, but don't blame me if we wind up in a divorce court." That she sounded childish, she knew, but at that point she no longer cared. Never had she encountered such an exasperating man!

"How charmingly you accept my proposal," Ben snarled. "If we do wind up in a divorce court, it won't be because I haven't tried." He turned away, as if he could no longer bear the sight of her. "We'll get the ball rolling tomorrow morning," he said when he turned back to her. His face was now washed clean of all expression and his tone was flat, deadly flat. "We'll get married as soon as it is legally possible."

"Tomorrow morning!" Vichy repeated, stunned. "But — but surely you want to go home and prepare Chad, don't you?"

"Chad will accept whatever I tell him," Ben informed her arrogantly. "When I go home, you will be with me. I really hate to say that I don't trust you, Vich, but I don't." His tone took on iron determination. "I will stay right here, in this very room, until after we are married."

"I am not going to run away, Ben," Vichy sighed. "I know when I'm beaten."

"Sure," he snorted. "Nevertheless, I'll stay here. I think we'll do it Saturday.

Now, put your coat on and we'll get things started."

"What can we do tonight?" Vichy squeaked. He was moving much too fast for her and the strain showed in her voice.

"Tell your parents," Ben told her coolly, shrugging into a Polartec jacket.

"I'll tell them," Vichy said shakily, beginning to panic. "You don't have to go with me."

"I know I don't *have* to go with you," Ben retorted, "but I am going. I helped make it, I'll face your family with you."

Half sick to her stomach, Vichy drove back to her parents' home, Ben, in the Lexus, right on her tail. She found both her parents and Bette in the kitchen having a before-bed cup of chocolate. Bette's cheeks flared red when she saw Ben, and her glance shied away from Vichy's. Biting her lip, Vichy fumbled for words to tell them about her condition.

"Mom, Dad, I — I —"

"Vich is pregnant," Ben said flatly over her inept stammering. "We are going to get married."

As subtle as a machine gun, Vichy thought, inwardly wincing at the expressions of shock her parents could not disguise. Surprisingly, they rallied quickly.

"It happens in the best of families," Luke murmured dryly after a short, tense silence. Getting to his feet, he extended his hand to Ben.

"I'm sorry for my bluntness," Ben apologized, accepting Luke's handshake. "But I figured the best way to get it done was to do it."

Strangely — at least Vichy thought it strange — Luke seemed to not only understand, but to agree with Ben.

"Know what you mean." Luke nodded. "So, when are you two going to tie the knot?"

"Saturday," Ben replied.

"It's best." Luke again nodded.

During this exchange Vichy, Johanna, and Bette stared from one to the other in confusion.

"Well, Johanna, don't you have anything to say?" Luke prodded his wife out of her near trance.

"What's to say?" Johanna asked calmly. "It seems to me you and Ben have already said it all." She drew a deep breath, which told Vichy she was not nearly as calm as she pretended to be. "I would have preferred a different, more conventional wedding for Vichy, but, as you say, these things do happen." She blinked and swallowed hard, and Vichy found herself blinking rapidly. "What plans have you made?" She glanced from Vichy to Ben.

"None really," Vichy admitted.

"Other than to get married as soon as possible," Ben added. "I have a young son at home and I would like to get back to him by the beginning of next week." His smile held heartwarming charm. "I know he is going to love Vich every bit as much as I do."

Vichy had to gulp back the gasp that rose to her lips. How dare he stand there and lie to her parents like that! When just a few weeks ago he had been celebrating with another woman! Fighting down the urge to slap his lying mouth, Vichy said quickly, "And I know I'm going to love him." *I at least mean what I say,* she thought smugly. *I will try very hard to be a good substitute mother.*

Ben stayed for over an hour. Johanna made more hot chocolate, then, the five of them sitting around the kitchen table, they discussed what Vichy and Ben would have to do before they could get married. Although Ben insisted they wanted no fuss, he finally gave in to Johanna's insistence that a small family party be held after the ceremony.

By the time Vichy got into bed, she was so tired she immediately fell into a deep sleep, only to toss and turn most of the night with dreams of herself decked out in full bridal attire, walking down the aisle while a church full of beautiful women laughed and took turns kissing Ben.

Vichy went to the breakfast table the next morning bleary-eyed and dull-witted. She and her mother were alone in the kitchen, as her father was hiding out in the barn and Bette had long since left to go back to school.

"You'd better have something to eat," Johanna advised, glancing at the clock. "Ben will be here in less then an hour."

How did it happen, Vichy wondered, that her mother spoke so easily of Ben? Oh, he had been utterly charming to her, as well as to her father and Bette, but Vichy had always thought both her parents were shrewd judges of character. Yet all three of them seemed to look on him as something special. Of course, they didn't know him the way she did, she told herself, conveniently forgetting she had thought him very special until the last night of her engagement at the hotel.

"I called Mattie and Josh a little while ago." Johanna startled her with that bit of news. "They will both be here early Saturday morning."

Vichy had to swallow to dislodge the tightness in her throat. "What did they say? Did you tell them that I'm pregnant?"

"Yes, of course I told them." Johanna sighed. "What could they say? I think Josh was more shocked than Mattie." She shook her head. "I really believe Josh thought of you as above that sort of thing."

Vichy winced and averted her suddenly teary eyes. God, she hated to disillusion Josh. He had always been so protective of her. So very much the big brother.

"Now don't go feeling bad about Josh," Johanna admonished, correctly reading Vichy's emotions. "He'll be fine as soon as he takes the time to think. We are all merely human, Vichy. Getting pregnant by the man you love is nothing to be ashamed of." Slipping an arm around her shoulders, she gave her a quick hug, then scolded, "Now eat something. You and Ben have a lot to do."

Saturday dawned clear and bitter cold, and Vichy wanted nothing more then to burrow under her covers and escape the day. She loved Ben. If possible more now than before. But she was selfish as far as he was concerned, and the idea of possibly having to share him with others was a torment she would just as soon not have to go through.

The arrival of Mattie and her family drew her out of her bed with a sigh of resignation.

Josh and his family arrived thirty minutes after Mattie and the house rang with voices, all talking at the same time, all, including Josh, teasing Vichy unmercifully. Her family might have been initially shocked at the news of her pregnancy and the need for a hurried wedding, but they were a close unit and they had closed ranks protectively around her.

In midafternoon they made a three-car convoy as they drove to the district justice's office. Ben was waiting for them, and Vichy made hurried introductions before they went inside. In less than fifteen minutes it was over, and Vichy's finger was adorned with a plain band of gold that proclaimed her Ben's wife.

The party began as soon as they got back to the house. Vichy, in an effort to avoid close contact with Ben, kept herself busy helping her mother with the food and her father with the drinks — which seemed to flow very freely. At one point she observed Ben in deep conversation with Mattie. At another, she saw Josh and Ben with their heads together. Quite sure her big brother and sister were cautioning Ben on taking care of her, Vichy steered clear of both conferences.

Vichy went cold all over when Ben declared it was time for them to leave. Moving stiffly, she went to her room to get her coat and overnight case — the only case that had not been stashed in her car. Fighting tears, she glanced slowly around the only room she had ever really thought of as hers and then, turning away quickly, she walked out and closed the door.

Their leave-taking was prolonged and noisy, but finally Vichy was behind the wheel of her car following Ben's Lexus to the motel.

As she trailed his red taillights, it suddenly hit Vichy that other than somewhere in central New Jersey, she hadn't the vaguest idea of where she was going. The plan had been for them to stop at the motel for Ben's things and then drive straight through to his home, Vichy following him in her own car. So, when they reached the motel, Vichy remained behind the wheel and frowned at Ben when he came around to her door and opened it.

"I'll wait here," she said tersely.

"I've changed my mind," Ben informed her coolly. "It's too late to start home today. We'll stay here tonight and get an early start in the morning."

"B-but —" Vichy stuttered, suddenly very, very nervous.

"I'm too tired to argue, Vich." Ben sighed, swinging the door wide. "Just get out of the car . . . please."

Knowing procrastination would be futile, Vichy slid from behind the wheel, thankful that the room had two beds.

"You may have the bathroom first," Ben

offered as soon as the door had closed behind them.

Not about to argue, Vichy opened her valise, removed her nightwear, and dashed into the bathroom. She drew out her shower and nightly routine as long as possible and then, belting her robe securely, she walked back into the bedroom and stopped in her tracks.

Twelve

Ben, looking tall and lean and altogether too naked in nothing but boxers, was turning from one of the beds where he had just folded back the covers.

"You look tired," he said softly, his eyes making a minute inspection of her face. With a wave of his hand he indicated the bed. "Why don't you turn in?"

The sight of him unnerved her and, breathing carefully, she murmured, "I am not sleeping with you, Ben."

"Why not?" he asked even more softly. "You enjoyed sleeping with me before."

"Yes," Vichy snapped. "Before I realized I was expected to share you with others."

Ben went rigid, a frown drawing a dark line between his brows. "I think you had better explain that remark," he rapped sharply.

His tone flicked her on the raw. How dare he play the innocent? she riled silently. Standing stiffly erect, she glared at him defiantly. He was totally unimpressed.

"I'm waiting, Vich," he ground out, sounding like a man who was hanging on to his patience by sheer willpower. Moving slowly, he crossed the room to stand in front of her, his eyes warning dire things if she did not speak quickly.

Vichy was suddenly very tired. She had been living on her nerves for weeks. Now, when she needed them most, her nerves gave up the battle. Closing her eyes wearily, she began speaking in a flat monotone.

"I was married when I was twenty-two. A very young, dumb twenty-two."

"What does that have to do —" Ben stopped speaking when Vichy went on as if she hadn't heard him.

"Although there is no resemblance whatever between you and Brad, he loved to gamble, much the same as you do."

"Now, wait a minute!" Ben exclaimed, but again she went on, his protest unheard.

"We were married six months. I was working one of the smaller rooms in Vegas and, again much the same as you, he showed up every night for my final set. Until that last night."

Here she stopped her narrative to open her eyes and stare at him. When she continued, her voice was even lower, flatter. "I hadn't even realized the parallel but, exactly like you, he did not show up that last night. And exactly like that last night in

Atlantic City with you, I was not concerned." Vichy paused to smile humorlessly. "The difference was, unlike that last night in Atlantic City, I did not find Brad in the casino. I didn't even look for him there." Her smile disappeared. "Positive he was planning a private celebration of our six-month-old marriage, I rushed to our room."

Vichy had Ben's undivided attention now. As if sensing what was coming, he was hanging on to her every word.

"Wanting to surprise him, I unlocked the door to our room soundlessly. When the door swung open, the bottom fell out of my life. The light was on, and Brad was in bed, but he wasn't asleep, and he wasn't alone." A shudder of remembrance shook her slender body and, with a muttered curse, Ben's hand grasped her upper arms.

"Vichy, stop."

This time his fingers inflicted no pain, for though his hold on her was firm, it was also tenderly protective. His tone reflected the emotions guiding his hands.

Ignoring his command, Vichy went on tonelessly. "The woman was a cocktail waitress in the lounge, and she was beautiful. They were in bed."

"Vichy, stop!"

This time his emotion-roughened voice drew her eyes to his. His were dark red with concern. Hers were opaque with sadness.

"Vichy." Ben's hands moved, giving her a gentle shake. "I'm sorry for what you had to go through, but I do not see what it has to do —" He broke off, his gaze narrowing on her face. "You said, 'Unlike that last night in Atlantic City, you did not find Brad in the casino.' What did you mean?"

"I did find you," she answered wearily.

"I don't understand." Ben shook his head. "I didn't see you again after you told me to get lost."

"I know, but I saw you." Now the blue eyes that gazed at him were misty with tears. "You were standing at the cashier's cage, having just cashed in chips to the tune of thirty-four thousand dollars. You were not alone. There was a young woman with you. She had her arms around your waist, and you were laughing and kissing each other."

"Vichy, for God's sake, that —"

"While I watched you I could see that hotel room, that bed." The low monotone was gone. With every other word Vichy's voice rose, building to an anguished cry.

"Only it wasn't Brad on that bed. Brad doesn't matter anymore. It was you I saw, Ben, you. And the pain I felt was unbearable."

"Vichy!"

"I couldn't stand it, Ben." Vichy was sobbing now, her arms wrapped tightly around her midsection as if to hold herself together. "Oh, God, Ben, I still can't stand it."

"Oh, good Lord." Ben's groan was a plea, not a curse. Sliding his arms around her, he pulled her against him, holding her tightly, as if to contain and absorb the sobs that shook her.

"Vichy, listen to me, listen," Ben said urgently. "That woman was Mike's wife, Shelly. Are you listening?" He felt her head move up and down, then he went on quietly. "She and Mike found me at the craps table just about the time I'd decided to quit while I was ahead. They had been looking for me throughout most of the day. If you hadn't run, if you had come to me, you'd have found Mike standing three feet away, grinning his damn fool head off." He bent his head and she felt his lips move against her hair. "If you had only come to me."

"Oh, Ben," Vichy moaned into his chest. "I could not have walked to you then. You can't imagine what I was feeling." Her weeping had subsided into hiccuping sobs.

"I have an idea." His arms tightened crushingly. "I know the rage and pain I felt when you intimated you had been with Mark Hartman." His voice dropped to a

496

raspy growl. "You were lying, weren't you?"

Her murmured response was barely audible, but the affirmative motion of her head was all the answer he required. Lowering his head farther, his lips brushed over her temple, then over her ear.

"I love you, Vichy," Ben whispered fervently. "I didn't know what to do when I couldn't find you that night. Then, when I went back to our room and found your bracelet and necklace on the bed and realized you'd gone" — his voice held a raw note, and Vichy felt the shudder that rippled through his long body — "I — I thought I'd go crazy. And then, when I couldn't find you in California . . ." His one hand came up to tangle in her disheveled mass of dark hair. Tugging gently, he forced her head back until he could stare into her tear-blurred eyes.

"After what you just said, you don't have to tell me you love me. I know you do. But I want to hear it just the same."

"I love you, Ben, desperately."

Her avowal, her parted, trembling lips proved too much for him. With a groaned "Oh, God, Vichy," he fastened his mouth onto hers.

Scooping her up into his arms, Ben carried her to the bed. "I've been like a wildman these last weeks," he murmured as he lay down beside her. "I haven't slept worth a damn." His lips teased hers into supplication. "I'd grown too used to waking and finding you beside me."

His tongue snaked out, searching for hers. Ben was quiet for some seconds as his lips, his tongue tasted the sweetness of her mouth. "I need you, Vichy. I forget how to live when I'm away from you. Love me, sweetheart. I'm so empty. Fill me with your love."

Ben's hands, moving with urgent restlessness over her responding body, evoked a familiar wildness in Vichy. Gasping his name over and over, she lost herself in the madness that seemed to affect them both in equal measure.

Time, place, the rest of the world lost all meaning as she took him to herself as greedily as he possessed her. With her mouth and her body and her enfolding arms and legs, she immersed herself in the sensuousness of Ben's driving need of her.

It was very late when Vichy stirred inside the warm circle of Ben's arms.

"Are you cold?" he whispered.

"No." Vichy moved her face against his hair-rough chest. "I'm — I'm frightened."

"Frightened?" Ben echoed in astonishment. His body stiffened, then jerked as he flipped her onto her back where he could look into her face. "Frightened of what?"

His tone reflected the baffled expression on his face.

"I was married to a gambler before, Ben." Vichy sighed. "I can't stand the idea of living my life on the highs and lows of the careless toss of a pair of dice."

"What the hell is this?" Jackknifing into a sitting position, Ben turned and grasped her naked shoulders to hold her flat and still. "I am not a gambler. I enjoy gambling occasionally, simply for the challenge. Lord, Vichy, life itself is a gamble."

"Are you telling me you don't gamble compulsively?" Vichy asked warily.

"Hell, no!" Ben exploded. "I told you I have a job. If you had asked, I'd have told you how I earn my living."

"But I thought it was just any old job, meaningless and unimportant," Vichy cried. "A stopgap for when the dice or cards are cold for you."

"Good grief, I don't believe this!" Ben exclaimed, shaking his head. "Vichy, I'm a research scientist."

"A what!" Vichy's eyes flew wide in astonishment.

"A scientist," Ben nearly shouted. "Does the name Princeton ring a bell?"

"Princeton?" Vichy repeated dumbly. Then, her eyes widening even more, she whispered, "The Princeton?"

"The very same," Ben drawled dryly.

"And that's where we're going tomorrow?" she asked hesitantly.

"You got it." Ben's tone now held amusement.

Vichy bit her lip in consternation, feeling unbelievably stupid. "Then that's why you were free to be in Atlantic City that first week?" she had to ask, even though she already knew the answer.

"Right on center." Ben nodded, obviously fighting laughter. "I was on Thanksgiving break."

"Oh, Ben," Vichy wailed. "To think I almost threw it all away! I feel like such a fool."

Her tone washed all sign of amusement from his face. Releasing his hold on her shoulders, Ben slid his hands out along the bed until he was spread-eagle on top of her. Touching her lips gently with his, he kissed her lingeringly.

"I love you," he whispered when he lifted his head. "And I don't care if you are a fool." His smile took her breath away. "As long as you are *my* fool."

The house, just off campus, was quiet and dark, except for a dim light in the small, centrally located room on the second floor. The leaves on the tree outside the room's one window, their brilliant fall colors reduced to a solid mass of black, rustled dryly in the pre-dawn breeze.

Inside the room the silence was broken by the rhythmic creak of rocking chair runners on the carpeted floor, and a muted, gurgling sound.

Sitting in the rocking chair, a softly tender smile on her face, Vichy gazed down lovingly at her hungrily feeding, perfectly beautiful infant daughter.

In her gulping greed, the source of the milky flow was lost, and her tiny bud lips opened in a wail of frustration. Her smile deepening, Vichy raised a hand to her breast to reinsert the nipple inside her daughter's searching mouth.

"Slow down, you little pig," she murmured laughingly. "As your pop-pop would tell you: The faster you go, the behinder you get."

A soft chuckle drew her bemused glance to the doorway. Leaning lazily against the door frame, wearing only a pair of tight faded blue jeans that looked like they'd been spray-painted onto the lower half of his body, Ben watched the feeding ritual.

As her eyes touched him, Vichy was struck by the expression on his face. She had seen an expression almost exactly like that before, but where?

"I'm sorry, darling, did we wake you?" Vichy asked softly.

"No." Ben's tone matched hers for softness. "I woke up and got to missing you." His eyes remained fastened on his daughter's ecstatic face. "I'm jealous of her, you know." Ben made the admission without inflection.

"Jealous!" Vichy gasped. "Don't be silly, Ben."

"I mean it," he insisted calmly. "Every time she stakes a claim on a part of you that I consider within my own territorial rights, I feel a stab of jealousy."

Vichy felt her cheeks grow warm with a combination of embarrassment and pleasure. She didn't know why she still blushed so readily at his outrageousness. She certainly knew by now that Ben said whatever was on his mind. If her husband was nothing else, he was open and completely honest. Of course, she had learned over the last months that he was much more than that. The words *tender, gentle, loving,* and *considerate* jumped into her mind.

"Well, you have one consolation, love," she said soothingly, teasingly. "Her claim is only temporary. You hold lifetime rights."

At her soft assurance he lifted his eyes to hers and the breath caught in her throat. The expression on his face was the same as before, only now Vichy knew where she'd seen it before, and what it meant.

She had caught that same kind of expression on Mattie's husband's face several times when he had thought he was unobserved. The expression was one of near adoration.

Trembling with reaction of her discovery, Vichy studied Ben's visage more thoroughly. More fully defined, his expression proclaimed more than love. Embodied within that expression was total commitment of heart, mind, and soul.

Shaken to the depths of her being, Vichy blinked against the onrush of warm moisture to her eyes. Ben could not miss seeing the gathering tears.

"Are you happy, sweetheart?" he asked anxiously, crossing the floor to stand before her.

"I'm very much afraid," Vichy whispered huskily, "that if I get any happier, I'm going to explode into a million pieces of joyousness."

Ben's relieved laughter surrounded her like a close embrace. Bending over the rocking chair, he kissed her tenderly on the lips, whispering, "I couldn't have put my own feelings into better words."

THE GAME IS
PLAYED

One

"You can get dressed now, Mrs. Ortega, and I'll see you in my office in a few minutes." Helen smiled gently at the timid young woman with the dark expressive eyes, then turned and left the examining room.

Ten minutes later, after seeing the beaming girl out of her consulting office, Helen leaned back into her desk chair with a contented sigh. Maria Ortega's delight in having her maternal expectations confirmed had given her an all-over good feeling. Even after five years of private practice Helen still felt the same satisfaction on diagnosing a wanted pregnancy as she had the first time.

A buzz and blinking light on her desk phone brought Helen upright in her chair, hand reaching for the receiver.

"Yes, Alice?"

The no-nonsense voice of her R.N., Alice Kelly, answered crisply. "Jolene Johnson is on the phone, Doctor. I think you'll want to speak to her yourself. I'll

507

have her chart on your desk in a minute."

"Thank you, Alice." A long, slender forefinger touched the blinking button and in a tone professionally confident she asked, "What's the problem, Jolene?" Automatically glancing at the clock, Helen noted the time: one fifteen. Fifteen minutes into her half day.

Every Wednesday Alice scheduled patients no later than twelve thirty or twelve forty-five, depending on the medical requirements, in order to have the office clear of patients by one o'clock, thereby giving Helen one free afternoon a week. Helen hoped to one day achieve that free afternoon.

Now as she glanced at the clock she gave a small sigh. She had so wanted to get to that lecture at Temple this afternoon.

"I don't know if it is a problem, Dr. Cassidy." Jolene Johnson's young voice wavered unsurely. "But Tim insisted I call you."

Thoughts of free afternoons and lectures banished, Helen replied soothingly, "Suppose you tell me why your husband insisted you call me and we'll take it from there."

"Well, I have this odd little trickle. It's the strangest sensation. It started after lunch when I stood up to clear the table and it happened twice while I did the dishes. It's not like the book says happens when the water sac breaks, and I have no pain or anything, but it does feel funny."

As the girl was speaking Alice quietly entered the room and placed the open folder on Helen's desk. Helen nodded her thanks, lifted her oversize, dark-framed reading glasses from the desk, and slid them into place, her eyes scanning the neatly annotated sheets for pertinent facts while a picture of Jolene Johnson rose in her mind. A pretty girl of average height and weight, she was twenty-three years old, married two years, and was one week into her ninth month of pregnancy.

"Your husband was right, Jolene." Helen's voice was calm, unhurried. "I want you to get yourself ready and go to the hospital."

"But, Doctor, I don't even have any pain!"

"I know, Jolene, but although you've had no gush of water, you are leaking and I want you in the hospital. I'll call so they'll be expecting you."

"Eh — I —" The beginning of fear in the young woman's voice was unmistakable. "Okay, if you say so." Then more softly. "Doctor, do you think something's wrong?"

"I doubt it, Jolene."

Helen's eyes had completed their perusal

of the girl's chart and her voice was confident with the medical data she'd read. Jolene's pregnancy had been normal so far, with no indication of any irregularities. She'd have to examine the woman, of course, but she felt sure Jolene and the baby were in no danger.

"Don't be alarmed. The hospital staff will take good care of you and I'll be in to see you later this afternoon."

Helen's quiet tone had the hoped-for calming effect, for the lessening of tension was evident in Jolene's voice.

"All right, Doctor, I'll do whatever you say, and thank you."

Helen sighed as she replaced the receiver and handed the chart to the silently waiting Alice.

"Trouble?" Alice asked quietly. The tall, rawboned woman had been a nurse for over twenty-five years. She had seen much, said little, and was impressed with very few. Helen Cassidy was one of those few.

"I hope not." Helen sighed again. Well, so much for free half days. "Jolene's leaking but has no pain. Nothing very unusual so far, but we'll see."

Alice nodded briefly, then turned and left the room. Helen sat staring at the clock. If she left now, she'd be able to hear some of the lecture, but hearing part of a lecture wouldn't do her much good, so —

she shrugged her slim shoulders resignedly — maybe next time.

In sudden decision Helen pushed her chair back, went to the closet, and removed her storm coat. January was being very unkind to the East Coast this year, and the coat, along with the knee-high suede boots she wore, were not only fashionable, but necessary.

She slipped into the coat, dug in her capacious bag for her car keys, slung the bag's strap over her shoulder, and left the room, slowing her steps but not stopping as she passed Alice's desk.

"I'm going for lunch." She named a restaurant. "And then to the hospital, if you need me."

"Why don't you do yourself a favor and have a good meal for a change?" Alice chided dryly. "You're beginning to resemble your own shadow."

Helen heard the words as she closed the outer door. She was still smiling wryly as she unlocked the door to her Camry and slid behind the wheel. Alice had been on a fatten-up-the-boss campaign for several weeks now, and although her remarks were often pointedly barbed, they had failed to penetrate Helen's composure.

She was slender. She always had been slender. She probably always would be slender. End of story. Helen frowned. True she had been skipping some meals lately in order to keep up with her increasingly heavy schedule. Also true she had lost a few pounds, but at her age that was better than gaining weight.

An hour and a half later Helen walked into Jolene Johnson's hospital room and paused, a smile tugging at her lips. The head nurse stood by the bed, one hand outspread on the expectant mother's distended abdomen, her voice a dry, reassuring drawl.

"It's still in the attic. Relax, honey, it's going to be a long day."

As Helen moved quietly into the room the nurse turned and stepped back from the bed, a warm smile transforming her otherwise plain face.

"Hello, Doctor." Her tone matched her smile in warmth. "Jolene's doing just fine. All prepped and ready to go. At Mother Nature's convenience, of course."

The tug at Helen's lips turned into a full smile. This brash young woman was the most flip, while at the same time the most efficient nurse she had ever worked with.

"Thank you, Kathy."

The nurse nodded at Helen, sent a bracing grin at Jolene, and swung out of the room, whistling softly through her teeth.

Laughing, Helen placed her fingers on

Jolene's wrist to take her pulse, eyes shifting to her watch. Jolene began speaking the moment Helen removed her fingers.

"Doctor, tell me the truth. Am I going to lose my baby?"

Helen paused in the process of adjusting her stethoscope, glancing at the girl sharply. "No, of course not. Whatever gave you that idea?"

"Well." Jolene's lips trembled, "I'm not due for almost a month and I have this horrible feeling that something's wrong."

"Just a moment," Helen murmured, then proceeded to give the young woman a quick, but thorough, examination. When she finished, she straightened and looked Jolene squarely in the eyes. "There is no indication that anything is 'wrong.' Now what I want you to do is relax. You may use the bathroom, but I don't want you out of bed for any other purpose. I want you to rest."

"All right, Doctor," Jolene said softly. Then hesitantly, "May Tim come in?"

"Yes, for a little while," Helen replied, then added firmly, "but I want you to rest. The nurse will be taking your temperature and blood pressure hourly. Don't be alarmed, it's a precautionary measure. You are open to infection now and I want a periodic check just in case. She squeezed the girl's hand before adding. "Now relax and don't worry. I'll be back later to check your progress."

Helen walked out of the room, paused a few minutes to speak to Kathy, informing her that she'd be in the cafeteria if needed, then left the section.

As she walked along the halls toward the lunchroom, Helen smiled, nodded, and spoke to several of the doctors and nurses she passed, totally unaware of the admiring glances cast at her retreating back.

Looking tall and slender, her honey-gold hair drawn smoothly back from her classically beautiful face into a neat coil at the back of her head, Helen presented a picture of cool, calm professionalism. She lived up to that picture completely. It seemed she had always known she would become a doctor and had worked steadily toward that goal. During premed she had decided to specialize in gynecology and obstetrics and, except for a few minor and one major emotional entanglements, had concentrated all her energy in that direction.

Now, after five years of private practice and a flawless record, Helen had the reputation of being brilliant in her profession and coldly emotionless. She knew it, and she didn't care. In fact she encouraged the attitude. Within her own sphere Helen had made it. If the cost was occasional weariness, due to a grueling workload, and periodic loneliness, due to her withdrawn attitude, Helen paid the bill and considered the price as minimal.

She had what she wanted. She led a well-ordered existence doing the work she loved. If, at rare intervals, the warm female inside yearned for male companionship, she squashed the yearning ruthlessly.

Helen was of the opinion that in any emotional encounter the odds were heavily stacked in the male's favor. She had been burned, badly, while still in her early twenties and had promised herself that never again would a man get the chance to hurt her. It had taken months for the emotional wounds to heal, and the scars still remained, a searing reminder of the arrogance of the male animal called man.

As she left the lunchroom, after having a soothing cup of tea, Helen heard her name paged. She went to the main desk in the lobby, lifted the phone, and gave her name. After a short pause Alice's voice came calm over the wire.

"Better put on your roller blades, Doctor. I think you are going to be a mite rushed. Mr. Darren just called. He's bringing his wife to the hospital now. Her contractions are four minutes apart. Good luck."

There was a small click as Alice hung

up. Replacing her own receiver, Helen turned away from the desk with a silent groan. Why do they do it? she asked herself as she stepped into the elevator. Why do some of these women wait at home until the last moment? Are they afraid and trying to put off the inevitable as long as possible? Or are they trying to prove how unafraid they are? Helen truly didn't know. What she did know was, she could live without these last-minute rush jobs. And she had thought Kristeen Darren had more sense.

By the time Helen walked into the delivery room, properly capped, gowned, and shod, Kristeen was only minutes away from motherhood.

"Good afternoon, Kristeen." Helen's voice filtered coolly through the mask, which covered the lower half of her face. Above the mask her hazel eyes smiled warmly at the pale young woman. "Longing to have it over with and hold your baby in your arms?"

"Yes, Doctor." Kristeen began a smile that turned to a gasp as a hard contraction gripped her.

Helen's eyes shot a question at the anesthesiologist, who nodded and murmured, "Ready to go."

Less than twenty minutes later Helen walked out of the delivery room, leaving behind a very tired but ecstatically happy mother of a perfectly formed baby daughter.

After cleaning up, Helen went into Jolene Johnson's room, evicted young Tim Johnson with the assurance that he would be called when the time came, and spent the following twenty-five minutes examining Jolene and talking down her renewed anxieties.

"I want you to rest," she reiterated as she was leaving the room. "Sleep if possible. Conserve your strength for when your labor does begin. And don't worry, I'll be back later."

She was standing at the nurses' station, making notations on Jolene's chart and talking with Kathy when a nurse and a young student nurse rushed up to the desk all flustered and excited.

"You should have seen what we just bumped into, Kathy," the nurse, a dark-haired, attractive young woman in her midtwenties, said breathlessly.

Kathy eyed the two in amusement. "Good to look at, was he?" she asked dryly.

"Good!" the petite student gushed. "He was totally awesome. Tall, red-haired, blue-eyed, and shoulders like a linebacker. What a hunk," she finished breathlessly.

Kathy, obviously unimpressed, shot a long-suffering glance at Helen, who, lips twitching, opened her eyes innocently wide and fluttered naturally long, silky lashes at her, then turned and walked away without a word. Behind her she heard Kathy laugh softly, and the student nurse proclaim, "No kidding, Kath, he really was a hunk."

A smile still tugging the corners of her mouth, Helen pushed through the heavy swing doors that separated the labor and delivery rooms from the maternity section, thinking that, as Kristeen Darren was probably settled into a room by now, she might as well look in on her before leaving the floor.

The smile left her face on hearing her name mentioned as she approached the nurses' station.

"If Dr. Cassidy walked in now, we'd all catch hell." The irate nurse, standing with her back to Helen, was so agitated, she missed the warning shake of the head from the gray-haired nurse she was speaking to. "But I can't budge them."

Before the older woman, who was facing both Helen and the angry nurse, could respond, Helen asked quietly, "What's the problem, Nancee?"

"Oh!" Nancee spun around, her face flushed with exasperation. "Doctor, it's the people in Mrs. Darren's room. There are five people in there, besides her husband. I've told them that, so soon after delivery, there should be no one in there *except* her husband, but they just ignored me. I understand that they're prominent people, and I didn't want to cause any trouble by calling security, but Mrs. Darren looks exhausted."

"There are six people around that bed?" The tone of Helen's voice sent a chill of apprehension down the spines of both nurses.

"I've tried to —" Nancee began.

"I'll go help her clear the room," the older nurse cut in.

"No, I'll do it," Helen stated grimly. "You two have more important things to do than trying to coax a group of unthinking people into behaving rationally."

Ignoring the anxious look the two women exchanged, Helen squared her shoulders and walked the short distance to the room in question. Pausing in the open doorway, Helen's eyes circled the room slowly, missing nothing.

Kristeen Darren did indeed look exhausted, even though her eyes were bright with excitement and pride. Her small pale hand was clasped tightly in a larger one, which obviously belonged to her husband, who, Helen noted with a frown, was sitting on the bed beside her. On either side of the bed were two older couples who Helen correctly identified as the respective grandparents. And at the foot of the bed was a young man, somewhere around thirty, Helen judged, who could be no one other than the "totally awesome hunk," the giddy young student nurse had been starry-eyed over.

Helen's eyes lingered long seconds on the man. Up to a point the student's assessments had been correct. But only up to a point. He *was* tall and his shoulders did look like they belonged on a linebacker. But this was no mere "hunk." This was more like bad news for all females. And his hair could not really be described as red. It was more of a deep chestnut-brown, the red highlights gleaming in the glare from the overhead light. And the face was shatteringly masculine. At least the profile, which was what Helen viewed, was.

"Is this party strictly family or may anyone join in?"

The caustic question, spoken in Helen's most professional, icy tone, jerked five startled faces toward her. Before anyone could protest or even open their mouths, Helen added, "As it seems to have slipped everyone's mind, might I remind you that this woman has just given birth, and although she did not have a very hard delivery, it is never easy. She is tired. She needs rest, and as I want to examine her, I will give you thirty seconds to vacate this room."

The startled expressions changed to embarrassment on all the faces but one. The "hunk" turned, giving Helen the full impact of rugged good looks, an ice-blue stare, and a voice loaded with cool, male confidence.

"You must forgive us, Doctor." The smooth, deep voice held not a hint of apology. "This is the first child born in both families for some twenty-odd years and I'm afraid we've all been slightly carried away with her advent." His eyes shifted briefly to Kristeen, clearly his sister, then swung back to Helen. "But I see you are right. Kristeen does look very tired." His eyes took on the glint of devilment. "If you would step out of the doorway, we will all file quietly out and leave you to do your job."

A shaft of hot anger stiffened Helen's already straight spine. This silken-mouthed young man was most assuredly overdue for his comeuppance. "Thank you," she snapped acidly, then turned away as if he were of no importance at all and addressed his brother-in-law in a pleasant tone.

"I'm sorry, Mr. Darren, but you really must leave now. If you have any questions about your wife's condition, please wait in the hall. I'll only be a few minutes."

As she was speaking she heard the muffled movements as the others left the room. When she finished, she favored the new father with her most disarming smile.

That young man grinned sheepishly as he grasped his wife's hand.

"No, Doctor, I'm sorry. We were all thoughtless and inconsiderate." He gazed down at his wife, his eyes warm with love. "I'm so proud of her, we all are, and yet we remained, tiring her even more. Our only excuse, as Marsh said, is that we got carried away. I have no questions, as you filled me in perfectly after the baby was born." He bent, kissed his wife lingeringly on the mouth, murmured a few love words to her, then straightened, released his hand, and stretched it out to Helen. "I'll get out of here now. Thank you, Doctor, for everything."

Clasping his hand, Helen laughed softly. "I didn't do anything. Kristeen did all the hard work."

The moment he was out of the room, Kristeen said quietly, "I must apologize for my brother, Dr. Cassidy. I know he made you angry, but you see, Marsh is used to issuing orders, not taking them."

"No matter," Helen brushed aside the subject of that young man. "Let's see how you've progressed." She did a routine check, asked a few questions, then, as she removed her stethoscope, pronounced,

"Very good. Now, if you behave yourself, get some rest, and eat a good dinner, you may have visitors this evening." She started to move away from the bed, then paused and glanced archly over her shoulder. "Two at a time, please."

"Yes, Doctor," Kristeen promised meekly.

The hall was clear of Kristeen's visitors except for the "hunk" who leaned lazily against the wall next to the doorway, speculatively eyeing the passing nurses. As though he were invisible, Helen stepped by him briskly and headed down the hall. Silently, effortlessly, he fell into step beside her.

"I'd like a word with you, Doctor," the deep voice requested blandly.

Helen felt her hackles rise, followed by shocked surprise. What was it about this man that put her back up? For in all truth she had felt it the moment she'd clapped eyes on him.

"What about?" She bristled.

"Temper, temper," he murmured, then, at the flash of her eyes, "my sister, among other things."

Helen's steps didn't falter as she turned her head and raised her eyebrows at him in question.

"I've been told I was rude and owe you an apology by" — he raised his left hand

and ticked off the fingers one by one with his right forefinger — "my mother, my father, my brother-in-law, and his most respected parents. By way of an apology let me buy you dinner."

Coming to a full stop in front of the doors into the labor and delivery section, Helen turned to face him, shaking her head. "No, thank you, Mr. —"

"Kirk, Marshall Kirk. Most people call me Marsh."

"I am not most people," Helen elucidated clearly. "Now if you will excuse me, I have a patient waiting." On the last word she pushed the door open, stepped through, and let it swing back in his face.

Jolene's condition was stable and unchanged. She had not had a twinge of pain, and as she was getting bored and restless with her confinement, Helen sat talking to her for some time. After briefly outlining the procedures she would take if Jolene did not go into labor within a reasonable length of time, Helen left her and stopped at the desk to speak to Kathy.

"Slow day," Kathy drawled, glancing at the clock. "And unless things start happening mighty quickly, I'll be off duty long before Jolene is wheeled into delivery."

Nodding in agreement, Helen's eyes followed Kathy's to the large wall clock, then flickered in surprise. It was almost six thirty! She had been in the section almost an hour and a half. No wonder she was beginning to feel slightly wilted and vaguely empty. Informing Kathy that she was off in search of sustenance, Helen left the section. The sight that met her eyes as she walked through the swing doors brought her to a shocked standstill. Propped against the wall, head back, eyes closed, stood Marshall Kirk, looking, strangely, neither uncomfortable nor out of place. On hearing the door swish closed, his eyes opened and appraised her with cool deliberation.

"Surely you haven't been here all this time, Mr. Kirk?" The frank admiration in that level blue stare put an edge on Helen's tongue.

"I assure you I have, Dr. Cassidy." The sardonic emphasis he placed on her name rattled Helen, giving an even sharper edge to her tone.

"But why?"

Sighing wearily, exaggeratedly, he closed his eyes. When he lifted the lids, he fixed her with an ice-blue gaze so intense that Helen felt a shiver curl up the back of her neck.

"I told you I wanted to talk to you about my sister. I also invited you to have dinner with me, by way of an apology."

Fighting the urge to rub the back of her

neck, wondering at the odd catch in her throat, she rushed her words just a little. "That's not necessary, we can talk in the lounge right here or in the —"

"I know it's not necessary," he interrupted smoothly. "But it is now" — he glanced at the slim gold watch on his wrist — "close to seven. I assume you're hungry. I know I am. Why not have our discussion in a congenial atmosphere and feed the inner person as well?"

Helen stared at him wordlessly for a long second. What was it about this guy? She felt unnerved, a very rare sensation for her, and she didn't know why. Which, of course, unnerved her even more. His attitude, of polite interest, could not be faulted. Nor could his tone, for he sounded pleasantly reasonable. So what was it? Unable to find an answer, or a reason for refusing his invitation, Helen hedged.

"Mr. Kirk, I —"

"Yes, Dr. Cassidy?" he prodded gently.

"Okay," Helen sighed in defeat, then added firmly, "but I cannot go far or be gone too long. I have a patient in there" — she nodded at the large swing doors — "that I want to keep an eye on."

"Is she in labor?" he asked interestedly.

"Not yet." She shook her head. "But that's why I want to keep an eye on her."

"Whatever you say, Doctor." He paused,

obviously thinking, then offered, "There's a small place, fairly close by, an old, renovated inn. Would that do?"

"Yes, anywhere, as long as it's close by." Unsure she'd been wise in accepting him, Helen's tone was almost curt. "I'll need a few minutes. I must get my coat and bag and —"

"Take your time," he cut in. "I'll go get my car and wait for you at the main entrance."

Without waiting for a reply, he strode off down the corridor.

Her teeth nibbling at her lower lip, Helen watched him walk away, an uncomfortable feeling of foreboding stealing over her. She opened her mouth to call him back, tell him she'd changed her mind, then closed it again with a snap. *Don't be ridiculous,* she chided herself scathingly, there is nothing the least bit threatening about this man. He is exactly as he seems. A well-bred, urbane young man interested in the welfare of his sister. That his eyes seemed to have the power to demoralize her she put down to the fact that it had been a long day and that hunger was making her fanciful. Giving herself a mental shake, she walked away quickly.

He was waiting for her, standing beside a dark blue Acura, hands thrust into the

527

pockets of a cashmere topcoat. As her eyes ran over the luxurious garment Helen realized, with a start, that it was the first time she'd noticed his attire. If asked, she doubted if she could describe what he had on under the coat. Strange, she mused, hurrying toward the car, she usually took note of the total person, so to speak. Indeed, she could describe what Kristeen's parents, her husband, and his parents had been wearing, down to the snakeskin shoes the older Mrs. Darren wore on her small feet. Strange.

Preoccupied with her thoughts, Helen was only vaguely aware he'd helped her into the car and slid behind the wheel beside her, when his quiet voice brought her musings to an end.

"Problems?"

"What?" She blinked in confusion, then laughed softly. "No. No problems. I was just thinking."

One dark eyebrow went up questioningly and she was again subjected to that strangely intent blue gaze, then, with a small shrug and a murmured "Good," he turned away and set the car in motion.

A nervous, panicky feeling invaded her stomach and Helen turned her head to glance out of the side window, her teeth again punishing her lower lip. *What in the world,* she thought frantically, *is the matter with me?* She caught herself edging closer to the door and sat perfectly still with shock, her thoughts running wild. *Surely I'm not afraid of him?* Her hands went clammy as her stomach gave a small lurch. But that's preposterous, she told herself sternly. Over the last few years she had met, and had been unaffected by, a number of prominent and powerful men, some of whom had been extremely good-looking. What was it about this man? That she would react at all to him would have been curious. But this! This moist-palmed, all-over crawly sensation was mind bending. And to top it all off, he had to be at least five or six years her junior.

"You really are lost in thought." Once more that deep, quiet voice cut into her thoughts. "Wondering what your husband will say when he finds out you've had dinner with another man?"

It was a deliberate probe and she knew it. For some reason it irritated her.

"I'm not married, Mr. Kirk." Helen paused, then added bitingly, "As I suspect you already know, since I wear no rings."

To her surprise he laughed easily, slanting her a quick, glittering glance.

"No, Doctor, I didn't know, as a lack of rings today is no indication of a woman's marital status." All amusement was gone, replaced by mild disgust. "Quite a few women I know refuse to adorn their fingers with anything as possessive as a man's ring."

The knife-edged sarcasm to his tone shocked her and she stared at him in amazement. What in the world was he attacking her for? Did he think she was lying? The thought that he might brought her chin up in anger.

"I assure you," — she bit heavily on the words — "I have no so mistreated male hidden away."

"Temper, temper." He repeated his chiding admonition of a few hours earlier, then, "Ah, saved by our arrival at our destination."

The inn was old, but beautifully renovated. The decor was rustic, the lighting soft, and the fire that blazed in the huge stone fireplace infused the room with a warmth and welcome that went a long way in draining the anger from Helen.

Sipping at a predinner glass of white wine, Helen studied him over the rim of the glass, taking deliberate note of his clothes. His brown herringbone jacket and open-necked cream-colored shirt looked casually elegant, as did the way he leaned back lazily in his chair, sipping his own wine. His eyes scanned the room disinterestedly, yet Helen had the feeling that not the smallest detail escaped their perusal. And for some unknown reason he scared the hell out of her.

"Will I pass muster, Doctor?"

Helen felt her cheeks grow warm at the amused taunt. She would have vowed he had not observed her study. Deciding attack was the best form of defense, she gave him a level stare.

"Does it matter, Mr. Kirk?" she asked dryly. "You are a very attractive man, as I'm sure you know. I'm sorry if I was staring, but I can't believe you give a damn if you pass muster or not."

The sound of his soft laughter was more potent than the wine. The words that followed the laughter hit her like a blast of sobering cold air.

"Oh, but that's where you're wrong, Doctor. Your opinion of me is very important. You see, I fully intend to rectify the nudity of your left ring finger by encircling it with my wedding ring."

Two

Stunned, speechless, thought and feeling momentarily turned off, Helen sat staring at him while the color slowly drained from her face.

Marsh stared back at her calmly, his cool blue eyes studying her reaction almost clinically.

She opened her mouth, then closed it again. How did one respond to a statement like that? If he'd issued it flippantly or teasingly, she'd have known exactly what to say, but he had been serious, deadly serious.

Feeling returned with anger that surged through her body and up under the delicate skin that covered her cheeks. Helen gritted her teeth against the hot, uncomfortable feeling.

"Mr. Kirk —" she began.

"Yes, ma'am?" Now he was teasing, the light of devilry casting a shimmery gleam on his eyes. Leaning across the table, he caught her hand in his, and when she tried to pull away, his grip tightened, almost painfully.

"If you call me 'Mr. Kirk' again, in that tone of voice, I swear I'll — The name's Marsh. Got that?"

Too angry to speak Helen nodded, glancing pointedly at the large hand covering her own. When she glanced up, her eyes were as cold as her voice.

"Yes, I've got that, Marsh." Her voice lowered, but lost none of its brittleness. "Now if you don't remove your hand, I swear I'll stab you with my salad fork."

His soft laughter rippled across the table, surrounding her in a sudden, surprising warmth. His fingers tightened, somehow adding to the warmth, then he released her.

"Beautiful," he murmured. "My instincts were right. No wonder I fell in love the minute you started snapping at me in Kris's room."

Staring at him in astonishment, Helen froze in her chair, her eyes wide with disbelief at what she'd heard, disbelief and a touch of fear. Was this man some kind of nut? What had she let herself in for, coming out with him? Glancing around the room like a cornered animal, Helen's eyes stopped on the waiter approaching the table with their dinner. Thoughts tumbled chaotically through her mind as she watched the waiter weave around the tables in the crowded room. Should she say she was feeling ill? Ask the waiter to call her a cab, while insisting Marsh stay and have his dinner?

"Relax." Marsh's soft tone cut gently into her thoughts. "And get that hunted look off your face. I'm not planning to abduct you or harm you in any way."

Helen's eyes swung from the waiter back to his and caught, held captive by the tenderness she found there. When the waiter stopped at the table, he sat back, his eyes refusing to release hers. The moment the waiter had finished serving and left the table, Marsh leaned toward her again.

"I promise I'll take you directly back to the hospital when we've finished." That blue gaze remained compellingly steady. "I also promise my pursuit will be ruthless." He smiled at the small gasp that Helen couldn't smother, then commanded gently, "Eat your dinner, you're beginning to look hollow-eyed. There is all the time in the world to discuss this later. By the way —" he paused, frowned. "What the hell is your first name?"

The very abruptness of his tone brought an automatic response from her.

"Helen."

"Helen," he repeated softly, his eyes moving slowly over her face. She could feel the touch of those eyes, and a tiny shiver trickled down her spine.

"Yes," he finally murmured. "I like it. It suits you." He picked up his fork, held it suspended in midair. "By the way, Helen, I must warn you. My intentions are strictly honorable."

Helen was trembling. This conversation, this whole situation, was unreal. She had never seen him before this afternoon, yet there he sat, coolly telling her that he intended to marry her. And those eyes! What was it about his eyes that set her pulses racing, caused this tight, breathless feeling in her chest? The room around her seemed to recede into a shrouded fog, the diners' voices grew dim and blurred. For a brief second out of time she was alone with him in that room. She did not know him, and yet it was as if she had known him forever. The mystical thought brought with it a dart of fear, followed by a shaft of excitement.

"Eat your meal before it gets cold, Helen." His tone was that of a concerned parent, coaxing a peckish child. It was exactly what was needed to break the spell of unreality surrounding her.

The room refocused, the voices took on human quality, and Helen began eating. Slowly, methodically, she made inroads into her food, tasting nothing. He watched her silently until she was almost finished.

"I didn't mean to frighten you, Helen. I only meant to make my position clear."

The very gentleness of his tone struck a nerve. Who the hell did he think he was? And did he think he was speaking to a toddling child? Or a doddering ancient? The food in her stomach infused steel into her backbone and her head came up with a snap.

"You haven't frightened me in the least," she lied. "I've been around a few years, Marsh." She hesitated, then underlined, "A few more than you, I think, and it will take a little more than a weird proposal of marriage to frighten me."

"Weird or not, I meant every word."

She had had enough. She was tired. It had been one very long day.

"If you don't mind, I'd like to go back to the hospital now."

"Of course." His sharp eyes contradicted his bland tone, and his following words gave her the eerie feeling he could read her mind. "You're tired and your day isn't over yet. Let's go."

As they made their way out of the room he placed a hand lightly at the small of her back. It was an impersonal touch, and yet Helen felt a tingle at the base of her spine that moved slowly, shiveringly up to her hairline. Annoyed, confused by her reaction to his slightest touch, she shrugged his hand away, quickening her step.

They were almost back to the hospital when she remembered the reason she'd gone with him in the first place.

"You said you wanted to talk about your sister." She glanced at his profile, sharply etched in the glare of the headlights from the oncoming traffic. A good profile; strong, determined, attractive. Trying to ignore her sudden lack of breath, she continued with a false calmness. "What is it about your sister's condition that bothers you?"

"Not a thing." The calm reply was directed at the street.

"But you said —"

"I lied." He shot a mocking glance at her. "I figured it was the only thing I could say that might get you to go with me, and I had to talk to you alone, tell you."

Helen felt that strange, disoriented feeling surrounding her again, and she shook her head violently to dispel it. "You don't even know me," she whispered hoarsely.

He stopped the car at the hospital's main entrance, then turned to face her.

"I will before too long." He lifted his hand from the steering wheel to cup her face, draw her to him. His thumb moved caressingly, disturbingly, back and forth across her cheekbone, then slowly to the corner of her mouth. "Don't look so shattered." His head moved closer, closer, and Helen couldn't tear her eyes away from his mouth. His lips a mere whisper away from hers, he murmured, "I don't understand it myself. If I believed in reincarnation, I'd believe we have been lovers for a long, long time. I don't know. Hell, I don't even care. But I do know this: While I stood waiting for you in that hall, I knew I loved you and that you were mine."

Stunned, Helen's eyes widened as he spoke those incredible words, one thought screaming through her mind: *I've got to get out of this car.* His eyes held hers, motionless, breathless. His breath was warm against her face, the smell of the wine he'd had with dinner, mingled with the musky scent of his cologne, was intoxicating. When he finished speaking, she moistened parched lips, gave a strangled "No."

Too late. His mouth touched hers in a kiss so sweet, so tender, it was almost reverent in its gentleness. It destroyed her resistance and with a sigh she went limp inside the arms that were suddenly around her, hard and possessive. His lips left hers, moved searingly over her cheek, ruffled the hair at her temple.

"You're trembling," he said softly into her ear. "I know how you feel. I feel it too.

Oh, God, Helen, I don t know what's happening. I've never felt like this before in my life."

Unsure, frightened, not at all the cool, self-contained woman she knew herself to be, Helen stirred, tried to move away from him.

"I — I must go. I have a patient."

"No." His arms tightened. "Not yet."

His mouth sought hers again, but she twisted her head, began to struggle. The word *patient* had pierced the curtain of mistiness that had covered her mind, tore the veil of enchantment that had encircled her.

"Let me go, Marsh." Her voice was steady, controlled, the moment of madness had passed. "I want to go in . . . now."

Marsh sighed deeply but loosened his arms, then reached across her to open the door. "Okay, go to work." Dipping his head quickly, he gave her a fast, hard kiss. "I'll call you tomorrow."

"No. Marsh, I don't —"

A long finger came up to touch her lips, silencing her. "I'll call you tomorrow. Now go."

She went. Out of the car, up the steps, through the door, and across the lobby, practically at a run.

Waiting for the elevator, Helen glanced at her watch then looked closer. Nine forty-five? That couldn't be the correct time! She swung around and her eyes flew to the large wall clock in the lobby. Nine forty-six. How could that be? The elevator doors slid back silently, and a frown marring her smooth brow, Helen stepped inside. She had been gone less than three hours, and yet it seemed such a long time since she'd left the hospital. Hours. Days. Half a lifetime.

A cold shudder shook her body as inside her head his voice whispered over and over again, "I don't know how. Hell, I don't even care. I knew I loved you and that you were mine."

The words jarred in her mind, tore at her nerves. Nails digging into her palms, Helen stared, sightlessly, as the doors slid open at her floor. The doors whooshed softly as they came together and the car gave a mild lurch before it began to move up again. The lurch, mild as it had been, startled Helen back to awareness. Looking up at the floor indicator, she grimaced in self-disgust and stretched her hand out to touch the button of her floor number again. *What a fool you are,* she told herself bleakly. *You must need a vacation very badly.* The doors slid open once more and this time she stepped out quickly, walked down the hall with a determined pace.

Kathy was leaving Jolene's room as Helen crossed the floor toward it.

"Hang in there, Jo, you're doing fine." The nurse spoke over her shoulder, then turning, she flashed a smile at Helen. "That lady means business, Doctor. She went into labor not long after you left and she's gone from one stage to the other like that." Raising her hand, she snapped her fingers three times in succession. "She just might have this baby before I go off duty, after all." She grinned.

Helen grinned back, a sense of normalcy returning with the easy flippancy of Kathy's tone. Marshall Kirk and the bizarre events of the last few hours were pushed to the back of her mind as Helen went into Jolene's room.

Several hours later Helen stood in another elevator, her fingers idly playing with the keys in her hand. Jolene's son, born less than an hour before, had weighed in at seven pounds two ounces, a lusty male, squalling his resentment of the whole procedure. Jolene was doing fine, sleepily content now that her fears were unrealized. A tender smile curved Helen's lips as she remembered the bubbling joy young Tim Johnson had displayed on hearing her news.

The car stopped at the sixth floor and Helen stepped out and walked slowly along the hall to her apartment at the front of the building, a sudden thought wiping the smile from her lips. Tim Johnson had seemed so very young to her, and yet he could not be more than a few years younger than Marshall Kirk!

Hand none too steady, Helen unlocked her door, stepped inside, then leaned back against the smooth panels in sudden weariness. Memories of the few hours she'd spent with him flooded her mind, while a small shiver raced down her spine. What had possessed him to say what he had to her? Closing her eyes, she could almost hear his softly murmured words, feel his warm breath against her skin. Remembering the way she'd melted against him, her breath caught painfully in her throat. What had possessed her?

Opening her eyes, Helen pushed herself away from the door, hung her coat in the closet just inside the door, then walked unerringly through the dark living room to the small hallway that led to her bedroom. A flick of a switch cast a soft glow on the muted green and blue decor in the room, lent a sheen to the expensive dark wood furniture. Moving slowly, Helen sat down on the vanity bench, unzipped, then tugged the boots from her feet. Uncharacteristically she tossed the boots in the direction of her closet, then lifted her hands to remove the clip that held her hair in a neat coil. Freed, her honey-gold mane flowed rich and full to her shoulders, and Helen's fingers pushed through it to massage the scalp at the back of her head, gasping softly as the same tingling she'd experienced earlier that evening spread up her neck and under her fingers.

Stop it, she told herself harshly. *Stop thinking about him. He's a young guy probably looking for a diversion, and an older woman is a challenge.* Her eyes shifted to the mirror, momentarily studying her reflection. The makeup she had carefully applied that morning, and touched up before going to dinner, had worn off, leaving exposed her clear skin, now pale and somewhat taut, with tiny lines of strain at the corners of her eyes and mouth.

It was a beautiful face and Helen knew it. She would be a fool not to know it and she had never been that. The honey fairness, the classic bone structure, the full, soft mouth were gifts from her mother. Her height, her clear hazel eyes, and her determination were gifts from her father. Helen recognized and accepted those gifts with gratitude.

Now staring into those hazel eyes, Helen silently told her reflection, *he'll find no challenge here.* She had no intentions of getting involved with any man, let alone a younger one.

The mirrored eyes seemed to mock her knowingly. There was an attraction between them; she'd be a fool to deny that. The antagonism she'd felt on first sight should have warned her. Yet, she had never experienced anything like that before. How could she have known?

There was very little Helen didn't know about sex, except the actual participation in it. And that, she thought, biting her lip, was the most important part. What she had garnered from textbooks and lectures hardly qualified her as an expert. She knew what happened and the correct terms to define it, but without any real experience she was, in essence, abysmally ignorant.

Without conscious thought Helen brushed her hair and prepared for bed, her mind refusing to let go of the subject. She had come close, very close, to that real experience but she had backed away, almost at the last moment. And because of that long-ago fiasco she was still, unbelievable as it seemed, even to her sometimes, a virgin at thirty-five.

Slipping into bed, Helen lay still, eyes closed, wishing she'd not allowed her thoughts to stray in the direction they had. If she was still innocent, there had to be a reason, and her wandering thoughts had

led to that reason. With a soft sigh of protest Helen saw a picture of a handsome,
curly-haired, laughing young man. Carl
Engle, the man she had been engaged to
while still in college.

Moving restlessly, she turned onto her
side, trying to escape the memories
crowding in on her.

She had been in love as only the very
young can be, misty-eyed, seeing only perfection in the chosen one. They had
seemed perfectly matched. They had
shared the same interests in books, plays,
music, movies, sports, and, most importantly, medicine. They had had wonderful
times together; even studying had been
fun, as long as they studied together. She
had been seeing him exclusively for some
months when he asked her to marry him
and she had accepted him with only one
condition: they would not marry until she
received her M.D. Carl, who was planning
on specializing in pediatrics, had agreed
with a laughing "Of course. We'll make a
great team. You'll deliver them and I'll
take over from there."

Helen groaned and rolled onto her other
side, her eyes tightly shut, as if trying to
shut out the past. She was so tired, why
did she have to think of Carl tonight? Marshall Kirk's face replaced Carl's in her
mind and with another groan she gave up.

Pushing the covers back, she left the bed, slipped into her robe, and walked to the large square window in the wall that ran parallel to her bed. She stared at the dark streets six floors below, lit, at this late hour, only occasionally by the headlights of a passing car. Glancing up, her eyes scanned the sky, following the blinking lights of a passing aircraft. The night was cold and clear, the stars very bright, seemingly very close. A shudder rippled through Helen's body. The stars had seemed very bright and close on that other night too.

She and Carl had been engaged six months and she was very happy, if vaguely discontent. Knowing what the discontent stemmed from was little consolation. Helen had been carefully brought up by loving, protective parents whose views on sex were rigid to the point of puritanical. She had been gently, but firmly, taught that a girl "saves herself" for her wedding night. The nights came, more often as the months went by, that Carl's foreplay became heated and his soft voice cajoled her coaxingly to give in. She had been tempted, filled with the longing to belong to him completely, to be part of him. But her parents had done their job well, and she had stopped him before reaching the no-turning point. In consequence she was left with mingled feelings of guilt and frustration.

Guilt for having the perfectly normal urges that seared through her body, frustration at having to deny those urges.

That was the emotional situation on, what Helen had always thought of since as, *that night.* They had driven over into Jersey to join friends at a beer and pizza bar to celebrate the end of first term. It had been a fun evening with lots of laughter, as they solved the world's problems, decided who would win the upcoming Oscars, and discussed the merits of the latest rock groups. By the time the party broke up, Carl was mellow with beer and feeling very friendly. Instead of heading straight for the bridge to Philly he found a country road and parked the car off the side of the road under the trees.

Another shudder, stronger this time, shook Helen's slim frame and her arms came up to hug herself, her nails digging into the soft flesh of her upper arms. To this day every word, every act that had occurred in that car that night, was as clear in her mind as it had been then.

"Why are we stopping?" she had asked, glancing out the window apprehensively. The area was very dark and desolate, and the idea of being stranded there scared her. "Is there something wrong with the car?"

Laughing softly, Carl had turned to her,

pulled her into his arms. "No, honey, there's nothing wrong with the car. I just couldn't wait to kiss you." His arms loosened, hands moving between them to undo the buttons on her coat. When the buttons were free he pushed the coat open, down, and off her shoulders, tugging it off.

"Carl!" she'd cried. "I'm cold."

The coat was tossed behind him as he slid from under the steering wheel, pushing her along the seat toward the door. "You won't be for long. I'm gonna keep you warm." His jacket followed hers, then his arms were around her again, jerking her against him with such force, it knocked the breath from her body.

"Carl, what —"

She got no further for his mouth crashed onto hers, jolting her head back with the impact. His lips were moist and urgent, his tongue an assault, and his hand moving roughly over her back, slid between them to grasp painfully at her breast.

Shocked and angry at his rough handling, Helen had tried to twist away, her hand pushing at his shoulders. Her resistance seemed to inflame him and his arm slid around her again, crushed her against him. His lips slipped wetly from hers, slid slowly down the side of her neck.

"Come into the backseat with me."

His slurred words caused the first twinge

of fear. It was not an invitation. It was an order.

"Carl, you know how I feel about that. I want —"

She gasped in shock and pain as his teeth ground together on the soft skin at the curve of her neck.

"Carl! Stop, you're hurti— Oh!"

She hadn't seen his hand move, only felt the pain as his palm hit her cheek. His mouth caught hers again, grinding her lips against her teeth. Near panic, blinded by tears, Helen struggled, pushing against him frantically. Suddenly she was free as, pulling away from her, he slid back across the seat, cursing as he flung her coat and his jacket onto the floor, out of his way. He pushed his door open, then slammed it so hard behind him that the car rocked.

Sitting huddled and trembling on the seat, tears running down her face, Helen had thought he'd gone to cool off and she jumped when she heard him yank open the backseat door behind her. The door next to her was flung open, and with a grated "Get out," he reached in, grabbed her arm, and dragged her out of the car and around the backseat door. "Get in," he grated.

Nearly hysterical, Helen hit out at him, screaming, "No, I won't get in. I want you to take me home, now. I —"

"Damn you, get in."

This time it was his fist that hit her face, and barely conscious, Helen didn't even feel her shins scrape against the side of the car or her head strike the opposite armrest when he shoved her in and onto the seat. The next instant his body was on hers, pressing her back against the upholstery, one hand moving up under her sweater to clutch her breast, the other sliding up her leg under her skirt.

Her face, her whole head, throbbed with pain and she couldn't seem to focus her eyes. She felt groggy and sick to her stomach and still she fought him wildly, silently

"It's your own fault, Helen. You and your damned wait-till-the-wedding-night bit. Well, I can't wait anymore, and I won't."

His mouth crushed hers and his larger body, pressing down on hers, subdued her struggles, cut off her air. Consciousness shipping away from her, Helen hadn't heard the car stop behind them, but she did hear the sharp rap against the window, did hear the not-unpleasant voice of the patrolman when he called, "Break it up, kids. You're not allowed to park here." Not waiting for a response, he strolled back to the patrol car.

Jerking away from her, Carl stared out the back window, cursing softly at the retreating, straight back. Then, turning, he looped his legs over the back of the front seat and pushed himself up and over. Glancing in the rearview mirror at the patrol car, obviously waiting for him to move, he cursed again, then snarled, "Well are you coming up or not?"

Curled on the backseat, swallowing hard against the sobs that tore at her throat, Helen didn't bother to answer him. He waited a moment, cursed again, shrugged into his jacket, threw her coat over the seat to her, then reached out to slam the door closed with a snapped "Will you shut the damned door?"

Moving slowly, Helen straightened and closed the back door. Then, pulling her coat around her shoulders, she rested her pounding head back against the seat and closed her eyes, gulping down the nausea rising from her churning stomach. They were almost back to her dormitory before Carl broke the strained silence.

"I'm sorry I hit you, Helen," he began softly, then his tone hardened. "But a man can take just so much. We're going to be married anyway, so what the hell difference does it make if we have sex together now? No normal man could be expected to wait years to make love to his girlfriend."

Again Helen didn't respond and she was ready when he stopped the car in front of her dorm. Without speaking, she pushed open the door, jumped out, threw his ring onto the front seat, and ran up the walk to the safety of the dorm, ignoring his call to wait.

Now, over ten years later, Helen stood staring out her bedroom window at a night very much like that other night, her face cold and uncompromising.

Over the years she had dated many men, had proposals from several and a few propositions, but something inside seemed frozen and she could not respond to any of them. Intellectually she knew that all men did not become brutal when frustrated, but emotionally she could not handle a close relationship, and when a light good-night kiss began to deepen into something more or a male hand began to wander, she withdrew coldly, her manner shutting the man out as effectively as if she'd closed a door between them.

She had never been able to control her withdrawal, nor had she tried very hard to control it. In her opinion any woman who'd put herself in the position of receiving that kind of punishment twice was a fool.

Moving around the room restlessly, Helen tried to figure out what had happened to her built-in warning alarm that evening. Not only had she relaxed in

Marshall Kirk's arms, she had, if only for a moment, returned his kiss. And the fluttering breathlessness that gripped her when he turned that steady blue gaze on her confounded her completely. *What the hell,* she derided herself, *got into you?* Strangely her mind shied away from delving too deeply for answers, and shaking her head sharply, she told herself to forget him. Which, of course, brought a picture of him to her mind.

Glancing at the clock, she groaned aloud. It was almost four and her alarm would ring at seven; she had to get some sleep.

As she slid under the comforter, Marsh's murmured words taunted her mind. "I knew I loved you and that you were mine."

"Not on your young life, Kirk," she whispered aloud, then closed her eyes and drifted to sleep.

Three

"I don't know what it is, Doctor." Alice's voice was heavy with exasperation. "But I think everybody has a bad case of the Januaries."

Including me, Helen thought, a small smile tugging at her lips at the nurse's caustic tone.

"What now?" she sighed, cradling the phone against her shoulder. As usual for a Thursday the office had been full all day and that, plus her lack of sleep the night before, was beginning to tell on her. By the tone of her voice Helen suspected Alice was also beginning to feel a little hassled.

There is a patient in the other examining room, there are four more still in the waiting room, and I have a Mr. Kirk on the line who insists on speaking to you. I've told him you are very busy, but —"

"It's all right," she cut in wearily. "I'll talk to him."

There was a short, somewhat shocked, pause and then a click.

"What can I do for you, Mr. Kirk?" she asked coolly.

Soft laughter skimmed through the wire to tickle her ear.

"Do you want the proper answer or the truth?"

"I'm keeping a patient waiting." Helen's tone plunged five degrees.

"Where have I heard that before?" he wondered aloud, then, "okay, I'll be brief. What time should I pick you up for dinner, and where?"

Caught off guard by his casual assumption that she'd go with him, Helen searched for words. "Mr. Kirk," she began after several long seconds.

"Yes, babe?" It was a smooth warning Helen couldn't ignore.

"Marsh." She bit the name out through clenched teeth.

"That's better," he crooned.

"Marsh," she repeated coldly, "I do not have time to play telephone games. I had very little sleep last night and a very busy day today *and* I won't be through here for another hour and a half. I am tired and I don't feel like going out to dinner."

"Okay," he replied easily. "Come right to my place when you leave the office and we'll eat in."

This man had a positive talent for striking her speechless.

"I certainly will not come to your place," she finally snapped.

"I'm inviting you for dinner, Helen." The amusement in his voice made her feel very young and naive. "Not for a long, illicit weekend."

"I don't —"

"Good Lord, Helen," he cut in briskly, all amusement gone. "You're not afraid of me, are you?"

"No, of course not, but —"

"No, of course not," Marsh mimicked. "I'll expect you in about two hours." He rattled off an address, then his tone went low with warning. "And if you're more than fifteen minutes late, I'll come looking for you."

The line went dead before she could answer him, and Helen stared at the receiver, anger, mixed with a flutter in her stomach she refused to acknowledge, bringing a twinge of pink to her pale cheeks. Of all the arrogant gall, she fumed. Just who in the hell did he think he was, anyway? Well, he could go fly a kite. She had no intention of going to his place for dinner, or anything else.

The following hour and fifteen minutes seemed to fly by and Helen caught herself glancing at her watch more and more frequently. By the time she ushered her last patient out of her office, Helen was having a hard time hiding her nervousness. Would he really carry out his threat to come looking for her? Of course he wouldn't, she told herself bracingly. Of course he would, herself chided positively.

Undecided, Helen fidgeted, moving things around on her desk aimlessly. Alice came to the door to say goodnight, a puzzled expression on her face at Helen's unusual behavior. Her mind playing a tug of war with "to go or not to go," Helen didn't notice Alice's concerned look.

The second hand on her desk clock seemed to be sweeping the minutes away in less than thirty seconds each. Finally, with barely enough time left to reach his apartment within the time limit he'd set, Helen dashed into the changing room that connected her two examining rooms. Fingers trembling, she smoothed her hair, tucked a few loose tendrils into the neat coil, then did a quick repair job on her makeup.

Tension kept Helen's fingers curled tightly around the steering wheel as she inched her way through the early evening traffic, her eyes darting to her watch at every stop sign and red light. The address Marsh had given her was a large, fairly new condominium just outside the city limits, with a spacious parking area off to one side.

A security guard sat at a counterlike desk just inside the wide glass entrance doors, and the first thing Helen noticed was the clock that sat on the desktop. She was two minutes inside his time limit. She gave her name and the security guard said politely, "Oh, yes, Dr. Cassidy, Mr. Kirk called down that he was expecting you. You may go right up. Apartment eight-oh-two, to the left of the elevator."

He indicated the elevator across the foyer behind him, then bent to write something in the sign-in book. *Probably my name and the time of arrival,* Helen mused as she crossed the dark red-carpeted floor.

A few seconds later, standing before the door marked 802, Helen drew a deep breath, held it, and touched her finger to the lighted doorbell button. The door was opened almost immediately, convincing her that the guard had announced her arrival, and once again she was held motionless in a hypnotic blue gaze.

"Perfect timing," Marsh murmured, pulling the door wide as he stepped back. "I had just decided to give you a few more minutes before going on the hunt." His mouth curving into a smile, he taunted, "Are you coming in or are you going to bolt for the exit?"

Giving a good imitation of a careless

shrug, Helen exhaled slowly, broke the hold of his eyes, and stepped inside. Every nerve in her body seemed to jump when the door clicked shut behind her and hum like live electrical wires when she felt his hands on her shoulders.

"I'll take your coat."

His soft voice, close to her ear, turned a mundane statement into a caress, and Helen bit down hard on her lip to try and still the shakiness of her fingers fumbling at her coat buttons.

When he turned away to hang up her coat, Helen's eyes swept the oversize living room, glimpsed the dining room behind an intricately worked wrought-iron room divider. The colors in the room merged and blurred before her eyes as she was spun around and into his arms.

"I thought you'd never get here."

Marsh's eyes had a dark, smoldering look and his voice was a rasp from deep in his throat.

Helen's arms came up between them, her hands pushing ineffectively against his shoulders.

"Marsh —"

His head swooped low and his mouth caught her parted lips, silencing her protests. His lips were hard with the demand for her submission, his kiss possessive, consuming.

Feeling reason beginning to slip away, Helen's mind sent an order to her hands to pull his head away. Her hands lifted, her fingers slid into his hair, but somewhere along the line the order became garbled and instead of tugging at his hair, her hands grasped his head, drawing him closer. At once his arms tightened, molded her against the long, taut length of his body. His mouth searched hers hungrily, making her senses swim crazily and igniting a spark that quickly leaped into a searing flame that danced wildly from her lips to her toes. Teetering on the edge of sur-render, Helen murmured a soft protest when his mouth left hers. Leaving a trail of fire, his lips moved slowly over her cheek. His teeth, nibbling at her lobe, sent a shaft of alarm through her, and reason scuttled back where it belonged. Her hands dropped onto his shoulders and pushed, using all the strength she possessed.

"Marsh, stop, I've got to call my ser-vice."

"Later," he growled against the side of her neck. "Helen, I've waited all last night and all day today to hold you like this. You can do that later."

His lips found, caressed, the hollow at the base of her throat, and Helen, her breathing growing shallow and uneven, knew that if she didn't put some distance between them her will would turn to water. She pleaded, "Marsh, please. I must let the hospital know where I can be reached. Let me go, please."

For a long moment she thought he was going to disregard her plea; then, with a low moan, his arms dropped and he stepped back, a rueful smile curving his mouth.

"Be my guest."

He waved his hand negligently at the living room, and turning, Helen's eyes sought, then found, the phone resting on an octagonal-shaped cabinet table at the end of a long leather sofa.

On legs she was none too sure would support her, Helen made her way to the phone. As she punched out the numbers, she heard Marsh walk across the room and glanced up to see him disappear into the dining room.

"Come into the dining room."

His call, obviously from the kitchen, came as she replaced the receiver, and drawing a steadying breath, Helen rose and walked into the room just as he emerged from an opposite door.

"I hope you like Chinese food." He grinned easily. "I stopped and picked it up on my way home."

He held a long-stemmed glass, three quarters full of white wine, in each hand

and moved with such casual ease, Helen felt a hot flash of anger. What had happened to all the tension that had tautened his entire body only a few minutes ago? She felt on the point of collapse, while he looked relaxed and unaffected. Could he flick his emotions on and off like a light switch?

"Are you going to take the wine?" His chiding tone made her aware of the glass he was holding out to her. "Or are you going to scowl at it all night?"

Embarrassed now, not only by her present vagueness but by her response and subsequent reaction to his advance, she lifted her eyes and stared into his with a steadiness she was far from feeling.

"Is white the correct wine for Chinese food?" Her attempt at lightness didn't fall too short of the mark.

"Who cares?" His shoulders lifted eloquently. "I drink what I like with whatever I choose to eat." His eyes glittered as he placed the glass into her hand. "I please myself and never worry about what others deem correct."

Positive his last remark held a double meaning, also positive she would not be able to eat a thing, Helen allowed Marsh to seat her at the table. When he went back into the kitchen for the food, she sipped tentatively at her wine, identified it as an excellent chardonnay, then drank some more in an effort to relax the tightness in her throat.

Marsh hadn't forgotten a thing. He began talking the minute they'd started on their wonton soup and kept up a steady flow of light conversation right through the chicken lo mein, fricd rice, and shrimp egg rolls. By the time she bit into her almond cookie, Helen had not only relaxed, she found herself laughing delightedly as he recounted the Christmas Day antics of a friend's youngster.

"Give me a minute to clear the table and stack the dishwasher, then we can have our coffee in the living room," Marsh said when the last cookie crumb had disappeared. "Or would you prefer more wine?"

"No, thank you." Helen shook her head emphatically. "I've had more than enough. But I would love some coffee and I'll help you with the cleaning up."

They made fast work of the table and dishes, then Helen preceded him into the living room, sat on the sofa, and watched as he placed a tray with the coffee things on the low coffee table in front of him, then turned and walked to the stereo unit along the wall next to the dining room entrance. He selected a CD, put it in the player, then came back to her and, to her amazement, instead of seating himself in the opposite chair or on the sofa beside her, he dropped onto the floor, stretched his long legs out, and rested his back against the cushion, next to her legs.

The opening strains of Tchaikovsky's *Romeo and Juliet* filled the room as she poured the coffee, handed him his, then sat back. They sat listening in silence, both of them held in quiet captivity to the composer's genius. Even when Marsh held up his cup for a refill, she filled the cup and added more to her own without either uttering a murmur. When he finished his coffee, he placed the cup on the tray, shifted his shoulders, and rested his head against her thigh.

Replete with food, heavy lidded from lack of sleep the night before, Helen let her head drop back against the sofa and closed her eyes, the hauntingly beautiful music moving through her body like a living thing. Unaware of her actions, her hand dropped idly to his head, and slim fingers slid slowly through the silken strands of his hair.

Trembling, her emotions almost painfully in tune with the music's throbbing finale, it seemed the most natural thing in the world when his fingers circled her wrist, drew her hand across his face to his mouth. His lips, moving sensuously on her palm, sent a spreading warmth up her arm, increasing the trembling, robbing her of breath.

"Marsh."

Her soft involuntary gasp set him in motion. Grasping her wrist, he levered himself up and onto the sofa beside her, drawing her arm around his neck as his head moved toward hers. His free hand caught her chin, tilted her head back, ready for his mouth. His kiss was the exact opposite of the night before. His lips, hard and demanding, forced hers apart, took arrogant possession of her mouth with driving urgency. His hands moved between them to expertly dispatch the buttons of her shirt. A sensation strangely like déjà vu flashed through her. It was gone in a moment, replaced by the new, exciting sensations his hands, sliding around her waist, sent shivering through her body.

Holding her firmly, he turned her, lowered her slowly to the soft cushions, and without knowing quite how he'd managed it, she felt his long length stretched out partly beside, partly on top of her.

His mouth released hers, went to the hollow at the base of her throat, his lips, the tip of his tongue, teasing a soft moan from her constricted throat.

"Marsh, you must stop. I'm so sleepy. I have to go home, get to bed. Oh, Marsh —"

His lips had moved down, in a fiery

straight line, to explore the shadowed hollow between her breasts.

"You don't have to go anywhere." His warm breath tingled tantalizingly over her skin as his mouth moved back to hover over hers. "Your service knows where to reach you. If you're that sleepy, you can sleep here, with me."

"No, I —" His lips touched hers lightly, fleetingly. "I can't stay here." Her lower lip was caught between his. "It's — it's out of the question." His teeth nibbled gently at the sensitive inner ridge of her lip. Her voice sank to a low cry. "Oh, Marsh, kiss me."

His mouth crushed hers, causing a shudder to ripple along the length of her body. The flick of his tongue against her teeth drove her hands to his chest, trembling fingers fighting his shirt buttons. When her palms slid over his hair-roughened skin, he lifted his head, groaned, "Stay with me, Helen. Sleep with me. Let me show you what you do to me."

"I can't — I — what are you doing?"

He was on his feet, lifting her in his arms. Turning, he carried her across the room, through a doorway. "You said you wanted to go to bed." He kicked the door closed, walked to the bed, then stood her on her feet in front of him.

"Not here!" Her hands were drawn back

to his chest as if magnetized. "Marsh, I can't stay here. Stop that!"

Disregarding her order, his fingers continued to tug the clip from her hair. When her hair was free of its confining coil, his hands dropped to her shoulders. With a minimum of effort her shirt was removed, dropped carelessly onto the floor. "Marsh, don't," she pleaded softly. "I want to go home."

Again that odd flash of déjà vu struck her. In confusion she wondered what had caused it, then her thoughts became blurred as Marsh's lips found a sensitive spot behind her ear.

"You're so beautiful, Helen." Her legs went weak at his low tone, the enticing movement of his lips on her skin. "Stay with me." His hands slid smoothly over her back. His fingers flipped open her bra with easy expertise. The lacy wisp of material landed on top of her shirt. "I want you so desperately." His hands slid around her rib cage.

"Marsh, no!"

His mouth silenced her weak protest at the same moment as his hands moved up and over the full mounds of her aching breasts. Reason fled and with a soft sigh she wound her arms around his neck, clinging as he slowly lowered her onto the bed. His mouth devoured hers, his tongue teased hers. Her skirt was twisted around her hips, and one hand deserted a hard-tipped mound to caress her thigh.

Moaning softly, barely aware of what she was doing, her hands came up to clasp his head, fingers digging into his hair ruthlessly to pull him closer, wanting more and more of his mouth.

She heard him groan before he moved over her, his solid weight pushing her into the firm mattress. Suddenly she froze. The feeling of déjà vu gripped her and she was being pressed against a cold car seat. Carl's face rose before her, filling her mind with fear. Tearing at his hair, she forced his mouth from hers with a hoarse cry.

"Damn you, stop it."

Marsh jerked away from her as if he'd been shot.

"Helen, what is it? Did I hurt you?"

Shaking with remembered panic, she didn't hear the words. All that registered was that the voice was male, and it terrified her. Cringing away from him, she brought her forearm up across her face, fingers spread to ward off a blow. The voice that whispered through her lips belonged to a younger woman.

"Don't hit me again, please."

Marsh froze, staring at her in disbelief.

"Hit you? Helen, what the hell —"

"Carl, please don't." She was sobbing now. "Please."

At the sound of the other man's name, Marsh's face went rigid, lids narrowing over eyes ice-blue with fury.

"He hit you?" He gritted. "This . . . Carl . . . he dared to hit you?" His tone went low with menace. "If I ever find him, I'll kill him."

His cold tone, the words that were not a boast or even a threat, but a statement in the absolute, broke the hold of memory gripping Helen's mind. The back of her hand slid down to cover her mouth.

"Oh, God, Marsh." Her eyes went wide to stare into his. "It was so real, so horribly real. It was all happening again."

Sitting up fully, he grasped her shoulders, pulled her up, over his legs. Cradling her in his arms like a child, he asked, "When did it happen?"

Closing her eyes, she sighed wearily, "Long ago. So very long ago, and yet it seemed so real just now, as if it were all happening again." A shudder tore through her body, and his arms tightened protectively. She buried her face in the wiry mat of curls on his chest, her wet tears making a few strands glisten.

"He raped you?"

The words came softly from his lips, but Helen heard the tone that spoke of tightly controlled rage.

"No. No." She shook her head, her forehead rubbing against his chest.

"A — a patrol car stopped. The patrolman told him he'd have to move along."

Helen felt the shiver that slithered through his tough body, heard the sigh that escaped his lips. His arms tightened still more.

"You called to the cop for help?"

"No." Silent tears slid down her cheeks. "You don't understand, Marsh, I was engaged to him." She shivered. "I thought I wanted to spend the rest of my life with him."

"Don't cry, sweetheart." His fingers brushed at her wet cheeks, smoothed the hair back from her temples "You've been afraid ever since?"

"I guess so." She gave a small shrug.

"This has happened before, when you've been with other men?" He paused, then added stiffly, "Or is it me that repels you?"

"It has never happened before because I've never been with any other men. I don't know —"

"What?"

He went completely still. After several seconds Helen lifted her head to see his face. The face he turned to her was one of total astonishment.

"You have never been — ?" He broke off, his voice mirroring his expression. "Helen, are you still a —"

"Yes." Helen rushed before he could say the word. "Yes, yes. There has never been anyone."

"Wow," he murmured softly. "I've changed my mind." He bent his head, kissed her lightly, a small smile tugging at his lips. "I'm not going to kill him. I'm going to thank him for saving you for me."

"He didn't save me for you or anyone else," Helen snapped. "I lost my head tonight but it won't happen again."

His hand caught her face, drew it close to his.

"Not for a little while, maybe. I'm going to give you time to get to know me. I'm going to get to know you. But it will happen again. Nothing can stop it. I told you, you are mine. Nothing you do can change it. A little while ago, before the memories caught you, you were mine. We're going to be fantastic together."

He released her abruptly and stood up. "But not tonight. Right now I'm going to get the hell out of here so you can get dressed. Then I'm going to take you home." Bending swiftly, he kissed the tip of each full breast, then brought his lips to her mouth. "You have a beautiful body," he whispered between short, hard kisses. "I love it and I love you. You may not be ready to face it yet, but you love me too."

Laughing softly at her outraged gasp, he

strode across the room, bathing the room in light by the flick of a switch as he went through the doorway.

The moment the door closed, Helen jumped off the bed. She was wide awake, all her earlier sleepiness banished by the events of the last hour. Moving slowly, she tried to explain away the strange experience, make some logic of it in her own mind. What she'd told Marsh was true; nothing like it had ever happened to her before. She'd had frightening nightmares for some months after the incident, but they had eventually faded. During the last few years she'd rarely thought about it, and when she did, the memory was triggered by odd, unrelated incidents. Even meeting Carl, which she did occasionally, had not disturbed her. Except, her reasoning qualified, that very first time, and she had come away from that meeting with her head high, her poise and cool composure intact.

Helen used the bathroom that was off his bedroom, absently admiring the masculine-looking marbled black-and-white tile, the large snow-white bathsheets. The long glass shelf under the medicine cabinet held just three items: his shaving cream, his aftershave, and the cologne that, on his skin, had the power to make her senses swim.

Fully aware of her surroundings now, Helen went back into the bedroom, her

572

eyes making a cool survey. The bed, which she'd only seen in semidarkness before, was king-size and, right now, very rumpled. Like the bathroom, Marsh's bedroom reflected the man. Totally masculine, with an understated core of warmth.

Agitated at herself for her softened attitude toward him, Helen tossed back her hair impatiently. Within minutes she slipped into her bra and shirt, then on hands and knees she retrieved the hair clip he'd dropped carelessly to the floor.

Rising to her feet, she raked her fingers through her tangled hair. Wincing at the twinge of pain on her scalp, she walked to the door, pulled it open and called irritably, "Marsh, will you hand me my handbag, please? I need my hairbrush."

Tapping her foot impatiently, Helen watched him scoop her bag off the floor beside the sofa, then saunter to her, a smile curving his lips at her disgruntled expression. His eyes slid over her slowly, thoroughly, before coming back to study her face, her hair.

"I don't know why you want your brush," he teased, his eyes glinting with devilry. "You look ravishing with your hair all wild around your face." He paused, head tilted to the side, considering before adding softly, "Or is the correct word 'ravished'?"

Giving him a sour look, Helen snatched the bag from his hand, rummaged in it for the brush, then, tossing the bag onto the bed, she turned her back to him and walked to stand in front of the large mirror above the double dresser.

His reflection told her that his eyes followed her every move and, made nervous by his perusal, she pulled the brush through her knotted mane with unnecessary force. Tears sprang to her eyes from the self-inflicted pain. Pausing in midstroke, she blinked her lids rapidly to clear her vision and thus missed the reflection beside her own growing larger. The sound of his voice close behind her made her jump.

"What are you punishing yourself for?" His fingers plucked the brush from her hand. "Nothing happened here tonight that shouldn't have happened long ago." Very slowly, very gently, he drew the brush through her hair. "Don't misunderstand. I am, egotistically, very happy that it did not. You are mine and the thought that you have belonged, however briefly, to another — or several others — has been tearing my guts apart since I left you at the hospital last night."

The brush was tossed onto the dresser, and with a shiver she felt his hand draw aside her now-smooth and shining mane, felt his lips caress the sensitive skin on the back of her neck. The shiver increasing in intensity, she heard him draw deeply the scent of her into his lungs, felt the delicious tingle of his breath as he exhaled slowly.

"I'm nearly out of my mind with love for you, Helen. And I want you so badly, I can taste it. But I can wait until my lovemaking doesn't activate the ugly memories. Until I hear, from your own lips, that you want me every bit as badly as I want you. But, dear God, I hope the waiting period is a short one."

As he spoke he turned her around, into his arms, his intense blue gaze staring into her wide, wary eyes.

"Marsh," she began firmly enough, "I wish you wouldn't talk like this. I don't want to get invol—"

His mouth covered hers, effectively cutting off what she'd been about to say. Undaunted, Helen began speaking again the instant he lifted his head.

"Marsh, listen to me. I don't want any kind of emotional involvement. Besides which —" she hesitated, wet her dry lips, then said flatly, "I'm older than you."

A deep frown brought his dark, beautifully shaped eyebrows together. A tiny fire leaped in his eyes.

"Did you think I was unaware of that?"

Just the sound of his quiet voice made her shiver. "Exactly how old are you?"

Helen's eyelids lowered, then came up again defensively. Never before had she hesitated about stating her age. The fact that this man could make her feel defensive about, resentful of, her years was a shocking bit of self-knowledge she didn't want to face. In retaliation she forced a note of pride into her voice.

"Thirty-five."

"And I'll be thirty-one in March." His shrug was eloquent. "I hardly think four years is just cause for argument."

His blithe unconcern angered her. Jerking her shoulder away from his hand, she turned away.

"Four years can be very important."

She was immediately swung back to face him. His hand grasped her chin, held it firmly.

"The only years that hold any importance for me any longer are the years we are going to spend together."

At her wince the pressure on her chin was eased, although he did not let her go.

"I'm not going to argue about this anymore tonight, Helen." He lowered his head and Helen's eyes became fascinated with his mouth. "I knew from the moment I laid eyes on you that we belonged together. Nothing you say, nothing you do, is ever going to change that."

His lips were almost touching hers and Helen tried to ignore and deny the warm curl of anticipation in her stomach.

"There isn't anywhere on this earth you could run to to get away from me, or yourself for that matter. Now close your eyes, because I'm going to kiss you."

And suiting action to words, he did, his arms sliding around her to draw her close against him. The kiss was long and deep and wildly arousing, and Helen could no more have stopped her arms from clinging to him, any more than she could stop the passage of time. She felt a tremor run through his body before he put her firmly from him. Eyes smoldering with smoky blue fire, he stepped back.

"I'm taking you home now. Because if I don't, I doubt you'll ever see the place again."

He drove her car, brushing aside her protest with a careless "I'll grab a cab back."

Before they were halfway to her apartment Helen was having trouble keeping her eyes open. Numb with fatigue, she finally gave up the battle and allowed her lids to drop, block out the hurtful glare from the headlights of the approaching cars.

"Where should I put the car? Do you have a designated space, or can you park anywhere?"

Marsh's quiet voice nudged her eyelids up. The car was motionless, the engine idling, at the entrance to the covered parking area adjacent to her apartment building.

"What? Oh, anywhere. It doesn't matter."

Even fuzzy-minded, Helen could not miss the indulgent expression on his face. A smile curving his lips, he set the car in motion and drove onto the parking lot.

Too tired to argue, Helen simply shrugged when he insisted on seeing her safely into her apartment.

While she hung her coat in the closet, Marsh used her phone to call for a cab to pick him up. Standing by the door, she watched him cradle the receiver, then walk to her, a tingle of apprehensive anticipation growing stronger with each step he took.

"I won't be able to see you tomorrow or Saturday." He stopped in front of her, his tone regretful. "I have previous commitments that I can't break without causing friction on the homefront."

"Marsh, you don't have to explain your actions to me." Helen was experiencing that trapped, panicky feeling again. "You owe me nothing."

He smiled, raised his hand to caress her face, then went on as if she hadn't said a word.

"I'll be bored out of my gourd, but I

can't get out of it without hurting my mother's feelings. But I want to spend the whole day with you Sunday — if you're free."

The feather-light touch of his fingers on her cheek set off a chain reaction along her nervous system. Her breathing growing shallow, she murmured, "Yes, but —"

"Out." Laughing softly, he shook his head at her. "I'll take you out somewhere. I'll pick you up in the morning at . . . ?" He lifted a questioning eyebrow.

"Not too early," she sighed, too tired to argue with him. "Unless I have a call, I sleep late on Sunday."

"Ten?"

Helen shivered with weariness, nodded.

"Okay." Feeling her shiver against his fingers, his eyes grew sharp. "Don't eat, we'll start the day with breakfast or brunch. How does a walk in the park sound?"

"In January?"

"Of course." He laughed again. "You'll see."

His eyes moved over her face, clung for a moment on her mouth, then came back to her eyes.

"You're exhausted. Go to bed and go to sleep. Don't think. Don't speculate. Block everything out and sleep."

His thumb stroked the dark smudges

under her eyes as he lowered his head to hers and said softly, "I love you, Helen."

His lips, though firm, held no passion, no demand. Comforting warmth spread through her, easing the beginning ache at her temples. All too soon the warmth was removed, as moving away, he opened the door, murmured, "Sleep well, sweetheart," and was gone.

four

Sunday dawned bright and cold. The end of January sunlight, glittering fiercely through Helen's bedroom windows, warned her not to go outdoors without her sunglasses.

Yawning hugely, stretching luxuriously, Helen glanced at the clock on her nightstand and gave a small yelp. Marsh would be arriving in less than an hour and here she lay, basking in the sun like a fat house cat. Scrambling out of bed, she grabbed her robe off the end of the bed and ran into the bathroom.

Helen felt good. Surprisingly she'd slept well the last few nights, including Thursday. She hadn't expected to — in fact, after Marsh had left her with his murmured, "Sleep well, sweetheart," she'd been convinced she wouldn't sleep at all. Contrarily she was asleep not three minutes after her head hit the pillow.

With two deliveries, plus the usual number of office patients, on Friday, and several hours in the operating room on Saturday, she'd tired herself enough to sleep on those two nights. The thought of Marsh, and what had happened in his bedroom, she'd managed to push to the back of her mind by concentrating fiercely on her work.

When, at the odd moments, the thought of him, the remembered feel of him, crept to the forefront of her mind, she'd gritted her teeth, fighting down the shakiness that assailed her. Afraid, and unwilling to examine exactly why, she'd silently battled against the memories using sleep as an ally.

Her door chimes pealed at exactly ten o'clock. Fastening her belt, Helen walked to the door and pulled it open, her breath catching at the sight of him. He was dressed for a day out of doors in brown corduroys, cream-colored heavy knit sweater, and a fleece-lined, high-collared parka.

Before she could speak, he dipped his head and placed his cold lips against hers.

"Good morning," he murmured, his breath fresh and tickly on her lips. "May I come in?"

"Yes — yes, of course." She stepped back to allow him to walk by, then added hurriedly, "I'm ready to leave. All I have to do is put on my jacket."

A grin slashed his mouth, revealing perfect white teeth. His eyes danced with gentle mockery.

"Although I'll admit to being tempted, I'm not going to jump on you and drag you into the bedroom, Helen, but" — his arm shot out, snaked around her waist, pulled her to him — "I am going to kiss you properly."

As he lowered his head his hands came up to cup her face, cool fingers sliding over the smoothed back hair above her ears.

"Marsh! Don't you dare touch that clip."

Laughter rumbling in his throat, the tip of one finger gently nudged the faux tortoiseshell hair anchor back into place under the neat coil.

"Spoilsport."

The word was murmured against her lips, which, unbidden, had parted to receive his. Several inches separated him and Helen, yet he made no move to get closer, as if deliberately denying his body the feel of hers. His hands on her face, his mouth on hers, was their only physical contact, yet Helen felt a warmth and security flow through her that could not have been stronger had he enfolded her in his arms, held her tightly against his strong, hard body.

When he lifted his head, she had to bite back the soft cry of protest that rose in her throat. Opening her eyes, she felt her breath cut off altogether at the intensity of his blue gaze. The fingers of his right hand trailed slowly down her cheek, over her lips, then with a sharp shake of his head he stepped back, a rueful smile twisting his mouth.

"I think we'd better get out of here," he clipped tersely, going to the closet to get her jacket.

Shaken, Helen stood mutely, automatically lifting her arms to the sleeves of her jacket when he held it for her. When his hands dropped away from her shoulders, she found her voice.

"I must stop at the hospital."

"Why?"

The sharp edge to his tone drove the fuzziness from her mind. The face she lifted to him was cool, composed.

"I must make my rounds. I have three post-op and four maternity patients to examine and release papers to sign for another —" Helen paused in midsentence, a look of concern shadowing her eyes. "Marsh, the patient being released this morning is your sister."

"I know that." One dark brow went up in question. "So?"

"Well — I — mm — I mean," Helen faltered, then asked quickly, "Were you planning to wait for me in the car?"

"Hell, no!" he snapped irritably. "Do you know how cold it is out there? And I sure as hell didn't consider wasting gas to keep the car warm. If you don't want me trailing around behind you, leave Kris till last and I'll visit with her while you make your rounds."

"But —" Helen hesitated, her fingers playing nervously with her coat buttons. "Marsh, what will your sister think?"

"Who cares what she thinks?" He pulled the door open angrily. "Now, can we go and get these rounds over wish? I'm hungry."

An uneasy silence rode with them all the way to the hospital. By the time Marsh stopped the car at the entrance, Helen's nerves were ragged.

"I'll park the car and see you later in Kris's room."

Helen chose to ignore the anger that still laced his tone. She didn't want him to wait for her in his sister's room, simply because she didn't want Kristeen Darren to know that they were together.

"Why don't you wait for me in the lunchroom? Have some toast and a cup of —"

"Helen!" he exploded. "Will you get on with it? At the rate we're moving it will be lunchtime before we get breakfast."

Hot anger shot through her, and not bothering to reply, she slammed out of the car and into the building. *I must be out of my mind,* she fumed. *Why did I agree to spend the day with him? Did I, in fact, actually agree?*

Thoughts of the same nature seethed in her mind as Helen made her rounds, her cool outward appearance giving no hint of the anger that boiled in her veins. Not since Carl had she allowed a man to upset her like this. And the fact that he was younger than she was an added thorn. She was doing the work she loved and was completely satisfied with her life. She didn't need any man, let alone a smooth-talking rich kid who could issue orders like a marine sergeant.

By the time she walked into Kristeen Darren's room, Helen was in a cold fury and ready to tell Marshall Kirk to go to hell. The scene that met Helen's eyes as she walked through the doorway brought an abrupt halt to her angry stride.

Kristeen was sitting on the bed fully dressed, an impatient frown on her face. Her husband paced restlessly between the room's only window and the bed. Her mother sat, back rigid, in a chair beside the bed. And in the corner, sitting on a func-tional, straight-backed chair, Marsh some-how managed to look lazily comfortable. Helen's eyes slid over him as if he were not there.

"I'm sorry I'm late, Kristeen." She apol-ogized briskly, drawing four pairs of eyes to her. "I've signed your release, and they'll be bringing your baby to you in a minute. How are you feeling this morning?"

Her fingers on Kristeen's wrist, her eyes on her watch, Helen smiled and nodded understandingly at the young woman's breathless tone.

"I'm fine, Doctor. Excited about taking my baby home."

"Of course," she murmured, adjusting her stethoscope. Satisfied with what she heard, Helen glanced at Kristeen as she removed the instrument. "Okay, you may go. Do you have any questions about the instructions I gave you yesterday?"

"No, Doctor, everything's clear."

"Fine. If you have any problem whatever, call my office." Except for the cursory glance she'd given him on first entering the room, Helen had not looked at Marsh. She did not look at him now as, smiling warmly at the other three, she wished Kristeen good luck with her daughter, said she'd see her in six weeks, and turned to leave. Marsh's voice stopped her a foot from the door.

"Helen."

The sound of her name in that smooth, too-soft tone sent a chill along her spine. Turning slowly, she met his eyes, her breath catching at the mocking slant of his lips, the flash of blue fire in his eyes.

Out of the corner of her eye Helen caught the confused glances that flew between Kristeen, her husband, and her mother. Using every ounce of willpower she possessed, Helen hung on to her cool.

"Yes?"

"You're finished now?"

Helen's teeth ground together at the warm note Marsh had inflected into his voice. Just what did he think he was doing? she thought furiously, noting the sharp glance his mother turned on him. Her tone went from cool to cold.

"Yes."

"Then can we go now and have breakfast? My stomach is beginning to feel di vorced from the rest of my body."

The soft gasps that came from the two women, the low whistle that Mike Darren emitted, grated against Helen's nerves. She could have happily hit him. Instead she nodded her head sharply and turned to the door. He was beside her before she had taken three steps, his arm sliding possessively around her waist.

"Take care, Kristeen," he said lightly, shepherding Helen out of the room. "I'll see you all later."

Too angry to trust herself with words, Helen maintained a frigid silence as she retrieved her coat and followed him to his car. Spitting like an angry cat, she turned to him as soon as both car doors were closed.

"Damn you, Kirk," she began heatedly, only to have him cut her off with a soft warning.

"Watch it, my sweet. I'll take just about anything from you, except your cursing me."

"I'm not asking you to take anything at all from me," she sputtered, growing more angry by the minute. "And I want nothing from you. Not a meal, or a walk in the park, or your company. I'm going home."

Helen turned to the door, hand groping for the release, and gave a sharp cry of pain when his hands grasped her shoulders, pulled her around to face him.

"You're not going anywhere," he growled, giving her a not-too-gentle shake. "At least not until you tell me what you're so mad about."

"Oh, I'm not mad, Mr. Kirk." Helen returned his growl. "I'm way past mad. Try furious. Better yet, try incensed."

"But why?" His confusion was unfeigned. As angry as she was, Helen had no doubt of that. For some reason it incited her even more.

"Why?" She choked. "Why? What were you trying to do back there in Kristeen's room? Do you know?"

"Yes, I know," he replied evenly. "I was

determined to make you acknowledge my existence. You would have walked out of that room without even looking at me, wouldn't you?"

"Yes," she answered bluntly.

"Yes," he repeated grimly. "And that's why I stopped you."

"And because I bruised your delicate ego, you mentioned our having breakfast together in a tone that suggested we spent the night together."

"Oh," he breathed out slowly. "Now we get to the real reason for your anger. You didn't want anyone — not just my family, but anyone — to know we were together because you were afraid they'd wonder if we were sleeping together. That's why you wanted me to wait in the car or cafeteria."

"Exactly." Helen's face had taken on her cool, withdrawn, professional expression. Her tone held frigid hauteur. "My reputation, both professionally and privately, is spotless. I fully intend to keep it that way. I will not have my name bandied about in speculative gossip."

The laughter that met her stilted statement wiped the composure off Helen's face.

"Bandied about?" he gasped, between whoops of delight. "Oh! I love it. Bandied about." With an obvious effort he brought his roars under control. "Where did you pull that chestnut from?"

Against her better judgment Helen felt her lips twitch with humor. What a pompous ass she sounded. Where *had* she pulled that chestnut from?

"Don't laugh at me, Marsh," she scolded quietly. "It's not polite to ridicule your elders."

Hot, swift anger wiped the amusement from his face, cut off the laughter still rumbling in his chest. The abrupt transition startled and frightened her.

"Helen," he snarled softly, fingers digging painfully into her shoulders, "what is this stupid hang-up you have about our ages? You are not my *elder*." Helen's eyes widened as his face drew close to hers. "You will not speak to me as if I were a naughty child." His eyes glittered with intent, robbing Helen of breath. "A naughty man maybe, but not a naughty child."

His lips, hard with anger, forced hers apart. The rigid tip of his tongue flicked against her teeth, stirring an unwanted curl of excitement in her midsection.

"You want a taste of the man, Helen?"

A seductive whisper, then his mouth crushed hers hungrily, his tongue plunged to extract the sweetness as a bee extracts honey from the blossom.

Helen's heart seemed to stop, then the beat increased to thunder in her ears like the hoofbeats of a wildly galloping horse. Good Lord! It was the last coherent thought she had for several seconds. His hands turned her, pushed her gently against the seat, and her breasts were crushed by the weight of his chest.

An ache began, deep inside, that quickly grew to enormous proportions. Giving in to the need to get closer to him, Helen's arms encircled his waist, tightened convulsively.

His mouth left hers reluctantly, came back as if unwilling to have the moment end. Between slow, languorous forays, he muttered, "How long, Helen? How long before you face reality and yourself? You want me. I know you do."

Helen brought her hand up, her fingers moving across his lips.

"Marsh, stop." Her breathing was uneven, erratic. "I don't want any emotional involvements. Oh, Marsh, please." His lips were busy against her fingers, his teeth nipped playfully. "There's no time in my life for a man."

"Too late," he murmured. His lips caught the tip of her ring finger, sucked gently. "You've got a man in your life. At the moment a very hungry man." He moved away from her, back behind the steering wheel, a rueful smile slanting his mouth. "A hungry man in more ways than one. Are we going to go eat or are you going to sit there and watch me slowly starve to death?"

Helen welcomed his return to humor with a sigh of relief. Although his anger had been brief, it had been fierce and he had really frightened her. What would he be like, she wondered fleetingly, if he really let loose? She could only hope she never had to witness it, let alone be the cause of it. The mere thought made her feel cold all over. Shrugging to cover the shiver that shook her slim frame, Helen gave in.

"All right, Marsh, you win. We'll go eat."

His smile grew into a rakish grin. "At the risk of sounding conceited, I think I'd better warn you that I usually do. Win, that is."

Later, sitting in a small restaurant, Helen toyed with her cheese omelet and watched, fascinated, while Marsh demolished a huge club sandwich and a double order of French fries. Their conversation had been minimal as he attacked the food like a man who was actually starving.

When he finished, he wiped his lips with his napkin indicated to the waitress that he'd like his coffee cup refilled, sat back, and turned that unnerving blue gaze on her.

"Are you from Philly originally?"

Helen blinked with the suddenness of his question after the long silence. Nodding to the waitress who held the coffeepot poised over her cup, her eyebrows raised questioningly, Helen matched his casual tone. "No, I was born up near Wilkes-Barre. My father was a G.P., had a surprisingly large practice considering the size of the community."

"Was? Had?" he probed.

"He retired two years ago. He and my mother sold everything and moved to Phoenix. She lifted her gaze from her coffee cup, unaware of the touch of sadness he could see in her eyes, the wistfulness of her small smile. "I miss them."

"Of course." His voice lost some of its casualness. "You have other family here? Brothers, sisters?"

"No." She shook her head. "I have a younger brother; he's also in Phoenix. That's the main reason Mother and Dad decided to retire there. He, Rob, has two small children. My parents wanted to watch their grandchildren grow up." Helen's smile twisted wryly. "They gave up the hope of seeing any grandchildren from me a long time ago."

"Why?" Marsh's tone sharpened. "You're not too old to have kids."

Helen breathed deeply, then said firmly, "I don't want children, Marsh."

His eyes narrowed at the calm finality of her tone. His shoulders lifted, came down again in an oddly resigned gesture.

"Okay." His tone was flat, but steady. "We won't have any."

"Won't have any! Marsh —"

Helen stopped herself on hearing her own rising voice. She glanced around quickly before continuing in a much lower, fiercer tone. "Marsh, what are you talking about? You know my feelings on —"

"Not here." Marsh rose, silencing her effectively. In the car she turned to him as soon as he'd slid behind the wheel. "Not here, either," he snapped with finality.

Helen was amazed at the number of people in Fairmont Park. It was very cold and the wind, though not strong, bit at her exposed skin with icy teeth. "Incredible," she murmured, after they'd been walking for some minutes. "Is it like this every Sunday?"

"Yes." He slanted a mocking glance at her. "Helen, I find it hard to believe you didn't know. Don't you ever watch the local news on T.V.?"

"I rarely watch T.V. at all," she replied, glancing around interestedly. "I did know the park was a favorite spot for joggers but I had no idea there were this many people into jogging, let alone all these other people here."

"You live a rather single-minded existence, don't you?" he chided.

"I never thought of it that way, but" — she shrugged — "I suppose I do. Which reminds me. Back at the restaurant you said — Marsh! What are you doing?"

He had taken her gloved left hand in his larger bare one. After tugging her glove off, he laced the fingers of his right hand through hers, then slipped their clasped hands into the deep fleece-lined slash pocket of his jacket. When she tried to pull her hand free, his fingers tightened until she cried out in pain. "Marsh, please."

"Stop fighting me." His fingers loosened, but not enough for her to slip free. "And back at the restaurant I said that if you didn't want children we wouldn't have any."

He was so unconcerned, so nonchalant, Helen was beginning to feel she'd get better results talking to one of the park's many trees. Fighting to hang on to her patience, she gritted slowly.

"That's right, *we* won't have any children. *We* won't have anything together for the simple reason we won't be together. What do I have to do to make you understand? I don't want a relationship. I don't want to be bothered by any man." During this entire tirade Helen's tone had not risen above a harsh whisper. Now she drew a ragged breath and added in a more normal tone, "Do I make myself clear?"

"Perfectly."

It was what she'd wanted to hear, so why did his prompt, careless answer cause a sharp pain in her chest? No sooner had the thought skittered through her mind than he added blandly, "There's only one problem, sweetheart. You are already bothered by a man. This man. And this man plans to bother you one hell of a lot more before he's through."

"Marsh," Helen began angrily, but he cut in in that same bland tone.

"Let's shelve the subject for now and enjoy our walk. Are you cold?"

"Yes. No. A little." Helen could have shouted at him; he had her so frustrated, she didn't know what she was saying. And his soft, delighted laughter didn't help much either. "I mean I am a little cold but I'm enjoying the walk."

"Good. Do you want to walk down to the river and see if there are any hardy souls crewing?"

Helen hesitated. If there were boats on the river, she'd like to see them. But then again, her nose was beginning to feel numb now and the wind off the water would be a lot colder, so she shivered and shook her head. "I don't think so. Another day per-haps."

"Chicken," he taunted softly. "Don't tell me you're a hothouse flower."

"Coming from Wilkes-Barre?" She laughed. "You have got to be kidding. Why, when I was in the sixth grade I was the undisputed snowball champ."

"Liar."

Helen's laughter sang on the cold air, bringing a bemused expression to his eyes, a deepening timbre to his voice. "What were you really like in sixth grade?"

"Quiet, studious, head-of-the-class type. You-know." She paused, looked away from him. "I never wanted to be anything but a doctor. My mother despaired at my nose in a book, but my father was delighted. He had similar hopes for Rob too, but Rob had his own ideas." She laughed again, a soft, reminiscent laugh. "Rob's a charmer. Always has been. He could talk the face off an eight-day clock. A born salesman. And that's exactly what he is. Makes an excellent living at it too."

"You miss him." It was not a question. "Were you very close?"

"Yes." Helen closed her eyes against the sudden, sharp longing she felt for her distant family. "While we were growing up we fought like a dog and cat. Nearly drove my mother mad. Our saving grace was that we also defended each other fiercely against outsiders." She laughed again at a particular memory.

"Tell me," Marsh prompted. "Let me share the laughter."

"It's silly." Helen shook her head, still smiling. "To this day Rob tells people that I was named Laura, after my mother, but I grew up a hell-en and it stuck."

"You *do* miss him." Inside the pocket his fingers squeezed hers, sending a shaft of exciting warmth up her arm. "When did you see him last?"

"I flew out for a week last spring for his birthday." She frowned, remembering. Her tone lost its sparkle, went flat. "His thirty-first. I've always thought of Rob as my baby brother, Marsh, and he's a year older than you are."

A tautness came into his body. She could feel it in the arm that rested against hers, in the tightening of his fingers. "Do you think of me in the same vein?" Even his voice was taut.

"Marsh, I —"

"Do you?" Harsh now, rough, he stopped walking, turned to face her.

"No." It was a shaken whisper, but she could not lie to him with that intent blue gaze on her. His deep sigh formed a misty cloud between them.

"It's a damned good thing," he grated. "Helen, unless you want to see some real fireworks, I think you'd better make a concentrated effort to forget the difference in our ages. Without too much prodding I could become positively paranoid about it."

He leaned closer to her and his voice went very low. Not in self-consciousness of the people passing by, but in sheer intensity. "I love you, Helen. I don't know *how* I know, but I *do* know that if there were ten or even fifteen years between us, I would still love you."

"Marsh, I — I —" Shaken by his declaration, unsure, Helen searched for words.

"Leave it for now," he said softly. The bone-crushing grip on her fingers was eased as the tension went out of his body. "We came here to walk, let's walk."

They had taken only a few steps when he jiggled her fingers, and requested, "Tell me some more about your family."

"No." The eyes that met his sharp look were teasing. "Tell me about yours. I'm curious to know what type people it takes to produce such a — a —"

"Bonehead?" he suggested dryly. "Bulldog? Bast—"

"Marsh!"

His head was thrown back in laughter. Joyful, enchanting laughter that stole her breath, doubled the rate of her heartbeat. And before she realized what he was doing, he turned, bent his head, and caught her mouth with his, unconcerned with the giggles that came from a group of teenage girls passing by.

Helen felt as gauche as a teenager herself, feeling her cheeks grow hot when he lifted his head, grinned at her, and whispered, "I do love kissing you."

"You're a fool," she whispered back, trying to sound stern, failing miserably.

"Yes, well, we'll go into that another time," he warned. "But now" — he resumed walking again, totally relaxed — "my family. My mother's beautiful, as I'm sure you noticed." He raised dark brows at her and she nodded. "My father's rich, and I mean old guard, Society Hill rich. Kris is a pet. She used to be a drag, trailing after me all the time, but even when she was a drag, she was a pet. I love them all, but I adore my grandfather."

Helen looked up quickly, breath catching at the softness in his tone, his eyes. The strong lines of his face, the russet hair, those incredibly clear blue eyes, were becoming too familiar, too heart-wrenchingly important. In an effort to shake off her thoughts, Helen prompted, "Your grandfather?"

"Yes." He smiled. "My grandfather. You'll like him," he stated emphatically. "And I know he's going to be crazy about you." He laughed softly at some secret

601

joke, then went on. "My grandfather is definitely not old guard. A real scrapper still, and he's close to seventy-five. Chews me out regularly, enjoys every minute of it too. He started sixty years ago with a couple of hundred dollars, which was all that was left after his father died, and built it into a small empire. It keeps me running, trying to handle the damn thing."

"Started what?"

"A small building and construction firm that is now a very large building and construction firm, plus assorted other interests he's picked up along the way."

"So you do work for a living," she chided "I did wonder. You're a construction worker?"

"Among other things." That devastating grin flashed. "My father wanted me to follow him into banking." He grimaced. "Can you see me as a banker?" Helen smiled, shook her head. "Yeah, well, neither could I. Cullen couldn't either."

"Cullen?"

"My grandfather. I've called him Cullen, on his insistence, for as long as I can remember. Drove my grandparents on my father's side up the wall."

"Cullen is your mother's father."

"Yes. Her mother died giving her life and although Cullen wanted a son, he never remarried. He told me there wasn't a woman alive who could replace his Megan. Anyway, after she died, he lived for his work and his daughter. I think he claimed me for himself about five minutes after I was born. My father didn't stand a chance against the old bear."

"Your father gave in to him without a fight?" Helen asked incredulously, thinking of the battle anyone would have had trying to claim her brother away from her father.

"Hell, no." Marsh chuckled. "Dad's no slouch. The tug-of-war lasted through all the years I was growing up, with me in the middle, catching flak from both sides."

They had retraced their steps back to the car and Helen was glad to slide onto the seat, out of the cold air. She waited until he'd started the car and driven into the flow of traffic before observing, "I'm surprised you weren't scarred by the war. Or were you?"

"It wasn't that kind of war." He stopped at a stop sign and turned to give her an encompassing glance. "You look frozen. Any warmth coming from the heater yet?"

"Yes, a little, but I'm fine." Helen turned to study his features. "What kind of war was it?"

"Friendly. Dad and Cullen get along fine, always did. I suppose you could say they fought their battle like a chess game, only I was the only chessman. One would move me this way, the other another way."

"And your grandfather made the deciding move?" Helen couldn't decide if she was fascinated or appalled by the story.

"No." Marsh grinned. "I did."

"But, Marsh, you said earlier that you ran the business, that must mean your grandfather's got what he wanted."

"You think so?" he taunted softly. "Ask him sometime."

Helen had been so caught up in watching the play of emotions on his face, she hadn't once glanced out the window. When he drove the car into a small parking area, she looked around in confusion. The parking lot was adjacent to a small Italian restaurant in a part of the city she was unfamiliar with. Her eyes came back to him as he turned the key, cutting the engine.

"Why are we stopping here?"

"This is one of my favorite haunts. I'm addicted to their shrimp scampi." Her widening eyes brought the grin back to his mouth. "I walked off my lunch," he defended himself carelessly. "I'm hungry." His eyes went over her face, dropped to her slim wrists. "Some good, rich Italian food wouldn't hurt you either. Were you always so thin?"

"Oh, for heaven's sake," Helen groaned, reaching for the door release. "You sound like Alice."

He was out of his door and around to hers in time to close it for her. "Who's Alice?"

"My office nurse."

"Oh, yes, the dragon I talked to on the phone Thursday." He held open the door into the restaurant for her to precede him inside, and as he helped her with her coat he asked wryly, "Does Alice look as daunting as she sounds?"

"And as bossy." Helen nodded. "She has been nagging me for weeks about my weight."

"I think I like Alice," he murmured as a tall, genial man approached, a huge smile revealing glistening white teeth.

"Hiya, Marsh, haven't seen you for a while." His bold, dark eyes slid over Helen appreciatively. When his eyes returned to Marsh they held a trace of envy. "Where've you been hiding out, *compare?*"

Marsh put his hand out to clasp the other man's, a taunting grin curving his lips. "Not hiding, Moe, working. Cullen's had me on the run for weeks."

Moe looked at Helen, letting his glance linger deliberately a second before remarking, "Not too much on the run. You've obviously had time for other things. Very beautiful other things."

Marsh laughed aloud, and Helen

couldn't help smiling back at the good-looking Moe. He was about the same age as Marsh, with black curly hair, dark brown eyes, and a sexy look about him that probably ensnared women in droves.

"Helen, this smart-mouthed Sicilian is Emilio Brenzini, Moe to you. He's the owner of this joint. He's also my best friend, I think." Marsh turned a sardonic face to Moe. "Moe, Helen Cassidy. Dr. Helen Cassidy, my future wife."

Helen's shocked gasp was covered up by Moe's shouted, "What? Hey, man, that's terrific. Come and sit down." They were ushered to a small table covered with a blood-red cloth, matching napkins folded neatly beside carefully arranged flatware. When Moe moved behind Helen to hold her chair, she glared at Marsh, who smiled back sweetly. Choking back the angry words she wanted to spit at him, she forced a smile to her lips when Moe was again facing them.

"I just can't believe it," Moe exclaimed in awe. "Marshall Kirk, man about town, heartbreaker extraordinaire, brought down in his prime by a female sawbones." His eyes glittered at Helen. "What the hell did such a gorgeous creature as you see in this big number-counting lady killer?"

"Knock off the comedy routine, Moe," Marsh drawled. "And break out the wine.

Helen and I were outside for hours and we need some warming up."

"Okay, sweetheart." Moe did a bad imitation of Bogart and walked away, chuckling to himself.

The moment he was out of sight Helen snapped, "How dare you tell him that."

"Why not?" Marsh answered blandly. "You are going to be my wife."

"No, I am not," she gritted furiously. "Do you understand? I am not. When Moe comes back, you tell him you were joking."

"No."

"Marsh, I'm warning you." Seething, Helen had trouble enunciating her words. "If you don't tell him, I will."

Marsh eyed her dispassionately. "Have fun," he drawled. "But personally I think you're going to seem pretty damned silly. Moe's going to wonder why you didn't deny it at once."

Helen opened her mouth, closed it again, trying to collect some control. Then Moe was back, grinning happily as he poured the ruby-red wine.

"To both of you." He lifted his glass, his face sobering as he turned to Helen. "I should say I hope you'll be very happy but with this one" — he jerked his head at Marsh, a soft smile touching his lips — "I don't really think it's necessary. He is the best there is, Helen. Only a very foolish woman would not find happiness with him." Then he turned to Marsh, glass going high in salute.

"Congratulations, *compare*. I begin to suspect that you are a very, very lucky man."

fiue

Sleep eluding her, Helen lay on her back, staring at the pale white ceiling. It was late, several hours since Marsh had left, and yet her mind hung on to the day's happenings as tenaciously as a baby monkey hangs on to its mother.

She had said nothing to clarify the situation to Moe, of course. How could she after the sincerity of his toast to them?

Positive she'd choke if she tried to force food around the anger waiting to explode from her throat, Helen had surprised herself by not only eating but keeping pace with Marsh. The scampi was every bit as delicious as Marsh had claimed, but then, the antipasto, tossed salad, large slices of crispy crusted bread, and spumoni were the best Helen had ever eaten also. When they had drained the last drop of wine and were preparing to leave, Marsh reached for his wallet. Moe placed his hand on Marsh's arm and shook his head.

"This one's on me, buddy. Bring Helen

over to meet Jeanette soon." He laughed softly before adding, "They've already got one thing in common."

At Helen's questioning look Marsh explained, "The medical profession. Jeanette is an anesthesiologist."

"Really? Where?" Those were her first unstrained words since Marsh had told Moe she was to be his wife. Moe named the hospital and Helen smiled, nodded. "Yes, I'm familiar with it. They have excellent facilities and a first-rate staff. Does she enjoy her work?"

"Most of the time." Moe's answer was laconic. "Sometimes it all gets on top of her. You know, the job, taking care of the kids, the house" — he grinned — "keeping me happy."

Curious, Helen asked, "How many children do you have?" His smug answer shocked her.

"Four. Five years of marriage and four *bambinos*. That's pretty good work, wouldn't you say, Doc?"

"Four babies and she keeps up the pace in the O.R.?" Helen returned incredulously. "Moe, you are married to a superwoman."

"Jeanette *is* a super person," Marsh put in, edging her to the door. "But don't think for a minute this buffoon doesn't take good care of her. She works by choice. and she has plenty of help in the house. The *gran signore* here gets his masculine ego kicks by giving people the impression he's got a master-slave marital arrangement. When in fact he'd drop onto his knees and kiss the hem of her uniform if she asked him to."

"Without hesitation" was Moe's emphatic response.

Even now, hours later, Helen shook her head in wonder at Moe's wife. A date had been set, for the following Saturday, for Helen and Marsh to join Moe and Jeanette for dinner at the restaurant. Helen was looking forward to meeting her.

When, finally, they had left Emilio's, Helen had withdrawn into a cold silence. Marsh had not made an attempt to break that silence, although he had cast several searching glances at her.

Helen was mad, and she wanted him to know she was mad. She simmered with indignation all the way home, while he parked the car, rode up in the elevator with her, stood behind her as she turned the key in the lock. When she turned to give him a frosty good night, he reached around her, pushed the door open, spun her around, gave her a gentle shove, and followed her into the room. Eyes blazing, she'd whirled back to face him. He beat her to the draw.

"Okay, you're mad." His voice was low,

steady, unrepentent. "So let's have it. Get it out of your system and then we'll talk calmly about it."

"I don't want to talk about it," Helen said coldly. "You will have to make my apology next Saturday night. I am not going with you. I do not want to see you again. I do not want you to call me." Breathing deeply, she stared into his impassive, expressionless face. "Is that understood?"

"You're nuts, do you know that?"

The soft, taunting amusement in his tone drew a gasp from her. Before she could form words of retaliation, he stepped in front of her, grasped her shoulders, and gave her a light shake.

"For all your cool, self-contained act, it doesn't take much to set you off, does it?" His eyebrows arched and a knowing smile twitched his lips. "Or is it me?" he chided softly. "I have a hunch that if any other man had made that statement, you would have, very coolly, called him a liar." His voice went softer still. "I get to you, don't I? I rattle you and ruffle your feathers. I make you mad, but" — he lowered his head to within an inch of hers — "I can also make you laugh." His mouth brushed hers, once, twice. "But what really bothers you is that I excite you." The tip of his tongue slid across her lips, parting them in a small, involuntary gasp. His mouth covered hers, his hands moved down her spine, molding her against him.

At first she struggled against him, clenching her teeth and jaw tightly. But what he said was true. He did excite her, and that excitement curled around and through her, loosening her jaw, weakening her knees, driving her arms up and around his neck to cling helplessly while his mouth plundered hers.

Helen moved restlessly on the bed. Just thinking about him sparked off that excitement, sent it scampering wildly through her body. The words he'd whispered against her lips now brought a low moan from her throat.

"I want to sleep with you, Helen. Let me stay. Let me exorcise, once and for all, the fears that have kept your emotions frozen all these years." He pulled her closer, his arms tightening. His breath danced across her ear. "Trust me, love, I won't hurt you."

"No, no."

Her words had a desperate, panicky sound, even to her own ears, and he allowed her to move out of his arms, away from him. He watched her pull the ragged edges of her composure together, then he sighed softly and walked to the door.

"I'll call you tomorrow."

"Marsh, I said —"

"Damn it, Helen," he flared, "don't fight me. Do you want me to come back over there? Prove to you that there's a woman inside that cool, professional veneer you've covered yourself with?"

She backed away warily, shaking her head in answer.

"All right then, play it cool for a while, see what develops. Now," he sighed again, impatiently, "what's the best time to call you tomorrow?"

"After six thirty. Here."

Why had she given in to him? Helen silently asked her ceiling. Why did she let him brush aside her protests as if they meant nothing? Her mouth twisted in self-mockery. Maybe, because, if she was honest with herself, they meant exactly that: nothing.

Helen went rigid, fingers curling lightly around the comforter. The self-truth was a shocking jolt her stiffened body tried to reject. *Face it, Dr. Cassidy,* she told herself derisively, *you're as human and vulnerable as the next woman. You* like *the breathlessness that intent, blue gaze causes. You* like *the feeling of weakness the touch of his hand on your body induces. You* like *the crazy riot of sensations his hungry mouth generates. For the first time in over ten years you have a physical need for a man. But why this particular man?*

Helen's mind darted in different directions in an effort to avoid answering her own question. It was quite true she'd felt no urges of a sexual nature since the night of Carl's assault. Filled with disgust, contempt, she had, for many months, withdrawn from any kind of personal contact with the opposite sex. As time passed and circumstances demanded she had some contact with men, the contempt lessened, and in a few cases was replaced by respect and admiration, but that was all. It was as if the part of her brain that controlled her emotional responses had closed shop — permanently. With the rest of her mind she could evaluate a man's potential and his accomplishments, and applaud them, but always as a contemporary, never, ever, as an interesting male.

Now, suddenly, this one man, this *younger* man, was arousing all kinds of needs and wants inside her.

"No, please." It was a whispered cry into the room's darkness. The stiffness drained out of her body, replaced by a longing ache that made what she'd felt for Carl, before *that* night, seem mild and insipid by comparison.

Head moving from side to side on the pillow, Helen's eyes closed slowly. After all these years the emotional control center in her brain was alert and functioning and sending out signals she could not deny. She wanted this man. She needed this man. *Damn it to hell,* she thought furiously, *I'm in love with him.*

No! I can't be, her reason rebelled. *I don't even know him and I never even found out what it is, exactly, he does.* Then, irrelevantly, *he's not even in the medical profession.* The irrationality of her thoughts struck her, and aloud she moaned, "He is right, I am nuts."

The comforter twisted around her squirming body as she fought against the insidious languor thoughts of him had produced. *I am not in love,* she told herself firmly. *Of course I'm not. This — this craziness is just that: physical craziness. Marsh is a good-looking — no, handsome — man. He has charm, and money, in abundance, and face it, he is downright sexy.* His eyes alone had the power to set off a chain reaction of sensations inside a woman. *And,* she rationalized, *I can surely handle my own physical attraction to him. I must. I cannot, I will not, expose myself to that kind of pain again. I'm a mature woman. not a silly young girl. And I certainly will not be an object of any man's pleasure. Most especially a young man.*

Helen winced. Why, when all the mature, sophisticated men she'd met had left her cold, did she react so strongly to him? His assertion that they were fated to come together she dismissed as nonsense. She was a physician. She was aware, if not fully understanding, of the age-old mystery of one person's chemistry striking sparks off another. But it was totally incomprehensible to her why his was the only chemistry able to ignite hers, after all this time. She would not have it. She had worked too hard to allow a man, probably going through a phase in which he was attracted to older women, to disrupt her life.

For a long time Helen's thoughts ran on in the same vein, always coming back to the same conclusion. Since she could not order him to stay away — he paid no attention to her when she did — she'd go along with him, keeping him at arm's length, until the phase, or attraction, wore itself out.

Finally the plaguing ache left her body and she relaxed, grew drowsy. Her last coherent thought was that he could not hurt her if she simply refused to allow herself to *be* hurt.

She held on to that thought all through office hours the next day, whenever Marsh invaded her mind. She was in the apartment not fifteen minutes when the phone rang. Going to the wall phone in the kitchen, Helen glanced at the clock, thinking it must be her service as Marsh was not due to call for a half hour.

"Dr. Cassidy." She spoke briskly into the receiver.

"I don't want to speak to Dr. Cassidy," the low voice taunted. "I want to speak to Helen. Is she there?"

Steeling herself against the warmth the sound of his voice sent racing through her body, Helen asked coolly, "Is there a difference?"

His soft laughter sent a shiver after the warmth. "A very big difference," he stated firmly. "Dr. Cassidy is a machine, Helen is a woman."

Stung by his jibe, surprised at the swift shaft of pain it caused, Helen murmured, "That wasn't very nice, Marsh."

"When did I ever say I was nice?" he mocked. "Oh, I have my moments, but not with you. I don't want to be nice to you. What I want to do is shake some sense into your rigid mind. But not tonight. I'll have to pass on that pleasure for the rest of the week." He paused and his tone took on an edge Helen didn't understand. "I'm going out of town for the rest of the week. I must make a circuit of several of my clients, clear up a few things." Now he sounded annoyed, as if angry at the claim to his time. "The damned incompetence of some bookkeepers today is not to be believed."

Again he paused, and his tone had a controlled, frustrated ring. "I'll be back sometime Friday. I'll call you."

"All right, Marsh." Helen's calm reply gave away none of the confusion she was feeling. After wishing him a safe trip and hanging up the receiver, Helen moved around the kitchen, getting herself something to eat, her mind nagging at his tone.

Why had he been so annoyed? she wondered with a vague twinge of unease. After forcing down a cold sliced roast beef sandwich and a small salad, she brewed a pot of herb tea and carried it into the living room. As she sipped the hot, green liquid Helen speculated on the reason for his anger. Was it really caused by the need to visit clients or was it connected in some way with her?

Cup in hand, Helen moved restlessly around the tastefully decorated room in a vain attempt to escape her thoughts. It didn't work. Her thoughts pursued her as she paced back and forth, into the kitchen to wash up her few dishes. He had been angry the night before. Angry and impatient and very likely frustrated with his failure at getting her into bed with him.

A shudder rippled through her body and she stood unmoving at the sink, the towel she'd been drying her hands on hanging forgotten in her fingers. Had he thought she'd be an easy conquest? Her behavior the previous Thursday might have led him to believe so. Did he think, like many other people, that an unmarried woman in her mid-thirties was so desperate for male companionship that she'd hop into bed with almost any male?

Wincing, Helen tossed aside the towel and went back to pacing the living room. Unlike most women, reaching thirty, thirty-five, had not bothered her. Why should it? She was performing at the peak of her efficiency and she knew it. She lived well and had a comfortable sum of money in the bank. Her life was evolving as planned. What more could she possibly ask for? Up until now her answer to that would have been an emphatic nothing. But now the answer that shouted in her mind shook her with its intensity.

She wanted Marsh. She wanted the feel of his mouth on hers, his arms tight around her, his body, hard and urgent, leaving her in no doubt that he wanted her as badly.

Becoming tired, yet unable to sit still, Helen continued to pace in a nervous, jerky manner that in itself was alien to her usual smooth movements. She did not feel like herself. She wasn't even sure what she did feel like. She didn't like it, but wasn't quite sure what to do about it.

Maybe, she decided clinically as she prepared for bed, she should have an affair with him, get him out of her system, let him get her out of his. She toyed with the idea a moment, then rejected it. No, she could not do that, for she felt positive that in an encounter or affair like that she would end up wounded if not crushed. While he, malelike, would blithely walk away, one Helen Cassidy forgotten, looking for new battlefields to conquer. No! She wasn't quite sure how she'd handle the situation, but she felt positive that if she played along with him, let him have it all his way, she'd be the one left torn and bleeding on this particular battlefield.

So ran her thoughts for the remainder of the week, and by the time her alarm rang on Friday morning she was thoroughly sick of them. Although it was an extremely busy week, with several deliveries and her office packed with patients, it had seemed like an endless one.

By the time her last patient left on Friday afternoon, Helen decided she'd been a fool to give the matter so much consideration. Without Marsh's proximity she had reached the point of observing the whole affair objectively and come to the conclusion that she was mountain climbing over molehills.

Her sense of balance restored, Helen

went home with the conviction that she could handle one Marshall Kirk with one hand tied behind her back. Her right hand at that.

She would, she thought smugly, do exactly as Marsh had recommended: play it cool. She would go with him to have dinner with Moe and his wife and start the evening with a flat denial of Marsh's assertions of the previous Sunday.

Helen waited for his call until after midnight, her hard-fought balance slipping away as each hour died a slow death. And when, in the small hours, she did finally drift into an uneasy sleep, she felt actually bruised, as if she'd been beaten, and her pillow knew an unfamiliar dampness.

Her phone rang before her alarm, and as she had two patients due at any time, Helen snatched up the receiver on the second ring.

"Good morning, sweetheart, did I wake you?"

Marsh's soft voice sent an anticipatory shiver through Helen's body, and she had to clutch the receiver to keep from dropping it. How, she wondered, did he manage to sound so seductive at this hour of the morning?

"Yes." And why did she have to sound so breathless and sleepy?

"I could tell," he purred sexily. "You

sound warm and cuddly and" — he paused
— "ready, and I wish like hell that I was
there right now."

Helen's mouth went dry, and she placed
her hand over the receiver as if afraid he
could actually see her wet her lips.

"No comeback?" Marsh taunted softly.
"No cutting reply? You must still be half
asleep." He laughed low in his throat. "Or
is it the other? Are you all warm . . . and
so forth?"

The jarring noise of her alarm broke the
spell his sensuous voice had caught her up
in. So much for firm resolutions and objective reasoning, Helen thought wryly, her
finger silencing the alarm's persistent ring.

"Actually" — how had she achieved that
detached tone? — "I was confused for a
moment as to who it was. It's been so long
since I heard your voice." A gentle, but effective, reminder that he'd said he'd call
the night before.

His laughter appreciated the thrust.
"You lie so convincingly, my sweet. Is it
one of your habits?" His laughter deepened
at the half gasp her covering hand was not
fast enough to blank out entirely. "I know
I said I'd call you last night but it was very
late when I got in and I didn't want to disturb you — or did I manage to do that
anyway?"

The soft insinuation brought a sparkle of

anger, self-directed, to Helen's now-wide-awake hazel eyes. Biting back the few choice names she would have found much pleasure in calling him at this safe distance, she snapped waspishly, "Marsh, I have to go to work. Did you call for a reason or just to annoy me?"

"Ah-ha, she's awake now, and the transformation has been made. There speaks the mechanical Dr. Cassidy."

"Marsh, have you been up all night?" Helen enunciated with exaggerated patience. "You sound somewhat light-headed."

"It's an affliction that attacks the minds of men when they're in love," Marsh replied seriously. Then he added wickedly, "And have the hots."

"Not men," she retaliated harshly. "Callow youths."

"Mind your tongue, Helen." The bantering tone was gone, replaced by steel-edged anger.

"Marsh, it's after seven thirty." Helen retreated quickly. "I have to get ready for work. What, exactly, did you call for?"

"To find out what your early-morning voice sounds like," he shot back smoothly. "And to tell you I'll pick you up at seven."

"All right, now I must go."

"And, Helen? Give me a break and let your hair down. Bye, love."

Fuming, Helen stood several seconds, listening to the dial tone before replacing the receiver, unsure if he had meant her to take his request literally or figuratively.

The morning went surprisingly well and before one thirty Helen found herself free for the day. About to leave the office, she turned back, picked up her phone, and called the hairdresser who occasionally cut and styled her hair. Yes, the young woman told her, if Helen could come right in, she could work her in.

When she let herself into her apartment several hours later, Helen's hair had been shampooed, shaped, and blown dry. It lay in soft curls and waves around her face and against her shoulders.

Later, as she was putting the finishing touches to her makeup, Helen paused to study the unfamiliar hairstyle. At first, the change being so radical from her usual smoothed-back neatness, Helen had not been sure if she liked it. But now, after living with it for some hours, she had to admit that the loose curls and waves framing her face softened the stubborn line of her chin, the curve of her cheek. Was she, perhaps, past the age for such a careless style? Her hazel eyes sharpened, searched thoroughly, but the thick mane, not quite brown, yet not quite blond, revealed not a sign of gray. Well, maybe for the weekends, the rare evening out, she finally decided. But never, never for the office, the hospital. The one thing she didn't want while she was working was to appear, in any way, softened or vulnerable. At one minute to seven Helen stepped out of the elevator into the apartment building's small lobby and came face to face with Marsh. Without speaking, she watched his eyes widen, flicker with admiration and approval as they went over her hair, her face, then move down to the muted red of her wool coat. She could actually feel the touch of that blue gaze as it slowly traveled the length of her slim, sheer nylon-clad legs to her narrow feet, not at all covered by the few thin straps of her narrow-heeled sandals. When he raised his eyes to hers, Helen felt her heartbeat slow down then speed up into an alarmingly rapid thud. The expression in his eyes, on his strong, handsome face, was so blatantly sensual, all the moisture evaporated from her mouth and throat.

"You are one beautiful woman." His voice was very low, yet each word was clear, distinct. "Why in the hell do you ever pull your hair back off your face?"

Helen stared at her own reflection in his eyes, suddenly filled with an overwhelming desire to lose herself in their blue depths. Her lips parted, the tip of her tongue skimming over them wetly, but no words came. She heard him draw in his breath sharply, saw him lift his hands, take a step toward her before he brought himself up abruptly, a rueful smile twisting his lips.

"We had better get out of here, love," he murmured hoarsely, "before I do something that would very likely delight the people in this lobby but embarrass you."

With that he stepped beside her, grasped her elbow, and hurried her toward the front entrance. It was only then that Helen became aware of the group of people in the lobby, laughing and talking about the evening ahead, calling a greeting to another couple as they came in the door and joined the group.

As they passed the group several pairs of eyes turned in their direction, and Helen could not help but see the sharp looks of interest and appreciation. Avid female glances took in Marsh's imposing figure; warm male eyes ran over her own.

With a jolt Helen realized that up until that point she and Marsh had been unobserved and that the eternity that had seemed to pass while she'd stared into his eyes had, in actuality, lasted only a few brief seconds.

Oddly shaken, Helen walked beside him in silence to the car, slid obediently onto the seat as he held the door. Her mind numb, refusing to delve for any deep meaning in the incident, Helen stared through the windshield as Marsh slid behind the wheel, started the engine, and drove away from the parking lot.

When the stunned sensation left her, Helen stole a glance at Marsh's set profile. Her glance froze and held for long seconds before, with a smothered gasp, she forced her eyes back to the windshield. But the windshield couldn't hold her gaze, and slowly, almost against her will, her eyes crept back to fasten hungrily on his face. She had not realized how very much she'd missed him. In something very close to pain her eyes devoured the sight of him, soaked the image of him into her mind, her senses.

"Stop it, Helen."

Helen blinked at the raw harshness of his voice, stammered, "W— what?"

"You know damn well what," he rasped. "I can *feel* your eyes on me. We have a date with Moe and Jeanette, but if you don't look away, I'm going to say the hell with it, turn the car around, and take you to my place."

"Marsh — I —" Helen began tremulously.

"I mean it, Helen." He cut across her words roughly. "The way I feel right this minute, I could park this car at the first empty spot I find and make love to you and not give a damn if we drew an audience."

A shiver of excited anticipation slid down Helen's spine, then shocked at her reaction to his threat, she practically jumped away from him and glued her eyes to the side window.

"That's better." His tone had smoothed out and it now held amusement. Helen gritted her teeth and a few moments later greeted with a sigh of relief the bright red neon sign that spelled out the name EMILIO'S.

There was an awkward stiffness between them as they left the car and walked to the restaurant, but the awkwardness soon dissolved when exposed to the sincere warmth of Moe's greeting. With unrestrained pride Moe drew his wife forward to introduce her to Helen.

At a quick, cursory glance Jeanette might have appeared simply pretty. But, as Helen's glance was neither quick nor cursory, she was struck by the beauty of Jeanette's mass of short, shiny black curls, her wide, dark brown eyes, which somehow managed to look both femininely soft and sharply intelligent at the same time.

With a flourish Moe ushered them to a table, telling them menus wouldn't be necessary as he and Jeanette had completely planned the meal from appetizer to dessert. When a small wiry waiter walked up to their table carrying a silver bucket containing a bottle with a foil-wrapped head, a happy grin spread across Moe's face.

"For my *compare* and his beautiful bride-to-be" — his hand grasped the neck of the bottle, lifted it to reveal the Dom Pérignon label — "nothing but the best."

In frozen silence, a strained smile cracking her pale face, Helen heard the muffled pop of the cork as it was forced from the bottle by Moe's hand, hidden beneath a towel. Watching the golden liquid as it cascaded, bubbling, into the tulip-shaped glasses, Helen thought frantically: *Now is the time to speak, put an end to this pretence.*

In cloying panic she had the uncanny feeling that if she did not speak before the toast was given she'd be trapped into a situation from which she'd never get free. *That's ridiculous,* she told herself scathingly, casting about in her mind for light, joking words that would correct Marsh's statement of the week before without putting a damper on the party. She knew, already, that she was going to really like Moe and Jeanette and she didn't want to begin a friendship with a lie.

Unable to find the proper words, Helen's mind went blank. The glasses were passed around, and Moe and Jeanette lifted theirs. Surprisingly it was Jeanette who offered the toast. Her smile, her entire face, revealing the affection she felt for him, she looked directly at Marsh.

"To our favorite man, who deserves the best." She then looked at Helen, drawing her into the circle of affection. "And to his woman, who obviously is."

"*Bravissimo, cara,*" Moe applauded as he lifted his glass to his lips.

"*Grazie,*" Marsh replied simply before leaning across the table to kiss Jeanette's smiling mouth.

Self-schooled to show as little emotion as possible, Helen had listened to the toast, observed Marsh's reaction to it, and stared openly as the two men embraced each other, with a growing sense of wonder. Did these people always display their feelings this openly? Then all conjecture was sent flying as Moe's amazingly gentle lips touched hers. Startled, Helen was about to pull back and away when Marsh's chiding voice saved her from making a fool of herself.

"Enough already, you greedy Sicilian. It's my turn."

The gentle lips were removed, replaced by an equally gentle pair. And yet there was a difference. A difference so electrifying, Helen felt the shock waves reverberate through her entire body. He must have felt it too for he lifted his head too swiftly, breathed, "Later, sweetheart," and turned a smiling face back to Moe and Jeanette.

The toast over, Helen relaxed and, before she was even aware of being drawn, found herself laughing and talking with Moe and Jeanette as if she'd known them for years. The minute they'd finished their after-dinner liqueur and coffee, Moe stood up, his grin directed at Marsh.

"Come with me, *paesano*, I got to show you my new ovens."

Marsh rose but stood still when Jeanette placed a staying hand on his arm. Turning to her husband, she sighed exaggeratedly. "Marsh doesn't want to see your ovens, Moe."

Moe's eyes, as soulful as a scolded cocker spaniel's, shifted from Marsh to Jeanette, then back to Marsh.

"Tell the heartless woman you want to see my new ovens, Marsh," he pleaded petulantly.

His lips twitching, Marsh stared into Jeanette's laughing brown eyes and said seriously, "I want to see Moe's new ovens, heartless woman."

Jeanette's carefully controlled features dissolved into laughter. Waving one hand dismissively, she cried, "Oh, for heaven's sake, go admire the new ovens, you two lunatics."

Shaking her curly black head, Jeanette turned back to Helen with a grimace that quickly turned into a smile. "I swear, sometimes I think that man loves his kitchens more than he loves me."

"Kitchens?" Helen queried.

"Yes." The black head nodded. "He has three restaurants, even though this place, being the first, is his favorite."

"Does he do any of the cooking?"

"Lord, yes!" Jeanette exclaimed. "Here and at home. And what a cook!" She placed closed fingertips to her lips and kissed them. "I have to starve myself during the working hours or there would be a lot more of me."

"Well, if he cooked tonight's dinner," Helen said laughingly, "I can understand your problem."

"You know, Helen," Jeanette's tone went low, serious, "when Moe came home raving about Marsh's beautiful woman, I thought, yeah, just another in a long line of beautiful women. But five minutes after we met, I knew you were not just a beautiful woman in any man's line. You're special, and that makes me happy, because Marsh is also special and his happiness is very important to Moe and me."

What could one possibly reply to a sentiment like that? Feeling anything she'd say would be vastly inadequate, Helen nevertheless began an attempt to tell Jeanette the truth.

"Jeanette, I don't know quite how to say this, but —"

"By your solemn expression, love," Marsh inserted, "I have a nasty suspicion my best friend's wife has been telling tales out of school."

"Every chance I can," Jeanette retorted. "We girls have to stick together if we hope to keep you guys in line."

The moment for taking Jeanette into her confidence was past, and Helen felt an odd relief at Marsh's interruption. Strangely she hated the idea of disappointing Moe and Jeanette.

Six

It was close to midnight before the party broke up. It seemed to Helen that they talked nonstop, one minute laughingly, the next seriously. There were even a few friendly arguments, which nobody won, ending happily with everyone agreeing to disagree. Helen amazed herself with her own participation. She couldn't remember the last time she'd entered into a free-for-all conversation so effortlessly, and she enjoyed every minute of it.

When the last of the other dinner patrons had left, Moe, Marsh, and a few of the waiters cleared a small area of floor space by moving several tables together, and Moe found some slow, late-night music on the stereo behind the bar.

He then came to Helen and, with a courtly, old-world bow, requested the honor of the first dance. Moe was a good dancer; in fact he was the next thing to expert. Never very proficient herself, Helen found it hard to relax. When the music ended and was followed immediately by another, slower, number, Helen swirled out of one pair of arms into another.

Although he moved smoothly, evenly, Marsh was not nearly as expert as Moe and as his steps were less intricate, Helen followed his lead more easily. As one song followed another and the tension of concentration seeped out of her body, Marsh's arms tightened. His steps grew slower until, locked together, they were simply swaying to the music, oblivious of the knowing smiles of Moe and Jeanette, the shadowy movements of the waiters as they unobtrusively cleared the tables.

On the way home, still in a mellow mood, Helen tipped her head back against the headrest and softly hummed one of the tunes they'd danced to.

"You like my friends?" Marsh's quiet tone blended with her mood, and she answered without hesitation.

"Very much."

"I'm glad." He was quiet a moment, then added softly, "Maybe you'll introduce me to some of your friends sometime."

The mood was shattered, and Helen sat up straight, alert and wary. Now she did hesitate, for although his voice was soft, his tone had tautened.

"Maybe," she said, hedging, "sometime."

His soft laughter mocked her but he

didn't pursue the subject. Instead he taunted, "Did you miss me this week?"

"Why?" Helen asked blandly, innocently. "Were you away?"

This time his laughter filled the car, scurried down her spine.

"That'll cost you also," he purred warningly. "You are racking up quite a bill, woman. And I fully intend to make you pay in toto."

"I don't have the vaguest idea what you're talking about." Helen managed a light tone, despite the lick of excitement that shot through her veins.

"Oh, I think you do," he mocked. "Now answer my question. Did you miss me?"

"Well, maybe a little." She returned his mocking tone. "Like one might miss a persistent itch after it's gone."

"Deeper and deeper," he said, chuckling. "You're going to need a ladder to get yourself out of the hole you're digging."

He parked the car on the lot close to the building and grinned when she turned to say good night.

"Save your breath, I'm coming up with you."

"But, Marsh, it's late and —"

"Save it." He cut her off. "I'm coming up with you, Helen. That almost kiss I got early this evening wore off long ago. Besides which, I thought you'd offer me a nightcap or at least a cup of coffee."

"Coffee! At this hour?"

"You forget, I'm still young," he teased roughly. "Coffee never keeps me awake. Now stop stalling and let's go."

They went, Helen at an irritated, impatient clip, Marsh at a long-legged saunter beside her. She only glanced at him once on the way up. One glance at his twitching lips, his blue eyes dancing with devilry, was enough to send her blood racing — with anger? — through her body.

Inside the apartment she flung her coat and bag onto a chair and stormed into the kitchen. His soft laughter, as he carefully hung up her coat, crawled up the back of her neck, made her scalp tingle.

She was pouring the water into the top of the automatic coffeemaker when he entered the room, and after sliding the glass pot into place, Helen turned, eyes widening. He had not only removed his coat, but his jacket and tie as well, and had opened the top three buttons of his shirt. Turning away quickly, she pulled open the cabinet door, shaking fingers fumbling for cups. Damn him, she thought wildly, trying to concentrate on getting the cups safely out of the cabinet. *How can I hope to keep him at arm's length when he's already half undressed? And how in the world do I handle a man who simply laughs at me and refuses to be handled? More to the point, how do I handle myself when I know that what I want to do is finish the job he started on his shirt, feel his warm skin against my fingertips?*

Angry with him, with herself, with everything in general, she slid the cups from the shelf and banged them onto the countertop. Glaring at the coffee running into the pot, she snapped, "Make yourself at home."

"I intend to."

She hadn't heard him move up behind her, and she jumped when his arms slid around her waist, drew her back against him. When his lips touched her cheek, she cried, "Marsh, the coffee's ready."

"So am I," he murmured close to her ear, his hands moving slowly up her rib cage. "God, I missed you," he groaned. "You may only have missed me like the absence of an itch, but this is one itch that is going to persist until you have to scratch, Helen."

Helen's mouth went dry and her eyes closed against the sigh of urgency he put into her name. She gasped softly when his teeth nipped her lobe, then her eyes flew wide as his hands moved over her breasts.

"Marsh, stop."

Her words whirled away as she twirled inside his arms. His hungry mouth, covering hers, allowed no more words for several moments. Feeling her resolve, her determination, melt under the heat of his obvious desire, Helen pushed at his chest, head moving back and forth in agitation.

"Marsh, the coffee."

"The hell with the coffee," he growled harshly. "Helen, I've barely thought of anything but this all week. Now will you be quiet and let me kiss you?"

"No." She pushed harder against his chest. "Marsh, you — you wanted the damn coffee and you're going to drink it or you're going to go home."

He sighed, but his hands dropped to his sides. "All right, I'll drink the coffee." He gave in, then qualified, "If you'll join me."

The room crackled with tension as she filled the cups, placed them, along with cream and sugar, on the table. Sitting opposite him, sipping nervously at the brew she didn't want, Helen could feel the tension like a tangible presence. When he spoke, the calm normalcy of his tone struck her like a dash of cold water.

"Were you very busy this week?"

"Yes."

Try as she did, she could not come up with any other words. The silence yawned in front of her again, and her head jerked up when he blandly asked, "What's that you say? Did I have a busy week? As a matter of fact I did." His eyes bored into hers. "Even though I seemed to spend as much time in the air as on the ground. Altoona, Harrisburg, Pittsburgh."

He stopped abruptly, his eyes refusing to release hers. But he had achieved his purpose, he had reignited her curiosity about his work.

"Your grandfather's building and construction firm extends throughout the state?"

The blue gaze softened and he smiled.

"No, but he does have business interests not only throughout the state but along the entire East Coast."

"I see."

Helen sipped her coffee, then stared into the creamy brew. She really didn't know any more than she had before. When she looked up, she was caught by the waiting stillness about Marsh, the hint of amusement in his eyes. *He's not going to volunteer a thing,* she thought frustratedly. *He's going to sit there, silently laughing at me, and make me ask. The hell with it,* she fumed, *and him. I don't even care what he does.*

With elaborate casualness she got up, walked to the counter, and refilled her cup with coffee she wanted even less than the first cup. When he held out his cup to her, his lips twitching, she refilled it and handed it back to him, fighting down the urge to upend it over his head. She was going to ask. She knew she was going to ask and she resented him for it. Why was it so important to her anyway? The less she knew about him the better. Right?

"Do you handle all your grandfather's interests?" Well, at least she'd managed an unconcerned tone, she congratulated herself.

"Mostly," he replied laconically. "But I wasn't on Cullen's business this trip. I was on my own."

Helen glanced up hopefully, but he was calmly drinking his coffee, his eyes mocking her over the cup's rim. *Damn him,* she thought furiously. *Why is he doing this?* "Because he knows," reason told her. *He knows how much I hate this need to know everything about him. God, can he read my mind?* It was not the first time she'd wondered about that, and the idea, as ridiculous as it was, made her uneasy. Placing her cup carefully in the saucer, Helen sighed in defeat.

"What is your business, Marsh?"

"Now, that hardly hurt at all, did it?" Marsh mocked softly. Then all traces of mockery were gone, but the amusement deepened, danced in his eyes. "I'm an accountant."

"An accountant!"

642

At her tone of astonished disbelief his laughter escaped, danced across the table and along her nerve ends. "An accountant," he repeated dryly. "Don't I look like an accountant?"

"Hardly." Helen had control of herself now; her dryness matched his. "Does King Kong look like a monkey?"

"Do I look like King Kong?" His laughter deepened and Helen felt a strange, melting sensation inside. Her own eyes sparkling with amusement, she answered sweetly, "Only when you're angry."

He was up and around the table before Helen even finished speaking, and still laughing, he pulled her out of her chair and into his arms.

"You want to play Fay Wray?" He grinned suggestively.

"To an accountant?" Helen taunted.

"Ah, but you see, love," he said in the same suggestive tone, "accountants know all about figures." His hands moved slowly down her back, over her hips. "And you've got one of the best I've ever handled."

"And you've handled so many?" Helen shot back, annoyed at the twinge of pain the memory of Jeanette's words about Marsh's women sent tearing through her chest.

"Enough," he admitted lazily. His arms tightened, drawing her close to his muscle-tautened frame. "Helen," he murmured urgently, "you're driving me crazy." His mouth was a driving force that pushed her head back, crushed the resistance out of her.

Feeling her body soften traitorously against him, Helen sighed fatalistically. She *had* missed him. She had missed *this*. Her hands, imprisoned between them, inched to the center of his chest. She heard his sharply indrawn breath when her fingers began undoing the buttons still fastened on his shirt, and when she paused, heard him groan, "Good God, love, don't stop."

His lips left a fiery, hungry trail down her arched throat; his hands moved restlessly over her shoulders, her back, her hips. His lips backtracked to the sensitive skin behind her ear. His voice was a hoarse, exciting seduction. "I love you. I love you. It's been such a long week. Helen, don't send me home, let me stay with you."

"Marsh, oh, Marsh." Helen could hardly speak. Her breath came in short, quick gasps through her parted lips. The shirt was open and she felt him shudder when her fingers tentatively stroked his heated skin.

"More, more." His mouth hovered tantalizingly over hers. Her hands pushed away the silky material of his shirt as they slid up his chest, over his shoulders. With a low moan his mouth crushed hers in a demand she no longer could, or wanted to, deny.

The ring of the wall phone, not three feet from Helen's head, was a shrill intrusion of reality. It was a call she couldn't ignore, and on the second ring she struggled against him. Cursing softly, Marsh released her reluctantly.

With shaking hands Helen grasped the receiver, drew a deep breath, and huskily said, "Dr. Cassidy."

"Sorry to waken you, Doctor," the voice of the never-seen person who worked for her service said apologetically. "I just had a call from a Mr. Rayburn. He said his wife's labor pains are ten minutes apart and she's spotting, and he is taking her to the hospital."

"Thank you." Helen's husky, sleepy-sounding tone had brisked to wide-awake alertness. Without even looking at Marsh, she swung through the doorway to the living room, calling to him over her shoulder, "Marsh, you might as well go home. I have to go to the hospital and I have no idea how long I'll be."

He caught up with her halfway across the living room, grasping her arm to spin her around to face him.

"I'll drive you and wait for you."

Impatient to be gone, Helen shrugged his hand from her arm. "Don't be silly! I told you I have no idea how long it will take. It's one thirty in the morning. Go home, get some sleep."

"But I don't mind —"

"Marsh, please," Helen interrupted sharply. Cold reality, and the knowledge of how close she'd come to sharing her bed with him, put an edge on her tongue. "I have to go and I want to change my clothes. Will you just go home?"

"Would you object if I wait while you change and walk down to your car with you?" Marsh asked sarcastically. "As you said, it is one thirty in the morning."

"Oh, all right," Helen replied ungraciously, turning to run into the bedroom.

When she came hurrying back a few minutes later, he was standing at the door, holding her coat and handbag.

"Marsh, I — I'm sorry I was so sharp with you," Helen apologized haltingly, sliding her arms into the sleeves of her coat. "It's just that I . . . well —"

"Don't worry about it." His hands tightened a second on her shoulders before he removed them and turned to open the door. "Had you scared for a minute there in the kitchen, didn't I?" he teased as she walked by him into the hall. His good humor was entirely restored and the devil gleam was back in his eyes.

"I don't understand." Flustered, Helen stepped into the elevator, then turned deliberately widened, questioning eyes to him.

"You understand perfectly," he said softly, tormenting her. "I'm going to get you and you know it. It's just a matter of time." He paused, grinning ruefully. "And an uninterrupted opportunity."

As they stepped out of the apartment entrance, for the second time that night, they were met by a swirl of snowflakes.

"I hope this doesn't amount to anything." Marsh frowned, looking up at the dirty gray sky.

"Why, don't you like snow, Marsh?" Helen had always liked snow.

"As a rule it doesn't bother me one way or the other," he answered, taking her keys from her fingers as they reached her car. He unlocked the door, handed her keys back, then opened the door for her and added, "But tonight, at who knows what time, my woman's going to be driving home in it, so I hope it doesn't amount to anything."

Before she could say anything he kissed her hard on the mouth and strode across the lot in the direction of his car, parked some distance away.

His woman! His *woman!* Helen wasn't sure if she was amused or angry. His woman indeed. As she drove off the lot Marsh's car was two bright headlights reflected in her rearview mirror. And the reflection was there, every time she glanced in the mirror, all the way to the hospital. Now she was sure she was angry.

After parking her car in the section marked DOCTORS ONLY, Helen flung out of the car and across the lot to where the blue Acura sat idling quietly. He slid out of the car when she reached the front fender. Walking with jerky, angry steps around the door, she snapped, "What do you think you're doing? I asked you to go home."

Without a word he pulled her into his arms, kissed her roughly.

"And I'm going home," he grated when he lifted his head. "I wanted to make sure you got here safely, and to tell you to call me when you get home."

"But I don't know what time it will be." She started walking toward a side entrance, Marsh close beside her.

"That doesn't matter," he stated flatly.

"Marsh, I do this all the time," Helen reasoned.

"And people get stopped and attacked in their cars more and more all the time." His tone was adamant, final. "Helen, I mean it. Promise you'll call or I'll wait right here."

"All right, I promise." Helen yanked open the door. "Now will you go and let me get to the delivery room before that baby does?"

"Okay, I'll go. Don't forget."

Helen was gone, practically running down the long hall to the elevators.

It was a hard delivery and Helen felt exhausted when she finally let herself into her living room close to three thirty. At least she hadn't had to face treacherous driving conditions, as the snow squall had moved off and the streets were dry.

The baby was a large one and had taken quite a bit out of his mother, not to mention Helen. Like a sleepwalker she went into the bedroom and undressed, thinking light-headedly that even at birth most males gave a woman an undue amount of trouble. After washing her face and hands, Helen sat on the side of her bed and picked up the phone.

"Helen?" Marsh's voice questioned after the first ring

"Yes, Marsh." Helen spoke softly, tiredly. "I'm home."

"You sound beat, sweetheart. Was it bad?" Deep concern laced his tone.

"For a while there," she sighed. "But Mrs. Rayburn is fine and so is her son and I'm half asleep sitting here."

"I can hear that," he murmured. "I wish

I was there to hold you, reward you. Go to bed. I'll call you tomorrow afternoon. By the way, my parents would like you to come for dinner tomorrow, or should I say tonight, but I'll tell you more about that when I call. Good night, sweetheart."

Helen murmured good night, replaced the receiver, then sat up with a start. His parents' for dinner! Whatever for? Good grief! Was she to be brought home to Mother and Dad for approval? Was Marsh out of his mind to think she'd stand for that? *And what did he mean by "reward me"?*

Too many questions in a mind too tired to search for answers. Helen switched off the light, crawled into bed, and was instantly asleep.

The phone remained considerately silent all Sunday morning, and Helen slept until after noon. She was glancing over the paper, sipping at her second cup of coffee, when the instrument issued its insistent cry. It was Marsh, and she was ready for him.

"What was all that business about dinner at your parents' home?" Helen began the moment he'd finished saying, "Good morning, love, did you sleep well?"

There was a long pause, then he asked smoothly, "Are you always this prickly when you first wake up?"

"Only when I've been sent to sleep with the threat of being paraded for approval, like a horse at an auction," she replied acidly.

"Only with the very best Thoroughbred fillies, sweetheart." He laughed softly. "What gave you the idea you were going to be paraded?"

"It smacks too much of 'bring the girl home for inspection before you do anything stupid, son,' " Helen retorted. "Really, Marsh, why else would they invite me?"

"Because they want to meet you? Get to know you?" His amusement curled along the line to her.

"Why now? All of a sudden?" she asked bluntly.

"All right, Helen." His voice sobered, grew serious. "I admit that Mother asked a few discreet questions after we left Kris's room together. I'm also sure she had already talked to my father about it, as he was there during the" — he paused — "questioning."

"And?" Helen prompted.

"I told them I'd asked you to marry me."

The calm statement almost had the power to curl Helen's hair.

"Marsh, you didn't!" Helen fairly screamed into the mouthpiece.

"Don't fall apart, love." He was laughing again. "I was honest. I told them you'd turned me down — for now."

"Marshall Kirk," Helen gritted, "if you're trying to get yourself strangled, you are going about it in the right way. I can't go."

"You'd better," he warned. "I've told them we'll be there at seven. It won't be all that bad. Kris and Mike will be there, and as an extra added attraction they've invited Cullen. You can sit back and watch my father and the old bear take verbal potshots at each other."

Good Lord, the whole family! Helen groaned. *Am I going prematurely senile? I must be or I wouldn't put up with this silliness. Why should I volunteer to endure this meet-the-family routine? I haven't the slightest intention of getting involved with him in any way, let alone marrying him.* The scene in that very kitchen the night before returned to mock her, and she groaned again.

"Helen? What's the matter?" His sharp query made her aware of how long she'd been quiet. His next question assured her that he'd heard her soft groan. "Are you crying?"

"I never cry," she answered bitingly. "I don't have the time."

"But you *do* have time for dinner tonight," he bit back. "And I *will* come for you at six thirty." The bite turned into a threat. "And you'd *better* be ready."

Helen simmered, just below boiling point, all afternoon. Marsh's parting thrust, "You'd *better* be ready," stabbed at her mind like the tip of a red-hot poker.

You fool! she berated herself unmercifully. *You stupid fool! You have no sense at all.* Silently, as if to another person, she dressed herself down as harshly as a tough top sergeant might a raw recruit. *You, a professional — whose very pride is in that cool professionalism — are you going to meekly submit to the dictates of a man? What can you be thinking of? You are* not *a twittering teenager. You are* not *a fresh-faced young woman, just starting out. You have earned your pride, your confidence, your independence. And you did it by yourself, without the support, the consideration of any male.*

Although the day waned, Helen's self-directed fury did not. As she went about washing the few dishes in the sink, making her bed, straightening the apartment, her mental tirade continued.

Now, now when you've reached the point in life where you hold that pride, that independence, tightly in your hands, are you going to fling it all away for the brief assuagement of your resurrected physical needs? And don't, for one minute, try to convince yourself it will be anything but brief.

At five forty-five, her soft lips twisted in self-derision, Helen stepped under the shower. Still scolding silently, she told her invisible target, *The very idea of a woman like you is a challenge to the Marshall Kirks of this world. He says he loves you. In all probability he would say or do anything to get what he wants.*

Helen stepped out of the shower, scooped up a towel, and began patting herself dry. *And what does he want, you ask?* Helen went still, a wry smile tugging at her lips as she gazed into the hazel eyes of the recipient of her condemnation, reflected in the full-length mirror on the back of the bathroom door. *Okay, you asked for it. I'll tell you exactly what he wants. He wants the power to make you come to heel, like a well-trained puppy, at his mildest command. He wants the exquisite satisfaction of knowing he has brought the very cool, so very professional, Dr. Cassidy to her knees. And when he is sated with that satisfaction, he will take a walk — and forget to come back. Are you willing,* Helen asked those watchful, reflected eyes, *to deny everything you've worked so hard for, for a few moments of mindless bliss that can only be found in this one man's arms?*

Helen blinked, and her head snapped up.

The answer was there, in the clear hazel eyes staring back at her. Silently, yet loud and clear, those eyes proclaimed, "No way."

Her self-denouncement completed, Helen dressed slowly, carefully, a secret smile softening the contours of her face. She had tried, and failed, to convince Marsh of her disinterest in any kind of male-female relationship. He had, figuratively, backed her into a corner. She refused to cower in that corner. Her intelligent father and gentle mother had not raised a female fool. She would play Marsh's game, and beat him at it.

The doorbell rang at exactly six thirty. Composing her features, squaring her shoulders, Helen went to open the door, a smile of welcome curving her lips. The smile wavered at the sheer, overpowering look of him, then strengthened at the memory of her resolve.

He was dressed in a dark suit and silk shirt, which matched exactly the color of his eyes, and a patterned tie, which contrasted, yet complemented, his attire. The overall effect was one of elegantly covered, raw masculinity. His gleaming, not-quite red hair had been slightly tousled by the wind. His gray coat had been tossed carelessly over one broad shoulder, and his casually arrogant stance gave him the look of a well-dressed hell-raiser.

"Good eve—" He broke off midword, a stunned expression on his face, as his eyes made a slow tour of her body, while her own expression returned the compliment.

Without speaking, Helen moved back to allow him to enter, then closed the door quietly and turned to face him.

After long deliberation she had dressed in a long, narrow black velvet dress that accentuated her figure. A single strand of milky-white pearls (a gift from her brother when she had graduated from medical school) glowed around her slender throat. The warm admiration in his eyes told her she'd chosen well.

"A little black dress," he murmured when her eyes met his. "Very effective with your hair, your fair skin, and the pearls." His voice deepened huskily. "You're beautiful, Helen."

A thrill of excitement shot through Helen, followed by a shaft of elation. He had called the game and dealt out the cards on the day they met. Now, she decided, was the time for her to pick up her hand and play her first card.

Helen's eyes lifted to his. "Thank you. You — you're beautiful too." She laughed softly. "I suppose a woman shouldn't tell a man he's beautiful, but you are, you know. A beautiful male animal."

A flame ignited in his eyes and he drew his breath in very slowly. As he exhaled, equally slowly, he moved to stand close to her.

"I don't know if a woman is supposed to tell a man that," he murmured. "But I know this man likes hearing it." His hands came up to cup her face. "Tell me more. Tell me why you think I'm beautiful."

"I don't know if I can explain, exactly." Helen searched for words. "Certainly you are very attractive, but you know that. You dress well. Instead of simply covering your body, your clothes enhance it, proclaim your masculinity."

His thumb moved caressingly over her cheek, and Helen paused to run her tongue over suddenly dry lips.

"An invitation if I ever saw one," he whispered, bending his head to touch his mouth to hers. "Is there more?" he whispered against her lips.

"You make me laugh, even when I'm angry," Helen whispered back. "And you make me breathless, most of the time."

"Are you breathless now?"

"Yes."

"And me." His mouth crushed hers, sending the room spinning around her head.

When he lifted his head and the room settled back into place, Helen drew deep breaths to calm her racing senses. "Marsh, we must go, your parents are expecting us."

"I know," he groaned. "Helen, will you let me stay?"

It was time to play the second card. Lifting her hand to his face, she trailed her slim fingers across his cheek, over his firm lips. "Marsh, please, be patient with me. Let me get to know you, feel . . . easier . . . with you. It's been a long time since I've felt safe with a man." She shuddered and felt his lips kiss her finger. "I don't want what happened that night in your apartment to happen again." She slid her hand from his mouth, across his face, and around his neck to draw his head close to hers. Her lips against his, she pleaded, "Please, Marsh."

Helen felt a ripple run through his body and heard his soft sigh before he answered tersely, "All right, sweetheart, I won't pressure you. But I think it's only fair to warn you that I want you very badly and I'm going to do every damned thing I can think of to warm that core of ice that's deep inside you."

He stepped back, his eyes devouring her, then he shook his head and muttered, "We'd better leave."

Seven

Helen shivered, but not from the outside cold. The warmth from the car's heater protected them from the biting winds and subzero temperature. The soft music from the CD player added to that warmth. The chill was inside Helen, deep inside. The shiver stemmed from two different sources. One of them was excitement, the other, fear. The elements of both those emotions had Helen at near fever pitch.

The feeling of power that had surged through her at Marsh's reaction to her small advance had generated an excitement Helen had never experienced before. It was heady, exhilarating, while at the same time, she realized, a little dangerous. And then there was the tiny fear that had begun with Marsh's words. Taken at face value they were innocuous enough. But could she take them at face value? There was the seed of her growing fear. *I'm going to do every damned thing I can think of to warm that core of ice.* A simple, straightforward promise? Or something more? Perhaps she was reading words between the lines that simply were not there, but his tone, everything about him, had been so intense that a small alarm had sounded inside her mind.

"You're very quiet," Marsh said softly into her thoughts. "You're not nervous about meeting the family, are you?"

All traces of his earlier intensity were gone, and telling herself she was being overimaginative, Helen turned to him with a smile.

"A little," she admitted. "Mostly of your grandfather. He sounds a very formidable character."

"Oh, he is that." Marsh laughed. "But he's a pushover for a beautiful woman. And an absolute lapdog for one with intelligence as well as beauty. You, love, will have him eating out of your hand fifteen minutes after you're there."

"Your confidence in my feminine prowess is overwhelming," Helen murmured dryly, secretly elated. He thought she was beautiful. He thought she was intelligent. She was a challenge to his manhood, and he wanted to overcome that challenge by possessing her physically. *Nothing very complicated or scary about that,* she assured herself. *You, Doctor, have been chasing shadows that just are not there. Relax and enjoy the game until the final card is played.*

Marsh's parents' home loomed large and imposing, the many brightly lit windows a beacon in the winter-night darkness. From the moment she stepped inside the door Helen could feel the wealth and good taste of its owners surround her. The family, the very correct butler informed Marsh, were in the small rear sitting room. Following his ramrod-straight back across the wide hall, Helen chanced a glance at Marsh and received a slow exaggerated wink in return.

The small rear sitting room was not really at the rear and not small at all, and very, very elegant. Helen judged that the furniture, paintings, and exquisite decorations in the room had probably cost more than she could earn if she worked flat out until she was ninety. A room definitely not for small children, she thought, wondering if Marsh and his sister had been barred from it while they were growing up.

Marsh's mother, a tall, attractive woman in her mid-fifties, came across the room to greet them, her head high, rich auburn hair gleaming in the room's soft light.

"Good evening, Dr. Cassidy." Kathleen Kirk's voice was deep and cultured, and held a note of real welcoming warmth that was reassuring. "I'm so pleased you were free to join us this evening."

"Thank you for inviting me," Helen replied softly, studying the older woman as she placed her hand in the one outstretched to her. Although she was tall, she was delicately formed and the fine skin covering her face still held a faint, youthful glow despite the fine lines around her dark blue eyes.

During the brief exchange two men had come to stand behind Mrs. Kirk, and as she released Helen's hand she stepped to the side, said pleasantly, "My husband, George," nodding to a sandy-haired, distinguished-looking man not much taller than herself.

Helen took his hand, searching in vain for a resemblance to Marsh, as she murmured, "Mr. Kirk." Then she turned her head and caught her breath at Mrs. Kirk's, "And my father, Cullen Hannlon."

The resemblance here was uncanny. Helen knew that Marsh's grandfather had to be in his mid-seventies, yet nothing about him betrayed that fact. As tall as Marsh, his shoulders almost as broad, Cullen Hannlon stood straight, his large frame unbowed by time. He fitted Marsh's name for him perfectly, for he was truly a bear of a man. The light blue eyes that held hers were the exact shade of his grandson's and they glowed with the same intent sharpness, and Helen would have bet her eyeteeth that his luxuriant shock of white hair had, in years past, been the same not-quite red as Marsh's.

Her hand was grasped, not taken, by his large, hard-fingered, brown one, which reminded Helen of tough old leather. His entire appearance contrasted oddly with his deep, gentle voice.

"Well, Helen." No title from this quarter, Helen thought with amusement. "We finally meet. Of course," he teased, squeezing her hand, "now that I see you I can understand why Marsh wanted to keep you to himself. You, my dear, are an extraordinarily beautiful woman."

Before Helen could find words to reply to this unbelievable old man, she heard Marsh laugh softly behind her and say sardonically, "You're wasting your time and breath, Cullen. Helen is immune to flattery."

Cullen favored Helen with a secret smile before turning suddenly fierce blue eyes on his grandson. "If you really believe that, son, you are a fool. And I know you are anything but that. No woman is immune to flattery, as indeed no man is; *if* it's the right kind of flattery."

Sauntering beside her as his mother ushered them into the room, Marsh's laughter deepened and he whispered close to her ear, "Imagine what he must have been like when he was young."

I don't have to imagine anything, Helen

thought wryly. *All I have to do is turn my head and look at you.* The thought that Marsh would very likely be exactly the same as Cullen when he grew old was a strangely exciting one, and Helen quickly squashed it by thinking, *I won't be there to see it.* Forcing her mind away from the oddly bereft sensation her thoughts created, Helen turned her attention to what Mrs. Kirk was saying.

"You know my daughter, Kristeen, and her husband, Mike, of course."

Helen smiled at the young couple, seating herself on the delicately upholstered chair beside the matching settee they shared. "Hello, Kristeen, how are you? Mr. Darren. And how is your daughter?"

"She's perfect, Doctor, thank you." Kristeen smiled shyly. "And I feel wonderful. I wouldn't dare feel any other way after the amount of fussing this family of mine has done over me."

"Fussing, hell!" Cullen snorted impatiently. "This family has lost one woman through childbirth. I don't want to live through that again, so behave yourself, young woman, and let us care for you."

Although a smile played at her soft mouth, Kristeen answered demurely, "Yes, Grandfather."

"Father, please," Kathleen murmured softly, silencingly.

On his first statement Helen's eyes, full of questions, had swung to Cullen's, and now, although he grasped his daughter's shoulder gently, he answered the question. "I lost my wife three weeks after Kathleen was born." His voice was steady, yet Helen could sense the wealth of sorrow he still felt from his loss. "Megan had had a hard delivery and she was very weak. I was just getting started in the construction business and couldn't afford a full-time nurse."

His eyes darkened with pain, and Helen said urgently "Mr. Hannlon, please don't. This isn't necessary." Her eyes flew to Marsh with a silent plea for help, but he didn't see her. His eyes were fastened on his grandfather, and incredibly Cullen's pain was reflected in them.

"She was so delighted with our daughter, she found pleasure in caring for her, even though it drained the little strength she had." He went on in that same quiet tone. "She was eighteen, I was twenty-one. Twenty-one," he repeated softly, then his eyes sharpened on Helen's. "Do you have any idea, I wonder, what losing his soul-mate can do to a man?"

Helen felt trapped, pinned by those intense blue eyes, and she had the unreal, weird sensation that he was trying to tell her something important. Mentally shrugging off the feeling as compassion for his still obviously deep grief, Helen searched for suitable words.

"I — I don't know, sir. I've never lost a patient or had to bring that kind of news to a husband. I can't even imagine —"

Marsh's soft voice saved Helen from floundering further, but in so doing he confused her even more, for there was a definite warning in his tone.

"Enough said, Cullen."

The old man's eyes shot a challenge at his grandson, one Marsh's very stance conveyed he was ready to meet. For several seconds the room seemed electrically charged and Helen could see her own confusion mirrored on the faces of the others as matching pairs of blue eyes silently duelled. Mr. Kirk relieved the tension with a dry gibe, addressed to Helen, but aimed at his son.

"May I get you an aperitif, Helen? You may need some alcoholic fortitude, as your escort seems to be spoiling for an argument."

"I'll get it." Marsh shot a grin at his father and a broad wink at his grandfather. "But let me assure you, she does not need it. I've tried arguing with Helen. I invariably lose."

"Good for Helen." Kathleen Kirk's smile stole the sting from her barb. "You are much too sure of yourself."

Later Helen was to wonder why she had hesitated over Marsh's parents' invitation. She had a delightful time. Kristeen and Mike were a lively couple, full of interesting and funny stories of times spent with their wide assortment of friends. Marsh periodically dropped dry, witty comments into their narrative as they shared some of their friends. Helen was surprised to find that Mr. and Mrs. Kirk were very well acquainted with several of her friends and colleagues, and that paved the way for further easy conversation.

But for Helen the most enjoyable part of the evening came from watching, in fascinated amusement, the thrust and parry between Cullen Hannlon and George Kirk. The play swung back and forth, George Kirk's wry, caustic lunges effortlessly deflected by Cullen's dry, acerbic ripostes. Helen had never witnessed anything quite like it before in her life.

Glancing at Marsh, Helen saw her own amusement mirrored in his eyes. That he got a kick out of watching the two men was obvious. Equally obvious was the deep love and respect he had for them. Knowing this warmed her, but for the life of her she couldn't figure out why. Why should it matter to her one way or the other, she asked herself, if he was capable of feeling abiding love, loyalty, respect?

When he took her home, Marsh kept to his promise not to pressure her. With a murmured, "I'll call you," he kissed her gently and left her staring after him in uncertain amazement.

It was toward the end of the following week that Helen first felt an uncomfortable twinge about Marsh's behavior. The fact that she couldn't exactly pinpoint what it was about his attitude made her uneasy. He was considerate and attentive, without actually dancing attendance on her, and yet there was something. It nagged her, but she couldn't quite put her finger on why.

January slipped into February and their relationship seemed at an impasse. Helen was seeing Marsh on an average of four nights a week, and surprisingly he did not call her on the nights she didn't see him. More surprising still was that he was adhering completely to his no-pressure promise. Was he losing interest? It was a question Helen asked herself more and more frequently as the days went by.

On the surface Marsh seemed as determined as before, at times more so. On the evening of Valentine's Day Kristeen and Mike were having a small get-together of friends, the first since their baby's birth, and they had asked Helen and Marsh to join them.

"I don't think so," Helen hedged when

Marsh relayed Kris's invitation.

"Why not?" he asked, surprised. "I thought you liked Kris and Mike."

"I do," Helen replied promptly, then hesitated. She couldn't very well tell him that she thought it unadvisable to get too involved with his family and friends, so she offered, lamely, "But it will be young married couples, won't it? I just don't think I'd fit in."

"Not fit in?" he exclaimed. "Helen, that's ridiculous. Of course you'd fit in. It will do you good to be around young women who are not your patients. Besides which" — he grinned — "I already told them we'd come."

He takes too much on himself, Helen fumed in frustration. *I really ought to put him back in his place.* She didn't at once, and then the moment was gone as he went on blandly to tell her who would be there. Not a large group, he informed her. Just a few close friends he shared with Kris and Mike.

On the fourteenth Marsh arrived at the apartment with a large elaborately decorated heart-shaped box of chocolates and a card, almost as large, that was covered with cupids and flowers and gushy sentiment. Reading the card, Helen frowned, unable to believe he really went in for that sort of mush; then, glancing up, she smiled ruefully at the devil gleam in his eye.

"There are times I'm convinced you are really quite mad, Marsh," she said, her tone deliberately crushing. It didn't work. He laughed at her, taunted, "I am quite mad. For you. I couldn't resist the urge to watch your face as you read it." He paused, then chided, nodding at the candy, "Aren't you going to offer me a piece?"

"You're impossible," Helen murmured, tugging at the end of the large bow on the ribbon that surrounded the box. Glancing up to smile at him, she felt her heartbeats quicken, her mouth go dry. The gleam had disappeared and there was a waiting stillness about him that warned her. Lifting the heart-shaped lid carefully, she bit her lip, then sat down slowly. At the *V* of the heart several pieces of the candy had been removed and in their place was nestled a small jeweler's box.

For a moment, thinking that the box contained a ring, pure panic gripped her. Then reason reasserted itself as she realized the box was larger, flatter than a ring box. With trembling fingers she removed the box, lifted the lid, a small gasp whispering through her lips. In the glow from the lamp beside her chair the gold inside the box seemed to glitter and wink at her. Very carefully she extracted the intricately worked and, at the price of gold, obviously expensive chains, one for the neck and a smaller one for the wrist.

Handling the delicate pieces gently, Helen looked up at the silently waiting man in front of her, her eyes unknowingly telegraphing her words.

"Marsh, they're beautiful, but I —"

"Don't say it, Helen," Marsh warned softly. He lifted the candy box from her lap and slid it onto the end table. "Stand up and I'll fasten them on for you."

Standing on legs that felt none too steady, Helen watched as he clasped the small chain on her wrist. The chain was loose and slid partway down the back of her hand.

"I didn't realize your wrist was so slender," he said softly. "Should I have it made smaller for you?"

A sudden, unreasonable feeling of possessiveness gripped her, and not even knowing why, she didn't want to remove the chain. "No!" Too hasty, she chided herself, tempering it with a small laugh. "I think I like it loose like that."

"Yes," Marsh murmured, studying the effect of the gold against her skin. "Something sexy about it." His eyes lifted to hers and what they told her sent her pulses racing.

Without waiting to see if she'd reply, he moved around her to fasten the neck chain.

He brushed her hair to one side, and Helen felt a chill at the touch of his fingers on the sensitive skin at the back of her neck. The chain was fastened, then his hands encircled her throat.

The chill turned into a strong shiver that zigzagged the length of her spine, down the back of her legs.

"Marsh . . . oh, Marsh, stop."

It was a strangled protest against his mouth, moving along the side of her neck; his hands, moving down the silky material of her blouse, over the firm mounds of her breasts.

"How long are you going to hold out, Helen?" his breath whispered against her skin. Then she was turned around into his arms, his hands holding her tightly to the hard length of his body, drawing her still closer, making her all too aware of his meaning.

His kiss was a hungry, urgent demand, and Helen's hands, which had grasped his wrists to pull his hands away from her hips, slid up his arms to his shoulders and clung. He hadn't kissed her like this in weeks, and until that moment Helen hadn't fully realized how much she'd wanted him to. The realization was a sobering one. Giving a firm push against his shoulders, she stepped back away from him.

"Marsh, stop it," she cried shakily. "If you think my accepting these gives you the right to —" She paused, fingers fumbling at the clasp on the wrist chain. "You can take it back."

"Leave it," Marsh snapped, his large hand covering her fingers, stilling their trembling. "There are no strings on it, or anything else I may give you. Not even on myself." He drew a harsh breath, then added more softly, "You know what I want, Helen. I made my feelings clear at the beginning. But you can set the rules, you make the conditions. Only, for God's sake, do it soon. Don't let me hang indefinitely."

Helen felt shaken and confused. Oh, yes, she thought wildly, she knew what he wanted. He wanted a bed partner, the triumph of subduing the cool, *older* lady doctor. Were there rules and conditions to that kind of relationship? If there were, Helen was positive that, for all his assurances to the contrary, he fully intended to set them.

He waited several minutes, and when she didn't speak or respond in any way, he spun away, walked to the closet, yanked her coat from the hanger, and snapped, "Let's get out of here. Kris and Mike are probably wondering where we are."

Still without speaking, Helen slipped into the coat, buttoned up with a calmness she

673

was far from feeling inside. He was angry. Really angry. His eyes held a chilling coldness he'd never turned on her before. His control seemed to crack when she returned his stare with a forced coolness of her own.

"You're enjoying every minute of this, aren't you?" he ground through clenched teeth.

"I don't know what you mean."

"Of course not," he taunted silkily. "Have your fun while you can, love, because your line's about played out."

Marsh maintained a cool, withdrawn silence during the entire twenty-five-minute drive to his sister's home. Helen's nerves, already frayed when they left the apartment, stretched and grew more taut as each silent second followed another. She was twisting the narrow chain around her wrist, on the verge of telling him to turn the car around and take her home, when he pulled up and parked along the curb in front of a row of fairly new, modern town houses. There were other cars parked along the curb and two, bumper to bumper, in the narrow driveway that led to a garage adjacent to the house.

When Marsh walked through the doorway of his sister's house, he left outside the cold, angry man he'd been for over a half hour. A slight widening of her eyes was her only outward reaction to his sudden change, but he saw it and shook his head once sharply at her before turning a smiling face to the people gathered inside the long living room.

Besides Kris and Mike there were four other couples in the room. Names were tossed at her casually, with an aside from Marsh not to worry, he'd sort them out for her later, but although the surnames were lost, she caught and held on to the first names. There were Bob and Donna, and Charles and Irene, all the same age as Kris and Mike. Then there were Ray and Betty, and Grant and Mary Ellen, a few years older than the others, more Marsh's age.

There were no awkward moments. The introductions dispensed with, Helen was drawn into the conversation so effortlessly, it had her wondering if the whole thing had been rehearsed. She would reject the idea a short time later.

Before many minutes had passed, Helen reached the conclusion that the affection these people obviously held for each other was a holdover from childhood. They accepted her without question because she was with Marsh, it was as simple as that.

Marsh slipped into a chair and the conversation with an easy camaraderie. Letting the conversation swirl around her, Helen observed him, as she had the evening she'd been at his parents' home. All traces of his earlier tension and anger were gone. He laughed often, a delightful sound that drew a reciprocal response from the others. It soon became evident to Helen as she watched him that, although he genuinely liked all the guests, there was a special bond between him and Grant.

Their banter back and forth, as they argued over a recent basketball game, was much the same as Marsh indulged in with Moe. Listening more to the tone of their voices rather than their words, Helen glanced up in surprise when Grant asked, "Don't you agree, Helen?"

"I'm sorry." Helen smiled apologetically. "I'm afraid I wasn't listening."

"Grant said that it looks like the team may have a winning year." Marsh's tone held a faint trace of annoyance. "He asked if you agree with him."

"I have no idea." Helen met Marsh's cool glance with equal coolness before turning to Grant with a warm smile. "I don't follow basketball at all." A teasing note covered her serious tone. "Does that make me a traitor to my city?"

"If it does, you have plenty of company," Mary Ellen answered for her husband.

"I thought you liked basketball." Grant's pleasant, ordinary face held an injured look that matched his tone.

"I do." Mary Ellen laughed. "I also like

watching football, hockey, and baseball, but not necessarily as a steady diet."

Grant turned to Marsh with eyebrows raised exaggeratedly high. "Do you get the feeling our conversation has been boring the ladies?"

"The thought has occurred," Marsh replied dryly. "Perhaps we should hit the ball into their court and let them choose a topic."

It was all the encouragement Mary Ellen needed. Eyes bright with amusement, she launched into a hilarious account of a comedy-of-errors skiing trip she and Grant had taken the previous year.

During the course of the evening Helen learned, from Mary Ellen, that her assumption about the closeness between Marsh and Grant was correct. They had been friends from grade school, were in fact closer than most brothers. Marsh had been best man at their wedding and was their son's godfather. A sudden stifled, closed-in sensation feathered over Helen when Mary Ellen finished, "Both Grant and I unashamedly adore Marsh and would love to see him content and happy with a family of his own." Her eyes sought the man in question; a gentle smile curved her lips as she studied him. "Marsh will be thirty-one next month," she said softly. "And though he claims to be having a ball in his bachelor existence, everyone who loves him knows it's a lie. He's a steady, roots-deep-in-the-ground sort of man; he's ready to settle down." Her eyes swung to Helen's face, and her smile deepened. "The problem *has* been finding the right woman."

Unease joined the stifled sensations rippling along Helen's nerves, and changing the subject quickly, she figuratively backed away from Mary Ellen's none too subtle revelations.

Midway through the evening Kris announced that a light supper had been set out on the dining room table. After serving herself sparingly from the wide assortment of food, Helen followed Marsh back to the living room and allowed him to draw her down onto a comfortable sofa.

"What do you think of Grant?" His bland tone didn't deceive her for a second. She could actually feel the intensity with which he awaited her answer.

"I like him." She answered with frank honesty. "And I think the easygoing manner he shows to the world is a facade that disguises a very determined man." She glanced up at him, smiled slightly. "I think he could give a woman a very bad time, if he was so inclined."

"Couldn't we all?" Marsh slanted her a wicked glance and laughed softly. "But

I'm inclined to think that Mary Ellen could probably give him a damned good run for his money, if *she* was so inclined." His grin was every bit as wicked as his glance. "You want to try *me* on?"

Ignoring the lightning shaft of excitement that zigzagged through her, Helen returned his stare thoughtfully, then replied coolly, "You'd lose, you know."

His soft laughter was a gentle assault on her senses. "Not on your stethoscope, sweetheart."

Even though his tone had been teasing, Helen felt a chill of warning replace the excitement deep inside. She had no time to analyze the feeling however, as he went on quietly, "I've invited Grant and Mary Ellen to join us for dinner at my apartment Saturday night." He arched an inquiring eyebrow at her. "All right?"

"Yes, of course," Helen replied. "But right now I think I'd better go home. I have a full schedule tomorrow."

After the usual time-consuming flurry of leave-taking and when they were finally in the car, Helen asked curiously, "Were you planning to cook dinner yourself?"

"And poison some of my best friends?" Marsh asked seriously. "No, love, I'll let Moe do the honors this time. Unless" — he shot her a teasing glance — "you'd like to do it."

For one insane moment Helen was actually tempted, then common sense reasserted itself. "I'll pass, thank you." As he stopped at a stop sign at that moment, she turned to look at him directly, her eyes cool. "I'm not in the least domestic." Another card, unplanned, was placed onto the invisible table between them.

Marsh played a trump. "It doesn't matter, I can always *hire* domestic help."

They both knew they were no longer talking about the upcoming dinner, and thinking it judicious to play her cards more carefully in future, Helen remained silent. Could he, she wondered, be aware that she'd dealt herself a hand in this game he was playing? The thought nagged at her for some minutes, then she dismissed it as ridiculous. He was far too sure of himself to ever consider the possibility.

Helen was late arriving for dinner. Marsh had said they'd eat at seven thirty but, as Grant and Mary Ellen were coming at seven for predinner drinks, he'd pick her up at six thirty.

Just before five Helen received an emergency call from the hospital. A self-induced abortion case had been brought in, she was informed. A young woman, still in her teens. As her mother, frantic with worry, was a patient of Helen's, she had insisted, hysterically, that Helen be called.

Helen recognized the woman's name immediately and said she'd be there as soon as possible. She left the apartment without a thought to Marsh's dinner, her mind on the possible physical damage to the teen, and the mental damage to the mother.

The woman had come to Helen with a minor problem the same week she'd opened her office and returned for twice-yearly checkups ever since. Honest, hard-working and unassuming, she had made a career of taking care of her husband, raising her family. Helen knew what the daughter's action could do to the woman. So much for the joys and rewards of family life, Helen thought cynically as she drove to the hospital.

It was not until she had parked her car, illegally, in the emergency entrance and was striding toward the wide glass doors, that she remembered Marsh.

Stopping at the nurses' station, Helen asked where the patient was, if someone could take care of her car, and would the nurse make a phone call for her. In that order. The nurse, a middle-aged veteran, echoed Helen's brisk tone. The patient was being prepped for the O.R.; she could rest easy about her car; and, certainly, the phone call would be made.

Helen asked for a piece of paper, on

which she scribbled Marsh's name and phone number, then she told the nurse tersely, "Just tell him there's been an emergency and I'll get there as soon as I can. And thank you."

The nurse's quiet "You're welcome, Doctor" floated on the empty air where Helen had stood. Moving at a fast clip toward the elevators, Helen glanced at the large wall clock. It was twenty-three minutes since she'd received the call.

It was messy and touch and go, and the hands on the O.R. wall clock moved inexorably from number to number, but Helen saved the young woman's life.

Exhausted, filled with rage and bitter frustration at the idea that in an age of almost instant legal abortion on demand, a young woman, terrified at the results of her own foolishness, would inflict such damage on herself rather than go to her parents, Helen cleaned up and went to the lounge where those parents waited.

On entering the room, Helen's eyes went first to the father. Of medium height, stockily built, the man held his face in such rigid control, it looked as if it were carved in stone. Shifting her gaze, Helen's eyes met the anxious, tear-drenched eyes of his wife. Lips quivering, the woman whispered, "Doctor?"

"She'll live," Helen stated bluntly,

steeling herself against the fresh tears that ran down the woman's pale cheeks.

"Thank God." The low, choked-out prayer came from the husband. "May we see her?"

Helen's eyes swung back to his, now suspiciously bright with moisture. "She'll be in recovery for a while." Compassion tugged at her heart, softened her tone. "You both look on the verge of collapse. Why don't you take your wife down to the cafeteria, have some coffee and something to eat." She underlined the last three words heavily.

"Was there much damage, Doctor?" The woman had gained control of herself. Her eyes were clear, steady.

"Some." Helen sighed. "But she is alive and will recover. We'll discuss the damage, both physical and mental, later. Right now I prescribe a strong shot of caffeine for both of you." She was rewarded with a weak smile. "The nurse at the floor station will tell you when you can see her. If you can arrange to be in the hospital tomorrow morning when I make my rounds, we'll talk after I've examined your daughter."

"We'll be here." The man beat his wife into speech.

After again advising them to have something to eat, Helen left the room and went to collect her coat and bag, not even bothering to repair her makeup.

Marsh opened the door seconds after Helen touched the bell and, after a quick glance at her face, murmured, "Was it bad?"

"Yes," she answered simply as she entered the apartment's tiny foyer.

Standing behind her, holding her coat as she slipped out of it, he asked, "A hard delivery?"

"No." Helen turned to face him, waited until he'd hung up her coat and turned around again before adding, "A teenager tried to commit suicide the hard way."

"Abortion?" Incredulity laced his tone.

"Yes."

His eyes, tinged with concern, searched her face. "Is she all right?"

"She's alive." Helen sighed wearily. "Oh, Marsh, it was grim." Without hesitation, without even thinking, she walked right into him, rested her forehead against his chest.

For a split second he was still, then his arms came around her, tightened protectively. "It's all right, love," he murmured against her hair. "You're home."

Too tired, for the moment, to think, she barely heard his words, let alone the meaning behind them. His hand moved and tugged at her hair to turn her face up to his. In fascination Helen watched his firm mouth lowering slowly to hers, lost to the presence of the two people sitting in the living room unashamedly watching the tableau with interest.

Marsh's mouth was tender, gentle with hers. As the kiss lengthened, deepened, Helen felt the tensions and frustrations of the last hours drain out of her. Sighing deeply, she returned his kiss fervently. Her hands were moving up his chest to his neck when he suddenly stepped back, a rueful smile curving his lips.

"We have guests, sweetheart," he said softly. "Come have a drink and relax a little before dinner."

Marsh turned her toward the living room, his arm, angled from shoulder to waist across her back, holding her close to his side. Helen felt the warmth of embarrassment mount her cheeks on encountering the expressions of concern for her, written clearly on the faces of Grant and Mary Ellen.

"Come sit by me, Helen, while Marsh gets your drink," Mary Ellen invited warmly. "You look completely shattered."

With a tired smile Helen sank onto the sofa beside Mary Ellen, accepted the glass of wine Marsh handed her, took a small sip, smiled her appreciation and thanks to him, then turned her attention to what Mary Ellen was saying.

"We couldn't help but overhear what you said when you came in. What a horrible thing to do."

"Yes," Helen agreed. "It was pretty horrible for her parents too. I am of the opinion that raising children can be heartbreaking at times."

"But rewarding as well," Mary Ellen assured firmly. "Grant and I have had a few bad moments with our two boys, but I wouldn't give them up for the world." She turned her serious gaze onto her husband. "Would you, Grant?"

"No," Grant answered simply. "I think that by the time they are fully grown the good times will have, by far, outweighed the bad."

"I think on that profound note, we'll go have dinner," Marsh said, quietly reaching for Helen's hand.

Conversation was easy and relaxed while they ate Moe's expertly prepared veal scallopini.

"Do you ski, Helen?" Mary Ellen asked suddenly, pausing in the act of spooning up the rich dessert Moe had concocted.

"Yes," Helen admitted, adding, "not expertly, but well enough to handle the smaller slopes."

"And I know Marsh is very good." Mary Ellen's eyes lit with an idea. "Grant and I, along with several other couples, are going up to the Poconos next Thursday for a long weekend of skiing. Why don't you two join us?"

"I don't think —" That was as far as Helen got with her refusal, for Marsh quietly interrupted her.

"Sounds good to me." He lifted an eyebrow at her. "What do you say, Helen? Do you think you could get someone to fill in for you? You could stand a break, especially after today."

"Well, I suppose I could, but —"

"The hospital won't fall apart in four days, Helen," Marsh urged.

"Well —" Helen hesitated, then gave in. "Let me see if I can arrange something."

Leaving the table, Helen went to the phone in the living room, dialed, then spoke quietly for a few moments. When she turned back to the others, she was smiling.

"All set." Helen's eyes sought, then found the blue ones. "Dr. Munziack will be on call for me. He owes me one." Her smile deepened. "As a matter of fact he owes me several. I can be ready to leave as soon as I've made my rounds Thursday morning."

The remainder of the evening was spent in making plans and generally getting to know each other. Marsh put on a CD, then waited for the music to begin to adjust the volume. Helen glanced up in surprise on hearing the opening strains of Tchaikovsky's Fifth Symphony. Marsh grinned at her, shrugged.

"What can I tell you?" His grin widened. "I'm a Tchaikovsky nut."

Helen managed to keep a straight face, but her amusement came through in her tone. "And all this time I thought it was a ploy you used when — ah — entertaining."

Laughing softly, he strolled across the room to her, placed a hand on her shoulder, and gave her a punishing squeeze, blandly ignoring the confused glances Grant and Mary Ellen exchanged.

It was not until later that night when Helen lay on her bed, tired yet sleepless, that the closed-in feeling returned. Only now it was so much stronger, so cloying, Helen sat up quickly, breathing deeply. Marsh was drawing her slowly, but inexorably, into his life. His words of earlier that night crept into her mind. "It's all right, love. You're home."

She slid down onto the pillows again, her mind worrying at his words. Calmer now, her thinking process coolly detached, Helen reached the conclusion that Marsh had decided to pull out all the stops. He had every intention of winning this particular game. *And you,* she told herself dismally, *are playing right into his hands.* Her last coherent thought as she drifted into sleep was that the last thing she should be considering now was a long weekend in the mountains with him.

Eight

That same thought nagged at her all day Monday and Tuesday, kept her unusually quiet during dinner Tuesday night. When, over coffee, Marsh finally commented on her preoccupation, she pleaded fatigue, lack of sleep. It was a perfectly legitimate excuse, as she'd had a late delivery Monday night and it had been after three when she'd dropped onto her bed to fall asleep immediately.

"You really do need a rest," Marsh said softly. "I'm glad we decided to go. You can take it easy for four whole days."

"On the slopes?" The "we" got to her, put a slight sting in her voice.

"There's no law that says you have to ski, Helen," Marsh admonished softly. "You can laze around the fireplace all day if you want to." His eyes narrowed on her face. "You look like you've about had it. I'm going to take you home so you can have an early night." His tone lowered, caressed. "We have the long weekend to be together."

Maybe if his tone hadn't been quite so caressing, hadn't held that hint of what he expected from their weekend away together, Helen would not have bolted. Oh, most definitely she had to get away. But from him, not with him.

It seemed that whenever Helen got a break between patients on Wednesday she had a phone call to make. The first one was to Dr. Stanley Munziack, who assured her it would be no hardship for him if she extended her four-day weekend into a full week. At her lunchtime break she called the airport and was informed that there was a seat available on the late-night flight to Phoenix. In midafternoon she called her mother and was told, "Of course your father will meet the plane." And finally, after her last patient had left, she called her answering service.

After a light supper that she barely touched Helen packed her suitcase, her eyes going to her small bedside clock every few minutes. Although they had agreed not to see each other that night, Marsh had said he would call. When the phone rang, Helen's hand clutched, crushed, the blouse she was holding and with a muttered "Damn," she let it drop into a silky heap on the bed before, taking a deep breath, she reached for the receiver.

"Dr. Cassidy." Helen's voice was over-

cool with trying to cover her guilty nervousness.

"What's wrong, Helen?" Marsh's tone
was sharp with concern. "Are you all
right?"

"Yes, of course I'm all right," she answered a little less coolly. "I'm just tired
and a little harried with the packing."

"You? Harried?" His tone held real astonishment. "You really are tired. Did I
catch you right in the middle of it?"

"Yes, and I would really like to get it finished, Marsh." Helen caught her lower lip
between her teeth, fighting down the urge
to tell him the truth.

"Okay." He laughed softly "I can take a
hint. I'll call you in the morning, early, to
make sure you haven't overslept."

Helen stood with her hand on the receiver long moments after she'd replaced
it. Without halfway trying, she could
imagine Marsh's reaction in the morning
when her service informed him that Dr.
Cassidy was out of town and no, they
didn't know where she'd gone.

The flight, late that night, was quiet and
uneventful, and although she didn't think
she'd be able to, Helen slept through most
of it. Her father, tall, slim, was waiting for
her, a smile of eager expectancy on his
sun-weathered face.

With a feeling of coming home, being

safe, Helen walked into his outstretched arms, closed her eyes against the sudden hot sting of tears.

"What's this?" Robert Cassidy felt the shiver that rippled through his daughter's slim frame, and grasping her shoulders, he held her away from him, studied her face carefully. Noting the brightness of her eyes, his brows rose slowly.

"A man, Helen?"

Helen didn't even consider pretense. He was the one person she could never fool with her cool exterior. In fact there were times while Helen was growing up that he seemed to know what she was going to do before she did. And now, her feelings raw and she more vulnerable than she'd ever been before in her life, she didn't even try.

"Yes."

That one softly murmured word spoke volumes to him, and his eyes sharpened while his tone softened.

"Want to talk about it?"

"No." Helen gave a quick shake of her head, then smiled ruefully. "At least not tonight." She paused before adding, "I have to think it through for myself first, Dad. Right now I'm uncertain as to how to handle this and I don't like the feeling; it's not me."

"That's for sure." One arm draped over her shoulders, Robert paced his long stride to hers as they went to pick up her suit-case. In tune mentally, as they had always been, they dropped the subject, Robert knowing that when she was ready Helen would tell him, if not everything, enough to put him in the picture.

Her mother was waiting at the door of the small ranch-style home her parents had bought on the outskirts of Phoenix, her still-lovely face mirroring her happiness at seeing her firstborn. For the second time in less than an hour Helen was enfolded within loving arms and again felt the quick rush of tears.

No less shrewd than her husband, Laura Cassidy was quick to notice the change in her daughter.

"Darling, what's wrong?" she asked anxiously. "Are you ill?"

The words, so similar to the ones Marsh had said to her just a few hours ago, brought a fresh surge of moisture. What was wrong with her anyway? Helen thought irritably. She hadn't been this quick to tears during adolescence. With a determined effort she controlled her features, steadied her voice.

"No, Mother, I'm not ill," she answered firmly. "The last couple of weeks have been hectic, and I'm very tired. Nothing more serious than that."

"Well, that's a relief," Laura sighed

deeply, her sentiments reflected on her face. "Come sit down. I have a pot of herb tea ready for you, and as soon as you've had a cup it's bed for you."

Helen's laughter was a warm, natural reaction to her mother's dictate. Not since her fifteenth year had she heard that note of firmness in her mother's voice.

"Oh, Mother." Helen bestowed a brief hug on her parent. "It's so good to see you."

Surrounded by parental love, cocooned within the silence of her father's tacit patience, Helen slept deeply and refreshingly, undisturbed by uneasy thoughts of a handsome young man bent on possession.

Rob's welcome was no less enthusiastic than their parents' had been, as was his pretty, somewhat flighty wife and their two fresh-faced boys. But as their mother and father had done the previous evening, he saw at once that all was not well with her.

"What's the problem, big sister?" Rob asked bluntly the first time they were alone for a minute.

"Mind your own business, sonny," Helen quipped gently, returning the grin he threw her at her deliberate use of his childhood nickname.

"The subject not open for discussion, Helen?"

"Not just yet, Rob," she answered softly.

They were standing together at the barbecue grill at the end of the large patio outside the kitchen of Rob's much larger ranch-style home a few miles from her parents'. In between brushing globs of sauce on the chicken sizzling on the grill, Rob slanted her a sharp-eyed glance.

"Will you answer one question?" He turned to face her fully, his gaze level.

"Depends on the question," Helen hedged.

"Daddy." The voice of Rob's eldest filtered through the kitchen screen door.

"In a minute, Chuck," Rob tossed over his shoulder, his eyes locked on hers. Then, his tone lower, he asked, "Is there a man involved?"

"Yes, but that's all I'm saying."

"Daddy, Mommy said you should come in for the salad things." Chuck's young voice was a shade louder.

"Paint your chicken, sonny," Helen gibed, grinning as she turned toward the house. "I'll help Chuck with the salad."

Rob's hand caught her arm, held her still a moment. "If you need me, want someone to tell your troubles to, I'm here, big sister."

Something lodged, painfully, in Helen's throat at his gentle tone. Her slim hand covered his, tightened briefly in thanks. Turning quickly, she hurried towards the house, a tiny break in her voice as she called, "Daddy's busy, Chuck. I'll help you."

In the general confusion of fixing a salad with Chuck, fussing over her youngest nephew, Mike, when he woke from his nap, and receiving a rundown from her sister-in-law of both boys' activities since she'd last seen them, Helen was able to bring her shaky emotions under control.

The week passed pleasantly and much too fast. As her tension eased and her usual confidence reasserted itself, Helen lost the urge to confide in her family.

In the afternoon of the day before Helen's scheduled return to Philly, she had a few minutes alone with her father in the tiny room everyone teasingly referred to as "Dad's study." Feeling she owed her father some sort of an explanation, yet not sure how to begin, Helen sighed with relief when her father ended the short, uncomfortable silence.

"Feeling better, Helen?"

"Yes, Dad, I —" Helen hesitated, searching for words. His astuteness made it unnecessary.

"You look better too." Robert studied her carefully, warmly. "If you don't want to talk about it, Helen, then don't. But just remember, I'm here for you if you need me."

Not for the first time, Helen gave silent thanks for the family she'd been blessed with. Her mother had fussed over her all week, coaxing her to eat, to rest, but though her eyes mirrored her concern, she had not questioned her once. And now her father's words had echoed Rob's. "If you need me, I'm here." They would not pry or in any way presume to infringe on her privacy, but quietly, lovingly, they let her know they were there for her. It helped.

"Thanks, Dad." Helen smiled her gratitude. "I'd really rather not talk about it. Right now I'm feeling a little unsure of myself with this man, who, if you don't mind, will remain nameless." Robert nodded his head briefly. "Please don't worry, and don't let Mother and Rob worry either." Her voice firmed with determination. "I'll resolve it."

"Of course you will." Robert's tone was equally firm. "We all need breathing space at times, Helen, when things seem to crowd in, threaten to overwhelm us. You have a good head on your shoulders. I doubt there's much you can't handle."

But then, Helen thought wryly, *you don't know Marshall Kirk.*

Her flight home was every bit as uneventful as the one west had been. She boarded the plane feeling more relaxed than she had in weeks, but tension began building as the big jet drew ever nearer to the East Coast.

There was Marsh's justifiable anger to be faced. What had been his reaction to her disappearance? Perhaps, after his initial irritation cooled, he had put her from his mind and gone about the business of finding a more accommodating companion. The mere thought of him with another woman brought a mixture of pain and self-derision. *Do you know,* she asked herself bitingly, *what exactly you* do *want?* Flipping open the magazine her father had bought for her, she thumbed through the pages, not yet ready to face a truthful answer to her own question.

It was early evening when Helen entered her apartment. After depositing her suitcase in the bedroom, she went into the kitchen, made herself a cup of tea, then called her service for messages left while she was gone. The crisp voice at the other end of the line rattled on for several minutes and ended with, "And a Mr. Kirk has called twice a day, morning and evening, every day. He was very put-out the first morning, insisted I tell him where you were. I had some difficulty convincing him I had no idea where you'd gone."

"Yes . . . well, I'll take care of it," Helen said softly. "Thank you."

Her finger pressed the disconnect button, then moved to press Marsh's number. While his phone rang, she drew a deep breath, steeling herself for his anger.

"Hello." The voice was so harsh, so ragged sounding, Helen was not sure it was he.

"Marsh?"

There was silence for a full ten seconds before Helen heard his breath being expelled very slowly.

"Where were you?" His very softness threw her off balance, robbed her of speech. "Helen, I've been damned near out of my mind. Where were you?" The tone was rough now, demanding an answer.

"With my family." Helen found her voice, even managed to keep it steady. "In Arizona. I was tired, Marsh, and I just couldn't face that skiing trip. I'm sorry but —"

"Who cares about the stupid skiing trip?" he cut in roughly. "Are you all right?"

"Yes, of course, but —"

"No buts," Marsh again cut in. "If you had to get away for a while, then you did. I told you no strings, Helen, and I meant it." His voice went low, held a hint of amusement. "I've got you running scared, haven't I?"

"Scared?" she scoffed, a little shakily. "Of you? You flatter yourself."

His soft laughter hummed along the wire to tickle her ear, tinge her cheeks pink. "Do I? I don't think so," he drawled. "Why don't you give up? You're going to lose, Helen."

"I don't know what you mean," she snapped. "I must hang up now, I have some more calls to make."

"Okay, coward." Helen shivered as he laughed again. "One more thing and I'll let you go." His tone softened. "Do you feel rested now?"

Suspicious of his tone but not sure why, Helen hesitated a second before admitting, "Yes."

"Good, then you'll be up to having dinner with Cullen tomorrow night." Before she could object, refuse, he whispered, "Good night, love," and hung up.

Cullen was the perfect host, charming and amusing. Helen knew, for she had seen at unguarded moments, that everyone was speculating about the seriousness of her and Marsh's relationship. Everyone, that was, except Cullen. In the relatively short amount of time they were with him, she was left in little doubt that the "old bear" was no longer speculating. He had reached the conclusion that the young "cub" had found a mate. He made no attempt to hide the fact that his conclusion pleased him.

Helen did not like deceiving anyone. But

most especially she did not like deceiving Cullen. If he was an "old bear," he was an extremely gentle one, at least with her. After that evening the game became not only nerve-racking but distasteful, and Helen told herself repeatedly to end it.

Curiosity kept her from following the dictates of her own common sense. How long, she wondered, would Marsh drag out the farce? As the weeks slipped by, Helen became certain that the game was losing its appeal for him, for he made no overt moves toward her. Since the night he gave her the gold chains and his promise of no pressure, he had not been in her apartment. When he brought her home, it was to the door, where, with a light, passionless kiss and a casual good night, he left her.

But still he made no indication that he was ready to either abandon or end the game, even though the challenge she had represented had apparently lost its allure. Helen, barely able to face her own accusing eyes in the mirror, doggedly followed his lead.

What did she think she was doing? The question repeated itself with monotonous regularity. He was becoming a habit; a habit, moveover, that was growing stronger with each passing day. Being with him was torment, being away from him was agony. She wanted him desperately and the intensity of that growing desperation confused and frightened her. At times she lost sight of what the game was all about and longed for the feel of his arms around her, his hard body pressed to hers. She had no basis of comparison for her feelings except the time she had spent with Carl, and even in that, the comparison was minute. At no time, either while they were dating or after they had become engaged, had her feelings for Carl ever made her lose sight of her goal. And so she worried. Worried about her own increasing need to be with him. Worried about the thoughts that tormented her late in the night, driving her out of her bed to pace the floor restlessly. Worried about the end that had to come soon if she was to retain a shred of her self-respect.

Marsh seemed in no way concerned with similar worries. And seemingly without being aware he was doing it, he was wearing down her resistance. He took it for granted that she would spend most of her free time with him and had taken to calling her at the office to inform her of the plans he'd made, the invitations he'd accepted for both of them.

Sundays they were together exclusively. Hour by hour, hand in hand, they walked. They explored Germantown, strolled on the cobblestone street by the brick houses in Elfreth's Alley, a one-block-long street near the riverfront that is one of the oldest streets in America. They spent hours in Independence Hall and the National Historical Park and seriously discussed the possibility of the first United States flag being made in the Betsy Ross House. Then they went back to Fairmont Park; this time Marsh succeeded in drawing her down to the river to watch the sculling crews working out. Sunday nights were the only nights Helen had no difficulty sleeping. With all the exercise and fresh air, she was usually out cold within minutes after sliding into bed.

By mid-March Helen had a problem. On Saturday afternoon, after ushering her last patient out of her office, she sat staring at the square, white, gold-embossed invitation she held gingerly in one hand. A frown creasing her forehead, she read, then re-read, the gold script. The invitation was for a retirement party on the following Saturday to honor the much-respected and very well-liked head of OB-GYN, at the hospital. True, it gave very short notice of the affair, but as she knew the man's decision to retire had been on the spur of the moment because of health reasons, this was not why Helen frowned.

Her problem was Marsh. As the invitation had been issued to Helen and guest, she was, of course, at liberty to ask him to escort her. But that was the fly in her particular ointment. Thus far she had deliberately avoided introducing him to any of her small circle of friends. At regular intervals he had chided her about it, but she had dodged his sardonic barbs with the excuse that her friends, most with full family lives, were in an after-the-holidays entertaining slump. As it was now over two months since the holiday season, Helen knew there were large holes in the excuse and she had been searching her mind for a replacement.

Now, tucked in with the usual mundane Saturday mail, was an invitation she could not very well ignore. Helen's friends, knowing her as well as possible, had thought little of her absence — except that she might be overworking. They knew that she was a very private person, that she preferred a quiet evening of conversation or a really good concert, to overcrowded parties, whether in private homes or the organized ones in large hotels or country clubs. But they also knew of the true affection she had for her department chief and would be surprised if she bypassed his party.

Tapping the card with a neatly trimmed, unpainted fingernail, Helen wondered what to do. She knew Marsh. She also knew that if she told him that she could not see him next Saturday night he would torment her subtly until she told him why. She could lie, of course, but somehow the thought of lying outright to him was repulsive to her. When her phone buzzed, Helen tossed the card onto her desk with relief. Lifting the receiver, she pressed the blinking button and said briskly, "Dr. Cassidy."

Without preliminaries Marsh inquired, "Are you almost through there, Helen?"

"Yes, why?"

"No little mother about to increase the population? No meetings? No hairdresser appointment or shopping to do?"

"No," Helen answered patiently. "Why, Marsh?"

"I'm stranded at a construction site and hoped I could coax you into picking me up." Marsh hesitated, then bribed, "I'll buy you lunch."

"What do you mean, you're stranded? Where is your car?"

"I put it in the garage this morning for inspection," he explained. "It won't be ready until later this afternoon. As a matter of fact you could drop me at the garage after we've had lunch, okay?"

"Yes, of course I'll pick you up," Helen agreed at once. "But what construction site are you stranded at, and why?" Helen's puzzlement was obvious. "I mean — why are you at *any* construction site?"

"It's one of Cullen's babies." Marsh laughed "There was a snarl up here, and as always, he called and told me to come straighten it out."

"And did you?" Helen asked dryly.

"Just about." He spoke with equal dryness. He gave her directions to the site, which was located some distance outside the city, then said, "When you get here, park the car and come into the trailer office." A hint of laughter touched his tone. "Just in case the unsnarler gets snarled."

As Helen prepared to leave the office her glance was caught by the white card on her desk. After a moment's hesitation she picked it up, slipped it back into its envelope, and stuffed it into the depths of her handbag. Giving a mental shrug, she thought, *I'll decide about that later.*

She found the site without difficulty, and after parking the car, she made her way carefully over the uneven and still frozen ground, pausing to read the large white sign posted on the wooden fence that completely surrounded the site. The sign informed her that the construction under way would result in a high-rise apartment complex, that it had been designed by the architectural firm of Wanner, Freebold, and Wanner, and was being erected by the Hannlon Building and Construction Firm, Cullen Hannlon, President.

A small smile curved Helen's lips as she read the last, then her eyes perplexed, her gaze returned to the name Wanner.

"Learning anything?"

Helen jumped at the sound of the teasing voice close to her ear. Not bothering to answer his question, she murmured, "That name Wanner seems vaguely familiar."

"I'm not surprised." Marsh laughed softly. "You were introduced to it a few weeks ago." At her confused stare he nudged. "Grant? Mary Ellen?"

"Oh!" Helen's eyes cleared and she smiled, remembering. "Last names barely registered that night. I was relieved I could hold on to the first."

"Grant's the second Wanner," he offered. "The firm was started by his father and uncle. Grant joined it as a very junior member when he got out of school. He's really very good," he added. "As a matter of fact he designed this building."

While he was talking, Marsh led her to a small trailer some yards away and guided her up the steps and into what appeared to be a shambles. Watching her expression as her eyes circled the mess, Marsh laughed aloud.

"Don't be deceived, sweetheart. I assure you the construction boss knows exactly where everything is and can lay his hand on whatever he wants at a moment's notice." Strolling into the trailer's tiny kitchen area, he asked, "Would you like some coffee?"

Helen opened her mouth to say "Yes, please," but nothing came out. Lips forming a large *O* her eyes went wide at the loud sound of gears grinding, tires screeching, and then the scream of a man. Before she could close her mouth or blink her eyes, Marsh was by her and lunging out the door, the last part of his growled "Son of a —" lost to her. In half an instant she was spinning around, running after him, stumbling over the torn-up, slippery earth.

Dodging ice-skimmed puddles of water, Helen tried to make sense of the blurred scene that met her eyes. Men were running from all directions toward a large piece of machinery lying drunkenly on its side. As she reached the fringes of the crowd of men, Helen could hear Marsh's voice, sharp, clear, issuing orders tersely. One man detached himself from the group, ran toward another large machine.

From inside the circle of men Helen heard the agonized speech of a man, heard him groan, and her hand pushed against a rock-hard male arm.

"Let me through," she ordered as sharply as Marsh had. "I'm a doctor."

Moving aside respectfully, the man tapped the shoulder of the man in front of him, relaying Helen's order. Moving through the men, Helen took in the situation. When the machine had toppled over, it had trapped the driver and crushed his leg against the ground, and now half in, half out, of the thing, the man lay in a crumpled heap in the driver's seat. His lips were twisted in pain, his eyes were glazed, and his face was gray with shock.

Helen dropped to the ground beside him, her fingers going to his wrist. Not liking what she felt, she ordered softly, "Marsh, you have got to move this monster off of him," not for a minute doubting his ability to do so.

"We will," Marsh said just as softly. "An ambulance has been called. I've sent for blankets and —" A man walked up beside him, handed him a white box with a red cross on it. "And here's the first-aid box. There's a syringe of morphine inside."

Without questioning or even looking up, Helen held out her hand. A saturated piece of cotton was placed in her fingers, and after swabbing the man's arm, Helen administered the injection. Working quickly, carefully, her hands firm, yet gentle, she covered as much of the man's body as she could with the blankets Marsh handed her. While she worked Helen was aware of the machine being backed into position beside the disabled one, of chains being fixed into place. When Marsh grasped her elbow, she stood up and stepped back.

In a strained hush everyone watched as, motor growling, chains rattling over winches, the shuddering machine was set aright. Whispering, "Oh, God," Helen watched the injured man's leg dangle crookedly over the side of the machine. Then with a barked, "Don't touch him," she stopped the men's move toward him. Marsh beside her, she walked up to that leg.

"Is there a scissors in that box?"

"Yes."

Seconds later Helen was snipping away, quickly but cautiously, at the blood-soaked material. Her eyes closed briefly when the leg was exposed. The leg was mangled, literally crushed, and with the weight of inadequacy pushing on her mind, she didn't know where to begin. She drew a deep breath, then gave a silent, thankful prayer of relief on hearing the scream of the ambulance siren.

The construction crew guiding the driver, the ambulance was backed as closely as possible to the injured man and two paramedics jumped out and went into action. Working with them, Helen helped cushion and immobilize the leg with an inflatable plastic casing, then the man was moved carefully onto the litter. Strangely, Helen knew one of the paramedics, as she had delivered his first and only child, and after sliding the litter into the long vehicle, he slapped the door shut, smiled, winked, and murmured, "Good work, Doc."

Feeling the praise unearned, Helen nevertheless returned his smile with a soft "Thank you."

As the paramedics climbed back into the ambulance, a hard arm slid around her back.

"I'd like to follow along to the hospital, if you don't mind. There'll be questions to answer, forms to fill out. And I'll have to call Cullen, give him a report on the man's condition."

"Yes, of course. But you do realize it may be some time before any definite word is given out." Breathlessly she moved beside him as, striding along, he half dragged, half carried, her over the rough ground toward her car.

"I know." He gave her a small smile. "But it's got to be done and I've got to do it. The man has no family here."

The drive was a short one, as they took the man to a local hospital. For the following forty-five minutes Helen stood with Marsh as he filled out form after form, answered questions. Helen was asked questions also, but at last it was all finished and the desk nurse said, "If you'd like to wait in the lounge, Doctor, Mr. Kirk, the doctor will have some information for you as soon as possible."

About to walk away, Marsh turned back to the nurse.

"If we're wanted, we'll be in the coffee shop." He paused, then asked, "There is a coffee shop?"

The nurse smiled, nodded, and gave them directions.

"Not exactly what I had in mind when I promised you lunch." Marsh smiled ruefully twenty-five minutes later when the waitress walked away after serving them their food.

"But I love chicken noodle soup." Helen smiled, indicating the steaming bowl in front of her. And with a wave of her hand, over her sandwich, added, "And I've been a cheeseburger freak since I was a kid." She sipped at the cup cradled in her hands. "The coffee is hot and really very good. It's an excellent lunch, Marsh." Her eyes teased him. "And you can't beat the prices."

"You're a cheap date." Marsh's warmly glowing eyes teased back. "Remind me to invite you out to lunch again sometime."

It was after four thirty when they returned to the waiting lounge, and after only a few tense moments Helen suddenly remembered something. Standing up, she held out her hand to Marsh, palm up.

"Give me your car keys."

Without question Marsh stood up, plunged his hand into his pocket, then, glancing up, curiously asked, "What for?"

"I'm going to go for your car," she answered simply. "I'll ask the desk nurse to call a cab for me and go get your car."

"Helen, that's not necessary," Marsh said softly.

"I know." Her eyes were teasing again. "But I hate hanging around hospital waiting rooms. Now give me the keys and the address of the garage and I'll be back before you can even miss me."

"I seriously doubt that," he drawled, dropping the keys into her hand.

It was after six when they finally left the hospital, relief on hearing the man would not lose his leg rendering a spring to their step. Marsh walked Helen to her car, unlocked and opened the door for her before asking, "Can you be ready by eight?"

"Ready for what?"

"For dinner." Marsh grinned. "Maybe a bowl of soup and a cheeseburger would hold you for hours, but I have a suspicion that in another hour or so I'm going to be looking forward to a steak. So can you be ready?"

"I'm really very tired, Marsh, and —"

"Nothing fancy," Marsh promised. "And I plan to take you home as soon as we've finished dinner."

Helen was vaguely unsettled by his words, but with a sigh she agreed.

There was nothing fancy about the restaurant Marsh took her to. But it was clean and quiet and the food was delicious and the wine was good.

Later, standing in the hallway in front of her open apartment door, Marsh cupped her face in his hands, kissed her softly.

"You were pretty wonderful today, Helen," he murmured. "Some day, very soon, you and I are going to have a long, serious discussion. But right now you look too tired to think properly, let alone talk." He kissed her again, then dropped his hands. "Go inside, go to bed. I'll call you late in the morning."

Lying in bed, Helen closed her eyes, as if by doing so, she could close out the certainty painfully searing her mind. He was ready to make his move, play his high card, and she knew it. And the knowing hurt, more than she had ever dreamed it would.

Nine

By midmorning Sunday Helen had come to terms with her emotions. Although, when embarking on this charade, she had not fully considered the possibly painful ramifications to herself, she could not throw in her hand now. No, pride demanded she play the hand to the last card, then pick up what emotional chips were left and go home.

When Marsh called, Helen was able to talk to him calmly, but she wasn't yet ready to see him. In an easy tone she could hardly believe she'd achieved, she told him she didn't want to go out that afternoon, as she had a hundred personal things she had to catch up on.

"A full hundred?" he mocked. "Are you trying to put off the inevitable, love?"

Helen felt a sinking sensation in the pit of her stomach. Marsh hadn't called her "love" in that tone for weeks. She was right. He was ready for the big play.

Her eyes closed against the renewed pain. She should have felt relieved, thankful that it would be over soon. She didn't. She felt sick, and suddenly very tired.

"Helen?"

She'd been quiet very long. Too long.

"Yes, Marsh."

"Are you all right?" The concern in his voice, which he made no effort to hide, deepened her pain. "I mean, are you feeling all right?"

"Yes, of course." Helen forced a light laugh. "I'm sorry, Marsh, I'm afraid I'm still a little sleep-vacant."

Helen winced at the lie. "I haven't been up very long and I don't have the mental process together yet."

"I can't wait to hear what you'll have to say when you get it together." He laughed, then chided, "Do you think you will have your hundred personal chores finished by dinnertime? I'll make reservations somewhere."

Again she hesitated, but only briefly this time.

"All right, Marsh, but I want to have an early night. I'm scheduled for the O.R. early tomorrow morning." At least that was the truth.

"Something serious?"

"Yes." She would say no more.

"Okay, love, you're the boss. I'll pick you up at six thirty and you can be back home and tucked in for the night by ten."

Alone, Helen added silently.

The restaurant was a new one for Helen. Spanish in decor, with a lot of black wrought iron complemented by dark red tablecloths and carpet. The menu was a disappointment, being entirely American. The closest Helen got to Spain was the bottle of imported sangría, compliments of the house, that was included with every — expensive — meal.

After dinner Helen played with the stem of her tiny cordial glass, staring at the Amaretto inside.

"Are you going to admire it or drink it?" Marsh teased.

Startled out of her reverie, Helen glanced up, saw his own cognac was gone. A red-jacketed waiter stopped at their table, re-filled the coffee cups. When he walked away again, Marsh pinned her with curious eyes.

"Something bothering you, Helen?"

"No." Her fingertip circled the rim of the small glass. *You are certainly not playing this very intelligently,* she told herself bleakly. *Perhaps it's time to throw a card that will put him off balance, just a little.* "I was just wondering if you'd care to escort me to a party Saturday night."

"Of course," he replied promptly. "Did you doubt that I would?"

"I wasn't sure." Helen shrugged. "I'm

afraid it won't be a very lively affair, but I don't want to miss it."

"What sort of party is it?"

"Retirement." Helen sipped her drink, smiled gently. "My chief in OB. He's a nice man and a brilliant surgeon. I'm going to miss him and I would like to go."

"So we'll go," Marsh said easily, then his eyes narrowed slightly. "But now something bothers me."

"What?" Helen answered warily.

"Why you even hesitated about mentioning it. Did you really think I wouldn't want to go with you?" He paused and his tone grew an edge. "Or were you hating the idea that you'd finally have to introduce me to some of your friends?"

"Marsh!" Helen's shocked tone hid the curl of unease she felt.

"Don't play the innocent with me, love," he rapped softly. "You didn't really think I'd bought those lame excuses, did you? I knew all along why you were dodging that particular issue. Part of it, the biggest part, was this damned hang-up you have about our age difference." He leaned back lazily in his chair; his eyes refuted that laziness. Very softly he warned, "I'm not exactly stupid, you know."

A chill of apprehension trickled down Helen's spine. She was sure he was giving her a definite warning about something —

but what? For a brief, panicky second Helen felt sure he knew she was playing him at his own game. Then common sense took over. She had made her position clear from the beginning, had told him bluntly that she wanted no involvement of any kind. There was no reason whatever for him to be suspicious. Once again his pride had been touched and he didn't like it. And so the warning; it was as simple as that.

When Marsh didn't pursue the subject, Helen convinced herself her diagnosis was correct.

During the week Helen changed her mind about what to wear for the party at least four times. At one point she even convinced herself she needed something new. Never had she been so nervous about going out somewhere. After long mental arguments she finally scrapped the idea of a new gown. She *had* a new gown. She'd bought it for the holidays and never worn it. And though the calendar said it was just about spring, the temperature said it was still very much winter.

On Saturday night, standing fully dressed in front of her mirror, Helen still wasn't sure of her dress. There was very little of it, at least the top part of it, and Helen wondered for the tenth time if it was right for her. Its cut was deceptively simple, with a rather deep *V* neckline and straight, clingy skirt. About the only thing that did please Helen was the shimmery midnight-blue color. Marsh's gift chains were the only jewelry she wore. She had coiled her hair back, telling herself the severe style offset the gown's more daring effect.

"Very elegant."

They were Marsh's first words when she opened the door to him and they echoed her thought about his appearance. In a black suit and black band-collared shirt, the only word to describe him was devastating.

The party was being held in the ballroom of one of the city's largest hotels. Helen had not been in the room five minutes before she saw her own opinion of Marsh's looks reflected in the eyes of a dozen women. The sudden mixture of feelings those devouring female eyes sent searing through her made her want to run for the nearest exit. Pride, jealousy, and, Lord help her, possessiveness surged through her like a raging bull gone mad. It made her feel a little sick. It made her feel a little angry. But, worst of all, it made her feel foolish, and that she could not bear.

With a smile on her lips that was pure honey and tasted in her mouth like straight acid, Helen introduced Marsh to friends as they moved around the room. Helen was aware of more than one pair of eyebrows raised over eyes full of shocked disbelief, and she could imagine what everyone was thinking. She was rarely ever seen with a man, and when she was, it was usually with a close friend who was the husband of a closer friend. People who were her friends knew she simply did not indulge. Now here she was, not only with a man they had never met before, but a younger one as well. Helen had a feeling of certainty that the postparty conversations between husbands and wives would be loaded with speculation.

Marsh seemed sublimely unaware of it all. The glittery, assessing glances from women of varying ages, the raised brows, even the sharp inspection from her chief, apparently went over his head. But Helen saw it, and she didn't like it, not any of it.

Along the one end of the long room a table had been placed for the retiree and his family. In front of that, placed informally, were the other tables. Beyond them a large space had been left clear for dancing, and at the other end a small band awaited their cue to begin playing. Along the far wall a long buffet table had been set up, and next to that was an almost equally long bar.

Marsh found a table, tucked against a

pillar, barely big enough for two, and that's where they sat, turning down, with a smile, the numerous offers from friends to join them. Helen knew it was real friendship that prompted the offers, friendship and a big dash of curiosity.

After the short speeches were made and the toasts given, the party's planner invited everyone to help himself to the food and the dance floor.

To the background music of a popular new song, Marsh asked, "Do you want something to eat or drink?"

"Not yet." Helen shook her head.

"Good, let's dance."

All the way to the dance floor Helen was called to, waved at, but Marsh would not let her stop. A smile on his lips, his hand firmly grasping hers, he kept moving, until, reaching the dancing area, he turned her into his arms with an exaggerated sigh.

"I had no idea you had so many friends," he groaned. "Didn't you mention that only some of your friends would be here tonight?"

"They aren't all close friends, Marsh." Helen laughed softly. "There are quite a few people here I only see at the hospital." Her smile remained, but her tone went dry. "I think you're the one causing all this sudden interest in me."

"I can't imagine why," he drawled. "I'm

really very ordinary."

Oh, sure, Helen thought, *about as much as Pavarotti is ordinary compared to other singers.*

An attractive young nurse, a Linda something-or-other, not at all shy or reticent, tapped Helen on the shoulder. Glancing around, Helen's eyes went wide with surprise at the young woman's words.

"Can I cut in, Doctor?" She smiled beautifully. "I was just saying to the girls I'm with that your escort is the best-looking man on the dance floor and — well — they dared me to cut in on you."

Astounded, Helen didn't know what to say until, flicking a glance at Marsh, she saw the amusement tugging at his lips.

"But of course," she purred sweetly. "I was dying for something to drink anyway." Moving out of Marsh's arms, away from his mocking eyes, she wiggled her fingers at him. "Have fun."

Helen accepted the glass of champagne from the bartender and took a large swallow, her eyes gleaming with fury. *And he says the difference in our ages doesn't matter,* she fumed. She swallowed some more of the wine, then looked at the glass as if seeing it for the first time. *No wonder I feel like a fool,* she thought bitterly. *I am one. And if I'm not careful, in another minute I'll be a smashed fool.*

"Good evening, Helen. It's been a long time."

The deep-timbred voice jerked her mind away from her own shortcomings and her head around to stare into the handsome face of Carl Engle.

"Oh! Hello, Carl." Helen smiled coolly. "You startled me."

"I'm sorry, I didn't mean to." He smiled warmly. "May I get you more wine?"

Helen frowned at the empty glass in her hand. She didn't even remember finishing it.

"Yes, please." Even though she didn't want it, Helen decided she'd look like even more of a fool standing around with an empty glass in her hand.

While Carl spoke to the waiter, then waited for a fresh glass of wine, Helen studied him unobtrusively. She had seen him at various functions over the last few years, but this was the first time she looked, really looked, at him.

There was not a hint of gray in the fair hair that contrasted beautifully with the deep tan on his handsome face. And he had matured into a handsome man, Helen admitted. Tall, still slim, his brown eyes bright and alert, he'd catch the eye of more than his share of females. Helen felt a strange sensation at the thought. If he had exercised some judgment, acquired a little maturity while still in college, he would probably be her husband today. For some unknown reason Helen was very glad he hadn't and wasn't.

"Are you here alone?" He turned back to her, the smile deepening, revealing even white teeth.

"No, I came with —"

"Me." Marsh finished the sentence for her, his eyes somber as they went slowly over Carl.

"Carl Engle, Marshall Kirk," Helen introduced quietly. Marsh's eyes narrowed a fleeting second, but it was the only indication he gave that he'd ever heard the name before. So much, Helen thought wryly, for his saying he'd thank Carl if he ever met him.

Two arms were extended, hands were clasped and almost immediately released.

"Kirk." Carl mused. "Any connection to the accounting firm of Kirk and Terrell?"

"The same Kirk," Marsh answered quietly.

"I've heard some very good things about your firm," Carl murmured. "You're connected with Hannlon Construction also, aren't you?"

"My grandfather," Marsh admitted.

"I know your sister, Kristeen," Carl said, then smiled at Marsh's raised brows. "I'm your niece's pediatrician." Before Marsh could reply, Carl smiled at Helen. "Another patient to thank you for, Dr. Cassidy."

"The choice is theirs." Helen shrugged. "If they ask for a recommendation, I supply three names."

"Well, thank you for including me in the three." Carl laughed. "Now, as the saying goes, may I have the next dance?"

"Excuse me," Marsh inserted before Helen could think of a polite way of saying no. "I promised Helen I'd take her to the buffet as soon as that dance was finished."

"Of course," Carl replied. "Maybe later."

Marsh smiled thinly in answer, grasped Helen's arm, and led her toward the end of the long table.

"I distinctly remember telling you I was not hungry," Helen chided coolly.

"I distinctly remember you telling me you were not thirsty," Marsh retorted, one eyebrow arched at her half-empty glass.

They ate in silence, Helen picking disinterestedly at the small amount of food on her plate. When Marsh had cleaned off his plate, he tossed his napkin on top of it and pinned her with very cool blue eyes.

"Did you want to dance with him?" His tone was cold and, Helen thought, somehow condemning. Her hackles rose.

"Would it have mattered if I did?" She

didn't wait for him to answer, adding sweetly, "Did you enjoy your dance?"

Watching his eyes narrow, Helen felt sick. Even to herself she sounded like a jealous, possessive woman.

"Not particularly," he finally answered. "I'm not turned on by gushy, clingy females."

"Too bad," she purred, looking beyond him. "There's another, probably the gushiest, heading this way. I imagine they'll all ask you now."

Helen recognized the girl coming toward them, for it was the student who had referred to Marsh as "totally awesome" on the day Helen met him.

When she stopped at their table, Marsh stood up, a charming, polite smile on his lips.

"Oh, Mr. Kirk." The girl actually did gush. "Doctor, I hope you don't mind, but Linda will be unbearable for the rest of the night if the rest of us don't get a dance."

"How many are the rest of you?" Marsh asked warily.

"Four," the girl answered brightly. "Including me."

Helen saw Marsh's lips tighten, but before he could say a word, she laughed softly. "Four's not many. Go along, Marsh." She dismissed him airily. "I'm perfectly happy here . . . by myself."

Marsh made a motion with his hand for the girl to precede him, then before following her, he turned a thunderous look on Helen. "You'll pay for this, woman," he whispered harshly.

Helen watched his retreating back, deriving a malicious pleasure in the stiffness of it. He certainly didn't like being manipulated.

"Time for that dance now, Helen?" Carl stood beside her, an expectant smile on his face.

"Yes, thank you." Helen smiled, thinking, *Well, why not? Anything's better than sitting here like the proverbial wallflower.*

Carl had always been a good dancer, smooth, easy to follow, and after a few minutes Helen felt some of the angry tautness leave her.

"You've matured into a beautiful woman, Helen." Carl's voice was low, oddly urgent.

A tiny smile touching her lips at his unknowing echo of her earlier thoughts about him, she glanced up.

"Thank you."

"Have you ever forgiven me, Helen?" he asked abruptly.

Helen's glance wavered, then grew steady again. "There's nothing to forgive, for nothing really happened." *No actual rape that is,* she amended mentally, *only two blows, the second with your fist.* "I never think of it," she lied. *Then what,* she chided herself, *were you sobbing about in Marsh's arms that night?*

"We could have made it together."

"What?" His incredible words shocked her out of her thoughts.

"You and I," he explained softly. "We could have made it very good." He drew her a little closer, and amazed at his cool presumption, Helen didn't resist. In fact she was hardly aware of him, for she had just caught a glimpse of Marsh with yet another girl in his arms, a little older, much prettier than the others.

"We still could, Helen." The urgent voice tried to draw her attention.

"How?" Helen wasn't even sure of what he was saying. All she was sure of was the hot jealousy running through her veins and the sick shame that jealousy spawned.

"Don't be naive, darling." Carl's lips touched her hair as he brought her closer still. "My wife would never know, and even if she did, I doubt if she'd care."

His lips, as well as his words, brushing her ear, brought her alert. She knew his wife and had heard of the number of mistresses he'd had.

"I find that a little hard to believe," she said carefully.

"You needn't, I assure you." Again his arms tightened, and Helen felt anger replace her jealousy. "My wife's a little girl playing house. Only in her case the dolls are our children and the playhouse furniture is life-sized. As long as her little domain is not threatened, she couldn't care less what I do." He paused, then added fatuously, "You do understand, I have no intention of threatening that domain."

Of course not, Helen thought furiously, *you're not stupid. Why lose the goodwill of a very prominent and influential father-in-law, if you can have your cake and eat it?* Helen placed her hands on his chest, about to push him away while she told him exactly what she thought of him. She didn't get a chance to do either.

"May I cut in?" Marsh's voice was low, deceptively quiet. "I believe you promised me this dance, Helen." His arm slid around her waist, his fingers gripped painfully.

"Yes, of course." Helen was suddenly breathless with apprehension. Good Lord, she couldn't allow him to make a scene *here.* "And then, if you don't mind, I'd like to go home."

Marsh nodded, started to turn her away, but Carl, seeming to think her words were a good sign for him, said softly, "I'll call you, Helen."

"No, you won't."

Flat, final, the words hung between the two men like a sword. Marsh's eyes cold, detached, bored into Carl's. Carl's dropped first as, with a shrug, he smiled faintly and walked away.

"Marsh, really, you —"

"Be quiet, Helen." Marsh's tone matched his eyes for coldness. "Do you want to dance or do you want to go home?"

"I —" Helen drew a deep breath. "I think we'd better go."

Without a word he turned on his heel, grasped her arm, and headed for the door. After hasty farewells to their host Helen found herself rushed to the cloakroom. Marsh asked for his car to be brought around, and as they stepped out of the door Helen gasped. There was at least three inches of snow on the ground and it was still coming down hard.

Driving was bad, requiring all Marsh's concentration, and the distance to her apartment was covered in silence. Helen could feel his anger beating against her like storm-tossed waves. Knowing there would be a confrontation when they got to her place, Helen almost dreaded arriving home. To her surprise he did not drive onto the parking lot, but pulled up, motor running, under the marquee that protected the entrance. She hesitated a second but when he didn't speak or even look at her, she slid across the seat, got out, closed the door carefully, and ran into the building.

Inside her apartment Helen went straight to her bedroom. She was wearing thin-strap evening sandals and her feet had gotten soaked in her short dash through the snow to the car. Now she felt chilled to the bone, not only from her foot soaking. She stripped, then took a hot shower, slipped into her nightgown and quilted, belted robe, and started for the kitchen to make a cup of tea.

The doorbell's ring stopped her in the kitchen doorway. Now who in the world? Helen glanced at the clock. At this hour? The ring came again, short, angry sound-ing. Helen walked slowly to the door, checked to see if the chain was in place, then opened the door two inches.

Marsh stood in the hall looking every bit as angry as he had when he'd dropped her off less than forty-five minutes ago. He also looked the tough construction worker he'd once been, dressed in a suede jacket, brushed-denim jeans, and what looked like logging boots laced almost to the knee.

"What do you want?" Slipping the chain, Helen stepped back. He walked in far enough to close the door. One eyebrow arched mockingly.

"There are a few questions I want answers to." He slipped out of his jacket.

"But why didn't you ask them when you brought me home?" She moved away from him edgily.

"I wanted to get the car home." He bent over, began unlacing his boots.

"But —"

"I have one of the company's four-wheel-drive pickups," he answered before she could ask. After tugging the boots off, he padded across the room to her. His eyes were cool, direct.

"Do you still feel something for him?"

Helen gasped. She didn't know what she'd been expecting, but it certainly hadn't been that.

"Carl?"

The confusion in her tone seemed to anger him even more. Grasping her shoulders painfully, he pulled her close to him.

"Yes, Carl," he gritted through clenched teeth. "While you were in his arms." His lips twisted, his tone grew sarcastic. "While you were held so very closely in his arms, dancing, did you find you still feel something for him?"

"No." It was stated simply, positively, but it didn't satisfy him.

"Then why did you allow him to practically crawl all over you?" he snapped. "What was he saying to you?"

Helen could have cried aloud. She didn't want to answer him. He was mad enough already. She hesitated a moment. It was a moment too long.

"Answer me, Helen." He gave her a little shake. "What did he say?"

"He suggested an . . . arrangement." She sighed. "He also assured me that his wife would not interfere. You men are wonderful creatures, aren't you?" she ended bitterly.

A flame flared in Marsh's eyes. "It takes two to play that kind of game. A man *and* a woman." His fingers dug into her arms. "What did you tell him?"

"I wanted to tell him to go to hell." Helen's eyes flashed back at him. "But you showed up before I could."

Helen could actually see the anger seep out of him. His face became less rigid; his fingers relaxed their punishing hold.

"If he calls you," he spat out, "or tries to see you —"

"I'm sure he won't," Helen said quickly, feeling his fingers tighten again. "I think you made it very clear that he shouldn't."

"He'd better not." He drew her closer, his fingers loosening again, massaging her tender skin. Then her eyes widened as he breathed softly, "You're mine, Helen. And the game is over."

"No, I'm —"

His mouth caught her parted lips, silencing her. If the kiss had been rough or hard, she could have fought him. It was neither. Gently, tenderly, his mouth put his stamp of ownership on her. Melting, trembling, she felt his hand slide down her back, his arm gather her tightly to him. His mouth left hers, moved slowly across her cheek to her ear.

"Helen, Helen." The voice that whispered her name was raw. "Oh, God, I love you. Hold me, love. Please hold me."

Helen's arms slid up and around his neck, and she closed her eyes against the quick, hot sting inside. Turning her face into the side of his neck, she breathed in deeply. His cologne, plus the male scent of him, confused her thinking.

"Marsh," she whispered, trying to hang on to her evaporating reason. "You — we shouldn't."

"Yes, we should." His warm breath feathered her ear, tickled its way down the length of her body. "We should have long ago."

His mouth left a fiery trace over her face, back to her lips. And now she was ready for the driving force that crushed her mouth, made dust of her resistance. Tiny little sparks burst into flames inside her. Flames that leaped higher and higher as his mouth grew more demanding.

Her own hunger aroused, Helen returned his kiss, barely aware of what he was doing, when she felt his hands loosen her belt, pull her arms down, slide her robe off. But she was aware of his hands moving over the silky material of her nightgown, was aware of the sudden need to feel those hands against her skin. The awareness brought momentary sanity. Tearing her mouth from his, she gasped for air, finally found her voice.

"Marsh, no." Helen couldn't breathe properly and she paused to draw a short, shallow breath. She shuddered as his lips nibbled along the strained cord in her neck. "Oh, Marsh, no." It was a feeble protest against his hands sliding the gown's narrow straps from her shoulders. The gown slid to the floor silently, and then Helen's body became electrically charged at the touch of his hands. His lips found the beginning swell of her breasts and she moaned softly. Moving lazily, the tip of his tongue driving the flame yet higher, his mouth retraced the trail to her lips. Reason was gone, common sense was gone; all that was left was the ache to be with him. Sliding her arms around his neck, she dug her fingers into his hair. Lifting his head, he stared down at her, his breathing ragged.

"Sweet Lord, I can't wait anymore," he

whispered hoarsely. "I won't wait anymore."

Bending swiftly, he swung her up into his arms and carried her into the bedroom. He laid her gently onto the bed, then straightened, his eyes caressing her as he pulled his knit sweater over his head and tossed it into a corner. When his hand went to the snap at the waistband of his jeans, Helen closed her eyes. He was beside her in seconds, his skin warm and firm against hers. "Marsh, I —"

"I love you," he whispered fiercely, his mouth closing off any further protests from her. His hands brought every inch of her skin tinglingly alive, his mouth drove her to the edge of madness. Aching, moaning deep in her throat, she opened her eyes wide when he ordered, "Tell me you love me."

"I love you," she repeated weakly.

"Again."

"I love you." A little stronger this time.

"Again."

"I love you. I love you. Damn you, I love you."

"Good." Blatant satisfaction coated his tone.

Her nails punished him, but he laughed softly. "You have a hunger almost as great as mine, love." He kissed her, his tongue probing until she arched uncontrollably against him.

"What do you want, love?" he teased.

"Don't," she pleaded.

"Tell me what you want," he demanded relentlessly.

"You," she sobbed. "I want you. Don't torture me, Marsh, please."

"Torture? You don't know the meaning of the word." His lips teased hers, the tip of his tongue ran along the outline of her upper lip. "I wanted to hear you say it, Helen. I had to hear it." His body shifted, blanketing hers, and with a whispered, but definite "Now," his lips ceased their teasing, became hard, urgent.

It was everything a younger Helen had once hoped it would be. And much, much more than her imagination had ever dared hope for. Slowly, gently, Marsh guided her through the first fleeting moments of discomfort, then, his passion unleashed, he introduced her to a world she'd never dreamed existed. A world of pure sensation, of tension almost unbearable, of pleasure so exquisite that it held a thread of pain. Finer, yet more defined, the sweet bud of agony slowly blossomed. When it burst into full bloom there was soaring joy, shuddering victory, and one brief moment of unconsciousness that filled Helen with wonder. And the most incredible thing was that the near perfection could be repeated, as Marsh proved at regular intervals, over and over again. It was after four in the morning before Marsh, with a softly taunted "Quitter," let her drift into sleep.

The eerie silence that smothers the world with a heavy snowfall woke Helen late in the morning. Without moving, she opened her eyelids slowly. The space on the bed beside her was empty. Turning her head, her eyes came to his tall form, standing in front of the window. Barely breathing, she studied that form, a sharp pain stabbing at her heart. He had pulled on his jeans, but nothing else, and with his fingers tucked into his back pockets, his muscles bunched tautly in his arms across his shoulders. Head up, somber-faced, he stared out through the window, a quality of waiting about him.

Waiting for what? To laugh? To crow over his triumph? To be prepared to smile indulgently as she meekly accepted his terms? Helen squirmed inwardly at her own thoughts, hating herself for her own weakness — almost hating him for taking advantage of that weakness.

Her eyes closed again, covering the pain and despair he could have easily read had he turned his head. She knew what she looked like in the morning. She faced that reality every day. Face pale, tiny lines of strain and years around her eyes and mouth. And this morning she would look even worse with her hair a tangled mess framing her pale face.

Helen would have been more shocked had someone thrust a mirror in front of her, forced her to open her eyes. The afterglow of love still tinged her cheeks; the tiny lines of strain had smoothed out, been partially erased by the release of tension; and the disarray of her hair gave her an untamed, sensual look. In essence the image she would have seen reflected in a mirror, and that Marsh did see when he turned his head, was of a breathtakingly beautiful woman. But no one did place a mirror in front of her, and Helen was convinced, on opening her eyes and finding Marsh's brooding ones on her, that what those hooded eyes observed displeased him.

Unable to bear those unreadable eyes on her, the taut, waiting stillness that held him, her hands curled into tight, determined fists under the covers. He had played his ace to her king, but if he thought he had won the game he was in for a shock. She still held one card and she would let *him* squirm awhile before she played it. The veneer of cool professionalism was pulled into place. In a voice withdrawn, detached from all the happenings of the past night, Helen clipped, "Are you happy now? Are you satisfied?"

Ten

Marsh didn't move. A flame leaped brightly in his blue eyes, then was instantly, deliberately, quenched.

"Am I satisfied?" His voice, devoid of emotion, had a frighteningly dead sound. "For the moment, yes. Am I happy? Now? No."

Well, Helen thought dismally, you certainly couldn't argue with a statement as definite as that. It wasn't quite what she had expected, but then, when had he ever done anything quite like she'd expected?

"Helen, about last night —"

No! a voice screamed inside her head. No, she would not listen to terms or possible plans or — maybe — rejection, not while she still lay on the battlefield of her own defeat.

"Marsh," she interrupted quickly, "I want to have a shower, get dressed." Dragging the sheet with her, she sat up.

"Helen," Marsh gritted impatiently, "we have got to talk about —"

"Marsh, please." She again cut him off. "Will you leave this room so I can get up?"

His body stiffened, and she could see the battle that raged inside him. Then, with a curt nod, he turned and strode across the room, scooping his sweater off the floor in passing, and left the room, closing the door with an angry snap.

Fighting the urge to run after him, to agree to everything and anything he wanted, Helen slid off the bed and ran into the bathroom.

Twenty minutes later she walked into the kitchen to face him, her resolve strengthened, her course clearly mapped out in her mind.

He had made a pot of coffee and stood leaning against the counter, a cup of steaming brew cradled in his hands. Her small kitchen radio played softly in the background. When she entered the room, he set down his cup, filled a matching one for her, handed it to her, then tilted his head at the only window in the room.

"I've just heard a weather report," he said quietly. "We had over a foot of snow during the night and it's still snowing heavily. The weather bureau is calling for another three to five inches."

A very safe subject, Helen thought cynically, the weather. Falling in with his lead, she murmured, "Driving is going to be a nightmare. It's a good thing you took your car home."

He nodded and polished off half his coffee in several swallows. The subject of the weather exhausted, a strained, uneasy silence vibrated between them. They both jumped at the sudden, discordant ring from the phone. Helen snatched up the receiver on the second ring, beating her service to it.

"Dr. Cassidy."

"Doctor, this is David Stewart. My wife fell a little while ago and is in labor," the man rushed all in one breath. Gasping quickly, he hurried on. "What the hell am I going to do? I can't even get my car out of the garage."

Conjuring up a mental picture of Cheryl Stewart, Helen asked calmly, "How far apart are the contractions?"

"I don't know," he answered distractedly; then, "just a minute, my mother-in-law is timing it now." There was a short pause, then, "Five minutes, Doctor."

"Mr. Stewart, give me your address, then go hold your wife's hand." Helen's calm voice soothed. "I'll send an ambulance out and meet you at the hospital."

"But can an ambulance get out here in this mess?" His voice was now frantic. Hearing an outcry of pain in the background, Helen knew why. This was the

Stewarts' first baby.

"I'm sure it can, Mr. Stewart, if you get off the line and let me call for one."

The line went dead. A small smile pulling at her lips, Helen put through the call for an ambulance. The dispatcher's harried "As soon as possible, Doctor" erased the smile, triggered a curl of unease. Her face thoughtful, Helen replaced the receiver. Glancing around at Marsh, she tossed the address to him.

"Can you get me out there?"

"Yes." He caught on at once. "You don't feel right about this?"

"I'm probably running you on a wild-goose chase." Helen smiled apologetically. "But no, I don't feel right about it."

"So jump into your boots, grab your coat, and let's go." He was already moving toward the living room.

Helen did exactly as he suggested. Less than ten minutes later, ready to go out the door, Helen paused, turned back to Marsh.

"In the closet, at the far end of the shelf, there's a black bag. Will you get it for me, please?"

Walking to the elevator, bag in his hand, Marsh lifted a questioning eyebrow at Helen.

"I don't even know what made me think of it. I've never used it," she explained softly. "My father gave it to me when I entered premed," She hesitated, a gentle smile curling her lips. "He had hoped I'd follow him into general practice."

As Helen had predicted earlier, driving was a nightmare. Even with the four-wheel drive, negotiating the truck through the heavy wet snow required all Marsh's concentration, and as Helen was busy with her own thoughts, the drive was completed in near silence. When Marsh turned onto the street where the Stewarts lived, Helen sighed with a mixture of relief and disappointment. She had hoped to see an ambulance, if only the retreating lights of one, but the street was empty, the snow virgin, smooth.

As he parked the truck Marsh grunted, "At least a path's been shoveled to the curb." Stepping out, he advised, "Slide under the wheel and get out this side."

David Stewart had the door open before they were halfway up the walk.

"Where the hell is that ambulance, Doctor?" His voice was heavy with strain, his face pale. "Her pains are getting closer."

"They'll get here as soon as they can." Helen's tone was soothing as she walked into the small foyer. She removed her coat, then went still at the outcry of a woman in pain. "Where is she? I'll —"

"I don't think this baby is going to wait

for an ambulance. Come with me, Doctor."

Helen moved automatically toward the older woman who stood in an archway that led off the living room. Without another word the woman turned and led the way along a short hallway and into a bedroom. Cheryl Stewart lay on the bed, her face drawn with pain, her brow wet with sweat.

"Oh, Doctor," she gasped. "I'm so glad to see you. The pains are very bad."

"She's been very good up until now, Doctor," Cheryl's mother offered. "I managed to get a plastic sheet and towels under her before her water broke."

Drawing the covering sheet away, Helen nodded her approval. It required the briefest examination to ascertain the truth of the older woman's statement. This baby was not going to wait for anything. Cheryl gasped with the onslaught of another contraction, and Helen urged, "Don't fight it, Cheryl, go with it."

About to call to Marsh to bring her bag, Helen smiled in gratitude when he placed it beside her, asking, "What can I do to help?"

"I think there's a packaged pair of gloves in there. Will you get them for me?"

After that she simply had to ask for what she wanted and it was handed to her. Sheets were draped, tentlike, over the girl's legs, and speaking quietly, encouragingly, Helen delivered the baby.

"Stop pushing now," Helen instructed Cheryl when she held the baby's head and one shoulder in her hands. Then to Marsh, "The syringe ready?"

"Right here," came the calm reply.

Guiding the small form with her hands, Helen drew the baby into the world, then taking the syringe Marsh handed her, she cleaned the tiny mouth and nostrils of birth mucus. The infant sputtered, then began to cry, and Helen placed the red-faced child on Cheryl's stomach.

"You have a beautiful son, Cheryl," she told the exhausted girl.

When she was satisfied that the baby was breathing spontaneously, Helen cut the lifeline cord, unaware that the ambulance had arrived or that the two attendants waited in the hall to take over.

They entered the room as she swabbed the blood from the baby's face.

"Okay, let's go," Helen ordered briskly, wrapping the baby up warmly while the attendants carefully covered Cheryl. "I'll suture in the hospital. Marsh, if you'll follow behind with Mr. Stewart, I'll ride in the ambulance."

Marsh nodded, holding her coat for her, and as she slipped into it he whispered, "That was beautiful, Helen. You're fantastic."

It had stopped snowing and the streets

were in somewhat better condition by the time they returned to the Stewart house several hours later. After dropping off a much happier-looking David, Marsh suggested they go to his apartment for something to eat.

"No, Marsh." Helen shook her head firmly. "There's plenty of food in my fridge. Besides which, I need a shower. I'm tired. I want to go home and get comfortable." She didn't bother to add that her tiredness stemmed more from her lack of sleep the night before than the events of the day. She wasn't quite ready to tackle that subject yet.

After a relaxing shower Helen prepared a quick meal of canned soup and bacon, lettuce, and tomato sandwiches. Although they kept the conversation light and general while they ate, Helen could feel the tension of the morning tautening between them again. When the supper things were cleared away, they carried their coffee into the living room. Coffee cup in hand, Marsh paced back and forth for several minutes, then came to an abrupt halt in front of Helen.

"Can we talk now?"

"There is nothing to talk about." Glancing up, Helen saw his lips tighten.

"Last night was nothing?" he asked sharply.

"I didn't say that." Helen stood up, walked to the window. Her back to him, she said, "What I meant was, it doesn't change anything."

"Really?" Marsh mocked dryly. "I'd have thought it changed everything." A small smile replaced the mockery on his lips. "Helen, I told you at the beginning that my intentions were honorable. I'm asking you to marry me."

"No," Helen answered at once, afraid to give herself time to think, to weaken. "It wouldn't work. My life suits me just as it is. I want no commitments, no strings."

"All right, we'll play it your way." His smile deepened as he slowly crossed the room to her. "We'll live together without ceremony. You can move into my place or" — at her frown — "I'll move in here." He shrugged, coming to a stop before her. "It doesn't matter where, as long as I know that when you leave the office or the hospital or wherever, you'll be coming home to me. There'll be no commitments, no strings, no pressures, I promise."

"No, Marsh." Feeling sick, Helen watched the smile leave his face, his eyes narrow.

"I believe you said you love me last night," he said quietly.

"That admission was forced out of me," Helen snapped.

"And that changes it?" he snapped back. "I also believe I told you I love you — at least fifty times."

"And *I'm* positive you believe it — now." Helen backed away from the sudden flare in his eyes. "And I'm positive you believe you could be content with the arrangement you've suggested." Holding up her hand to prevent him from interrupting, she hurried on. "But I'm also very positive that the day would come when that arrangement would not be enough, when you'd ask for more, and I'm not prepared to play the three traditional roles. Not even for you."

"What are you talking about?" Marsh was obviously confused. "What three roles?"

Her heart feeling like a lead weight in her chest, Helen looked him squarely in the eyes and coldly, flatly, threw down her ace of trump.

"The cook in your kitchen, the madonna in your nursery, the mistress in your bed. For whether you believe it now or not, Marsh, I'm positive that the day will come when you'll come home hungry at dinner-time and I won't be here, either to make a meal or go out with you for one, and you'll resent it. And I don't need that."

"Helen."

"And the nights will come," Helen went

on, as if he hadn't spoken, "when, after I've been called out, you'll lay alone on the bed and the dissatisfaction will grow. And I don't need that."

"Helen."

There was a low, angry warning in his tone now, and yet Helen went on.

"And the day will surely come when the desire for an extension of yourself, in the form of a child, will bring that resentment and dissatisfaction to an angry confrontation. *And I don't need that.*"

Finished now, Helen stood before him, waiting for his reaction. Finally, when she was beginning to think he would not reply at all, he said softly, "In other words you don't need me. Is that what you're saying?"

Helen's throat closed painfully, but telling herself she had to say it, she lifted her head, pushed the word out.

"Yes."

His face went pale and for one flashing instant seemed to contort with pain. In that instant Helen thought she saw raw agony in his eyes; then his head snapped up arrogantly, his jaw hardened, and his eyes went dead.

"Well, that's clear enough." His tone was devoid of expression. "I won't bother you again, Helen."

Fingers curled into her hand, nails digging into her palm, Helen stared into the empty space where he'd stood. Eyes hot with a sudden sting, she heard him stamp into his boots, open the door. Teeth biting down hard on her lip, she kept herself from crying out to him to stop.

Let him go, she silently wept. *Now the game is played.*

For the following two weeks Helen worked at a grueling pace. When she wasn't at the hospital or in the office, she attended every lecture offered — on her own subject of OB-GYN as well as others. She spent as little time as possible in her apartment and saw nothing at all of her friends. Telling herself that the empty, dead feeling inside would pass more quickly if she kept herself busy, she kept busy for all she was worth.

She had just returned home from the hospital on Monday night, two weeks after she had sent Marsh away, when she answered her doorbell and found Kris in the hall.

"I'm sorry to bother you so late, Helen." she apologized after Helen had asked her to come in, "but I've been here several times in the last couple of days and you've always been out."

"I've been rather lousy," Helen said warily "What did you want to see me about?" Helen knew, of course. She hoped she was wrong, but she wasn't.

"Marsh," Kris answered bluntly.

"Kris, I don't —" Helen began.

"Helen, I don't know what happened between you two and I have no intention of asking. But I love him and I'm worried about him and there's something I think you should know."

Helen had continued to stand after asking Kris to sit down, but now, fear whispering through her mind, her legs suddenly weak, she sank onto a chair.

"Worried about him? Why? What's wrong with him?"

"I don't know if anything is," Kris answered distractedly. "Oh, let me explain. Two weeks ago today I took the baby over to Mother's and went shopping. When I returned, I heard voices from the library, and as the door was partially open, I thought Mother was probably in there with Dad, so I walked toward it. Just before I reached the door, the voices became louder and I stopped." Kris wet her lips. "I did not mean to eavesdrop, but I was so shocked by what I heard, I couldn't seem to move."

"Kris," Helen inserted quickly, "if you overheard a private family conversation, I don't think you should be repeating it."

"I have to, Helen," Kris pleaded, "so you'll understand why I'm here." Helen started to shake her head, but Kris rushed on. "I heard my father say to Marsh, 'What do you intend? Good Lord, son, this woman has an excellent reputation. Are you going to marry her?' I would have moved on then, Helen, really I would. But the odd sound of Marsh's voice kept me motionless. 'She doesn't want me' was all he answered then, but he sounded so strange."

"Kris, please." Helen stood up again, moved around restlessly.

"Then Dad asked him what he was going to do, or something like that," Kris went on relentlessly. "And Marsh almost shouted at him." Kris bit her lip. "Helen, I've never heard Marsh raise his voice to my father before. Still in that odd tone he said, 'I don't know. Right now I'm bleeding to death inside and I simply don't care.' He walked out of the room then and right by me, as if I weren't there. When he got to the door, I called to him, asked him where he was going. He turned and looked through me. Then he smiled very gently and said, 'Very probably to hell.'"

Helen felt as if something had given way inside, and she sat down again very quickly.

"That was the last any of us saw of him. We haven't heard a word from him and have no idea where he is. I know Mother is very upset, and although he doesn't say anything, Dad's beginning to worry too. But there is one person who may know where he is."

Cullen. The name flashed into Helen's mind at the same moment Kris said, "My grandfather. I've been to see him, but all he'll tell me is Marsh can take care of himself and I'm not to worry."

"Then don't," Helen advised, now more than a little concerned herself.

"Oh, Helen," Kris sighed. "How does one not worry about the welfare of someone they love? I can't help but worry. This is just not like Marsh." She hesitated, then suggested tentatively, "If you went to Grandfather, I think he might tell you."

"I can't do that, Kris." Helen was out of her chair again. "I — I have no right to question your grandfather about Marsh."

"Just think about it, please." Kris stood up and walked to the door. "I must go. Mike is waiting in the car." Before she walked out of the door, she urged, "At least think about it, Helen."

"I can't, Kris," was all Helen could find to say.

Three days later Helen stood in front of the large door of the imposing edifice Cullen Hannlon called home. Kris had called her at the office that afternoon to inform her that there had still been no word from Marsh. Unable to bear her own fears and uncertainties any longer, Helen had come to the house directly from the office.

The door was opened by a pleasant-faced woman close to Cullen's own age. Helen asked to see Mr. Hannlon, then gave her name and was ushered inside and along a wide, beautifully paneled hall so swiftly that she almost felt she had been expected. The woman stopped at a door midway down the hall, tapped lightly, then pushed the door open and motioned Helen inside.

Cullen Hannlon stood beside a long narrow window, a smile on his still handsome face.

"Ah, Helen, come in, come in," he urged. "I've been standing here enjoying the sunshine. This more springlike weather feels so good after that snow a few weeks ago. But come, sit down. Can I get you some coffee or a drink?"

"No, nothing, thank you," Helen murmured, wondering where to begin. "Mr. Hannlon, I — I —"

"Kris has been talking to you, hasn't she?" He smiled knowingly. "I was afraid she would."

"Do you know where he is?" Helen asked bluntly.

"Yes." He was equally blunt. "But I can't tell you. I gave him my word."

"But —"

"No, Helen, I'm sorry." He really did sound sorry; he also sounded adamant. "I don't know what the problem is, but I do know my grandson's hurting. He went away on my suggestion and with my word that I'd tell no one where he is. I don't think you would ask me to break my word to him."

"No," Helen whispered. "Of course not."

"But I can tell you this," he said gently. "He will be back within two weeks. Should I tell him you were here?" this last was added hopefully.

Helen rose quickly. "No, please don't. I need some time myself." She paused, then admitted, to herself as well as him, "To re-organize my thinking."

I love him. Nothing has changed that; nothing ever will.

Helen lost count of the times she faced that fact during the next two weeks. With a suddenness that was shattering, she realized that without him her work, her independence, everything she had counted as precious, had very little meaning to her. She longed to see him, feel his strong arms draw her close against his hard body. It was spring and she wanted to walk in the park with him. She didn't hear a word from, or about, him.

Toward the end of that week Helen had

a rough delivery. Rough in two ways. The breech birth in itself was difficult. The fact that her patient was her oldest and closest friend made it doubly so.

She had first met Estelle while in her first year of premed. Being the daughter of Helen's favorite professor, Estelle had been at home the first time Helen had been invited to his house. They had very few similar interests, and yet they became fast friends. The friendship had endured the years.

Estelle, scatterbrained and happy-go-lucky, surprised everyone, except possibly Helen, by marrying a serious-minded English professor ten years her senior. Everyone said the union could not possibly work. Everyone was wrong. Estelle and John balanced each other perfectly. There was only one unhappy note in their marriage: Estelle's inability to carry a child full term. After her third miscarriage, at the age of thirty-three, Estelle was strongly advised by Helen not to get pregnant again.

Estelle, being Estelle, disregarded Helen's advice and came to her two years later to confirm her pregnancy. And Helen, being Helen, was determined to see this child born. And now, after a pregnancy spent almost entirely in bed, a very long, hard labor and an extremely difficult delivery, Helen smiled with joy at both mother and son.

The new father was gently adoring when he was allowed a few minutes with his exhausted wife, proud as a prancing stallion when he viewed his offspring, and full of praise when he rejoined Helen in the waiting lounge.

"I want to buy you dinner." He grinned as he crossed the room to her. "I want to buy you champagne." Pulling her to him, he gave her a bear hug. "God, Helen, I want to buy you the moon."

"I'll settle for dinner," Helen told him solemnly, her eyes teasing.

He picked the most expensive restaurant in one of the largest hotels. As they had no reservations, they were informed they could be served if they didn't mind a short wait. His high spirits undaunted, John told the maître d' they'd be in the bar and led Helen to it. Some forty-five minutes later they were called to their table. Told they should take their drinks with them, they left the bar with drinks in hand. Crossing the threshold into the dining room, Helen came to a jarring stop.

Coming toward her, a lovely, young brunette on his arm, was the man Helen had spent almost four weeks being sick over. In the few seconds it took for Marsh and the girl to come up to her, Helen noted detail.

Marsh looked well, relaxed, and, as he was smiling, happy. The girl, chattering away, looked equally happy. And why not? Helen asked herself bitterly. The girl's left hand rested on his forearm and on the ring finger rested a diamond solitaire big enough to choke a small horse.

The advantage was Helen's, as she had time to compose her features. Smiling down at the girl, Marsh didn't see her until he was practically on top of her.

"Good evening, Helen."

Nothing registered on his face. No emotion, nothing. Helen went him one better — she smiled. "Marsh."

Marsh's cool blue eyes swept their glasses, then Helen's and John's smiling faces.

"A celebration?" His tone was mildly curious.

"Of the best kind," John answered for her. "This beautiful woman has just made me the happiest man in the state."

Helen didn't bother to correct the wrong impression John had given.

"Congratulations," Marsh said dryly, his eyes mocking Helen and the words she'd spoken against marriage just a few weeks before.

"Thank you." John grinned, accepting Marsh's good wishes at face value.

"Excuse me." The brunette's voice was

soft but insistent. "Marsh, we have to go. I don't want to be late for my own engagement party."

"Of course," Marsh said at once, then with a brief nod at Helen and John, he led the girl from the room.

Three hours later, pacing back and forth on her living room carpet, Helen was still amazed at the way she'd handled herself. Not only had she eaten her dinner, she had laughed and held up her end of the conversation. Now she wasn't at all sure her dinner would stay down and she was a great deal closer to tears than laughter. In an effort to keep the tears from escaping, she whipped herself into a rage.

You are not only a fool, she silently stormed, *you're an absolute nitwit. For weeks you've been dragging yourself from day to day, aching for the sight of him. Like an innocent child you talked yourself into believing every word he said. Convinced yourself your life was pointless without him. While he's out getting engaged to a young girl.*

Hands clenched into fists, she paced. Never had she known such anger. Anger at Marsh? Anger at herself? Her mind tried to shy away from the questions, not quite ready to face the final self-commitment. With no place left to hide, exposed to herself, her mind screamed,

Dammit, he is mine.

When the doorbell pealed, Helen swung blazing eyes to the door. It was Marsh. She knew it and she was tempted to ignore it. When it rang again, she strode across the room, flipped the lock, and yanked the door open. Without a word Marsh stormed by her, tossed his coat at a chair, then, eyes blazing as hotly as hers, turned to confront her.

"Who the hell is he?" he rasped harshly.

"None of your damned business," Helen snapped.

Biting off a curse, Marsh closed the space between them. Grasping her shoulders, he pulled her against his body with such force the air exploded from her lungs.

"It is my damned business," he snarled. "You are mine, Helen." He jerked his head in the direction of the bedroom. "I made you mine in there. Now get on that phone and call what's-his-name and tell him to run along. He can't have you."

Sheer fury ripped through Helen. Of all the arrogant swine. Talk about wanting to have your cake and eat it all at the same time. He actually came from his own engagement party to tell her that she belonged to him and couldn't have another man.

Twisting out of his arms, she spun away from him, then spun back, her voice icy.

"You — you . . . boy." She flung at him. "Get out of here right now." Incensed, raging, no longer thinking, she cried, "To think I went to that old man."

"You went to Cullen? Why?"

She was long past noticing how still he'd grown, how tight was his tone.

"To find out where you were." Helen was near to shouting. She didn't care. Her laughter was not pretty. "I was ready to crawl on my knees to you. I must have been out of my —"

She was pulled against him, her words drowning inside his mouth. It was heaven. It was hell. And though Helen didn't want it to ever stop, she pushed him away.

"I told you to get out of here." Her voice was cold, flat, all signs of her fiery anger gone. "Go back to your party, your friends, your fiancée."

"My fiancée! I don't —" Marsh went silent, his eyes incredulous. "You're jealous?" The incredulity changed to wonder. "Helen, you're jealous."

Helen stepped back warily, unsure of his awed tone, the light that leaped into his eyes.

"Helen, love," Marsh murmured, "that girl is Grant's sister. She's been another Kris to me. That engagement party tonight was for her and a young guy named Robert, who decided he couldn't live another day without her. Just exactly as I decided the same about you in January." He walked to her slowly, drew her gently into his arms. "Nothing's changed that," he whispered. "Nothing ever will."

Tiny fingers crawled up Helen's scalp, and she experienced that eerie sensation he'd caused before.

"Oh, Marsh."

"What's-his-name has got to go," he groaned. "Helen, love, haven't you realized yet that we belong to each other, together? I won't let you send me away again. I can't and continue to function normally."

"What's-his-name is the husband of my best friend," Helen explained softly, her hand going to his face with the need to touch him. "She and I together successfully brought their first child into the world late this afternoon. He insisted on buying me dinner. That's what we were celebrating."

"Oh, God." His mouth moved over her face as if imprinting her likeness on his lips. "I don't ever want to live through a period like the last couple of hours again. Helen, I was so mad, I thought I'd blow apart. The thought of you with another man —" He shuddered and brought his mouth back to hers to kiss her violently.

"I know," she whispered when she could breathe again. "I was going through the same thing." Her voice went rough. "Marsh, where have you been these past weeks? I was sick with worry." Before he could answer she slid her fingers over his lips, shook her head. "No, it doesn't matter. I love you. I want to spend the rest of my life with you. With commitments or without. With strings or without. That doesn't matter either." Then, very softly, she repeated his words of weeks ago. "The only thing that does matter is when you finally do come, from the office, or wherever, you'll be coming to me."

The sunshine, streaming through the bedroom windows, had a golden autumnal glow. Marsh, whistling softly, came through the bedroom door.

"Coffee's ready and the juice is poured, love. Are you going to laze away half the holiday in bed or are you going to get up and have breakfast with me?"

At the mention of food Helen groaned and rolled onto her side away from him.

A smile curving his lips, Marsh sauntered to Helen's side of the bed, dropped onto his haunches, leaned forward, and tickled her ear with his tongue.

"If you're not up in thirty seconds, I'm going to crawl back in there with you, and I don't care if we never make it to Mother's for Thanksgiving dinner."

With a murmured "Good morning," Helen slid one arm around his neck and sought the lips now teasing her cheek. When his wake-up kiss started to deepen, she pushed gently against his shoulders. "Go back to the kitchen," Helen whispered breathlessly, evading his still hungry mouth. "I'll be with you in a minute."

Marsh grinned, stole another quick kiss, then rose and strolled out of the room, again whistling softly.

After rinsing her face and brushing her teeth, Helen followed him to the kitchen, impatient with the weariness of her body. As she entered the kitchen the room swirled before her eyes, and groaning a soft protest against the light-headedness, she grasped the back of a kitchen chair.

"Helen?" Marsh's sharp tone barely penetrated the mistiness, but she felt his strength when he scooped her up into his arms. "What's the matter? Are you coming down with something?" The questions were rapped anxiously at her as he strode through the living room into the bedroom.

"No, Marsh, I'm not sick." Off her feet she felt the fuzziness pass and she smiled weakly at him. "I'm pregnant."

Marsh froze. Even his face looked frozen. "How?" At her arched glance he sighed, "I mean, you were taking precautions."

"I stopped."

"Why, Helen? I told you it didn't matter."

"It suddenly mattered very much to me." She hid her face against his chest as he set her on her feet. "I wanted to have our baby, Marsh."

The sound of his sharply indrawn breath came clearly to her as he turned her around in his arms, then spread his hands wide over her still flat belly. "Is it safe for you, love?"

"Yes, Marsh. I'm seeing an excellent obstetrician."

"Are you sure?" he murmured against her hair. "Are you very, very sure?"

"Very, very sure." Helen's hands covered his, the narrow gold band on her left ring finger brushing against its counterpart on his. "It will be all right, I promise you. We are going to have a beautiful baby, Marsh."

The employees of Thorndike Press hope you have enjoyed this Large Print book. All our Thorndike and Wheeler Large Print titles are designed for easy reading, and all our books are made to last. Other Thorndike Press Large Print books are available at your library, through selected bookstores, or directly from us.

For information about titles, please call:

(800) 223-1244

or visit our Web site at:

www.gale.com/thorndike
www.gale.com/wheeler

To share your comments, please write:

Publisher
Thorndike Press
295 Kennedy Memorial Drive
Waterville, ME   04901